Mistletoe Mischief

Mistletoe Mischief

Codi Hall

Podium

Cover design by Wendi Chen

Mistletoe image designed by Freepik (www.freepik.com)

ISBN: 978-1-0394-7822-0

Published in 2024 by Podium Publishing
www.podiumentertainment.com

This book belongs to Sarah Jane and Cass Dolan,
who patiently guided me through each editorial step to make
this book grand. Thank you for your grace.

Mistletoe Mischief

Chapter One

"The turquoise of the water drew me in, calling to me like a siren, and I was unable to resist taking that final step. I was so surprised by the warmth of the water, I stumbled back and landed on my butt in the sand. The people on the beach probably thought I was an idiot."

Pike Sutton chuckled at the image his favorite travel podcaster, Alia Cole, created about her first visit to Aruba. Pike had never been anywhere farther than the states surrounding Idaho, so listening to Alia's accounts of fascinating and beautiful places worldwide was his favorite thing to do on his way to work. Someday when Adventures in Mistletoe took off, he planned to travel, to explore some of the places Alia talked about on her podcast. But until then, the guided outdoor sports business he'd opened with his best friend, Anthony Russo, was his main focus.

"When I got my bearings again, I stepped into the clear, sparkling water. It was warm and inviting, but I'll admit, I could only handle it for a short time. When it's hot outside, I want my water to be colder than the temperature around me."

I'm the exact same way.

"Although, if I'm in a colder climate, I want a scalding bath or sauna and a cup of hot cocoa to warm me up."

Not a man? He couldn't imagine a woman like Alia was single unless it was by choice. What man in his right mind would meet an adventurous, funny, stunning woman and not shoot his shot? She probably had daily DMs from men like Zac Efron.

Pike knew it was pathetic to fantasize about a celebrity as if they were really who they pretended to be, but Alia's sense of humor, goofiness, and ability to laugh at herself had drawn him to her. He'd even checked out the podcast's Instagram and discovered that not only was Alia the entire personality package but a knockout as well.

Although he'd read every post, Pike had only commented on a few, lest he give off Joe Goldberg vibes. When she'd responded to every comment with a small detail about the photo she hadn't included in the podcast, he fully admitted that his stomach somersaulted like some lovestruck hero in a romance novel. As if she had saved those special details for him.

Pike had no illusions that Alia and he were meant for each other. He was an average guy with a great sense of style, a fastidious grooming routine, and a big personality. He used to hate his red hair and even tried to dye it black in his teen years, but he'd slowly learned to accept it. It was thick and shiny, and his beard was trimmed and full, which pulled attention away from the freckles he tried to hide. Alia had been seen with some of the most beautiful people in Hollywood; if they ever got a chance to meet, Pike knew she'd never fall for a man who'd been called "Lucky Charms" all through elementary school.

Not to mention the awkward middle school years when he'd been as round as he was tall, but those times were behind him. He spent hours in the gym every week, keeping everything hard and tight. There was no way he'd give others any more ammunition for mockery.

Besides, while fantasies were always fun, Pike was pursuing something real with Delilah Gill. She was best friends with his friend Nick Winters' youngest sister, Holly, and according to gossip, Delilah had been infatuated with Pike for years. He'd known her since she was twelve, but maturity looked good on her now that she was in her late twenties. He'd finally gotten the chance to dance with Delilah and spend a little time with her, only to have her leave early without a goodbye. He'd thought about getting her number from Holly and cold-contacting her, but Pike didn't want to overplay his hand. Although she'd been sweet and fun to talk to, she could be weighing her options, which was her prerogative. Pike had waited nearly fourteen years to make a move, so if she wanted to make him work for it, he'd do it. It was a minor setback, but considering his disastrous relationship history and the fact that he was over thirty in a small town where the dating pool was turning into a puddle, he needed to act fast.

Pike parked a few blocks down from Adventures in Mistletoe. It was Anthony's turn to head out with clients while Pike helmed the store, but he hated being stuck inside on days like this. It was bright and beautiful outside with a slight bite in the air, the first hint that the weather was going to turn. Fresh powder meant better experiences for the clients who enjoyed skiing and snowboarding.

He rubbed his tired eyes and leaned back against the seat with a sigh. His coffee had come out with a heap of grounds in it, and he had no idea what happened. Pike wanted to stop in at Kiss My Donut, but he was afraid if he did, Anthony would be late to meet the clients, which would reflect badly on them both. Coffee would have to be forgone unless he could convince someone to bring him some. Maybe Holly or Nick would drop by with a cup.

While Pike would love to sit in the car listening to the rest of the podcast, he needed to get inside and talk to Anthony about the Mistletoe Christmas festivities. Merry Griffin was heading up the planning committee and had handpicked Adventures in Mistletoe to organize the first ever Mistletoe Winter Games. This was huge for the business, and he was anxious to have everything sorted before the deadline on Friday.

"The best part of the trip was what happened later that night . . ." Alia's voice cut off as Pike pulled the keys out of the ignition.

"To be continued," he murmured, pulling up the podcast's Instagram. Pike scrolled through the posts as he exited the car and stepped onto the sidewalk, making his way to the front door. The top post on his feed caught his eye, and he paused outside the glass double doors.

"Where Should I Go Next?" Contest
Post a location in the comments and include three exciting attractions that make your destination stand out!
Contest closes Monday, November 25 at 10:00 a.m. EST.

Pike checked the time on his cell phone. Shit, that was in fifteen minutes! If he entered now, would she even consider him?

If you don't enter, she won't have the chance to consider Mistletoe! Better to try than not!

Pike's thumbs tapped at lightning speed, pushing back the negative voice that scoffed at him. *She is never going to choose Mistletoe, Idaho.*

You should come to Mistletoe, Idaho, as your next destination. Gorgeous landscapes, perfect for outdoor sports like snowboarding, snowmobiling, and snowshoeing, surround the small town. Adventures in Mistletoe would be happy to give you guided tours around the area. The town hosts various holiday activities, including lights displays, parades, concerts, and an epic Winter Games. I would also encourage you to try one of our natural hot springs. They have magical powers!

Pike tapped the send button and opened the door to Adventures in Mistletoe. He stepped over the threshold, almost bumping into Delilah. She was wrapped in a puffer jacket, her dark hair up and off her face. Maybe it was the flush in her cheeks or the way those black cat-eye frames drew attention to her blue eyes, but she was looking mighty delectable. Pike knew what was under that coat and imagined what it would be like to spend date nights curled up on the couch to stay warm, talking about their days and what they should do for dinner. Although he knew Delilah as an acquaintance, he looked forward to learning all her likes and dislikes, to forging a bond.

He just had to get her number first!

"Hey! Is it weird if I say I've been looking for you?" he asked.

"Hi. No, I mean, depends," she said, giving him a small smile. "I don't owe you money, do I?"

"Funny," he said, taking a few steps toward her, "but no, I wanted to check in and see how you were feeling."

"Feeling . . ." Delilah hesitated, her forehead furrowed for a split second before she gasped, "Oh, after the other night. You know, drank too much. Needed to sleep it off."

Pike noticed she hadn't stopped moving since he walked in, fidgeting with her hands and hair, and he smiled at the tell. It was cute that he made her nervous, but he wanted to put her at ease. "Great, then, if you're fully recovered, maybe we could have coffee sometime?"

"Um—"

"I'm going to take off," Anthony said abruptly, coming around the counter. It didn't surprise Pike that the bigger man was in a hurry, since it took a good twenty minutes to reach the ski resort lodge, but his brusque exit probably had something to do with Pike not acknowledging him. He hadn't meant to be an ass, but was so surprised and delighted to see Delilah, he had tunnel vision.

"Alright, man." Pike almost stopped him to talk, but he wanted to be alone with Delilah. He patted Anthony on the back as he walked by. They could talk about the games later.

Pike returned his attention to Delilah, pulling his cell phone from his back pocket. He opened his mouth to ask Delilah if he could get her number, but—

"By the way," Anthony said from behind him, "thanks for bringing my blanket back, Delilah."

His blanket? What the fuck?

Delilah's mouth dropped open, her big blue eyes staring over his shoulder. Pike spun around to ask Anthony what he was talking about, but he was already out the door. Finally, he turned to face Delilah again and noticed her flushed face. Suspicion scratched at the back of his mind. Had something happened over the weekend after she left the bar?

And if so, why hadn't Anthony said anything?

"Why did you have his blanket?" Pike asked, keeping his voice even.

Delilah's mouth snapped closed, and he realized that he sounded like a jealous boyfriend.

Idiot.

"Sorry," he said with a laugh. "You don't have to answer that. You don't owe me any explanation."

"No, you're fine," she said, tucking a strand of hair behind her ear. "When I got a little sick the other night, I threw up on myself. It was really embarrassing. Anthony gave Holly the blanket to help me clean up, and I washed it at home. That's why I had it."

Pike wanted to crawl into a hole. If Anthony was interested in Delilah, he would have told him. His straight shooter best friend was the last person on Earth to lie and sneak around behind Pike's back.

What the hell is wrong with you?

Pike hated to make excuses for bad behavior, but as a guy who'd lost most of his girlfriends to other more successful, attractive men, he might have a complex. But to start off acting like a jealous asshat before they'd even had a date? Bad form.

"Man, that sucks. I haven't been that sick in years, but it took me a long time to figure out my limits." Pike cleared his throat, shooting her a sheepish grin. "So, you and Anthony aren't secretly hooking up then?"

Delilah snorted. "No, definitely not."

"Good, then, could I snag your phone number before I miss my chance again?"

"When did you miss your chance before?" she asked, a slight edge to her voice he couldn't decipher. He'd heard it before when they danced on Saturday night, as if his interest irritated her.

"On Saturday, before you disappeared."

"Right," she said, her face relaxing into a smile. "Yeah, sure, you can have my number."

Pike held out his phone for her to take, his skin humming with excitement as she typed in her information. This was his moment, a story they could tell their grandkids about. *Your granddad thought I was too young, and he almost waited too long, but he came in a clutch, and I fell for him all over again.*

At least, he hoped some variation of that took place because Pike was pinning a lot of his future romantic hopes on Delilah.

His notification sound went off, and she handed it back to him with wide eyes. "Sorry, I didn't mean to look, but you have an Instagram notification."

Pike snatched the phone back, his hands shaking as he opened the app. Alia would be announcing *Excursion*'s next destination any minute, and he couldn't wait to see it. Even though he knew the chances were slim, it was still exciting to imagine her picking Mistletoe and maybe even booking a snowmobiling outing with them. The publicity alone would be enough to shoot their company to the moon, so long as she had a good time. If she did come, he would make sure it was absolutely perfect.

I need to stop dreaming so big.

Too often he hoped for the incredible and ended up crushed when it didn't work out.

When he saw the @ExcursionsPC handle in his notifications, he started jumping up and down. "Oh fuck! Holy shit!"

"Are you okay?" Delilah asked, eyes widening when he whooped loudly. He'd clicked on the post, and there it was!

Thanks to @PikenAround for the excellent recommendation, @ExcursionsPC will be trading out the bikinis and suntan lotion for beanies and snow boots! We're headed to Mistletoe, Idaho, for the holidays!

"Fuck yeah, I am good! She picked us! She's coming here!" Every word was an out of breath shout, but he was too excited to dial it back.

"Who?" Delilah asked.

"Alia flipping Cole!" She stared at him blankly and he followed it up with, "From *Excursions*, the travel podcast! This is huge!" Pike stopped jumping and took several deep breaths as he scrolled through his contacts. "I gotta call Anthony! He is going to flip out!"

"Alright, I've got to go, too," Delilah said, taking a step around him with a pat on his arm, "but congratulations."

"Thanks," he said, barely looking up from his phone as he scrolled for Anthony's name, bringing it to his ear, "I'll call you!"

Delilah waved as she headed out the door, but Pike was too excited to think about anything but sharing the news with his best friend. The first time his call went to voicemail, but he tried again, frustration clawing up his throat as he hollered, "Come on, motherfucker, pick up your phone!"

On the third try, Anthony picked up with an impatient, "What?"

"Is that any way to talk to the man who just got us our biggest business break?"

"What are you talking about?" Anthony asked.

"I entered an Instagram contest and suggested for Alia Cole from the *Excursions* podcast to come to Mistletoe for the holidays, and she fucking picked us! She is coming here, man!"

Silence stretched on the other line. Finally, Anthony whispered, "Are you serious?!"

"As a damn heart attack!"

"Holy shit!" Anthony laughed and whooped, and Pike started jumping again, ignoring the stares from passersby.

"We are celebrating tonight, my dude!" Pike hollered. "Come by my place after work, and we'll finalize the list of events for the winter games. I'll grab the beer and pizza!"

"I can't believe this," Anthony said.

"Me neither, but I will never doubt the power of positive thinking ever again!"

Anthony chuckled. "Nice job, man. We'll talk soon."

"Later," Pike said, ending the call and clicking on the Instagram post and reading it one more time.

So far today, he'd snagged a cute girl's number and was about to meet his favorite podcaster. Things were definitely coming up Pike.

A message popped up in the upper right-hand corner of the app, and Pike clicked on it, shocked to see a DM from Alia at the top.

Dear Mr. Sutton,

I am Ms. Cole's assistant. Thank you for bringing Mistletoe to our attention. While I was born and raised in Idaho until I was twelve, I admit that I had never heard of your little town. We are excited to explore and experience all the holiday fun it has to offer. You mentioned Adventures in Mistletoe, and after exploring some of the services you have listed on your website, we'd love to book the four excursions package for four people. I am arranging our travel now and should be in town and ready to explore on Friday, November 29. We will be staying in town until Christmas.

I would also like to know more about these hot springs! I googled pictures, and while the settings are amazing, that water doesn't look habitable.

Sincerely,

Ryler Colby

Excursions Podcast

Ryler, huh? Strange name. Although Pike was hoping it would be Alia reaching out, it was nice to talk to another Idahoan who would at least be familiar with the area.

Pike checked his calendar and responded to Alia's assistant, his fingers flying across the keyboard.

Dear Ryler,

Please, call me Pike. It's not surprising that you haven't heard of Mistletoe, as we're a relatively small town tucked back in the mountains above Fairfield. Most people pass through for a few hours and move on.

I've confirmed your adventures. Please let me know if the dates attached work for you and if I can be of any other assistance to you. I'm happy to give your group a tour when you arrive and tell you all the secrets about the area. By the way, you're definitely going to want to try Lord of the Fries while you're here. Best food in town.

I realize that sometimes the shallow pools look orange, but I'll be taking you to one like this. (I'm attaching a photo.)

Sincerely,

Pike

He scrolled through his phone for a picture, and although it had him and his friend group shirtless, Pike sent it. Hopefully the guy didn't think anything of it.

The bell above the door rang, and Pike put down his phone, his smile genuine as he greeted them. Pike was riding such a high, there was nothing in the world that could bring him down.

Chapter Two

The sand under Ryler Colby's feet disappeared as the ocean drew away, readying for another wave to build up and crash against the shore. It was a beautiful morning in Bali, with the sun hovering over the oceanic horizon, a brilliant beacon of light amid the light peach, lavender, and yellow sunrise that rose from the water and bled into the dark blue sky, which still sparkled with a few stars.

It was paradise, and yet Ryler was restless to move on.

Removing her phone from the pocket of her yoga pants, she snapped an Instagram-worthy photo of the sunrise before putting it away. She stepped back out of the reach of the incoming waves and made her way along the sandy trail to the bungalow she'd been staying in for the better part of a week. The lush greenery hid the rental from view until she crested the hill, the trees giving way to the spectacular view of the beach below.

Maybe it was the Hallmark movies she'd been binging since the plane ride from Aruba, but with Thanksgiving only a few days away, Ryler couldn't help thinking there should be a slight nip in the air at least. Instead, she was sweating already, and it was only six thirty in the morning.

Which was why seeing @PikenAround's comment on her post fifteen minutes before the contest ended last night seemed like kismet. She'd been curled up in bed unable to sleep, when her alarm went off at midnight, reminding her to choose a winner. She'd happened to see Pike's comment, since he was the last one to enter, and curious about the town's name, had googled pictures. It was the perfect winter retreat and a break from all the sunshine and sand. She'd reached out to him and immediately started booking their travel. She hadn't told the rest of the crew yet, as they'd been out last night having fun. While she didn't imagine any trouble from Kit or Neil, her cousin, Alia, would be another story.

Ryler unlocked the front door and stepped inside the quiet home. Alia would sleep until the afternoon if Ryler let her, but they needed to be out the door and at the airport by one p.m. Everyone was used to a spontaneous schedule, so Ryler wasn't worried about it.

Ryler's room was the only one upstairs, while the other three bedrooms were downstairs. She'd skipped the team-building over tequila in favor of dinner and dessert in bed, wrapped up in a streaming romance between a wine maker and a distributer. The cozy movie was set among hills of gorgeous fall foliage, and a pang settled in her stomach as Ryler remembered the smell of her parents' kitchen at the holidays. The sweet aroma of apples and cinnamon wafted around her as her mother hummed Christmas carols and her dad stood on the back porch with her uncles, drinking beer as the turkey fried.

Ryler opened the fridge with a shake of her head. It had been a long time since she'd thought of those memories. Why was she suddenly so nostalgic?

She pulled out some fresh fruit, washing and peeling the items before cutting up an array into a bowl. Ryler carried her snack into her bedroom and onto the balcony, where she took a seat on the simple metal chair. She settled the bowl into her lap and poked the colorful fruit salad with her fork absently as she opened up Instagram. She saw the message from @PikenAround and looked at the picture he'd attached of him and a few friends sitting in a blue-green pool of water with green grass and spring flowers surrounding them. In the distance was a craggy, snowcapped peak.

Ryler shot back a message. Now that is the kind of hot springs I'd be down for.

Someone knocked on her door, and Ryler glanced up from her cell and called out, "Come on in."

Neil poked his head in, tsking. "You're really just letting anyone into your bedroom without asking who it is?"

"I was hoping for Dylan Wang, but I guess you'll do."

"Ain't you sweet," he said, coming inside with a paper bag in his hand and closing the door behind him. Neil was her best friend and producer.

Although they'd dated for a hot minute in college, they'd realized early on they were better off as friends. When they had graduated six years ago, Ryler took her communications major and launched *Excursions*, her travel podcast, with Neil by her side. They'd started small, driving around the country in a secondhand camper, visiting obscure and commercial locations, posting pictures of landscapes, local cuisine, and events. It had been a simpler time, and sometimes she missed it.

"I went out to get breakfast," Neil said, setting the bag on the corner table by the window and launching himself across her bed, his dark skin and shirt standing out against the white comforter. "And how are you this fine morning?"

"I'm great. I went for a walk." She waved her hand to the plate of fruit on her nightstand. "Ate some fruit. Booked our next destination."

Neil grabbed the half-eaten fruit bowl off her side table and took a bite. "Where to?"

"There's this little town in Idaho called Mistletoe. It's in the mountains, and they have all these Christmas traditions!" Ryler leaned over, handing him her phone. "Check them out. I got us this beautiful four-bedroom log cabin in the woods that will be perfect for privacy."

Neil nodded. "Looks awesome. Alia is going to hate everything about it." Neil got up from the bed and cocked a hip, pouting his full bottom lip and mimicking in a high voice, "Why would you cover all this up?"

He waved a hand over his length, and Ryler grimaced. He was right. Alia opted for tropical destinations every time, but Ryler was burnt out. The only reason she'd picked Bali was because an old friend from college had invited her to visit. It was nice to catch up, but damn, she was ready for a change.

"I know, but she will get over it. Mistletoe will be the perfect place to wrap up the podcast before the holidays. Give us a couple weeks to pick our New Year's destination."

Neil scrolled through the pics she'd downloaded on her phone, nodding his head. "You know I'm down for anything, even the potato state."

"Kit will love the backdrop for photos," Ryler said.

He handed her back the phone, his dark gaze holding hers. "If she throws too big a fit, maybe that's a sign to come out of hiding. Before the truth comes out and bites you in the ass."

Ryler got up to grab a water bottle from the minifridge in the corner of the room, Neil's words circling her like a rope, tightening around her chest until she struggled to catch her breath. The thought of announcing to the world that she was the voice behind *Excursions* left her ready to give up the podcast altogether, and it was her life. She couldn't even focus on a relationship because she was never in one place long enough to let herself fall.

But telling the world that beautiful, perfect Alia Cole had never been the voice of *Excursions*, and that it was actually mousy Ryler behind the mic, using her cousin's name and face to hide behind? She'd rather just stop posting, but they couldn't do that either. They had sponsors and advertising that paid their bills.

Ryler twisted off her water cap with a huff. "If I came clean now, it would still take a big chunk out of my behind." Ryler slapped her butt to emphasize her point. "Starting with the sponsors and advertisers, who would pull their money and support."

Neil scoffed. "You put too much stock in appearances. Your listeners love you. They get wrapped up in your passion for these places. True fans don't care what you look like. They were obsessed with the show before we ever posted on Instagram."

"They do not want to look at a midsize woman with wavy hair she can't control and freckles dotting all over her cheeks and nose."

"Really? I thought I just saw a tutorial on TikTok on how to give yourself freckles? I think they're in."

"I'm an average woman, nothing remarkable. Definitely not Instagram worthy."

"Okay, that is what *you* see." Neil got up off the bed and crossed the room to hug her. "I see my gorgeous, successful friend who shines when she walks into any room. Who can set someone at ease with a smile." He chucked her under the chin, dark eyes meeting hers. "You are perfect, Ryls. I wish you could see it."

Ryler didn't have it in her to argue. She never wanted to be in the spotlight. She loved her podcast and sharing the places she explored with the world, but she didn't want to put herself on display for strangers to pick apart. She'd seen it happen a thousand times to celebrities who kept their identity a secret for years and then the big unmasking occurred. Suddenly, everyone had an opinion on what they should have looked like. While Ryler was confident in who she was, enduring society's insults wasn't something she wanted to open herself up to.

Ryler gave Neil a hard squeeze and released him, heading back to sit crisscross at the head of her bed. "While I appreciate your support, I'm happy with this arrangement. I get to do what I love without all the stress of public appearances."

"Fine, I'll shut up about it." Neil sat down on the edge and stared at her with solemn brown eyes. "I just worry."

"That's what I keep you around for," she teased.

"You also keep me around to intimidate interested males."

Ryler groaned and fell sideways on the bed. "I thought you went drinking with the others."

"I did."

"Then why aren't you miserable and hungover instead of lecturing me about my life?"

"I stuck to beer and water. I basically played babysitter, keeping the others from doing something stupid."

"Should I make you a shirt that reads *Papa Bear*?" she asked, running her finger over the front of her chest to demonstrate.

"I'll never wear it, but knock yourself out. Back to you though . . . When is the last time you talked to Ollie?"

"Yesterday," she said, fudging the truth a bit. Ryler had called and left a message . . . a few weeks ago.

"And is he going to make plans to spend the holidays with you in snowy paradise?"

"We haven't discussed it." In all honesty, Ollie and Ryler hadn't had a conversation longer than two minutes for a few weeks now. Ryler knew that was a sign to pull the plug, but she didn't want her friends to start chucking single men at her like basketballs to a hoop.

Neil grunted. "You need to stop dating these boring accountant types. They are never going to give you the life and love you deserve, or the fire."

"Ollie has heat," Ryler protested.

"Seriously, that kiss he gave you when he met you at the airport gate three weeks ago? Tepid at best!"

"Anyway!" Ryler laughed, sitting up and reaching for her phone. She tapped on Instagram again, when she saw there was a message and read Pike's response. I'm telling you, *Excursions* made the right choice picking Mistletoe. We will take care of you, trust me.

Ryler checked out the picture of @PikenAround's hot spring one more time. She knew from his profile pic that he was the guy with red hair and the beard standing up in the pool. Ryler couldn't help admiring the wide shoulders and sculpted chest, arms, and stomach. The guy probably lived at the gym.

"So, what does the winner of your contest get?" Neil asked, interrupting her ogling. "The one who suggested Mistletoe as a destination?"

"I thought picking their destination suggestion was enough," Ryler said, clicking on @PikenAround's profile picture. He was smiling for the camera with a backdrop of trees, hands in the pockets of his dark blue coat. His neat red beard was vibrant against the dark of his jacket. He had a nice smile and eyes, although he was too far away to tell the actual color.

"Oh, come on. He or she should get something extra. Who is this person?"

Ryler followed the link for Adventures in Mistletoe and scrolled through the different services. "He owns an outdoor sports tour company. Snowboarding lessons. Snowmobiling."

"Hey, that could be fun. We could hire his company's services while we're out there. When is the last time we hit the slopes?" he asked.

"Years, and I already did." She turned her phone around to show him the confirmation emails. "We have four activities booked, but I have a feeling we could do more." Ryler groaned. "I don't know about snowboarding. I'm totally out of practice."

"Stop acting like you're old," Neil said, snapping his fingers. "I'll make some sponsorship calls, and we can get everything we need shipped and waiting for us at the house when we arrive." Neil pulled out his phone, pausing with his fingers on the keys. "You said the house was a four-bedroom, right?"

"Yes, why?"

"Just wanted to make sure I wasn't sharing a room with Kit. He has one string cheese and he can clear a building with his noxious gas."

"Gross!" Ryler laughed, although she knew firsthand about Kit's dairy intolerance. Being stuck in a car with someone over the course of five years, you get real familiar with what they can eat on the road.

"By the way," Neil said, sobering, "I smoothed things over, but Alia insulted the man with the corner food cart and a waitress at the bar we were at last night."

Ryler grimaced. Although she loved Alia like a sister, Ryler knew she could be abrasive and tactless. Alia called it honesty, but no one else took it that way.

"Thanks for taking care of it."

"You don't have to thank me. *Excursions* is as much my baby as it is yours, and I'd never want people to think badly of us."

"I know," Ryler said, thankful that Neil was always there to support her. He was the only other constant in her life besides Alia and *Excursions*. He was her family.

"We fly out at three today," Ryler said, setting her phone down, "and I figured that would give you guys a couple days with your families before you fly out Friday to join us."

"When are you two going to arrive?" he asked.

"We will land with enough time to run back to the town house, pack, and get a good night's sleep."

Neil frowned. "Are you sure you don't want to come home with me? My mother loves you, and you know there's plenty of food." He cleared his throat, adding casually, "Alia could even come with you."

While Ryler enjoyed visiting with Neil and his family, she avoided major holidays with people, preferring to keep things low-key. Less likely to experience a rush of memories. However, she didn't like to tell Neil that kind of thing and have him pity her.

"Oh boy, that will be fun," she deadpanned. "Refereeing the two of you during Thanksgiving dinner?"

"Now, hang on, if Thanksgiving with my family has taught me anything, it is how to keep the peace for even the most contentious relationships."

Ryler patted Neil's arm. "I appreciate it, but you know I like to dig in ahead of everyone else. Get a feel for the place."

"Fine," Neil said, stretching. "Do you want me to stick around to break the news to Alia, or are you good if I head out for a run?"

"I'm not scared of my cousin," Ryler said.

"Shit, I am. She throws a tantrum like a three-year-old who wants more juice."

Ryler smothered her laugh. "You're mean."

"Maybe, but I'm just saying. She's gotten a little spoiled over the last few years."

Ryler knew Neil had issues with Alia. He hadn't been shy about telling her daily. Hiring Alia to be the face of *Excursions* gave Ryler the freedom to relax and continue to be herself without dealing with the politics. Dealing with Alia's dramatics was a small price to pay.

Especially after everything Alia and her family had done for Ryler.

"Maybe you're jealous because you want to be in front of the camera in a speedo?"

Neil hopped up from the bed with a grunt, the corner of his mouth curled up. "I'm a board shorts man, but no. I just want you to be happy."

"Enough." Ryler laughed, holding her hands out for him to take and help her off the bed. "Should we wake up the others and tell them the good news?"

"If you do, your cover girl might be an ogre for the trip home."

"Point taken. Better if we surprise her."

Chapter Three

"This is absolutely amazing, guys," Noel Winters said after reading the message from Alia's assistant. She handed Pike's phone back to him with a grin. "Congratulations, Fish!"

Pike couldn't even glare at his friend for using that stupid nickname. He was walking on sunshine. *Excursions* had signed up for four different experiences with Adventures in Mistletoe over the next few weeks, which meant that they were going to be featured on the podcast and Instagram. He'd spent most of his downtime in the store today looking at ornaments for their tree, hoping he could convince Anthony to do something awesome for the Festival of Trees. While they didn't have time to decorate, at least they could order the stuff and have one available for people to see. They were about to get a shit ton of exposure, and they needed to be out there, soaking up all of it.

"Thanks." He took his phone back and slipped it into the pocket of his jeans.

"I'm still amazed that she picked Mistletoe," Nick said, shaking his head. "With Sun Valley a stone's throw away? Aren't her parents big-time Hollywood actors? You'd think that would have probably been more her speed."

"Hey now, let's not jinx ourselves!" Pike said, pointing at Nick. "Yes, her dad is the CEO of Cole Studios, and her mom was a big rom-com queen in the late nineties, but she is coming here, and this is where she is going to stay."

"Whoa, now, let's not get too intense," Anthony joked. "We don't want to scare her away."

"Speaking of scaring women away," Noel said, smirking, "Nick said you've finally noticed Delilah Gill. What brought that on?"

Pike groaned softly. When he'd invited his three friends over to celebrate and brainstorm over pizza and beer, the last thing he expected was to be questioned on romantic pursuits.

"I guess the timing kind of fell into place." Pike reached out and slugged Anthony in the arm.

"Ow! Asshole!" Anthony glared at him.

"That's for fucking with me earlier with the blanket thing. Why did you make it seem like you were hiding something?"

Anthony's cheeks darkened, and Pike could have sworn he was blushing. "I was just thanking her. I can't help it if you took it weird."

"Whatever, it was a jacked-up thing to do." Pike straightened his tie, grinning. "At least she didn't let your bullshit affect her feelings toward me."

"So, this is happening?" Nick asked.

"I got her number, at least. Now I just got to figure out where to take her."

Noel and Nick exchanged a glance, and Pike frowned. "What was that?"

"Nothing," they chorused.

"Bull, that was a *look*," Pike said, his focus shifting between the two of them. "Do not start doing that married mind meld thing! What don't you want to say?"

Noel glanced at Nick, who shrugged. She leaned forward and steepled her fingers, her hesitation making him crazy.

"I wonder if you are pursuing Delilah for the right reasons," Noel said slowly, as if she were picking every word carefully.

Pike scowled. "What are the right and wrong reasons?"

"Are you finally noticing Delilah because you really like her and want to get to know who she is?" Noel asked, holding her hands out like a scale and dropping her left hand lower. "Or are you kind of at a loss for who to date, and she fills a void?"

Pike sat back, his mouth hanging open. "Wow, that's what you think of me? That I use people because I'm bored?"

"We don't think it's intentional," Nick said quickly.

Noel nodded. "I just know you've had a tough couple of years with dating and relationships, and I don't want you to jump into something that could cause complications later."

Anthony sat quietly drinking his beer, and Pike turned to him expectantly. "Is this what you think, too?"

He held both hands up in surrender, his beer clutched in his fist. "Hey, your love life is your business."

Pike snapped his fingers and pointed at Anthony. "Uh-uh, none of that shit. You said something Saturday about me just liking her because of a dress. You've got opinions. Share with the class."

Anthony took a long pull of his beer, finally admitting, "I think that you're looking for something, and Delilah happened to catch your eye at the right moment. You two are a lot alike."

"Shouldn't that be a good thing? We'll have things in common."

"Except," Noel interjected, reaching out to take Nick's hand, smiling sweetly. "I've found that opposites tend to attract."

Pike made a face. "And sometimes being too different leads to friction."

"We just don't want you to settle, regret it, and then someone gets hurt," Noel said.

"Well, despite your low opinion of me, I'm not using Delilah." When Noel started to interject, Pike held up his hand. "Let me finish. I think she's beautiful and funny and sweet. It just took me a little longer to wrap my head around it because she is Holly's friend and the timing was off."

"And that's fine," Noel said quickly. "We just wanted to check in and make sure that was where your head was at."

"Fine." Pike picked up the notepad and pen off the coffee table where he'd left it and settled back into his couch. "If we're done dissecting my romantic motives, maybe we can get this list started for the winter games."

"Sure," Nick said, snatching another piece of pizza from the box. "What about a holiday baking cook-off, like they had in *The Grinch*? I volunteer as fudge judge."

The group collectively made a sound between a chuckle and groan, breaking the tension.

"I do agree that food is a must," Noel said, patting her husband's knee. "What about food trucks? You're having it at the park, right?"

Pike nodded. "Yeah, we could have a line of vendors along the edge. I'll reach out to them tomorrow." Pike started writing down the ideas and to-do list. "And despite his dorky-ass comment, I do like the holiday food contest. What about games and activities?"

"I think it should be an accumulation of events," Anthony said, finishing off his beer and getting up to throw it away. Over his shoulder, he said, "We can have some strange demonstrations, like chainsaw ice sculpting or something, in one tent. Maybe a hockey game."

"We definitely want to do a winter relay," Pike said, the wheels already turning.

"What do you have in mind? It will be too cold to swim," Nick said.

Noel nodded. "You could sled for one leg."

"Maybe that hill past the elementary school?" Pike offered.

"I've seen people ski on roadways. We have to hope for fresh snow, but that could be fun," Anthony said.

They sat quietly for several beats, before Noel laughed. "We have lived here our whole lives and can't come up with winter activities? Lame! What are some other things you do when it's cold outside?"

"Make snowmen?" Nick said.

"Snowball fights?" Anthony added.

"Maybe the skier could dodge snowballs while picking up snowman supplies." Pike saw Noel's skeptical expression and pressed on, "Hear me out. The last leg could be a sprint to a designated finish line where they have to build their best snowman."

"It has to be more than just a sprint," Nick said.

"What if they have to suit up in a Grinch costume?" Noel joked.

Pike stroked his chin. "That's not a bad idea."

"*You* can do that!" Anthony laughed.

"Fine by me," Pike said while writing down their ideas. "Food trucks. Holiday baking contest. Best sculpture. Hockey championship. Winter relay race. Snowball toss competition." Pike's mind was now racing with ideas. "Anything else?"

"I think that's enough to send to Merry and get her final input," Anthony said.

"Then the committee meeting for the first annual Mistletoe Winter Games is concluded." Pike held up his beer bottle, waiting for his friends to tap theirs to his. "Now, what should we do?"

"I don't know about the two of you but we," Nick said, climbing to his feet, "are going home."

"We are?" Noel asked.

"Yeah, we have that thing to do, remember?" Nick waggled his eyebrows, and Noel's face lit up.

"Right, that thing."

"Y'all are so obvious," Anthony muttered.

"Nasty," Pike agreed.

"Says Single-Dee and Single-Dum," Noel said, sticking her tongue out at them. She got to her feet and gave them a little wave. "Enjoy your bromance, my dudes."

"You are a couple of smug, married assholes!" Pike yelled after them as they headed for the door. Nick and Noel laughed, and Pike shook his head as the door shut behind them. "Can you believe those turds? Flaunting their happiness in our faces and mocking us?"

Anthony chuckled. "Come on, man. They're newlyweds. You can't tell me you wouldn't be doing the exact same thing if the roles were reversed."

"You know I would, but that's not the point. I don't like it when it's done to me."

"Well, too bad." Anthony got up off the couch, and Pike scowled.

"Are you going to ditch me, too?"

"Man, I am tired and sore, so yeah, I'm going home to take a long, hot shower."

"That's fine." Pike sniffled. "I'll just sit here, alone in my apartment, letting loneliness overtake me." Changing up the forlorn tone for a cheerful one, he added, "Or maybe I'll text Delilah, too. Set up our first date."

Anthony grabbed his coat off the back of the chair, but Pike could have sworn he was frowning. "Whatever floats your boat."

"Hey, don't be all gloomy!" Pike slapped him on the back with a grin. "Remember, we're about to be featured on *Excursions*. Millions of listeners. Exposure and advertising. This is going to be big."

Anthony returned his smile. "That is pretty cool, man. Thanks for taking the chance."

"I'm glad it paid off. Did you happen to look at those ornaments I sent?"

His friend scowled. "Yeah, and we are not shelling out fifty bucks per ornament. If you want to do the Festival of Trees, you better find something cheap. I'm not saying that the *Excursions* thing isn't going to be amazing, but let's not count our chickens before they hatch."

"Understood."

"Night," Anthony said, ducking out the door.

Pike locked it behind his friend and started cleaning up, putting the boxes of leftover pizza into the fridge. He dumped out any remaining beer down the sink before tossing the bottles in the recycle bin. Flipping off lights as he made his way back to his bedroom, he considered heading out to Brews and Chews for a little bit, but Pike hated going to the bar alone.

He sat on the edge of his bed and sent Delilah a text. It was only nine, so it's not like she'd mistake it for a booty call.

Hey. I hope you had a good day. Let me know what your schedule looks like. I'd love to take you out.

He stared at the message for several minutes, waiting for her to read it, but finally set his phone aside and stripped down. Pike went to the bathroom and brushed his teeth, thinking about what his friends had said about settling. Just because he finally felt like the age difference between them didn't matter and that they were in a good place to start something up didn't mean he wasn't truly into Delilah. Everything he'd said about her was true and then some. The fact that she'd been into him for a long time made it better. Less of a chance for him to get hurt.

Pike climbed into bed and checked his phone again. She still hadn't read it.

Is this what lonely feels like?

Pike leaned back against his pillow, the knot in the pit of his stomach continuing to twist on itself. For whatever reason, the walls seemed to be closing in on him the last few months, and he'd realized a few days ago that his inadequate love life was making him antsy. Not his sex life, which was probably a little too healthy, but finding someone who didn't use him as a placeholder for something better was more challenging than it should be. Pike liked to think he was a decent guy with a thriving business, but for whatever reason, the women he dated seemed to have one foot out the door, ready to run after whatever lawyer or doctor looked their way next. If he didn't know better, he'd think he was Good Luck Chuck or something, helping women find their true love after dumping his ass.

All his friends had taken the plunge and found someone special except for Anthony and Clark's brother, Sam, but the elder Griffin wasn't looking to settle down. They were the last single men standing in their group of friends. Pike couldn't wait to find someone to spend his life with, but discovering something lasting continued to elude him. His last meaningful relationship with Sally ended over a year ago, and he'd heard rumors the guy she was with now might pop the question.

Meanwhile, he was staring at his phone as if willing it to ping with a notification.

Pike noticed the Instagram icon at the top of his phone screen, indicating someone had commented or messaged him. He tapped on the DM symbol sporting a little red number one. It was from Ryler.

That picture of the hot springs looks awesome. I saw that you offer snowshoeing and guided hikes, but what about hot springs? Could we book one more day of your time? I think we could all use a little relaxing with the holidays approaching.

Damn, they were going to make out like bandits this year. Even without *Excursions* coming, they had nearly a full schedule starting next week. If things continued like this, they might have to hire someone to work behind the counter during store hours so that Anthony and Pike both could take clients out.

Of course, the thought of seeing Alia in a bikini up close and personal was just an added bonus.

Absolutely. I'm attaching a few available dates. Let me know what works best for you.

He sent the message and smiled when Ryler immediately read it. The dots popped up, and then the assistant's reply popped up.

I filled it out. We are on the plane headed home from Bali, so we might be a little jet-lagged when we arrive. Does your Lord of the Fries make lattes? ☺

Pike chuckled, typing, No, but Kiss My Donut does. And their maple bars are fantastic.

Mmmm, I haven't had a donut in months! Thanks for the tip. 😉

Pike reeled back, smacking against the headboard, and yelped, "Ow!" Pike rubbed his cranium as he stared down at the emoji. Winks were flirtatious, right?

Anytime, my dude. It was a bro response, but he didn't want to give the guy the wrong impression. While he may be an ally and joke around with his friends, Pike was a breast man to his core.

Pike backed out of the messages and tapped on the *Excursions* podcast, starting the season over. The new episode should drop next week, and Pike couldn't wait to hear about Bali. In all honesty, Alia Cole could talk about mud drying, and he'd still listen. Her voice was like a warm cozy blanket on a cold winter's night, and he closed his eyes, enjoying the comforting sound as he drifted off.

Chapter Four

"Idaho!" Alia griped for what felt like the billionth time since Ryler told her where they were headed next. "Why would you want to go back to that crap show?"

Ryler sat in first class next to Neil and ignored his raised eyebrow, which acted as a silent *I told you so*. She leaned across the aisle to address her cousin, who hadn't bothered to remove her sleep mask while she whined. The dim lighting of the plane allowed the passengers traveling overnight to sleep, so Ryler tried to keep her voice low, although irritation coursed below the surface. Alia had rarely visited Ryler's home state when they were younger, so how could she talk about it that way?

"I have fond memories of it," Ryler said tightly. "Besides, don't you want to celebrate Christmas where there's actual snow?"

Alia pulled off her sleep mask and sat up, her blue eyes narrowed. "Not really. I would rather spend the holidays sipping coconut drinks somewhere I won't get frostbite."

Ryler knew Alia was hungover and tired, especially since she had to be roused from her stupor in order to make their flight, but this was a bit overdramatic, even for her.

"Well, I can cancel your ticket and let you spend the holidays at the condo, if you prefer."

For a moment, Alia's eyes burned with frustration, but it faded just as quickly. It was a reactive quality that Ryler had gotten used to after sixteen years living with her cousin. Alia's moods shifted swiftly, giving most people whiplash, but Ryler had learned early on if she remained calm in the face of her cousin's emotional outbursts, they didn't escalate. Ryler chalked up Alia's behavior to her parents always jet-setting around the world, leaving her with nannies most of her life. When Ryler came to live with her aunt and uncle, Alia had been there for her, and Ryler had poured her broken heart over her parents' death out to her cousin. It was the two of them against the world.

Even when Alia had started modeling and traveling as much as her parents, she'd Skyped Ryler daily. Alia stopped going home during breaks in her schedule once Ryler got into UCLA; instead, Alia crashed at her cousin's off-campus apartment. After her fifth agency dropped her and she showed up on Ryler's doorstep four years ago, they'd spent the night sharing a bottle of Malibu and talking about their futures. It was during that coconut-infused night of drinking that Ryler had come up with the plan: Alia would be the face of the podcast on Instagram and Ryler would continue to be the podcast's voice. It gave Alia an adoring fan base and Ryler peace of mind, but above and beyond, it meant being with her family.

However, there was no way Ryler was going to let her ruin this holiday with a tantrum.

"I'm sorry," Alia whispered, releasing a long breath. "I know I'm acting like a brat."

Ryler reached across the aisle and squeezed her hand. "You're my brat, and I love you."

"I love you, too." Alia slipped her mask back into place and turned her face away.

Ryler settled back in her seat, and Neil leaned over to whisper, "Way to lay down the law."

"Shut up," she said, playfully smacking him. Neil chuckled, placing his headphones back on and pressing play on whatever podcast he was binging this flight. Ryler sometimes worried Neil was bored with *Excursions* and longed for a change of pace, but she was too afraid to ask him outright. They'd started the podcast together, and Ryler couldn't even imagine *Excursions* without Neil.

When she'd first brainstormed *Excursions*, it was a way to run from the fact that she didn't have anything to stay in LA for. After losing her parents and moving from Boise to LA, she'd poured her love into her cousin, but her aunt and uncle's mansion was never a home. Although they'd been good to her and she'd never wanted for anything but their time, Ryler wanted somewhere to belong. Her parents' life insurance had come to her in a trust on her eighteenth birthday, a substantial amount that paid for her college, her condo in El Dorado Hills, and had bankrolled the first few years on the road. With what her sponsors and advertising brought in now, she was able to leave her inheritance alone.

Still, Ryler kept searching for that sense of belonging and home she was missing.

Too wired to sleep, she logged on to the airline's Wi-Fi and tapped on Instagram. She hadn't responded to Pike's last message, unsure how to reply. It took her a bit to realize that Pike probably thought she was a guy and that winky face was a come-on. If that was the case, at least Ryler could say Pike had handled it with semi-professionalism.

Ryler clicked on @PikenAround's Instagram and read his bio again.

Pike Sutton.
Life is an adventure. Enjoy the ride.
Co-Owner of adventuresinmistletoe.com

Scrolling through his pictures, her thumb hovered over several, tempted to like the gorgeous landscapes, but Ryler didn't engage with her listeners like that, mostly because they would get the wrong idea about Alia being interested in them. Although Alia was the face of @ExcursionsPC, Ryler was the only one who could access it. While she loved Alia, her writing consisted of shorthand text styles—not exactly the branding Ryler was going for. However, there were numerous comments daily about Alia's face and body, which is another reason why she never engaged.

Ryler studied the beautiful pictures of mountains and trees, but it was the people that caught her attention.

The first post was obviously Pike's friend group, dressed up in Halloween costumes and sitting around a table. Pike was a pirate, sitting between Indiana Jones and Frankenstein. Ryler zoomed in on the pic, noting the dark eyeliner and charms in his beard, immediately appreciating his commitment. Ryler loved going all out for Halloween, too.

There were more posts of the same friend group, although she paused on a black-and-white photo of the man who'd been dressed as Frankenstein, now decked out in a tux and dancing with a beautiful woman in a simple white dress. Pike stood behind them, cheering, and Ryler read the caption.

When Noel asked me to be her bro of honor, I knew that this wedding was going to be epic. How could it not be, watching two of my best friends walk down the aisle and pledge to love each other until they kick the bucket? It was a day we weren't sure would ever happen, but I fully admit, seeing two people I love so damn happy made me weep like a fucking baby. Congrats, @NoelWins365 and @NickW2345! I am over the moon for you both!

Ryler laughed softly. Although not exactly eloquent, it was sweet and obviously heartfelt.

She scrolled again, lingering on a photo of an older woman with red hair cut short, wearing a pink birthday crown. A man with silver hair sat next to her, while Pike and a younger woman with strawberry blond hair stood behind them, all smiling. The caption was short and sweet.

Happy Birthday to the woman who ruined her body to give me life! Love you, Mom!

"What a trip," Ryler said aloud, grinning.

Neil turned her way and removed one side of his headphones. "Did you say something?"

Ryler's face warmed. She didn't want Neil to find out she was Instastalking their guide. "No, I was just talking to myself."

Neil gave her a funny look. "Is that a new thing? Should I be concerned?"

"Funny guy. Maybe you should quit being a producer and start a stand-up career."

"Don't think I haven't thought about it. I would kill it on the circuit."

"You mean bore your audiences to death?" Ryler said, smirking. "I agree."

"Damn, Salty Sally, you came locked and loaded."

"Don't dish it out if you can't take it."

Neil turned toward her, a wicked grin on his face. "Oh, I can take it—"

"Will you two shut up," Alia snapped, lifting her eye mask to scowl at them. "Some of us are trying to sleep!"

Neil leaned across Ryler and shot back, "Maybe don't stay out all night getting wasted with a Ken doll, and you won't be so cranky, Medusa."

Alia cocked her head, mouth hanging open. "Ken doll? What are you—" Her eyes flared wide. "Seriously? The guy bought me one shot and I do not turn down free top shelf."

"Whatever you say, princess."

Ryler arched a brow. If she didn't know better, she'd say Neil sounded jealous.

Alia hung in the aisle, closing the distance between their faces. "It's not the hangover. It's your voice grating on my nerves like nails on a chalkboard."

"My voice is grating?" Neil growled. Ryler leaned back as far as she could, Neil practically lying across her lap as he added, "Your voice is like a mermaid out of the water; high-pitched and painful!"

"I have no idea what you're saying! Mermaids have beautiful voices."

"Not according to Harry Potter! They're ugly, horrible creatures that screech outside of the water depths."

"Listen, nerd"—she punctuated the insult by pointing her finger—"just because you read a bunch of books does not make you smart!"

"Says the woman who thought Jane Austen was a clothing designer! Maybe if you actually cracked a book open, people would take you seriously."

"If people is you, I'd rather watch *Love Island* than read some boring, pretentious..."Alia kept ranting, the two of them were nose to nose, and Ryler could hear their harsh breathing in the quiet of the airplane. This was extreme behavior, even for the two of them. Although Neil and Alia hadn't always gotten along, it was mostly veiled insults, snark, and sarcasm. This was like something out of a sitcom, just before two characters started kissing and ripping each other's clothes off.

Ryler burst out laughing at the thought. Hell would freeze over after an asteroid hit Earth before Neil and Alia touched each other. Unless it was a prize fight where they got to hit each other.

"What's funny?" Alia asked.

Ryler was about to answer, but she saw the flight attendant peek around the corner and start toward them. Ryler put her hand in front of Neil's face, pushing him back into his seat. "You two look ridiculous. Enough of this."

"Is there a problem?" the flight attendant asked, glancing between Alia, who had buckled herself back into her seat, and Neil, who was removing Ryler's hand from his face.

"Yes, they were just in a heated debate about which comeback is superior, Backstreet vs 'NSYNC. Your thoughts?"

She gave Ryler a puzzled expression. "Uh, Backstreet."

"Not who I would have guessed, but good choice," Ryler said, smiling.

"Do you require anything?" she asked.

"No, we're good. Thanks." The woman walked away, and Ryler muttered, "Obviously not a pop culture fan."

"The next time you put your hand in my face, I'm going to bite you," Neil grumbled.

"Watch out, Ryls!" Alia sniped. "He probably has rabies."

"You know what—" Neil started to get out of his seat, and Ryler poked him in his ribs. He convulsed and fell back into his seat with a gasp. "Did you just tickle me into submission?"

"Yes, I did. The two of you have been going at it for weeks, way worse than normal, and it needs to stop. What is wrong with you?"

Neither one of them said much, and Ryler shook her head, addressing Neil, "Stop calling her Medusa."

"It's not like she knows who it is," Neil muttered.

"Actually, she's a mythological creature who was once a beautiful maiden until a jealous goddess cursed her with snakes for hair." Ryler snorted at Neil's slack-jawed expression, while Alia sniffed. "What? It's like you've never heard of Google."

Alia snapped her mask back into place and replaced her AirPods in her ears. Ryler turned to Neil, who had recovered from his initial shock.

"Do you want to explain what is going on with you and my cousin?"

"There's nothing going on," Neil said, opening up the sliding cover over the window, turning his back on her to look out into the darkness. "It's the same mutual loathing we've always had. We're just more vocal about it now."

"Uh-huh," Ryler said, looking at her phone screen once more. "Whatever you say."

Neil closed the window with a thwack. "What are you insinuating?"

"I'm just wondering if there is a bit of repressed lusting going on neither one of you wants to admit to," Ryler teased.

Neil's gaze flicked beyond her to Alia, then back to Ryler. "Nope."

He replaced his headphones, and Ryler left him alone, grinning to herself. They were complete opposites, and the only thing they seemed to have in common was Ryler. Imagining them going at it was so unbelievable, it bordered on comical.

Diving back into her Instagram observing, she continued to look through Pike's feed. His relationship with his family and friends was tight knit, which spoke to a likable person.

Plus, he had a really nice smile.

Guilt zipped through her, realizing she was ogling a strange man on the internet instead of shooting a message to the man she was dating to let him know she was excited to see him. The truth was, Oliver was nice and checked all the boxes for a good boyfriend; he had a busy career, his own place, and he didn't mind her being gone several weeks of the month. Which in itself was an issue, because if you wanted to be with someone, you should miss them and not want them gone all the time, right?

Ryler exited out of Pike's profile and typed Oliver York into the search bar in the Instagram app. Maybe she could get him on video call before he left for work.

Her thumb hovered over the message icon, when she spotted several new pictures he'd posted. Instead of initiating the call, she clicked on the newest picture. Ollie's slight build was decked out in a pair of bike shorts and a tank top, his balding head shiny as he held on to a petite Latina woman in hot pink running shorts and a tie-dyed sports bra, her hair styled in a short pixie cut.

The caption underneath explained everything. My beautiful girlfriend @claudialo916 and I enjoying an early morning run on the path.

They'd been making out on his couch several weeks ago, and suddenly he had a girlfriend?

When was the last time you actually spoke to him though? Two weeks? What man is going to think you're still interested after ghosting him for that long?

Ryler wanted to crawl into a hole, embarrassed at her arrogance. She'd just gone off without keeping in contact with him and assumed he'd be around when she got back.

Damn, what a jerk she was when it came to relationships. She couldn't even remember the name of the guy before Ollie, just that he liked to talk about his expensive aquarium and the fish inside.

"Ryls?" Alia whispered, breaking up her self-loathing.

Ryler turned to her cousin, waiting expectantly. "Yes?"

"I think I've come up with some even better options than Mistletoe *if*—"

When Ryler opened her mouth to protest, Alia spoke rapidly, "If you'll just hear me out."

Ryler pressed the button for the flight attendant. "I'm listening."

"Australia. We haven't hit all the cities on your list—"

"I lost interest after watching that giant spider jump on Neil's back."

Alia giggled. "It made for a good episode though, right?"

"Next?" Ryler said impatiently.

"What about New Zealand? It's Aussie adjacent, which means hot accents, but without the PTSD."

The attendant stopped in front of her, a bland expression on her face. "Yes?"

"Could I get a Moscow mule, please?" Ryler asked, figuring the alcohol might help her sleep.

"Right away," the attendant said, turning to Alia. "Anything for you, miss?"

"No, thank you."

When the woman walked away, Alia dived back in. "I've also heard Costa Rica is nice this time of year."

"Alia—"

"Oh, come on! We could go to flipping Finland if you want snow! Idaho is so . . . blegh!"

Forget the mule, Ryler thought, *I think I need something straight up*.

"I know you grew up there, but what are we going to do for three weeks or so in a cabin in the woods? That is how too many horror movies start, and I'm not about to be the star of *White Christmas No More*." The flight attendant returned with Ryler's drink, and Alia explained, "You know, because the snow turned red because of all the blood and murder."

Ryler swallowed the drink down and handed the glass to the attendant. "Another, please." The liquid burned down her esophagus and settled like a warm infusion in her stomach. The woman smiled, an understanding passing between them.

"I'll be right back."

"Thanks," Ryler said, collecting herself and taking a deep, bracing breath. "Alia, I just discovered that the guy I thought I was dating has a girlfriend because I forgot to call or text him for weeks. Now, does that mean that if I had kept in contact, maybe I'd be his girlfriend? Who knows, but it is obvious that I am lackluster when it comes to relationships. This holiday, I would like to reconnect with my childhood a bit and celebrate a traditional Christmas with the people I love, in a place that goes all out for the season. Can you just give this to me, please?"

"Is that why you're drinking? Because Ollie has a girlfriend?"

No, I am drinking because you are aggravating me. Ryler wasn't about to say that to Alia and start a full-blown argument on an international flight.

"Yes, I am drinking so I can fall asleep and stop berating myself for taking another nice guy for granted."

Alia laughed. "Come on, Ryls. You didn't actually like that guy."

Ryler sighed. "He was fine."

"But not *fiiiiiine*!" Alia said, dragging the word out.

Ryler fought a smile. "You're the worst."

"Sometimes," Alia admitted sheepishly. "I'm sorry I've been a pill lately. I just feel a little . . . useless, I guess?"

"What do you mean?" Ryler asked, accepting the new drink from the flight attendant, but the need to down it had passed with this new information. Her cousin felt useless? Since when?

"Look, I was a model for years. I'm used to smiling for the camera and playing a part, but lately I've felt like—people love *Excursions* because of you. Your voice, your antics. I'm just the eye candy."

"But they think you're me, so they technically love you," Ryler said.

"Yes, but not because of anything I did. I want to do something. Create something, you know?"

"Like what?"

Alia released a breathy laugh. "I'm not sure. I don't have any talents, really, except being pretty."

"That's not true. I've seen your watercolors. They are beautiful."

"And they look like a thousand other ones." Alia sighed.

Ryler snorted. "Do you know how many travel blogs are out there? I'm just lucky people fell in love with *Excursions* instead of one of the many others. Right time, right subject." Ryler reached out and squeezed her cousin's arm. "Seriously, you should do what makes you happy."

"I guess when I figure out what that is, I'll let you know." Alia grabbed her water bottle and held it up in a toast. "Until then, I guess we're going to Idaho!"

Ryler clinked her glass to Alia's water bottle. "To Mistletoe and a Christmas to remember!"

Chapter Five

On Wednesday, Pike stood between rows of trees at the Winters' Family Christmas Tree Farm, holding an axe in his hand. Every year, Pike, Anthony, and a bunch of their friends helped the Winters family get ready for the busy opening weekend after Thanksgiving. Most of the townspeople would make their way over throughout the weekend to get their choice of trees, which meant the flocking machine had to be checked, the wreaths stocked, and some precut trees scattered about for seniors who had ordered their trees for delivery. They'd set up the flocking tent and were now split up across the property to cut down delivery orders.

While Nick, who'd been partnered with Pike, walked ahead of him, studying the trees for the best-looking ones, Pike kept searching out Anthony. His business partner was off in the distance with Declan, and Pike watched them curiously. Anthony had been off the last few days, almost as if he were avoiding Pike. Which was strange and hard to do since they worked together.

"You think something is going on with Anthony?" Pike asked Nick abruptly.

Nick peeked his head around a fluffy noble fir, quirking a brow. "How so?"

"He seems more morose than usual."

Nick followed Pike's gaze to their mutual friend and shrugged. "It's the holidays and the first year without his mom. If he's down, he's got good reasons for it."

He knew Nick had a point. Anthony and his mom were close, and losing her devastated him, even if Anthony knew it was coming.

Still, there was this nagging sensation in the back of his mind that thought there might be something more going on.

"I feel like there's this cloud hanging over all of us."

"Not me," Nick said, stepping away from the tree with a nod. "I'm happy as a clam. This is the one."

Pike rolled his eyes as he lined up with the tree and brought his axe back. "Yeah, I know." He took a hard swing at the trunk. "Amazing wife." He dislodged the blade and wound up again. *Thwack!* "Great job." Pike let the axe fly again. "Getting ready to buy a house." Nick caught the tree as it fell with a crack, and Pike grinned, adding playfully, "Fuck you and your perfect life."

Nick's brown eyes sparkled. "Don't be mad, bro. You'll find someone."

And there it was. The asinine words of encouragement whenever his singleness was brought up. He couldn't even be mad about it because Nick really believed it. His friend thought that everyone's life would work out with a soul mate and a happily ever after, the damn romantic.

Pike wanted that, but he'd also wanted someone who loved him more. It might sound selfish, but he'd always been the one to fall first, fast, and hard. He was an average guy with a big personality, and he didn't do things half-assed, so if he was going to jump in, he didn't even consider how deep the water was or if there were sharks. He'd go in blindly and ignore the red flags. Like his ex attending "yoga class" every night after work when the schedule said Mondays and Wednesdays. Pike didn't think of himself as an idiot, but after being dumped for what his exes considered an upgrade several times—it made a guy wonder.

Pike could keep going out, hitting the bars, but he didn't want a random hookup with a stranger who would be leaving in a week. In addition, as a thirty-one-year-old man, many of the women hitting Brews and Chews were closer to twenty-one. Dating someone barely out of high school sounded exhausting.

What he needed was someone attractive and around his age who didn't look at men like meal tickets. That shouldn't be too hard, right?

Someone like Delilah.

"Well, I'm still waiting," Pike said.

"It's the holidays," Nick said, grinning as he picked up the tree by the trunk. "Aren't miracles kind of expected?"

"You keep having hope, Cindy-Lou," Pike said, stepping out of the way and grabbing the other end.

"How are things going with Delilah?" Nick asked.

"I'm not sure. I think Delilah is an interesting character. She doesn't care what anyone thinks about her, which I appreciate in a woman."

"You appreciate breathing in a woman." Nick laughed.

Pike gasped, pretending affront. "That is not fair. I also appreciate other normal bodily functions."

"You're an idiot."

Pike didn't argue. If he were a smart guy, he would have already set a date and time to take Delilah out. Instead, he was hoping to catch her and pin her down before she left the bachelor auction planning meeting at the main house today. From everything he'd heard over the years about Delilah's crush on him, Pike hadn't expected it to be this hard.

Pike knew that his friends thought he was this confident guy who couldn't be torn down, but that was all self-preservation. He'd really liked Sally, his ex, but everything he'd said to her had been twisted in a negative way, making him the bad guy. He could have fought it and told the truth, but what good would it do? His friends still loved him, and it wouldn't get Sally back. Even though they'd been broken up for over a year, during their time together, he'd thought they might be endgame. He'd ignored the red flags and the petty fights because, for the first time, he'd dated someone within the inner circle of their friend group. His relationship with Sally should have cured him of ever wanting to cross that line again, but having brought around enough women his friends despised, Pike still thought dating someone his friends knew and liked was the way to go.

They set the tree down inside the tent and had barely finished netting and tagging it when Pike's phone rang. Although he was tempted to let it go to voicemail, he answered his mother's call.

"Hi, Mom."

"Hi, honey. Are you still upset with us for driving out to Arizona tomorrow for the holiday?"

Pike grinned. "Nope, have a blast. Give Flora a hug and a middle finger from me."

"I'm not going to do that," she monotoned, used to his sister's and his outrageous behavior toward each other. Maybe it was the fact they were Irish twins and had never really had time to enjoy life without each other that made their love-hate relationship so virile.

"You know that you could have come with us," his mother said.

"Yes, but I have a business to run."

"I thought you were taking the weekend off?"

Damn, had he told her that? Stupid.

"True, but I also hate Arizona. It's hot and dry and full of cranky old people."

"Be careful who you're labeling old," she said, a clear warning in her tone.

Pike smirked. "Not you, Mom. You're timeless."

"Mm-hmm. We'll be back on Saturday, and we'll swing by with your sister's gift for you."

"Her gift? For what?"

"Christmas. She couldn't wait for you to have it."

Pike lost his smile. Any time his sister was excited about something, it usually did not bode well for him. "If it's a snake, I don't want it."

"Oh, don't be silly! As if I'd deliver a snake to you!"

"I just don't get why she's so anxious for me to have it unless it is something that will make me uncomfortable."

His mother scoffed. "Can't she just be happy that she found something you will love?"

"No, because she's my *sister.*"

"I'm not going to debate your sister's love with you," his mother grumbled. "I'll see you Saturday, and I hope you have a happy Thanksgiving."

"Happy Thanksgiving. Give everyone my best."

"I will. I love you."

"Love you, too. Bye." Pike ended the call at the same time Clark said, "And that's the last one! Who is ready to get cleaned up and eat?" The men in the tent cheered, filing out the entrance, and Pike ended up falling into step with Anthony.

"You still put out about your parents ditching you?" Anthony asked, a smirk turning up the corners of his mouth. The ball cap he wore hooded the upper half of his face, obstructing the view of his green eyes. Pike had caught himself wishing for his friend's big, muscular build and brooding good looks more than once, but being handsome hadn't brought Anthony any luck in the love department. Pike always felt like a ginger Kevin Hart among his friends: the short, funny guy that women always noticed last, but for whatever reason, Anthony got noticed and his relationships didn't last.

"No, I'm more concerned about the Christmas present she'll be bringing home from my sister."

"Maybe it's a sparkling new thong you can wear for the bachelor auction."

"Uh-uh, Merry said no nudity."

Anthony chuckled. "When have the rules ever stopped you?"

"Alas, my short time moonlighting in an all-male review is done and over with. While I'll relish the chance of getting back onstage to show the ladies of Mistletoe that I have a lot of love to offer, it will be in a vintage suit."

"I don't understand why we can't wear whatever we feel comfortable in," Anthony grumbled.

"It's about putting our best foot forward. You've seen what some of these guys wear to Brews and Chews. No woman in her right mind would waste her money on greasy hair and a barbecue-stained shirt." Pike clapped him on the back. "Look on the bright side, maybe you'll attract the attention of someone great, and you'll spend the holidays snuggled up under a blanket, talking about all the Christmas traditions you'll implement with your future kids."

Pike could tell by Anthony's expression that he wanted to say something snarky, but he refrained. His friend had been in a funk lately, especially when it came to dating, and Pike didn't know how to snap him out of it. If he looked like Anthony, Pike would eat up the attention at the auction.

Pike's phone went off, and he checked the notifications. It was an Instagram message from Ryler.

We're in the rental car on the way. Where are the trees? This does not match the pictures!

Pike laughed at the photo he'd attached of sagebrush and rolling hills.

"What's funny?" Anthony asked.

"Oh, the assistant for Alia Cole. He's in the valley on the way here and asking where the trees are."

Anthony's eyebrows shot up in surprise. "You're messaging with the male assistant, huh? You got something you want to share?"

"Oh, knock it off. Did you really think I'd be organizing all the details with Alia? She's got people for that."

"Yeah? What's her assistant's name?"

"Ryler," Pike said as they cleared the hill and crossed the gravel parking lot toward the main house. He tapped out a response and hit send.

Keep heading north. You'll find them.

RYLER

"What in the charming *Sons of Anarchy* town have you brought me to?"

Ryler ignored Alia's apt description of the adorable town, taking in the close buildings and elaborate window displays of each business they passed. Alia's exclamation was brought on by the group of men sitting outside of the coffee shop called Kiss My Donut, their long, graying beards nearly identical.

"Oh, stop being dramatic. This is beautiful." Although Ryler had doubts on the drive up that the place existed, Mistletoe was everything she'd been hoping for. Pike's assurance that the trees were there did not disappoint. Pine trees rose up on both sides as they exited the town limits, the GPS announcing, "In one thousand feet, make a right onto Blue Spruce Way."

"The mutant cannibals watching us from the trees are laughing," Alia sang as Ryler took the turn.

"Alia," she laughed, flicking her cousin's arm. "I'm going to make you walk to the house."

"Um, you can't. If the cannibals and biker gang don't get me, a bear definitely will," Alia said, pointing to a large sign that read *Bear Country* with a huge paw print on it. "You know I look like I'm filled with sweet cream."

"I don't want to know what you mean by that." Ryler laughed.

"I wish the guys would have just flown out here with us." Alia's voice trembled slightly, and Ryler's head whipped her way.

"I'm sorry, did you just say you wished *Neil* was here? Don't tell me after years of trading barbs and insults, he's finally grown on you."

Alia snorted. "Of course not, but having men around can be helpful. Someone to carry bags. Fetch firewood." Alia lowered her voice, but Ryler heard her clearly. "Trip them to give ourselves more time to escape from doom."

Ryler shook her head, grinning. Alia tended to ridicule her boyfriends, and the strangest thing about it was the meaner she acted, the more they loved her.

"If I didn't know that your animosity toward Neil was one hundred percent genuine, I'd think you were into him."

"Which would make you delusional, and I would worry for your sanity," Alia snapped.

"Relax, I'm only teasing."

"You have arrived at your destination," the robotic voice announced as the trees cleared and the gorgeous log home came into view. Ryler pulled up to the two-car garage and parked, twisting in her seat to face her cousin with a grin.

"This is perfect. The profile said it even comes pre-decorated with outdoor Christmas lights. We can get a tree and order some ornaments and garland—"

"When did you become Old Saint Nick?" Alia asked.

"I just think it will be fun to celebrate a traditional Christmas."

"I think the closest I've had to a real Christmas was that first year you came to live with us. Remember we cut down a tree in the front yard and dragged it inside? Mom and Dad came home from that gallery opening and were so pissed off. I think that is the only time I've ever seen my mom frown." Alia used her fingers to pull her skin up to her hairline. "Wrinkles."

Ryler burst out laughing, remembering that Christmas. After that, her aunt and uncle bought a fake tree, and the staff erected it every year for them, but it never felt like the holidays with just the two of them. Which didn't bother Ryler because Christmas became a special memory of her parents.

"This year we're going to make new memories," Ryler said, stepping out the driver's side. "We're going to look up traditions and try them all out, and it will be the start of something we do every year."

"Alright, Santa Ryler," Alia teased, opening up the passenger door. "Let's get inside before we're carted off by Fae folk."

"Please, nothing ever happens when the characters first arrive at the rural destination. We have a few hours at least." Ryler stretched her arms over her head. "Let's check out the house before we bring in the luggage."

Alia looked up, squinting at the trees. "It's getting dark. I say we bring them in now."

Ryler rolled her eyes but didn't argue, grabbing her backpack and large roller from the trunk. Alia grunted as she hauled the first of her massive suitcases out of the back.

"I told you this place had a washer and dryer," Ryler called over her shoulder. "You didn't have to bring your whole closet."

"This isn't even a quarter of what I needed," Alia grunted, lifting the second suitcase out and setting it on the ground with a clack. "That's coming from Amazon tomorrow."

"Oh lord," Ryler laughed, stopping at the top of the stairs with her two bags and looking down on her cousin. "You're about to lose a bag."

Alia squealed as she chased after her smallest rolling suitcase with the wobbling gait of a woman in stiletto boots. The blush-pink hard-sided case had started to take off down the driveway and she managed to catch it when it hit a rock and toppled onto its side, the sound of plastic scraping across the asphalt.

"Oh no!" Alia lifted the case, running her hands over it like an injured child. "She's all scratched up."

Ryler rolled her eyes and continued to climb the stairs, ignoring her cousin's vocal exertion behind her for as long as possible before she stopped to check on her.

Alia's face was ruddy, and her forehead and nose glistened with the sweat of exertion. Suddenly, she stopped halfway up the stairs and bent over the largest bag as she glared up at Ryler, her arm gripping the handle of the second bag behind her. Her third, injured suitcase had been abandoned at the bottom of the stairs.

"You could"—Alia wheezed, her words high and tight between gulps of air—"help, you know."

"Oh, absolutely not. This is your burden, as I told you multiple pea coats were ineffective and absurd."

Alia launched the suitcase behind her onto the step next to her, panting. "You'll be singing a different tune when they pop in the dreary, snowy pics Kit is going to take!"

Ryler rolled her eyes. "You would have been better off with one puffer jacket."

"I'm not looking like a fluffy marshmallow!"

"Narcissist!" Ryler teased.

"I just care about my image, which is also *your* image!"

"Please, you'd look beautiful wearing a dress of dead fish."

"Ew, why would you even use that example?"

Ryler shrugged. "I could have said 'wearing a boa constrictor.'"

Alia shivered. "I'll take the fish."

Her cousin hefted her bags and grunted the rest of the way up the stairs, making Ryler giggle. Although the clothes changed, packing a suitcase was almost muscle memory for her. Seven pairs of underwear and socks. Several bras and a set of workout clothes. Jeans and tees, a few hoodies, and sweaters. A simple black dress, just in case.

Ryler smiled, remembering her mother dressing for date nights with her dad. She'd never worn jeans, always donning a dress and heels. Ryler would stand behind her, watching her put on her makeup in the vanity mirror. Once, she smiled and said that dressing up made her feel special, which added to the magic of being with her husband.

If Ryler's aunt hadn't gotten her into therapy right away or if Alia hadn't been waiting for her, needing her, maybe her parents' death would have affected her differently. Although she'd been devastated and missed them every day, she'd been lucky to have had them and equally blessed to have ended up somewhere safe when they were gone.

They hauled their bags up through the front door, and Ryler put in the code, popping open the lockbox to retrieve the two keys inside. Once she unlocked the door and pushed it open, Ryler released a happy sigh as she took in the wooden beams and high ceilings.

"It's perfect."

"Great, can I get by you?" Alia slid her bag into the house with a deep breath, and Ryler stepped aside so she could bring the other over the threshold.

"You good?" Ryler smirked. "You're breathing kind of hard."

"I'm fine," Alia wheezed, straightening up. "Want to help me carry my other two bags up the stairs?"

"Um, no."

"That's rude," Alia muttered.

Ryler threw her arm around her cousin and gave her a smacking kiss on her cheek. "But I will 'cause I love you."

They finished bringing in the luggage and located their rooms on the second floor. Ryler had been about to place an online grocery order, but it wouldn't be there until Saturday, so she'd scrapped it with the plan of doing her grocery shopping in person.

"I'm going to head to the store and grab a few things," Ryler said.

Alia groaned. "It's six o'clock. Can't we just order food and go out tomorrow?"

"Tomorrow is Thanksgiving. Nothing will be open."

"What about Starbucks?" Alia asked, hopefully.

"Did you see a Starbucks when we drove in?" Alia shook her head, and Ryler held her hands up. "There's your answer."

"You mean we are going to be stuck here until Friday morning with nothing to do?"

"Of course not! I'm going to head into town now and get some groceries. Maybe we could even find a restaurant to hit for dinner."

"Preferably one that doesn't serve roadkill," Alia muttered.

"Let's go," Ryler said, holding the door open for Alia, who passed through slowly. Ryler locked up the house, and when they were back in the car, she did a three-point turn in order to get out of the driveway. Alia sat in the front seat, staring out the window, sulking.

"Do you want to look up a grocery store for me? I remember seeing one, but I'm not sure where."

Alia tapped the screen of her phone, silently searching as Ryler read the signs of businesses they passed.

"Oh! Pike said that Lord of the Fries diner is good."

"Who is Pike?" Alia asked without taking her eyes off her screen.

"He's the guy who recommended Mistletoe."

"What kind of name is Pike?"

"I don't know, a name his parents gave him?" Ryler heard the edge in her voice and took a deep breath. Alia never paid attention to the details or the people that made their trips possible. "He's the one who owns the guided tour company. I signed us up for a couple of adventures, like snowboarding, snowmobiling—"

"I found the store," Alia broke in. "Take a left at the next street."

"Alright," Ryler said, giving up on convincing Alia this would be fun. "Neil and Kit should be here early afternoon Friday. I figure that will give us plenty of time to get up Friday morning and find a Christmas tree."

"Sounds like a plan."

Ryler ignored her sarcasm and parked toward the front of the store, noting the limited number of cars. As they exited the SUV, Ryler spotted a woman in a police uniform leaving the store and called out, "Excuse me, Officer?"

The woman turned their way, her delicate features friendly. "Hi, can I help you?"

"Yes," Ryler said, moving closer. "We're staying in a house just outside of town for the holidays, and I was wondering if there is a place we could grab dinner and maybe a drink?"

"Sure, Brews and Chews Bar and Grill. You just follow this road," she said, pointing to the right, "and it will be on your right-hand side about a mile up."

"Thank you, Officer"—Ryler read her name tag—"Wren."

"My pleasure. Enjoy your stay."

"Not likely," Alia muttered, but Ryler ignored her snark. They were going to have a great time, even if she had to force the fun down her cousin's gullet.

Ryler's phone pinged, and she pulled the device out of her purse. An Instagram notification flashed on the top of her screen, and she noticed @PikenAround, so she clicked on it. She smiled as she read his comment on her picture of the Mistletoe sign.

Mistletoe is ready to give you the warmest welcome! Thank you!

Ryler almost snorted at the professional message. She preferred the funny, candid Pike to the guy trying to play the role of the proper business owner. Ryler couldn't wait to meet him in person and find out if he was as funny offline. The fact that he was probably expecting a male assistant tempted her like crazy to mess with him, but the last thing she wanted to do was offend him when they would be there for several weeks. Although Ryler planned on staying at least through Christmas, Neil and Kit would probably duck out earlier than that to spend the holidays with their families. Her aunt and uncle were spending the holidays with friends and hadn't extended invitations to Alia or Ryler to join them, but that was fine. Her aunt and uncle behaved more like doting benefactors than family to their only child, let alone their niece, and while Ryler had felt bad for Alia at first, she realized that her cousin didn't mind being away from her parents. Their complete detachment was the opposite of Ryler's upbringing; she was surprised Alia was able to form attachments at all as an adult.

"I need to find the bathroom," Alia said as they walked through the automatic doors. "I'm feeling a bit nauseous."

"Do you want me to come?" Ryler asked.

"No, please get started on the shopping. I'm tired."

Ryler watched Alia disappear into the bathroom before she grabbed a cart and headed for the produce first. She passed by a cold case with a mirror angled down at her. Ryler saw a woman with an oval face, her wavy hair pulled back in a ponytail with wispy strands escaping the confines. Freckles dotted her cheeks and the bridge of her slim nose, the only feature she shared with her cousin. Her lips were full and her chin slightly pointed. Her generous chest stretched the words on her cropped T-shirt, which brushed the top of her high-waisted jeans. The denim hugged her hips and thighs, showing off the curves that had made her self-conscious in middle school and high school. Being midsize in the fashion world was like being in limbo, especially when it came to certain styles that were so popular. While the hipster pants of the early 2000s were coming back in style, Ryler refused to give up her mom jeans, no matter how many times Alia tried to get her to conform.

She'd never been able to hold a candle to her taller, slimmer cousin, but after her initial bout of teenage insecurity, it didn't matter. Ryler was a tomboy, practical and driven, and Alia was bougie. They'd never competed over men or accolades, supporting each other instead. That is why their working relationship had lasted so long. They complemented each other well.

Ryler pulled out her phone and leaned across the handle of the shopping cart, tapping out a message to Pike. Made it to our rental. Going to grab some food and catch up on sleep. See you Friday and Happy Thanksgiving.

She slipped her phone into her back pocket again, smiling. The radio in the grocery store was playing holiday music already, large green boughs of garland hanging high on the walls. Cartoon Christmas characters were taped below and above the greenery. Ryler stopped in front of the dairy case and grabbed a carton of eggnog, setting it in the cart.

"Ew, eggnog?" Alia groaned, coming up alongside her. "Don't make me throw up again."

"You puked? Why?" Ryler asked.

Alia shrugged. "Probably still hungover."

Ryler knew that wasn't it, since it had been two days since Ryler had seen her drink anything. "So, you're not hungry?"

"I am," Alia said, grabbing a half gallon of nonfat milk.

"Then how about we get this done fast, go get some food and drinks"—Ryler bumped Alia with her hip—"flirt with a few guys."

"Ha, if we find one doable guy in this town, I'll die of shock."

I know at least one exists.

The thought of Alia showing interest in Pike, however, didn't sit well with Ryler.

Are you seriously calling dibs on a man you don't even know?

"Let's hope that doesn't happen."

Chapter Six

Wednesday evening had taken an unexpected turn for Pike when their friend group finished helping Nick get the Christmas tree farm ready for the Friday after Thanksgiving. They'd headed back to the house to find out what Mrs. Winters was making, only to discover Merry, Holly, and Delilah planning the holiday bachelor auction. Since he and Anthony were going to be a part of it, Pike was completely invested in how it should turn out. After they'd gone to Anthony's trailer to clean up, the group of men returned to brainstorm. Even Victoria and Chris Winters got into it, tossing out names like trivia answers.

Getting Delilah alone had been impossible until this point, but the plan he'd devised in the meantime was sure to score him a date. Fingering the sprig of mistletoe he'd slipped in his pocket, Pike waited for Delilah to finish her goodbyes with the Winters. Like all their children's friends, Victoria and Chris treated Delilah like one of their own.

"Delilah, you are allowed to call us by our first names." Victoria gave her a hug, a sheepish grin on her face as she added, "Pike and Anthony have been calling me Victoria since they were seniors, and I like you better than them."

"That hurts me!" Pike gasped.

Victoria scoffed. "She doesn't come in and eat all my food."

"It's a compliment to your culinary skills," Pike protested.

"Thank you, Victoria," Delilah said, giving the rest of the room a wave. "Good night, everyone. Holly, I'll text you when I make it home."

Holly hopped up from the couch to hug her, whispering something that Pike couldn't hear. But as Delilah responded, "Of course. That's what besties do," he assumed it was to thank Delilah for her help.

As everyone else called out their farewell, Pike stood up. "I'll walk you out."

Pike rounded the couch, his steps faltering when he caught her expression. Why did she look like he'd offered to walk her into the woods and leave her there?

Despite her less than enthusiastic response, Pike grabbed the front door and held it for her. "I'll be back in a minute," he said, catching Anthony's stony expression. Pike thought he'd at least have gotten a thumbs-up or some form of encouragement from his friends, but only Noel was smiling.

He shut the door behind them, pulling at his bow tie as he caught up to Delilah at the bottom step. She was facing him with her hands in her pockets, her breath fogging from the cold.

"What's up?" she asked.

Straightforward and to the point. A lackluster segue, but he'd take it. "I just wanted a chance to talk before you took off. It was crowded in there."

"It always is when the family gets together," she said, starting to walk down the pathway.

He chuckled. "Fair enough." Her pace was brisk, and when she started pulling ahead, Pike took a few longer steps, stopping in front of her. She pulled up short, that wide-eyed deer-in-headlights look making his palms sweat.

"I know you've got places to go," he joked, nervousness tickling the back of his throat, "but I need to get this out there. I want to make plans with you before another man beats me to the punch."

A shadow passed over her face, and she frowned. "Why are you suddenly interested in me, Pike?" she asked, her voice laced with annoyance. "I mean, why now? I wasn't exactly subtle in my adoration all these years."

His mouth flopped open, completely stunned by her honest assessment. He couldn't fault Delilah for her suspicions, but had she needed to bring them up so bluntly?

It took him several beats to collect himself, and then he stammered, "I mean, it's hard to pinpoint the exact moment—"

"Come on, be honest," she broke in.

"I am! You've always been an attractive woman"—her eyes narrowed, and he realized that was the wrong thing to say, so he pressed on—"but I guess if I had to give you a reason, you caught my attention the night at Brews. You walked in, and it was like seeing you for the first time."

Delilah laughed bitterly. "Do you understand how insulting that is? I mooned after you for years. I've been the same size for at least ten of them, so it's not that I lost weight or something. All this pursuit is because of a dress?"

Rising irritation at her tone warmed the skin on the back of his neck, and he frowned. "I'm confused. Did you not wear that dress because you wanted attention?"

"Technically, yes—"

"Then why are you mad at me for giving you what you wanted?"

"Because it's superficial!" She exploded, her voice rising, and he glanced at the doorway, hoping no one heard her outburst. "You don't know anything about me. You liked how I looked Saturday night, but can you tell me a single fact about myself that makes you think, 'Wow, I want to pursue that girl'?"

"I—you're a good dancer."

"I took dance classes until seventh grade, so fantastic observation," she said, crossing her arms over her chest. "Anything else?"

Come on, man, think! "I need a minute."

"You take all the time you need," Delilah deadpanned. "I've had men who weren't interested in me romantically, but they didn't write me off as a person. You wrote me off until you liked the way I looked."

"No, I just thought of you as a kid! The best friend of Nick's little sister. I was graduating high school when you were just starting. You went away to college for four years and came back when I was with someone. It took me a long time to get over my first love, and now I am ready to find something real. There hasn't been a time for us until now."

"Except I'm not feeling it, Pike," Delilah whispered.

Pike stared at her, disappointment settling in the pit of his stomach like a stone. He'd pinned all his hopes on her, on this chance to find someone who would give him her whole heart and then some, but he'd missed the moment.

Or had he?

Pulling the mistletoe from his pocket, Pike asked, "Are you sure?" He took a step toward her and held the sprig of greenery above their heads. "Should we put this to the test to be sure?"

Delilah laughed. "Why do you have mistletoe in your pocket?"

"Victoria always hangs a few sprigs around the farm during the holidays, and I thought it might be useful. What do you say?"

Delilah barely finished her nod before his mouth dropped to hers, soft lips melting under his. His tongue swept inside, seeking hers, and she kissed him back sweetly. It was a nice kiss, but there was no fire. No explosion of lust that made him want to back her against the nearest surface and rip her clothes off.

From the way Delilah broke the kiss and stared at him, the little lines of her forehead furrowed, he could tell she felt the same.

"You still not feeling it?" he asked.

"Don't let me interrupt," Anthony said, coming down the front porch steps.

Delilah gasped, and Pike wanted to punch his best friend. "You've got some timing there, bro."

"Like I said, carry on. It's not my fault you picked the only exit to make a move."

He passed by, and Pike saw Delilah glance after him, worrying her bottom lip. Was she embarrassed that Anthony had caught them?

When she finally met his gaze, she asked, "Sorry, what did you say?"

Ouch. Might as well get this over with. Pike wasn't sure his pride could take any more indifference.

"I asked if you were still not feeling it."

"I—" She cleared her throat, the noise inaudible over the roar of Anthony's truck and the crunch of gravel under tires. "I'm sorry, Pike. I think we missed our boat."

"Wow," he said, running a hand through his hair. "I thought the mistletoe was charming."

"It toed the line between charming and corny. I think it would work wonders with the right girl."

"But that's not you, huh?" he asked, slipping the mistletoe back into his pocket.

"It's not. I'm sorry."

Pike gave her what he hoped was a rueful smile. "Well, nothing ventured, nothing gained, right?"

"Yeah."

Delilah stood awkwardly, and he didn't want to prolong the rejection any longer, so he took a step back toward the house.

"I'm gonna head inside and grab another slice of pizza for the road," he said.

"Good night, Pike."

"You, too. Safe travel tomorrow."

"Thanks."

Pike backed up as he watched her continue down the walkway and through the gate to where her car was parked. Once she'd driven off, Pike was left with a conundrum. Did he bravely go back inside and admit to his friends and the Winters that he had struck out? Or dip like a coward and head to Brews and Chews for a self-pitying binge?

Pulling out his phone, he chose the latter, shooting Nick a text.

Suffered a painful rejection, so I'm ducking out. Tell your parents thank you and I'll see you all tomorrow.

His phone chirped as he climbed into his car.

Sorry, man. You need me to come meet you?

While he'd have loved Nick coming out to chill with him, being around Nick and Noel's love would only pour salt in his open wound.

Nah, you hang with your fam. Night.

RYLER

Ryler finished off her burger with gusto, moaning happily. "I think that was the best burger I've ever tasted."

"It was pretty good," Alia admitted, absently nibbling on a French fry as she stared at her phone screen. They'd taken the groceries home and headed back out to the bar in the pines. While Alia had originally balked at the honky-tonk atmosphere of Brews and Chews, Ryler had ordered her cousin's favorite cocktail, and all had become right with the world.

Ryler's foot tapped along with the song blasting over the speakers, although she couldn't remember the name or artist. The dance floor was empty with the exception of one couple who were getting down and dirty. A few guys sat at the bar, chatting up the gorgeous bartender, and two women sat at a table near the exit. Otherwise, they were the only ones in the place.

"I guess the day before Thanksgiving isn't exactly a party night," Ryler joked, watching her cousin for the hint of a smile, but she didn't even glance up.

By the way her thumbs were moving, Alia was texting someone, but she finally responded, "It's also eight on a Wednesday."

"That is true," Ryler said, pausing to see if Alia would notice her irritation before adding, "Which one of your many admirers are you chatting up?"

Alia blushed, finally looking up from the phone, although she didn't exactly meet Ryler's eye. "No one special."

"Then why is your face so red?" Ryler teased.

"Because it's really warm in here," Alia said, suddenly getting up from the table. "I'm going to the bathroom."

"Alright," Ryler said, watching her leave. It wasn't like Alia to be cagey about her conquests. Was she recycling an ex Ryler didn't approve of? Oh man. The list of sucky former boyfriends was long, and Ryler hoped she was wrong.

Ryler's notification beeped, and she checked her Instagram DMs. Glad you made it safely. If you and the crew want to meet up, I'm headed to Brews and Chews for a drink.

Rylie's pulse kicked into high gear. Pike was going to be here? Tonight?

Sure, she'd imagined there was a possibility he'd show up, this being a small town and all, but the knowledge that he was coming . . .

Not to mention he thought she was a guy and was probably in lust with her cousin, but details.

The pretty bartender waved at someone behind Ryler. "Hey, Pike."

Ryler straightened at the name, turning discreetly in her chair to get a look at him. He appeared disheveled compared to his Instagram pics, as if he'd just gotten out of the shower. His hair was brushed back like he'd just run his fingers through it. The collared shirt he wore was unbuttoned at the top, and there seemed to be something hanging from it she couldn't make out. His shirt was untucked, covering up his jean-clad backside.

Not that she was looking.

"Hi, Ricki, how are you?" he asked, taking an empty stool with his back to Ryler.

Ricki shrugged, her smooth tan shoulders exposed in her muscle tank top. "Same old. Want a beer?"

Pike shook his head, and although she could only make out his profile, Ryler thought he may have winced. "Something stronger."

"Rough day?"

"I'd say so."

"Whiskey it is, then." Ricki grabbed a bottle off the shelf and brought it back over to the bar tap with a glass full of ice.

Alia came out of the bathroom, and Ryler held her breath, hoping that Pike wouldn't recognize her yet. Ryler wanted to have a little time to watch him before introducing herself . . . and Alia.

Yeah, that doesn't seem stalkerish at all.

Ryler could freely admit that she found the guy intriguing and the last thing she wanted was to watch him drool all over her cousin, which was bound to happen. Every guy lost their mind when they met Alia, except for Neil and Kit, but they were atypical. Pike definitely seemed like the type of guy to be struck dumb by big blue eyes and a killer smile.

Alia managed to make it back to the table without being recognized by Pike, probably because she was bundled up in a sweatshirt and jeans, her blond hair haphazardly thrown on top of her head. It wasn't her normal look, but he also seemed distracted by the need for another drink and was hyper-focused on the bartender, Ricki.

"Are you about ready to go back to the house?" Alia asked, standing behind her chair with her back to Pike.

Ryler glanced from her cousin to Pike's impressive shoulders. "Not particularly."

"Really? Because I'm feeling kind of funky."

Ryler noticed her cousin's pallor and wanted to kick herself for being a selfish tool. Alia obviously wasn't feeling well, and Ryler kept railroading her into staying because Ryler wanted to check out their guide.

"Of course, we can go. Sorry, I was just people-watching."

"That's okay, you stay. I'm sure I could get an Uber to take me back to the house."

Ryler laughed. "An Uber here? I doubt it."

"Oh, you want to bet?" Alia said, holding up her phone. "Check that out."

Ryler saw the little white car that would cost Alia fifteen dollars to hail and shook her head. "You don't have to do that. I'll just finish my food, and we can bounce."

"Ryler," Alia exhaled. "I am giving you an out. I know I have been a crabby Patty all day and you are sick of my ass. I will go back to the house, take a Tums and a bath, and go to bed. If I don't wake up rejuvenated and cheerful, you can push me out a window tomorrow."

"Man, that is a tempting offer," Ryler joked. "You're sure you feel safe?"

"With the Uber driver named Tessa?" Alia asked, smirking. "Yeah. I'm still gonna be watching the tree line, though, for bears and cannibals."

"Alright, I won't be long." Ryler handed her the key. "Text me when you get inside and lock the door."

"The whole point is to stay long, you weirdo." Alia grinned when her phone beeped. "And she's here."

"Damn, she's quick."

"I actually ordered her when I was in the bathroom." Her smile widened, eyes sparkling mischievously. "You seemed to be in your element among the mountain folk, and I didn't want to disturb."

Ryler shook her head with a laugh. "Be safe."

"You, too."

Alia got up and headed for the door, leaving Ryler alone at the table, her gaze flicking to Pike's flannel-clad back and shoulders. He was turned in the stool, speaking to the man next to him, and Ryler realized how crazy this was. What was she hoping to accomplish by staying behind and watching him?

Ryler got up from the table, heading to the bathroom. She passed through the door with the *Cowgirls* sign and locked it behind her. She stared at herself in the mirror, a small part of her wishing she'd at least put on a little makeup today. She took her ponytail out, fluffing her hair around her shoulders. The natural waves hid the kink the band had made in her strands. Her simple cropped tee stretched across her breasts and dipped into a V, giving a hint of cleavage.

Oh my God, have you lost your mind? You can't hook up with this guy!

Ryler shook her head, reaching for the door. The little voice was right. She had booked five excursions, and it was a small town. Besides, what if she hit on him and he rejected her? Or worse, he hooked up with her but spent the remainder of the trip drooling over her cousin.

Ryler opened the door and stepped out, running smack into a wall of muscle that smelled like whiskey and cedar. Ryler bounced off him, catching herself on the wall. A soft, strong hand cupped her elbow and she looked up into heavy-lidded blue eyes.

"Sorry, I didn't see you," Pike said.

"Yeah, I kind of charged out of there, huh?"

"I had tunnel vision myself," he said, reaching for her other arm to help her upright. "You good?"

"Thanks." Ryler noticed that the string she'd seen hanging from his collar earlier was an undone bowtie, and she smiled. She'd noticed the bow tie in some of his pics, but thought it was due to special events. The fact that it was part of his style was adorkably hot.

He returned her smile with a nod. "Sure. Have a good night."

Pike continued down the hallway to a door at the back of the building. "You, too."

Something small fell out of his pocket, and Ryler trailed behind him, picking it up from the ground. It was a bushel of mistletoe.

Ryler followed him out the door, realizing she'd left her coat inside. The minute she stepped into the dimly lit courtyard, the icy breeze pricked along her skin. She spotted Pike along the edge of the fence, a lone figure in the dark.

"Hey," she called out. He turned around to face her, smiling quizzically.

"Hey again."

"You dropped this," she said, crossing the patio and holding the greenery out to him.

Pike looked down at it and laughed. "You keep it. Maybe it will bring you better luck than it did me."

"Oh, what? Were you walking around trying to get a bunch of girls to kiss you, and they said no?"

Ryler noticed his strained smile and wished she hadn't been so flippant. "Just one girl, but it didn't work out."

Ouch. "I'm sorry."

Pike shrugged. "You can only have one soul mate, right?"

"You believe in soul mates?" she asked, her stomach doing a little flip. It was such a romantic notion she wouldn't expect from such a burly guy.

"Sure. There are people out there we can be happy with but only one person who truly matches us." He leaned against the table with a heavy sigh. "Mine just seems to be eluding me."

Ryler liked that he was only five inches or so taller, not a huge difference, so she didn't have to break her neck to meet his eye.

She fiddled with the little plant in her hands, her mind screaming to turn back, but she ignored the warning. "So, you just hold this up above your head"—Ryler lifted her arm above them, dangling the leaves from her finger—"and you're guaranteed a kiss?"

Pike's gaze flicked from the mistletoe to her face, his expression unreadable. "Is that what you're looking for out here?"

Ryler's heart hammered at the gravelly edge in his voice, like the Big Bad Wolf tempting Little Red. "Yes."

Pike hesitated, his gaze traveling over her face, and when it dipped to her lips, heat swirled in the pit of her stomach. His hand cupped the side of her neck, warm fingers tangling in her hair.

"What's your name?" he whispered.

She smiled softly, stepping into him. "Does it matter?"

Ryler's eyes fluttered as he dropped his head, soft lips crushing hers. The whiskers of his beard tickled her skin, and gooseflesh exploded along the surface. He tasted like whiskey, and she opened her mouth wider, taking his thrusting tongue. His hands slipped over her shoulders and down her back, pressing her body flush with his, and her nipples puckered against the cups of her bra. She arched closer, kissing him back, returning each drive of his tongue.

Shit, Pike can fucking kiss.

Ryler wrapped her arms around his shoulders, lost in his taste and touch. How long had it been since she'd made out like this? Since a man had made her lower back tingle and her body ache for more. Being physical with someone was about release, satisfactory and efficient, but the way Pike's hands splayed against her back, gliding over her denim-covered hips, made her think there was something missing in her sex life.

She gasped when he lifted her onto a nearby chair, holding on to her thighs and stepping between her legs. She'd had a few one-night stands and on-the-road hookups, but this was the first time she'd ever initiated intimacy with a stranger. Ryler wasn't sure what it was about Pike, but even before she'd seen him headed for the bar, his pictures, his profile, the way he talked about his friends and family had drawn her to him. To Mistletoe to meet him. While yes, the idea of a snowy, traditional Christmas setting for the podcast had sounded perfect, she could admit that meeting Pike had also been a draw.

Ryler locked her ankles against his back, relishing the hard bulge of his erection pressing into her. She couldn't remember the last time a man had kissed her like he couldn't get enough of her, and here was this virtual stranger giving her the type of kiss she'd only ever heard about.

Pike jerked his mouth from hers abruptly, his breath rushing out hard and fast across her lips. "Fuck, I'm sorry."

"For what?" she whispered.

"You asked for a kiss and I practically assaulted you."

Ryler tightened her ankles. "Trust me, if I didn't want this, you'd be a sobbing heap on the ground."

Pike chuckled. "Is that a fact?"

"Absolutely. I've taken over a dozen self-defense and martial arts courses. I could take you out with a well-placed finger."

Pike brushed her hair back, grinning at her. "I think I'm already a goner."

While the line was cheesy as hell, the emotional undertones of awe and desire matched her energy, and she brushed her lips over his. Ryler strayed from his mouth, exploring the skin of his neck, the lobe of his ear. His hands squeezed her thighs when she nipped at his pulse point, and she gasped when he rolled his hips, lust pulsating in her pussy.

"Seriously, what's your name?" he murmured, one hand now cradling the back of her head. She leaned back into his hand, meeting his gaze and shooting him a saucy grin.

"Hmmm, guess."

His lips grazed her cheek. "Stephanie."

"Nope."

He nipped at her earlobe, and she closed her eyes against the zing of pleasure. "Paula?"

"You'll never guess."

The hand still on her hip skimmed up her thighs, and dipped between her legs slowly, giving her ample time to say no. When he finally cupped her, his finger stroking her through her jeans, she arched against his caress with a low moan. Anyone could come out and discover them, but she didn't care.

"Tell me," he said, his fingers rubbing against her harder, creating a tingle of need inside her core, "and I'll kiss you somewhere else."

Holy shit! This wasn't her. She didn't dirty talk with strangers on cold dark nights, and she especially wasn't tempted to let them do exactly what they promised in a public area.

He pulled down her T-shirt and sucked at the skin of her collarbone.

She gasped, holding on to his shoulders as he withdrew his mouth with a pop, kissing a trail along her chest until he reached the top of her left breast.

"Your name?" he coaxed, rubbing her in an upward motion through her jeans.

Her pussy tingled, her desire soaking her panties, and Ryler forgot why she should tell him any other name. His touch was like a truth serum, and she whispered, "Ryler," a second too late and froze.

"Ryler, that's—"

Suddenly, he jerked away, his jaw hanging slack. "Ryler?"

She held on to the stool, nodding.

"With *Excursions*?"

"Yes."

"Shit, I'm Pike." Pike ran his hands through his hair, staring at her. "I thought you were a guy."

Ryler laughed softly. "I had a feeling you did."

"Why didn't you tell me?" he asked.

Ryler slipped off the stool and approached him, frowning when he backed away from her. "I thought it would be a pleasant surprise."

She reached for him, but he took her hands, shaking his head. "You're Alia's assistant."

Ryler bit her lip. "So?"

"We can't—you're here with—" He released her and rubbed his hand over his face, laughing. "Damnit, this has not been my day."

"Wait, two minutes ago you were fingering me through my jeans, and now you're dipping because I didn't tell you I was a girl?"

"No, you don't understand. I cannot mess this up, and sleeping with you, with Alia Cole's assistant?" He held his hands up. "You don't know this, but I piss off nearly every woman I become romantically involved with."

"At this moment, I can understand why!" Ryler tried walking past him, humiliation gnawing inside her. How had she never considered that Pike would have kept things professional no matter what her gender was?

"Are you going to tell Alia?" he called after her.

A flash of hurt pinched her chest until it was replaced by fury. Was he actually asking her, after offering to go down on her, if she was going to tell her cousin because he what—thought something was going to happen between him and *Alia*?

"Why? You think you have a chance with her?" Ryler asked waspishly.

"No, I told you. This is the chance of a lifetime for my business partner and me. Letting him down isn't an option."

Ryler deflated and swallowed back her disappointment and humiliation, reminding herself that she'd done this to herself. Why the hell had she made a move on Pike in the first place? Now she was stuck here for three weeks, participating in activities that would throw them together, and all the while, she still wanted to kiss him.

Concealing her barrage of emotions with a wry smile, Ryler gave him a thumbs-up. "Don't worry, Skip. Your secret is safe with me."

Chapter Seven

There was a ringing in Pike's ears, making his whole head vibrate with pain, and as he blinked his eyes opened, he let out a strangled cry. What the hell had happened last night, and why did he feel like death?

He remembered having a couple drinks at the bar while he was waiting for Anthony to meet him at Brews. He went outside to get some air, and that woman followed him out . . .

Ryler.

Pike rolled onto his back, gripping his throbbing head. He'd kissed the assistant to the woman who was going to change all their fortunes—hell, he'd been about to do more than kiss her. If she told her boss, Alia would think he was a womanizing, philandering lout and probably take her podcast and business elsewhere.

Damnit, what had he been thinking?

That you were sad and lonely and a pretty girl was standing in front of you, asking you to kiss her.

And what a kiss.

How was he going to be in the same room with the woman and not think about the way she'd melted into him, wrapped herself around him, and followed his lead, a hot and willing participant, playfully teasing him?

And now his dick was hard. *Fan-fucking-tastic.*

That blaring ring erupted again, and Pike realized it was his phone. He blindly reached for it, squinting at the screen to see it was his mom calling. He slid his thumb over the green phone icon and cleared his throat.

"Hi, Mom."

"Happy Thanksgiving, sweetie."

Pike winced at the high-pitched volume of her greeting, holding the phone a few inches away from his ear. "You, too. How is Dad?"

"He's fine. He's in the kitchen helping your sister."

"That's nice."

"Why do you sound all stuffed up? Are you sick?" she asked.

"Nope, just woke up."

"Really? It's almost ten-thirty."

"So it is," he deadpanned.

"Well, I can let you go. I only called because we miss you."

"I miss you, too. See you when you get home."

"Bye."

Pike ended the call and let out a shaky breath. He needed a shower and something greasy to soak up the sourness in his stomach from too much whiskey. After Ryler had called him Skip in that snarktastic tone, she'd spun around and went inside before he could get his bearings. He'd thought about chasing after her and apologizing, but the part of him that could still feel the warmth of her on his fingers and the taste of her on his tongue thought that was a bad idea.

Pike swung his legs over the side of the bed, heading for the bathroom. When he'd finally gone back inside the bar, Pike ordered another drink and sat down with a couple of women by the door and proceeded to get rip-roaring drunk until Anthony arrived and cut him off.

The rest of it was a bit of a blur.

Pike tried calling Anthony, but when it went straight to voicemail, he decided to hop in the shower and clear his head. As the warm water sluiced over him, his mind drifted back to Ryler and those full, pouty lips.

Nope, damnit, it was one night. One fucking kiss, an incredible kiss, but that was all it was going to be.

Still, those lips were haunting him, and his cock was a turgid reminder that it had been weeks since he'd had his pipes cleaned.

Wrapping his hand around his girth, he stroked it up and down, twisting and pulling. He leaned his head back against the tile, imagining Ryler on her knees, those incredible lips wrapped around him, sucking him. Teasing him. Lapping at him. Her soft hands playing with his balls, squeezing him.

"Fuck yeah," he moaned as his dick surged. Pike imagined her swallowing his come, licking him clean like he was a fucking lollipop, and he sagged in relief. It had been a long time since he'd fantasized about any woman in the shower.

Pike finished showering and got dressed. Dinner at the Winters' farm was at two in the afternoon, and he wanted to get rid of this hangover before heading out there.

He was making eggs and bacon when his phone rang again and Anthony's name flashed across the screen. Pike answered on the second ring. "Finally. Where have you been?"

"Driving to Boise."

Pike reeled back and stared at his phone for a moment before asking the obvious question. "Why?"

"I decided to take my old man up on his offer and join them for Thanksgiving."

Pike's jaw dropped in surprise. Anthony and his dad had almost come to blows at his mother's funeral, and now he was spending the holidays with him? He had some major questions, but his brain was too foggy to articulate them without starting a fight, so he refrained.

"You mean I gotta go to the Winters' Thanksgiving hungover and alone? Do you know how depressing it is to be the only single guy in a room full of happy couples?"

"Actually, I do, but you won't be alone. I'm sure Clark's brother, Sam, will be there."

Pike shook his head. "Sam is way too cool for me. I can't carry on a conversation with that guy."

"I don't know what to tell you, bud. I left early this morning. I'm about fifteen minutes from his house."

Shit, was he really going to be on his own? "You could have brought me as backup! Someone is going to have to drag your ass out of there if he starts running his mouth again."

"I hope this is a peace offering, but if not, I'll leave."

"We could have gotten a hotel downtown and gone barhopping!" Man, he sounded like a desperate, petulant child, when Anthony was probably a jumble of nerves. He cleared his throat, adjusting his tone to one of concern. "Why didn't you tell me you'd changed your mind?"

"It was a last-minute decision, and I figured you needed to sleep."

"I did, but I would have been there for you. I know how hard it is seeing your dad. Besides, my mom called, and it reminded me they are bringing back my sister's Christmas present to me this weekend. I'm terrified."

"Why?" Anthony asked.

"My sister is evil, and my mom thinks it's hilarious."

He chuckled. "I like your sister."

"Because the two of you enjoy giving me rations of shit!"

"That's true. Still, I think you're worrying over nothing."

"We'll see." Pike grabbed a plate and scooped his eggs onto it. "So, will you be back tonight?"

"I'm not sure. I might get a hotel for the night and drive back tomorrow."

Pike picked up his bacon with tongs and set the slices on his plate. "Let me know what you decide, or I'll come looking for you. I can't run this business without you."

"I will."

"It's funny. I heard Delilah is in Boise this weekend, too. If you see her, talk me up. Maybe she'll regret her decision." Pike had no idea why he'd said that, especially after what happened with Ryler. If he'd really been broken up about Delilah, would he have almost taken Ryler home?

Maybe he *had* gone after Delilah because she was available and checked off all the items on his list. Sweet, pretty, funny . . . interested in him?

Unfortunately, he'd missed the mark on that one.

"Sure thing, man."

Pike heard the GPS announce, "You have arrived at your destination."

"Sounds like you're there." Pike grabbed a fork from the drawer and as he sat down at the table, he added, "Have fun with your brothers, at least. I might stay home and drown myself in pie and whiskey."

"You'll have fun with the Winters. Don't be a sad sack. When you meet the right woman, everything will fall into place."

"How do you know?" Pike grumbled.

"Because, like you said, even assholes have soul mates."

"Fuck you, bro," Pike laughed. "Later."

"Later."

Pike ended the call and set his phone on the table. He continued eating, his gaze moving over his empty apartment, a heavy weight settling in his stomach. Until last night, he'd thought his life was looking up, and things were going his way, but here he was on a major family holiday, alone. No family. A pity invite. No girlfriend.

"Happy Thanksgiving, you sad sack," he muttered, dropping his fork back onto his plate. Pike leaned back in his chair and picked up his phone again, tapping on the Instagram app. When he ended up on *Excursions* profile, he searched through all the pictures, looking for any of Ryler, but there was nothing. He checked out who *Excursions* was following, and of the ten people, she was number seven.

@rylerroams345 didn't have a plethora of smiling selfies on her profile. Her main photo was a big, white flower with green foliage in the background. As he went through her pictures, he noticed most of them were of scenery. Two guys kept popping up throughout, either drinking together or paddleboarding or lying on the beach. One of them was a tall Black man with his head shaved, and the other was a shorter man with spiky black hair. Further back in her posts, he found a photo of Ryler with her cheek pressed against the face of the taller guy, their eyes crossed and mouths wide open, tongues hanging out.

I love traveling the world with my partner in crime @TheRealNeilDeal34

Pike clicked on the guy's name, grinding his teeth when he saw that Neil's Insta was mostly pictures of Ryler and Alia, although the other man, @KitsgotPics90 showed up in a few. There was one picture that caught his eye of Ryler slung over the back of The Real Neil's shoulder, pushing herself up and laughing at the camera as he seemed to be carrying her into the ocean.

Was this guy part of the crew? Were they dating? Had she come on to him while her boyfriend wasn't in town yet?

Pike set the phone face down with a groan, dragging his hands down his face. One brief interaction with this woman, and he was Insta-stalking her and all her friends? Not to mention his jaw was aching because he'd been clenching it for a good ten minutes without realizing it. What was wrong with him?

Get it together, man. Tomorrow, you're going to take Alia and the rest of the Excursions *crew out and pretend like last night never happened.*

Chapter Eight

Ryler stepped out of the rental car with a smile as she scanned the Winters' Christmas Tree Farm. There were quite a few cars in the gravel parking lot, and Ryler could see people popping out between the rows of trees in the distance. Despite Wednesday night's disappointing interlude with Pike, she'd had a great time yesterday with Alia, eating junk food all day and watching seasonal rom-coms. Although Alia had scoffed at the predictable storylines and cheesy romantic moments, it was the first time they'd had a girls' day in a while.

Now that Thanksgiving was over, Ryler was ready to light this Christmas season up!

"Do you smell that?" Ryler asked, breathing deep.

"I smell dirt." Alia pushed her sunglasses on top of her head and sniffed. "Maybe a hint of pine."

Ryler closed her eyes and took another long breath before she murmured, "I smell Christmas."

"Of course you do," Alia deadpanned.

"Let's go!" Ryler pulled her purple knit cap over her ears and headed down the marked trail to the trees. She could see a large, white tent at the bottom of the trail and figured that was where they needed to go.

"Hey, Ryler," Alia called, and when she turned around, Alia had her phone up. "Smile, babes."

Ryler smiled, throwing her hands up in the air. Alia laughed. "Perfect. We should post it to the *Excursions* Insta."

Ryler shook her head. "No, I'll take one of you when we find the perfect tree."

Alia frowned. "The podcast feed doesn't just have to be me. We could include pictures of Neil, Kit, and you."

Ryler stopped, waiting for Alia to catch up before she asked, "What's wrong with you?"

"Me? Nothing. I'm doing what I promised and trying to be full of holiday cheer."

"I get that, but you're also someone who loves the camera. Why you trying to give up the spotlight?"

Alia snorted. "You make me sound like such a witch."

Ryler pulled up short and reached for her cousin's hand. "Hey, I didn't mean it that way at all. I was kidding."

Alia blinked her lashes rapidly as if she were trying not to cry. "Ugh, don't mind me. I've just been in my feels lately."

"Do you want to talk about it? Is it about a guy?"

"No," Alia said, her gaze shifting away. "None worth mentioning, at least." Alia squeezed her hand and gave it a tug. "Come on, let's get our tree."

Ryler let Alia drag her along, curious about her shifting moods. Was it the holidays making her cousin act so out of character? Maybe she was asking too much. While Ryler had warm memories of her parents during Christmas, Alia didn't.

"It really is pretty here," Alia admitted.

When they reached the white canopy, Ryler poked her head inside. It was bustling with people getting their trees flocked and shoved into cocoons of netting, and Ryler kept her eye out in case a familiar redhead popped up.

Alia gave her a little shove from behind. "Are we going in or what?"

"Yes, I was just trying to figure out who to talk to."

"Isn't that the dude from Instagram?" Alia asked, resting her arm on Ryler's shoulder, her finger stretched out past Ryler's nose. She followed Alia's finger, and sure enough, Pike was standing next to a taller man with brown hair, a saw in his hand. Pike wore a gray beanie and a navy work jacket, looking like a sexy hipster lumberjack or whatever the equivalent was. Ryler's mouth suddenly went dry as she imagined him peeling off his jacket and shirt to chop wood bare-chested.

Mmm, that beanie's working for him. He can keep that on, too.

Ryler shook herself, gritting her teeth against the lustful thoughts. "Yep, that's him."

"So, why aren't we asking him for help? He's the whole reason we're here, right?"

"Hmmm, debatable," Ryler grumbled, backing out of the tent, which meant pushing Alia with her butt.

"Hey!" Alia griped, stumbling back.

"Oops, sorry."

When her cousin got her bearings, she crossed her arms over her chest. "What did you do?"

"What?" Ryler feigned shock. "I did nothing!"

Alia watched her with narrowed eyes. "Then why are you being all squirrely?"

"Because I don't want to bother the man? He's busy." Ryler studied the landscape, the sky, but after several moments of avoidance, she couldn't stop herself from meeting her cousin's suspicious gaze. "Fine, something happened between me and him at the bar on Wednesday after you Ubered out."

"Really?" Alia went back to the tent opening and poked her head in. Ryler imagined Alia's blue eyes traveling all over Pike, probably imagining what he looked like naked.

Ryler clenched her jaw. "Stop being obvious."

Alia came out grinning. "You gonna tell me what happened, or should I guess?"

"I flirted. He seemed interested." Ryler's cheeks burned as she continued vaguely, "Things got hot fast until I told him my name."

"Why did your name cool things off?"

Ryler grimaced. "Because he recognized it from the email I sent as your assistant. He was afraid hooking up with me would ruin his chance to get to show you around Mistletoe."

"Except the person he should be trying to impress is you," Alia said, tapping her perfect French-tipped nail to her bottom lip. "Good kisser?"

Ryler couldn't lie. "Phenomenal."

Alia's eyebrows rose. "A man with a good mouth should never be wasted. Maybe you should tell him the truth."

First Neil and now Alia, telling her to out herself. Were they secretly conspiring against her and only pretending to hate each other?

"I think not," Ryler said.

"Hello." A cheerful blonde stepped out of the tent, shifting her dazzling smile between them. "Can I help you ladies?"

Alia seemed to be staring at her adorable pregnant belly, which pushed out the front of her gray sweater dress. Ryler stepped forward, shooting her cousin a warning look. Whatever Alia was thinking, Ryler hoped it wasn't completely tactless, and if so, she'd better keep it to herself.

"Hi, we were looking for a tree," Ryler said.

The blonde laughed, her hand waving toward the rows of green trees. "We have no shortage of that. Do you know what kind you want?"

"Actually," Alia said, shooting a sly look at Ryler. "We could use some big, strong manly help. Perhaps a strapping lad with red hair?"

Ryler would have to work on her alibi on the way back to the rental house, because she was going to murder her cousin.

"Pike? Sure, let me grab him for you," the woman said, disappearing inside.

"I seriously hate you," Ryler hissed.

"What?" Alia's tone was high and sweet. "I want to meet this steamy kiss-giver. Make sure he is good enough for my cousin."

"That's unnecessary, as it was just a fluke, a moment of lust that shall not be repeated."

Alia lifted the flap of the tent, grinning. "Well, don't look now, but Mr. Fluke is coming this way."

Ryler scurried to watch the activity over her cousin's shoulder, wishing a crack in the earth would open up and swallow her whole. The blond woman reached Pike, speaking and pointing their way. When he looked over and met Ryler's gaze, her face burned. His attention shifted to Alia, and his eyes widened. He started for them with a purposeful stride, and Ryler's heart sank.

Of course he's rushing over. He's excited to meet his favorite podcaster.

Man, even her inner voice sounded bitchy.

"Hmmm, I think I see it now," Alia whispered, glancing back at Ryler with a twinkle in her eyes. "Yeah, the shoulders. Wait, on second thought, as he gets closer, maybe it's those eyes. They're practically burning your clothes off."

"Shut up, they are not. If anything, he's excited to meet you. He's a big fan."

Pike reached them, his smile wide and friendly. "Hi, Miss Cole, it is a pleasure to meet you. I'm Pike Sutton, the one who suggested you come to Mistletoe. I'll also be taking you out on several guided experiences, courtesy of Adventures in Mistletoe."

Pike held out his hand, and Alia took it, returning his smile. "Pike, yes, Ryler speaks highly of you and your business."

Pike glanced her way briefly and back at Alia, making the hackles on Ryler's neck stand up. Was he going to just ignore her, then?

"I don't want to come on too strong, but I've listened to every single podcast multiple times, even the newest one. You've got a real knack for telling stories."

Ryler secretly beamed at the praise, even though it was directed at Alia.

"Aren't you sweet?" Alia said, taking Ryler's arm and pulling her forward. "Have you met my assistant, Ryler? I know you've exchanged emails . . ."

Pike cleared his throat, hesitating as his gaze held hers, but when she didn't admit their acquaintance, he said, "No, not in person. Hi, Ryler."

Ryler took his outstretched hand, squeezing it as hard as she could. "Hello, Pike."

His eyes narrowed, and his grip tightened slightly, not enough to hurt but to show her his strength, and she smirked, releasing his hand. "You can tell a lot about a man from his handshake."

"Oh yeah? Care to elaborate on mine?"

"Like a wet noodle."

Alia coughed, covering up a laugh, and to Ryler's surprise, Pike chuckled. "I'll have to work on that."

Damn, that wasn't the reaction she'd been looking for. Apparently, his need to make a good impression on Alia outweighed everything else.

Alia clapped her hands. "Any chance you're available now to help us find a tree?"

"It would be my pleasure," he said, and Ryler almost heaved at his fanboy drooling.

"Unfortunately, I didn't wear the right shoes to go traipsing around on uneven ground," Alia said, pointing to her high-heeled boots. "But Ryler knows what kind of tree I like."

Death was too good for her cousin. Maiming would be better.

"Sure, I'd be happy to help your assistant," Pike said pleasantly.

"Wunderbar. Is there somewhere I can sit and wait, maybe get a cup of hot cocoa?" Alia asked.

Pike pointed inside the tent to the pregnant blonde. "Just let my friend Merry know who you are and that I sent you. She'll take care of you."

"Thank you. Ta-ta, you two."

Torture. Maim. Kill. In that order.

"I take it she knows something happened?" Pike's tone was frosty to say the least, and Ryler glared at him.

"Don't worry, if she thinks you're hot, kissing me won't cockblock you."

"That is not what I care about—"

"Whatever," Ryler said, stomping toward the first row of trees.

She'd made it five steps when he caught up to her and muttered, "Anyone ever called you a brat before?"

"Not since I was five."

"Then you're long overdue."

Ryler snorted.

"What I was trying to say is that I don't want to sleep with your boss."

"Really?" Ryler spun around, crossing her arms over her chest. "You don't find her attractive?"

Pike spluttered. "That's—I didn't say that!"

Ryler hiked her eyebrows. "So, you do find her attractive?"

"This is a trap," Pike muttered.

Ryler snickered. "There's no trap. You think Alia is attractive. You're a heterosexual male, so that's a given. Therefore, you don't need to deny wanting to sleep with her."

Pike threw up his hands, saw and all. "I can find someone attractive and not want to have sex with them."

"Fine."

"Fine?" Pike's voice rose an octave, and she imagined he was ready to tear his hair out.

"I accept what you're saying. Isn't that what you wanted?"

Pike stormed past her, cursing under his breath. "Exasperating woman."

Ryler smiled behind Pike's back. For some reason, annoying the man was almost as fun as kissing him.

Chapter Nine

Pike walked ahead of Ryler, trying to rein in his temper. Whether she was deliberately messing with him about lusting after her boss or seriously believing he was trying to get into both their pants, he was tired of explaining his position. He just wanted to take them around Mistletoe and show them why the area was so special and worth exploring. Was that too much to ask?

The fact that Alia hadn't wanted to accompany them to find a tree was a bit disheartening, especially since at the top of the hill past the trees there was a great view of Mistletoe Peak.

"So, what type of tree do you want?" he asked, motioning with his saw at the rows of Douglas firs and noble firs. "Tall and skinny? Full?"

Ryler took a few big, rapid steps to catch up, and Pike tried not to notice how the purple of her hat made her brown eyes pop.

"The house we're staying in has a vaulted ceiling, so tall and full would be good. Maybe twelve feet."

"Okay, we'll have to go farther out then. There's a great view of the mountain just over the hill if you want to see it."

"Sure, lead the way."

Pike could feel the heat of her gaze following him; whether she was glaring at him or checking him out, he wasn't sure.

They walked in silence for several minutes before he asked, "I can't believe you knew who I was the whole time at Brews and didn't say anything."

When she didn't respond, Pike turned, and saw the telltale red in her cheeks. "You knew who I was, suspected I thought Ryler was a guy's name, and you came on to me anyway. Were you just messing with me?"

"No, of course not."

"Then why did you kiss me?"

"I guess I didn't want the mistletoe to go to waste," she said sharply.

"So it wasn't my sparkling blue eyes or sunny smile you couldn't resist?"

"Actually," she said flippantly, finally meeting his eyes, "it was a pent-up libido and the fact that I wouldn't break you in bed."

Pike reeled back, slightly impressed. "Well, that was brutally honest."

"Is that not what you wanted?" Ryler shrugged, marching ahead of him. "I have no other excuse except that you are an insanely attractive man, and when I saw you sitting there, drinking whiskey like you were trying to drown out the world, I thought we could . . ." She trailed off, her voice so soft he almost didn't catch it when she finished, "help each other."

Pike caught up to her, taking her arm in his hand to stop her. "You wanted to make me feel better?" Her admission touched him. That Ryler would feel bad for a buzzed guy alone in a bar was sweet.

"And myself. I'm not a saint."

"Obviously not." He laughed.

"Anyway, it's a moot point now because you ran scared; plus, now my boss knows, so absolutely nothing could happen between us even if I wanted something to."

Pike resented her presentation of the events, but he let it go for the sake of keeping the peace. "Then I guess we can stop all this snarktastic fun we're having and be professional?"

"Nah, I like snarky," she said, shaking off his hand. "I think I'll stay here awhile."

She took off again and Pike watched her as she pulled up her coat collar, hiding the cute pigtails peeking out from below her cap. While she might be a major brat, Ryler carried herself with an abundance of confidence he found incredibly sexy.

Damn it, was it the fact that she was off-limits making him want to cross the line? Or just that her demeanor fascinated him? Pike kept thinking of the guy from Instagram carrying her into the water.

Pike knew he wasn't Chris Evans irresistible, so why had she picked him to kiss?

"Where is this mountain view?" Ryler called over her shoulder.

"At the top of this trail." He jogged to catch up to her, taking the lead. When they reached the top and the break in the trees, Pike waved his arm with flourish. "There it is. Mistletoe Peak."

Pike watched Ryler stare at the craggy mountain, her face splitting into a soft smile. "Breathtaking. Like a Greek Titan bursting from the earth, reaching for the sky."

Pike chuckled. "You sound like Alia."

Ryler spun toward him, frowning. "What?"

"On *Excursions*. The way she describes things."

"Ah, well, we do spend a lot of time together." Ryler pulled out her phone, holding it up. After several shots of the mountain, she put her phone away and released a heavy breath. "Let's get a tree."

Pike followed her down the hill and through the trees, wondering if being compared to Alia bothered her. She'd made several comments about him wanting to hook up with her boss, but while Alia was gorgeous, he hadn't been struck with a bolt of electricity shaking her hand. Not the way touching Ryler's palm to his had singed, leaving a warmth on his skin that lingered.

"What about this one?" Ryler said, stopping next to a tree that was twice as tall as her, with thick poofy branches that tapered all the way to the top.

"If that's the one, sure."

Pike squatted down at the base and had his saw against the trunk before she cried out, "Wait!"

He looked up and spotted her a few rows down, standing next to another tree. "I think this one is better."

Pike climbed to his feet and crossed the dirt trail, eyeballing the tree that was at least a foot taller than the other. "You sure?"

"I think so."

Pike went down once more, the muscles of his thighs protesting the motion after his post-Thanksgiving workout this morning.

The rapid sound of her footfalls preceded her exclamation of "Hold on!"

Pike shuffled his feet to turn, still crouched down. By the pinch of her lips, Ryler appeared to be holding back laughter, and he scowled.

"You know, this whole up and down motion is bad for my knees."

"Womp womp," she mocked. "What are you, thirty-two? I think you're fine."

"Whoa, who you calling thirty-two?" he asked, climbing to his feet. "I'm thirty-one."

"Good for you. Now, if you please," she said, waving her hand like a benevolent queen.

"You know what?" he said, reaching for her hand and placing the handle of the saw in her palm. "I think you've got this."

Ryler's eyes widened. "You're really going to make me cut down the tree?"

"Why not? You look like you can handle it."

To his surprise, she grinned. "You're right." She squatted down on her haunches, calling from the ground, "Hold the trunk steady, will you? I don't want it to fall on me."

Pike did what she asked, smiling at a man and woman walking by. The man gave him a once-over and muttered something to his companion, who stared at him in a judgy way that made him squirm. They probably thought chivalry was dead, but Ryler had this little lesson coming.

"She's got this," he called out lamely.

They ignored him and kept walking. Pike felt the vibration of Ryler's saw easing back and forth against the trunk, and not long after, the tree shifted, cut free from its base. She climbed to her feet, standing just a foot away from him with a wicked smirk. She held out the saw to him, and he took the handle silently.

"There," she said brightly. "That wasn't so hard."

Pike grunted.

"Since it's so tall, I'll grab one end and you take the other. That way we don't lose pine needles dragging it."

"Look at you taking charge," he grumbled.

Ryler shrugged. "I'm used to making sure everything is perfect."

Pike got a better grip on the trunk and tilted it so she could grab the other end. Her arm disappeared between the branches.

"Ready?" he asked.

"Yep."

As they carried the tree, Pike asked, "So, you ever cut down trees before?"

"A couple of times. Last year, *Excursions* traveled to Oregon, and we visited a lumber mill. They had me try scaling a tree, which was terrifying and exhilarating at the same time."

"I remember that podcast." He laughed. "Alia found a squirrel family living in one of the trees she scaled and refused to let them cut it down. It turned into a huge fight, and finally, they compromised by hiring a wildlife rescue crew to come out and relocate the squirrels."

Ryler smiled at him over her shoulder. "It may have only been one family saved, but the owner got good publicity from working with the rescue. I hope he kept his promise to check trees before felling them, but people have to make money, right?"

The way Ryler talked about it had a familiar ring, and he was pretty sure Alia had said the money thing during the podcast. Could Excursions be partially scripted and Ryler helped write it? Pike wasn't sure why the thought disappointed him, but he'd always thought Alia sounded so genuine, like she spoke from the heart.

"Right," he murmured.

When they hefted the tree through the tent opening, Pike saw Alia sitting with Merry, having an animated conversation in the corner. Pike got a real good look at those ridiculous heeled boots on Alia's feet with her leg crossed over one knee, and he frowned. Why would an experienced hiker like Alia wear something like that to a tree farm?

Maybe she didn't realize it was cut-your-own-tree.

"Looks like Alia and your friend are hitting it off," Ryler said.

"Yeah, Merry's good people. Her family owns the farm."

"Awesome. I'll have to schedule a tour with her. It would be good for the podcast."

"Alia doesn't plan her own interviews?" Pike asked, confused.

Ryler shrugged. "She's only one woman, which is why she has me."

Pike couldn't imagine giving up that kind of control at Adventures in Mistletoe. It was hard enough compromising with Anthony on all of the holiday events, but if he didn't trust Pike to handle the clients alone? He'd lose his mind being micromanaged.

"Oh, good, you two are back," Alia said, climbing to her feet. Her shiny blond hair fell around her shoulders in waves, held off her face by a thick headband that covered her ears. Her smile created delicate lines by her eyes that did nothing to detract from her beauty.

It was funny that Pike had spent years looking at her photos and thought when he met her, he'd be tongue-tied around her, but it was almost like seeing a work of art in a museum. He could admire it without wanting to covet it.

"Hello, my arm is going to fall off," Ryler barked. Pike realized she was glaring at him and probably thought he was staring at Alia for all the wrong reasons.

It still didn't give her the right to snap at him.

"Go to that table, and we'll get a net around it," Pike shot back darkly.

"Whoa, everything okay over here?" Nick asked, coming up alongside Ryler. "I can take that for you, miss. I'm old hat at this job."

Ryler smiled up at Nick sweetly. "And here I thought chivalry was dead in Mistletoe."

"Only for some of us," Nick said, giving Pike a quizzical look.

"Please, she cut down the tree all on her own. She's not dainty and delicate."

Ryler gasped. "Wait, are you fat-shaming me now?"

Every female within hearing distance swung their way, and Pike shrank under the full weight of their disapproval. "What the hell? No!"

"Pike," Merry whispered, frowning at him. "What has gotten into you?"

Before he could articulate a response, Nick motioned with his head toward the netting table. "I think I'm going to take Pike over here before he shoves his foot farther down his gullet."

Pike followed Nick with the tree but caught Ryler's wicked grin as they passed. The little minx had set him up again.

"I'll get you for that later, Kitten," he whispered.

"Meow," she said, making a clawing gesture before hissing, her nose scrunching up.

Pike turned away before she saw him laugh. The damn woman caught him off guard, and a part of him loved that she kept him on his toes.

"What was that about?" Nick asked, setting his end of the tree on the silver rollers.

"Nothing, she's just a pain in the ass."

"Who is she?"

"Alia Cole's assistant. She likes to get under my skin."

Nick chuckled. "Is that all she likes to get under?"

"Slide the tree, idiot."

His friend did so without another word, but Pike noticed he didn't lose his shit-eating grin.

Once they finished sliding the tree across the table and through the net, they returned to the group of women, who were discussing the upcoming Christmas activities.

"Do you ladies have a vehicle to haul this home?" Nick asked Alia.

Alia turned to Ryler, who answered, "We're in a rental. It's a Nissan Rogue."

Pike couldn't believe Alia didn't even know what kind of car they had rented. "You got tie-down straps?"

"No," Ryler said.

Nick slapped Pike on the back. "Lucky for you, we deliver. Pike will follow you home with your tree."

"That would be wonderful, right, Ryler?" Alia smiled at her assistant, and Pike got the feeling Alia was enjoying teasing Ryler.

"Swell."

Pike covered his surprised laugh with a cough when he saw Ryler flash a double bird at her boss. It was strange how the two of them behaved more like sisters than employee and employer.

Ryler made a face at him when she caught him staring, and he grunted. "If you've paid, the two of you should go warm up in the car. I'll be right behind you."

As Alia and Ryler headed toward the tent exit, Pike could have sworn he heard Ryler mutter, "Bossy motherfucker."

He smirked. *Baby, you have no idea.*

Chapter Ten

Ryler watched Pike in the rearview mirror, questioning her behavior toward him. She'd always lectured Alia on how she treated the locals when they visited places, and here she was, practically declaring war against the man who had brought them here. What was it about Pike that pressed every button she didn't know she had?

"You're quiet."

"So?" Ryler asked.

"Is that because you're thinking about Christmas decorations or world domination?"

"Why can't it be both?" she quipped.

"Or, does your pensive state have something to do with the man currently following us in a big daddy truck."

"It's not his truck. He's borrowing it from the farm."

"Doesn't mean he can't be Daddy."

Ryler laughed. "Dude, that's your kink, not mine."

"And what is wrong with throwing a little kink in the bedroom play? What, are you seriously telling me you like straight missionary, all eye contact?"

"Oh my God, why are we talking about this?"

"Why not? You hit on a man in a bar, ready to pull the trigger on a casual encounter, which I am ninety-nine-point-nine percent sure is a first for you—"

"It's not," Ryler interjected.

"Excuse me?"

Alia's high, skeptical tone sounded so offended, Ryler glanced at her and burst out laughing at her slack-jawed expression. "I have enjoyed a handful of one-night stands. I'm just discreet and tight-lipped about my sex life."

"Well, then, if it's not that you swung and missed for the first time, I think that man seriously gets under your skin."

Ryler didn't answer, frustrated by Alia's analysis because it was too close to the truth. Something about Pike intrigued her from the first time she'd checked out his Instagram, and now that she'd met him in person, despite his initial rejection and her assurance that she was no longer interested, he still sent her pulse racing.

"I can neither confirm nor deny your accusation, but what I can say is that the moment has passed and there will be no more lapses."

Alia sighed. "Too bad. He's hot in a small-town, blue-collar way." Ryler eyeballed her suspiciously, and Alia was quick to add, "Not my type."

Ryler's shoulders sagged in relief. "I don't think we've ever shared a type."

"True, but there is a first time for everything."

"Ew, please no. I've gone through sixteen years without having to compete with you. Let's not start now."

Alia squeezed her arm. "I love you."

"That came out of nowhere," Ryler said, releasing the wheel to reach across her chest and cover her cousin's hand, "but I love you, too."

"I was just thinking that you're my only real family and the best friend I've ever had." Her voice seemed to choke on the last word, and the rest of it had come out kind of wobbly. "I would never want to lose that."

Ryler released her hand after another reassuring squeeze. "You're being really doom and gloom today. Something you want to share?"

"No," she sobbed. "I was just thinking about how important you are to me."

Her stomach bottomed out at the sound of her cousin's emotional meltdown. Alia rarely cried, especially for sentimental reasons.

"And now I'm officially freaked out," Ryler said, making the right-hand turn into their rental's driveway. "Are you dying?"

"Can't a cousin just show her love and appreciation without something drastic occurring?" Alia wailed, wiping at her eyes frantically.

"Alright, I'm gonna let this emotional breakdown slide for now because we are about to stop and I gotta save all my wits for my nemesis," Ryler said, wagging her finger at Alia as she steered with the other hand. "But we're going to come back to this later, and do not blame your period!"

Alia didn't respond for several beats and finally asked, "Are you telling me that Pike guy is your nemesis now?"

"Absolutely." Ryler noticed the silver SUV in the driveway when the trees cleared and smiled. "Speaking of nemeses, the guys are here."

"Great," Alia said, with no real bite to her tone.

Ryler pulled up behind them, saving the closest spot to the walkway for Pike so that they wouldn't have to go around a car to get the tree up the stairs and into the house.

Ryler rolled down her window and pointed to the empty spot, motioning for Pike to park there. He pulled up past her and the guys' rental car, and Ryler got out before the truck fully stopped. She paused in the doorway, staring at her cousin's obvious tear-stained face with a frown, worrying her bottom lip.

"Seriously, are you okay?" Ryler asked.

Alia released a wet laugh. "Yeah. Honestly, it's probably just this time of year. Nothing like an entire season meant for being with family to remind you how shitty your parents are."

Or that yours are gone.

Ryler knew that it wasn't the same thing, which is why she kept it to herself. Ryler had experienced a warm, loving relationship with her parents, whereas Alia spent hers with nannies and a staff in a mansion.

She came around the back of the truck and reached for the tailgate, but suddenly Pike was there.

"I got it," he said, lowering the tailgate. "That way, if it gets scratched, Nick will want to kill me instead of having to hide his rage for you."

"Thanks for looking out, but I'm not afraid of Frankenstein," Ryler said before she could catch herself.

"Frankenstein? Why would you—" Pike's eyes widened, his face splitting into a grin. "Stalker!"

"I don't know what you're talking about," she said with a sniff. "He's tall, and his head is kind of a rectangle shape."

"I'll let him know you said so," Pike said, his voice shaking with laughter, "but that's not why you called him that." Pike leaned in close and whispered, "You've been creeping on my Instagram."

"I have—only glanced at it briefly, looking for pictures of the town."

"Uh-huh."

"I'll grab Neil and Kit to help," Alia said as she passed by them. "It was very nice to meet you, Pike."

"Nice to meet you, too."

Ryler caught him watching Alia walk up the stairs and kicked his calf. "Perv."

"Ow," Pike yelled, bending over to rub the wound. "What was that for?"

"Checking out my cousin's backside."

"I was not."

"Please, I watched your eyes click like a camera shutter taking a mental picture for later."

Pike folded his arms and leaned against the tailgate, grinning down at her. "You're jealous."

"No, I'm disgusted."

"I'm a single guy, and I was trying to be discreet."

"You failed." Ryler noticed Neil coming down the stairs with Kit following close behind, and her face split into a wide, welcoming grin. "Hi!"

"Hey, we were ordered out here to help carry in a tree?" Neil said, holding out his hand to Pike. Neil was several inches taller, but his build was slimmer, and Pike's shoulders were nearly double Neil's width.

He took Neil's hand, pumping it. "I'm Pike. I work for Adventures in Mistletoe."

"Right, the guy whose comment brought us here. I'm the producer for *Excursions*." Neil released his hand and patted Kit's shoulder. "This is Kit, our cameraman."

Kit stepped forward and took Pike's hand. "Hey, man," Kit said softly. Kit was the quiet one of the group, whom Neil had introduced to Ryler their sophomore year. Kit had black spiky hair and tan skin. His family had moved to the U.S. before he was born, and when he graduated high school, they'd moved back to the Philippines but visited several times a year since Kit and his siblings had stayed in the States.

"Really great to meet you both," Pike said.

"Likewise," Neil said, coming around to sling an arm around Ryler's shoulders. "Ryler's been talking up this place and saying how excited she is to be here, so we're looking forward to exploring."

She noticed Pike's gaze linger on Neil's arm around her, and although she'd never thought about it before, she realized her friendship with Neil was very touchy-feely. They were always hugging and wrestling, and she wondered briefly if Pike thought there was something more to it.

"I've got plenty of places to show you," Pike said, his gaze shifting toward the stairs before his gaze met hers. "Hopefully Alia is as excited as Ryler. Mistletoe is a special place, and I think *Excursions* will see it has a lot to offer."

"Eh, we don't tell everyone this, but Ryler's the one who wears the pants at this show," Neil said, grinning down at her. "We're all her puppets, even Alia, going here and standing there and picking photo spots— Ow!" Neil released her to hop on one foot, grabbing the tip of his shoe where Ryler stepped on him. "I was kidding."

"Don't feel bad; she does that," Pike said, his lips twitching. "I don't know what kind of tread she has on those boots, but it is hard!"

Neil shot Ryler a disapproving look. "Ryls, what have you told us about being rude to the locals?"

"First of all, you both deserved it," Ryler said, counting off on her fingers, "and second, my boots are made from recycled tires, which means they are long lasting and good for the environment."

It wasn't an epic comeback, and she knew it, since all three men wore identical amused expressions. Well, Kit's was a little more impatient, and she imagined her type-A cameraman hadn't finished unpacking and setting up his gear, so he was eager to get back inside.

"Speaking of the environment," Neil said, addressing Pike, but when his dark gaze met Ryler's, they sparkled mischievously. "Love the pics of the hot springs. When can we hit that?"

Her cheeks burned as Pike turned her way, eyebrows raised, a slow grin spreading across his face. He turned his focus back to Neil. "Anytime, man. I'll keep an eye on the weather, and we can plan a day."

"Great, let's get this tree," Neil said before hopping into the truck.

Pike caught her gaze and mouthed, *Stalker.*

Humiliation crawled up her throat and settled like a lump, and she needed to escape. Ryler stomped past the three of them toward the stairs.

"Aren't you going to help?" Pike called.

"I think you three strong guys got this." Ryler stopped on the third step up, hands on her hips. "After all, I cut it down, so feels like my job is done."

"Do we have a tree stand for this?" Kit asked.

Ryler paused with her foot in midair and her hand on the banister, making a face. When she turned to face them, she plastered a sheepish grin on her face. "That would be a no."

"A Shop for All Seasons will have one," Pike said, shrugging. "Can't say how expensive it will be."

"What is that?" Neil asked.

"A little shop on Main Street. There's ornaments and Christmas decorations." Pike snapped his fingers. "Actually, have you checked the garage? I bet the Gimbles have one in there."

"The Gimbles?" Ryler climbed back down the stairs and trailed behind him.

"Yeah, the people who own this place," Pike called over his shoulder as he rounded the corner of the garage. "They're snowbirds, so they spend six months in Arizona and come back for the summer months."

Ryler shot Neil a death glare, and he responded by making a heart shape with his fingers. The shit.

She caught up to Pike on the side, who was turning the doorknob with a rattle. He looked up when she approached. "Do you have a key?"

Ryler reached into her pocket and pulled out the key, holding it out to Pike. He unlocked it and shoved the door open, and Ryler followed him inside. "Yep, they still have the basics in here." Pike picked up the green tree stand and held it out to her. "Check your rental agreement or shoot them a text, but I bet it's fine. If not, I can ask the Winters if they have an extra."

"Thanks, I'll do that and let you know," Ryler said.

He handed her back the keys. "You should really pull in your cars before the snow hits. Branches have been known to snap when we get a heavy snowfall, and I'd hate for you to file an insurance claim."

"Thank you," she whispered.

Ryler passed through the door ahead of him but turned around too fast to lock it and bumped into Pike. "Sorry."

"No problem, I'll just get out of your way."

Pike tried stepping to the right as she reached for the door, and she poked him in the stomach with the keys.

"Ow, jeez, what is this overwhelming desire to injure me?" he grumbled.

Ryler laughed. "That time was an accident."

"Sure it was." Pike put his hands up as he sidestepped her, giving Ryler full access to the doorknob. "I'm not making any sudden movements."

"Man, you are a drama king." Ryler locked up, and he let her go first. As she walked along the cement path, the back of her neck tingled, and she turned around really fast. Pike jerked his head up, looking off at the trees with a guilty expression.

"Excuse me, were you just looking at my ass?"

Pike met her gaze finally, the corner of his mouth curling up in a smirk. "On the off chance I'm about to be called a perv again, I'm going to go with yes."

Ryler laughed. "At least you're honest."

"There's no other way to be."

His words triggered a small measure of guilt for Ryler, who wasn't being honest with him. Not that she owed him or the world that piece of herself, but she appreciated honesty and knowing exactly who someone was. There was nothing worse than being blindsided.

Both Neil and Kit were gone when they made it back to the truck, as was the tree.

"I guess they didn't need me after all," he said.

"Or me," she joked.

Pike lifted the tailgate up and latched it. "I better get back to the farm. If you do decide to go into town and check out A Shop for All Seasons, tell Holly that I sent you."

"My, don't you have all the connections."

Pike grinned. "She's another Winters. And if you were wondering, we never dated."

"I wasn't." *I was.*

"Hey, Pike!" Alia called from the top of the stairs.

Ryler followed Pike, who stopped on the first step. "Yeah?"

"If you're around this weekend, maybe you could give us a tour of the area?"

"Alia, I told you his calendar was blacked out—"

"Only because it was a holiday," Pike interjected. "My parents are coming back tomorrow, and I plan on spending the day with them, but what about Sunday?"

"Sunday works. Thank you." Alia ducked back inside.

Pike turned to Ryler with a grin. "I guess I'll see you Sunday."

"Maybe," she said casually. "Unless I have a headache that day."

"Suit yourself, Kitten," he said, booping her nose with the tip of his finger.

"Next time you stick that in my face, I'm going to bite it off."

"Oh yeah?" Pike brushed past her, close enough for his shoulder to nudge her as he headed for the truck. Before he climbed inside, Pike called over his shoulders, "You should know, I bite back."

Chapter Eleven

Pike stared into the bonfire in the Winters' front yard, Anthony's message weighing on his mind. Anthony had texted early that morning, letting Pike know that he was staying in Boise with his brother Bradley for the weekend and he'd be back early Sunday. Both brothers had ducked out of the family's Thanksgiving due to high-stakes drama, but Anthony wasn't ready to come back yet. Of all his siblings, Pike knew that Anthony was the closest with Bradley, but it was still weird that his frugal friend would drop several hundred dollars at the last minute on a hotel for the weekend. Especially with Alia and the *Excursions* crew in town.

Although Pike had tried calling him on his way back from dropping off the tree at Ryler and Alia's rental, Anthony hadn't answered his phone and still hadn't returned Pike's call. Anthony didn't usually shut him out, but Pike kept thinking about the meeting with Merry and how put out Anthony had been. Then he'd been bitchy in his responses to Pike's ornament suggestions for their tree on Tuesday, and when Pike suggested wrapping their snowmobiles in lights and riding them in the Parade of Lights, Anthony had snapped that they couldn't do everything. Maybe he was sick of Pike, and this weekend was an intended break from him?

On a whim, Pike pulled up their location app. When they'd started Adventures in Mistletoe, Pike insisted they download it just in case either of them had an accident while out with guests. Anthony agreed it was a good idea, and the two had even gotten Nick and Noel to join them.

Pike tapped on Anthony, and it showed him in Boise, but when Pike zoomed in, it wasn't at a hotel. Anthony was in a residential neighborhood. Had he decided to go back and try to make amends with his dad after all?

Or he's hooked up with someone and is chilling at her house.

Pike glanced around the firepit, taking in the happy couples except for Sam Griffin, Clark's very single older brother; he wished he'd had a date to run off to tonight. Everyone was sitting in chairs, close together or holding hands. Sam and his nephew, Jace, were roasting marshmallows, and Jace laughed when his uncle set one on fire and started puffing on it hard.

"You should let me teach you how to roast a marshmallow correctly, son," Clark said, turning his marshmallow slowly in the coals. "Patience is the key."

"I like mine burnt," Jace argued, grinning up at Sam.

"Yeah, see, he likes it this way. You just mind your business."

Clark rolled his eyes but didn't say anything else about it.

Chris Winters stood and held a steel travel mug in his hand. "I just want to take a moment and say thank you to everyone for being here. I know some of you have other jobs, and this was your day off, but still, you showed up here to help out. I am a lucky man to have such an amazing family and circle of friends." Chris held up his cup and said, "To family and friends."

The group chorused, "To family and friends," and Chris sat down, leaning over to kiss his wife's cheek.

"I was comparing the numbers earlier," Clark said, sandwiching his marshmallow between two graham crackers as he talked. Clark was the Winters' foreman and helped handle the business side of things. "We did roughly twenty-five percent more sales today than we did on Black Friday last year."

"That's awesome," Nick said, popping an uncooked marshmallow into his mouth. "It was interesting how many new faces showed up."

"I was particularly intrigued by your new friends, Pike," Merry called, grinning at him slyly. "How do you know a travel blogger?"

"Alia's a podcaster, but I entered her contest on Instagram and suggested she come to Mistletoe because it's an awesome place to visit, especially for the holidays."

"She was not what I was expecting for a world traveler," Merry said, licking her fingers. "Her boots were more for looks than for hiking the trails."

"I thought her friend was going to castrate Pike for a second," Nick joked.

"That's her assistant, Ryler."

"Ah, that makes sense," Merry said.

"What does?" Pike asked.

Merry shrugged. "It's not a bad thing. She probably makes her assistant do all the heavy lifting, and she comes in for the photo op."

Pike frowned. "I've listened to her podcast. It would be hard to describe things the way she does without firsthand experience." Although, he'd wondered the same thing earlier, he didn't want to bad mouth Alia.

"Sorry, Pike," Merry said, pulling her blanket around her shoulders. "I didn't mean to besmirch her. I was just thinking out loud."

"Have you heard from Anthony?" Nick asked.

"He texted me. He decided to stay the weekend in Boise with his brother."

"Huh," Noel added to the conversation. "I'd have thought he'd come rushing back with all these celebrities here because of you."

"I thought the same thing," Pike said, wiping off his hands with a napkin. "But he hadn't seen his brother in a while, so I can't blame him."

"That's weird," Clark said.

"What's weird?" Pike asked.

"I was driving back from a delivery and thought I saw his truck in town."

Pike frowned. "Are you sure it was his? Because I checked his GPS location, and it says Boise."

Clark shrugged. "Maybe he took a different car."

"Ant doesn't have another car," Noel said.

"Maybe he decided to carpool with Delilah," Holly offered. "She was heading to Boise to visit her parents."

Pike stiffened. "Why would they do that? They don't even get along."

"With gas prices the way that they are, I'd carpool with my worst enemy if it meant being able to save money." Holly laughed.

Doubt niggled at the back of his mind. Yes, Delilah had rejected him and he'd taken it like a champ, but he'd asked Anthony multiple times if he was interested in Delilah and he'd said no. Why would it even cross his mind to carpool with a woman he couldn't stand and not say anything about it?

Pike shook his head. Anthony was his boy, his partner. There was no way he'd tell Pike he had no interest in Delilah and then go for her anyway. If there had been something going on, he would have told Pike.

"It probably belonged to someone else," Pike said, cleaning off his skewer and sticking it in the coals. He climbed to his feet and yawned. "I'm going to call it a night. My parents are coming back tomorrow, and I feel like I need to be mentally prepared for whatever they brought home for me from my sister."

"Good night, Pike," Victoria and Chris called.

Nick stood. "I'll walk you to your truck."

"That's so kind of you," Pike said. Then he addressed Noel as he pointed at Nick. "You hang on to this one, missy. He's a real gentleman."

"Back off my husband, Fish," Noel teased, bringing her fists up. "He's mine."

Pike wrapped his arms around Nick's waist and grinned. "I had him first."

"Are you seriously fighting over me in my parents' yard?" Nick asked.

"Hey, you are a catch! I'd fight for you in front of the pope!" Pike said.

"So? You're not Catholic," Nick said.

"True."

"You are all a strange bunch," Sam muttered.

"You know, Sam, I've been thinking of getting a tattoo—"

"No," Sam cut Pike off firmly.

"Why not?"

"Because I'm not tattooing any of my brother's friends and listening to you scream and cry about the pain. I'll never be able to tolerate you lot again. I'll make a recommendation, but I'm not going anywhere near you with my tattoo gun."

"Fair enough," Pike said, letting Nick lead the way to his SUV. "I probably would scream and cry."

"What do you want a tattoo of anyway?" Nick asked as they headed around the house to the driveway where all the cars were parked. The front yard was filled with festive blowups, Christmas lights flashing along the trim of the farmhouse.

Maybe he should get a wreath at the very least for his front door. It might be enough to shake the holiday blues.

"I don't know. Something that makes me happy. It's hard because it just kind of popped into my head the last few months that without my family and you, Noel, and Anthony, I don't have much going for me."

"Is this the start of a premature midlife crisis, because if so, maybe hold off a few years. I think the minimum age is thirty-five for that kind of breakdown."

Pike chuckled. "You're not going to spoon feed me positivity and tell me things will get better?"

"I've tried that and it doesn't seem to be working, so I figured I'd let you wallow a bit." Nick nudged him with his shoulder. "If it lasts much longer though, we're having an intervention. I don't know what I'll do if this gloominess persists."

Chapter Twelve

Ryler woke up Saturday morning ready to go to town and do some shopping and exploring. She knocked on Neil's door, but he said he wanted to sleep in a little while, and Alia didn't answer. She must've been wearing her noise-canceling headphones to bed. Kit was the only one game to check out the area. The two of them drove into the town of Mistletoe and parked in front of Kiss My Donut.

"This looks like a good place to start," Ryler said.

Kit smiled. "I would kill for an oat milk latte. Think they'll have that?"

"I'm sure with the tourists that role through here they will."

"Good, because I've seen some gorgeous places already, but I need caffeine if I'm going to get to all of them. Between the jet lag and jumping time zones, I'm zonked."

"Zonked is a word?" Ryler teased. "Isn't that from *Scooby Doo*?"

"That would be zoinks," Kit quipped.

Ryler appreciated that Kit was best in one-on-one interactions, rather than group settings. They got out of the SUV and walked toward the entrance. Ryler stopped before they went inside to admire the store window of a cute cartoon couple enjoying a latte together. Kit held the door open, and Ryler passed through.

People took up nearly every table and comfy chair in the place, and the inside of the shop was bustling with their conversations. The line was five deep, and Kit and Ryler scooched forward so there was room for anyone who came in behind them.

Ryler recognized the blonde from the tree farm standing a few people ahead of them in the line, and when their gazes met, she waved.

"Who is that?" Kit asked.

"She helped us at the tree farm yesterday. I think her name is Merry."

"She's cute," Kit said.

"And very pregnant." Ryler laughed.

"Married?"

"Pretty sure."

"Damn," Kit said, grinning, "well, there goes my chance to live out my pregophile fantasy."

"I wasn't aware that was even a thing." Ryler laughed.

"Maybe not the true technical term, but it exists."

"Aren't you still with Mae?" Ryler asked, studying Kit's face.

"No, we broke up right after Halloween."

"How did I not know this?" she asked.

Kit shrugged. "We don't really talk about relationship stuff."

That was true. While Kit was fun to be around and was incredibly talented with a camera, they didn't have deep conversations about love and the meaning of life.

"Are you doing okay? You and Mae were together for a long time."

"Yeah, you know, we just drifted apart. We met in college, and even though it's been six years, I wasn't ready to take the next step. So she ended things, and it's for the best."

"How come you weren't ready for the next step?" she asked.

"We're on the road so much and gone for a week or more at a time," he said, shoving his hands in his coat pockets. "If I want to get married, that means sticking in one place and settling down in a house with all the responsibilities that come along with it. I don't know if I'm ready to do that. I honestly don't know if I'll ever be ready to do that." The line moved, and they both took a step forward before Kit continued, "What about you? Things didn't work out with that lawyer from your condo?"

"No, things didn't work out with him. Turns out that people don't just pause and wait for you to get back when you leave on an extended trip to Bali," she said with a bitter laugh. "If they don't hear from you, they tend to move on."

Kit chuckled. "Strange how that happens."

"I know, right?" she said, feeling better about what happened with Ollie. It was a learning experience, one she would keep close to her heart so that she didn't take anyone in her life for granted again.

They ordered their coffees and stepped to the side of the pickup counter. Merry walked over to them with a red-haired woman in tow, smiling brightly.

"Hi, Ryler," Merry said. "This is my sister, Holly. Ryler is the assistant on that podcast Pike loves so much."

Ryler's heart fluttered at the secondhand praise and held her hand out with a smile. "It's very nice to meet you." Ryler waved a hand toward her companion. "This is Kit, who is the wizard behind the camera and video shots we use on Instagram."

Kit shook both their hands and greeted them with a shy "Hi."

"Hello," Merry said.

"Hey," Holly said, splitting her attention between Ryler and Kit. "Are you enjoying your stay so far?"

"Absolutely," Ryler gushed.

"It's a beautiful area," Kit added.

Ryler nodded. "And such a cute town."

"Wonderful. You'll have to come by my shop," Holly said, reaching into her purse and holding out a card for each of them. "It's called A Shop for All Seasons. It's about three doors down on the left."

"Oh, that's funny," Ryler said, tapping the card with her finger. "Pike actually suggested that we should check out your shop today and get some ornaments for our tree. He was talking it up big-time."

"Well, hopefully we don't fall short of your expectations," Holly said, smiling. "I'll be down there in about fifteen minutes, and I'll be more than happy to help you find everything you need."

The barista called Holly's and Merry's names, and they excused themselves to grab their drinks.

"It was very nice to meet you," Merry called out, addressing Kit.

"Likewise," he said.

"See you soon," Holly said with a wave, before the two women left the shop.

Kit grinned. "I didn't see a ring on Holly's finger."

"Except she's got a business and family here, so you know she isn't leaving town for anyone. If you're going to win her heart, you'll have to stay here," Ryler teased.

"I could think of worse fates," Kit said, stepping forward when their names were called.

When he handed Ryler her coffee, she said, "If you're thinking about leaving me to chase after your dream girl in Small-town, Idaho, you might want to say something."

"Are you kidding me?" Kit said, getting the door for her. "I get to go explore the world with my friends and get paid to do it. What is better than that?"

Ryler almost agreed with him, although it would be nice to find someone to love and share her dream with. As they strolled out onto the sidewalk and down the street, Ryler took in the scenery around them. Men were up on ladders, changing over the fall foliage that had been wrapped around each lamppost and stretched across the main road for greenery with red bows and white lights. Although it was just the day after Thanksgiving, it was the first indication that Christmas would be here in just a few weeks.

"You would think they would wait until at least December first," Ryler said, pointing to the lit Merry Christmas sign the bank was hanging in their window display. "Give Thanksgiving time to breathe."

"I'm pretty sure in America, Christmas starts on November first," Kit said, smirking, "and Thanksgiving is just thrown in there because they haven't figured out how to do away with it yet."

"Maybe for some people, but I believe that the holidays should have their own time without encroaching on each other," Ryler said.

"Good for you," he said, giving her a short, slow clap. "My mom is big on Christmas and starts listening to Christmas music the day after Halloween. She also collects Santa Claus figures and displays them all over the house. It's kind of creepy if you're not prepared for it."

Ryler laughed. "I have my mother's little nativity scene that she painted as a girl, but it's tucked away in a box in my closet."

"You should've brought it, and you could've set it out to enjoy this Christmas."

"No," Ryler said, sharper than she intended and softened her tone to clarify, "I always thought that when I found someplace I wanted to settle down in, I would bring it out to celebrate finally finding my home again."

"You don't like your condo in California?" Kit asked.

"It's just a place to lay my head in between trips."

"See, you and me, we're rolling stones," Kit said, talking more animatedly than she'd ever seen him. "We like to travel, although eventually, we will find a home to settle down, but we're not in any hurry."

"I guess that's why we all love *Excursions*," Ryler said.

"Except Neil and Alia aren't like us."

Kit's firm declaration surprised Ryler. "They're not?"

"No," Kit said, averting his gaze, but she wasn't having it.

"Kit, if you've got something to say, share."

Kit sighed. "Alright, he's going to murder me for telling you this, but Neil's been talking a lot about how he wants to buy a place and settle down."

"Really?" Neil hadn't said anything like that to Ryler, and she thought they talked about everything. "Is he dating someone I don't know about?"

Kit shrugged. "I'm not sure. I think he's just tired of the vagabond lifestyle."

"And Alia?"

"Oh, she's been ready to quit the show for a long time. I'm just not sure she knows how to tell you."

Dread rushed through Ryler's veins. If Alia left, Ryler could go back to posting scenic and food pics, but people would ask questions and wonder why she stopped posting pictures of herself. They'd built something together, but if Alia and Neil were thinking about leaving, what would that mean for *Excursions*?

"How do you know that?" she asked.

"People tend to talk a lot when I'm around," he said, smiling sheepishly. "I don't know if it's because I'm quiet or if they just don't care, but I hear a lot of stuff."

Alia's bad moods lately made a lot of sense if she didn't want to be the face of *Excursions* anymore. But why wouldn't she just say something?

"I wish they would be honest if they are both feeling this way," Ryler whispered.

Kit patted her shoulder. "I'm sure it's because neither one of them wants to disappoint you."

Ryler paused in front of the window for A Shop for All Seasons, contemplating Kit's revelations. The last thing she wanted to do was alienate the people she loved most, and if they were only doing the show for her, she didn't want to hold them back. Of course, if Alia no longer wanted to be the face of *Excursions*, Ryler would figure it out.

Or you could come clean, like Neil said. There may be some backlash, but it would free Alia.

And put Ryler in the hot seat.

"I didn't mean to bum you out," Kit said.

Ryler shook her head. "No, it's better if I know."

The blinds on the door of A Shop for All Seasons were up, and the sign was flipped to open, so Ryler turned the knob and held the door for Kit. The shop smelled of cinnamon and apples, and Ryler experienced another bout of déjà vu. Would that smell always remind her of her mom's baking and the holidays?

Holly looked up from behind a small counter and smiled. "Long time no see."

"This place is amazing," Ryler said, taking in all the colorful décor. The store had shelves of knickknacks and several different Christmas trees with gorgeous ornaments adorning every branch. There were baskets of Christmas plushies and stockings hanging on the wall. Holiday wall art and advent calendars were strategically placed around, catching Ryler's eye. Her parents had given her a chocolate-filled advent calendar every year on the first of December, but it might be fun to get a refillable one for the future.

"Thank you for saying so," Holly said, coming around the counter. "We switched over from fall to Christmas yesterday. It's a lot of work, but it brings others joy, which makes me happy."

Kit wandered over to one of the shelves, looking at a row of Santa statues, while Ryler headed to one of the trees, admiring the ornaments.

"Do you have some ideas on what you might be looking for?" Holly asked.

"I was thinking about doing some stockings and maybe writing our names on them with a Sharpie." Holly's horrified expression caught Ryler off guard, and she giggled, "Or not."

"Sorry," Holly said, her slack jaw transforming into a sheepish grin. "I've often been told I wear every thought on my face. We offer personalization and could embroider them for you. It takes about a day, and there's an extra charge, but they won't look funky."

"Oh, are we against funky? Because maybe that's the look I'm going for."

Holly laughed. "I heard you were a little feisty."

"Huh. I wonder who told you that," Ryler mused.

"A red-haired birdie."

Ryler arched a brow. "Would this redhead happened to be male and bearded?"

Holly touched her nose. "Bull's-eye."

"Well, he shouldn't dish shit out if he can't take it."

Holly clicked her tongue against her teeth. "I've been telling him that for years, but he still hasn't learned."

"Do men really ever learn?" Ryler asked, fingering a glittery red-and-white globe twisted to look like a peppermint.

"Hey!" Kit said.

Both women laughed. "Sorry, Kit. You were so quiet over there."

"Uh-huh," he grumbled.

Ryler plucked the ornament off the tree and held it up. "I love this one. Do you have an ornament box I could put my choices in?"

"I do," Holly said, taking the orb from her. "Let me grab one."

"Thanks," Ryler said, following Holly toward the back of the store and waiting outside the door to a back-room Holly had disappeared into. Ryler didn't want to make things awkward, but her curiosity got the best of her when Holly re-emerged with a cardboard box with slats.

"I'll set this by the register, and if you fill it up, we'll grab another."

"Thank you." Ryler lowered her voice, trying to avoid Kit overhearing, and asked, "So, if you don't mind me asking, what's Pike's deal?"

Holly set the box down and turned to face her, cocking her head to one side. "You'll have to be more specific."

"I mean, is he just a dog who goes after every woman he meets?"

Holly gave her a long, pensive look, and Ryler squirmed under her scrutiny, losing her nerve. "You know what? It's none of my business, and I am so sorry for being nosy."

"I'm just curious about why you're asking," Holly said slowly, leaning on the counter with a grin. "Did something happen between you two?"

"Now who's being nosy," Ryler said, chuckling, but she knew her cheeks were burning. "A mild flirtation when we first met."

"I see." Holly hadn't lost that amused expression, and Ryler wanted to kick herself for letting her curiosity overwhelm her good sense. What was to stop Holly from running back to Pike and telling him she'd been asking personal questions about him?

"Pike's had several long-term girlfriends, but the relationships haven't ended well," Holly said softly, heading over to the farthest tree away from Kit, and Ryler followed her, absently studying the ornaments.

"When was his last relationship?" Ryler asked.

"He dated one of Merry's friends for a while, but they broke up right before the holidays last year."

Ryler picked up a glass camera with sparkles on it, intending it for Kit. She walked it over to the box, and when she came back, she whispered, "Why did they break up?"

Holly hesitated, probably worried she'd say too much and Ryler would tell Pike. "Sally was looking for something else, and when Pike put his foot in his mouth big-time, it gave her an out. Pike really is a sweet guy, but he can be tactless."

"I don't mean to put you in an awkward position," Ryler said, nodding at a beautiful ornament shaped like a Christmas tree with string lights on the branches that Holly was holding up.

"No, you're fine. If you're curious about Pike, I don't mind sharing. Better you know what you're getting into with him."

"Oh no," Ryler protested, catching herself when her voice rose. "I'm not interested in Pike."

"You're not?" Holly asked.

"No, not like that." Holly touched a plaid shirt ornament that reminded Ryler of Pike but left it on the tree. "I just find him intriguing."

Holly giggled. "Well, I guess that's one word to describe him." Holly reached out suddenly and touched Ryler's arm. "I don't want to give you a poor impression of him due to his dating history. Like I said, his last relationship ended because the woman was looking for someone who was a little more financially stable and ready to settle down. Pike wanted to start a business, and at the time was working road construction. She wanted to get married. Be a stay-at-home mom."

"No offense to your friend but that sounds a little . . ."

"Shallow?" Holly asked.

"Oh, I am so sorry, there I go again sticking my foot in my mouth," Ryler said, quickly clarifying, "I just mean dumping a guy because someone else has a better job. You should be with someone because they match your energy and make you happy, not for what they can provide for you financially."

"I understand what you're saying, and we're all good. I don't like to mince words either." Holly held up another ornament, this one a snowman, but Ryler shook her head. Holly put the ornament back and continued, "I think it's human nature to crave stability and someone that matches what you're looking for in life. Some might call that shallow but, in the end, they just weren't meant to be."

"And he hasn't dated anyone since?" Ryler asked.

"Well, he tried," Holly said, leaning around the tree to get closer. "He asked out a friend of mine this week who's had a thing for him since we were kids, but for whatever reason, she turned him down."

Ryler's stomach bottomed out. When they'd met that first night, Pike had said, *Just one girl, but it didn't work out.*

Holly shook her head. "He must have been pretty upset, because he didn't even come back inside where we had been hanging out."

No, he went to the bar, and I threw myself at him.

Ryler felt like a heel. When he'd said that he'd used the mistletoe on someone, she hadn't thought it was that serious at the time, but it sounded like he really liked her. He'd been rejected, sad, and vulnerable, and she'd tried to take advantage of him.

"Did I say something wrong?" Holly asked.

"No, of course not." Ryler smiled. "I was just feeling bad he didn't get a date."

Holly laughed. "Oh, I'm sure Pike will bounce back fast."

I'll say, Ryler thought, remembering their kiss and what could have happened if she hadn't told him her name. Was that how he dealt with heartache? Get over someone by hooking up with someone else?

A thought crossed Ryler's mind that she really didn't like. When she'd left the bar, it had been filling up. Had he found someone else to scratch the itch?

"I don't suppose we can keep this conversation between us, can we?" Ryler asked cautiously.

Holly smiled warmly and held out her pinky for Ryler to take, which she did with a chuckle.

"Your secret is safe with me."

Chapter Thirteen

At half past noon on Saturday, Pike opened the door for his parents, his smile fading when he saw the small ball of fur in their arms.

"What the hell is that?" he asked, staring at the puffball with abject horror.

"This is your Christmas present from your sister," his mom said.

"Absolutely-the-fuck-not!" Pike roared.

"Watch your mouth and your tone." Tracy Sutton held out the red Pomeranian expectantly. "Here, take her."

"Uh-uh."

"Pike . . ." she warned.

"Moooom," he drawled back.

"Pike, take the dog from your mother so we can come in. It's freezing out here," Dale Sutton barked, his blue eyes narrowed at his son.

Pike took the animal grudgingly, holding it at arm's length. The little body was warm and trembling in his hands, and he hoped to God it didn't decide to pee on him.

"Isn't she adorable?" his mom asked, pushing past him into the house. "We have all her supplies in the back of the car, but we can get them later."

Pike shot his father a desperate look, but the man only chuckled. *Traitor.*

"Don't look at me," his dad said. "This was all your sister and your mother."

Pike turned to face his mother, who was removing her coat. "Why did you get me a dog?"

"It was your sister's idea, but I agreed. She'll be a good companion for you."

"I don't need a companion."

"Nonsense. You live alone," his mother said, settling onto his couch.

"I like living alone."

"Plus, she can go on all of your excursions with you, which will help you get a girlfriend. Women are goners for men who love animals."

"I don't love animals, especially pint-sized ones. And how am I going to take this thing to work with me? Strap her to the back of the snowmobile?"

His dad closed the front door and offered, "They make those little dog car seats."

"Don't help, Dad," Pike snapped.

"Do not talk to your father that way," his mother clapped back.

Pike took a deep breath. "I am sorry, but I'm not putting a dog car seat—" Pike stopped himself. "Do you know what? Never mind. I am not going to argue about this." He walked over to his mom and set the dog in her lap. "Thank you for thinking of me, but please take that thing back to wherever you got it."

"Your sister got it from a breeder in Arizona, so I cannot take it back." His mom handed the dog to his father, who passed it back to Pike.

"Then you keep it," Pike said, heading back for her, but she held up her hands.

"No, I will not keep it. This is your dog."

Pike looked to his dad for help, but the other man just shrugged. "Women, what are you gonna do, huh?"

Pike looked down at the fluffy puppy, who stared back at him with big brown eyes. The little puffball was cute, but this wasn't something he'd been looking for.

"I don't even think I can have a dog here."

"Well, maybe that'll be the incentive you need to move out of this bachelor pad," his mother said. When her husband sat down next to her, his parents faced him like a united front, although Tracy did all the talking. "Really, Pike, don't you think it's about time you bought a house and started planning for the future?"

"Why do I need to buy a house when it is just me?" he asked, bringing the pup against his chest when his arms got tired. The tiny beast snuggled against him, sticking its wet nose in the crook of his neck.

"Now it isn't just you," she said, pointing to the dog. "And eventually, you're going to get married."

"Considering how my last few relationships worked out, the odds are not really in my favor," he said.

"You never know what the future will bring."

This time, Dale acknowledged Pike's silent plea for assistance and interjected, "Honey, do we have to dive right in to this the minute we see our son?"

"Yeah, Mom, do we?" Pike said snarkily.

His father shot him a glare, and he shut his mouth.

"I'm sorry," Tracy said, sighing. "It's just with your sister getting married—"

Pike cut her off. "She's engaged? Since when?"

"It happened right after Thanksgiving dinner," his dad said.

"Yes, he proposed to her in front of his family and us. It was so lovely. They're thinking about having the wedding in August."

"Wow, good for them." Pike's sister was two years older and had been dating her boyfriend, Rick, for four years. Pike knew his sister was getting impatient with Rick not popping the question, and she voiced her concerns that he didn't want to marry her often. Pike was happy to learn that wasn't the case.

"I'll have to say congratulations when I bring this monstrosity back to her," Pike said, stroking the puppy's soft fur.

"You should give it a few weeks and see if she grows on you," his mom said.

"I don't think so."

"Oh, I don't want to argue about this with you," she said, waving her hands in the air like a queen banishing her subject. "Tell us about your week. What did you do? Lonely without us?"

"It was fine," Pike said, sitting down on the couch. He tried to shift the dog into his lap, but she cuddled deeper into his neck, so he gave up. "I went to the Winters' for Thanksgiving. And everyone loved my macaroni and cheese."

"Oh, you didn't do the Brussels sprouts this year?" his mom asked.

"No, Anthony said no one liked them."

"That's too bad. I thought they were tasty," his mom said.

"I thought they were foul," his father said.

Tracy smacked him on the shoulder. "That is because you don't like anything good for you."

"That's incorrect. I like Jamba Juice."

"That is pure sugar," Tracy said, shaking her head. "Go ahead, Pike. Don't mind your father."

"Not a lot happened this week. I went over to the Winters' Christmas Tree Farm yesterday and helped with opening day." Pike racked his brain for something else to talk about. "We had a bonfire afterward, and then I came home."

"It sounds like a busy week," his dad said.

"Well, you won't be alone for Christmas," his mom said, smiling. "Your sister is talking about coming up with Rick through New Year's and looking at places here to have the wedding."

"Really? They don't wanna have a wedding down in Arizona where all of his family are?" Pike asked.

"No, it'll be too hot in August. And his family has money, so they're willing to travel."

"Well, I guess if they have money, we should make sure they spend it unnecessarily." Pike knew his mother picked up on the sarcasm from the icy stare she sent him.

"Would you rather we spent our money traveling down to Arizona to sit in the hundred-and-thirty-degree weather?" his mom asked.

"You're right," Pike said, adding, "They can come up here."

"That's what I thought," she said.

"Oh, there was one more thing that happened this week," Pike said. "That travel podcast I listen to is doing an episode about Mistletoe. They booked Adventures in Mistletoe for several outings."

"Wow, congratulations," his dad said.

"Honey, that's incredible," his mom said. "I hope you made a good first impression." Pike rolled his eyes.

The puppy squirmed in his hands, and his mom said, "You might want to take her out. She hasn't gone potty in a few hours."

Pike grumbled as he took the puppy out the front door and set her on the grass. She sat there for a minute, not moving.

"Go on," he said.

She finally took a tentative step forward and then another and then she squatted.

"Make sure you praise her," his mother called from the doorway.

"Praise her for taking a piss?" he asked.

"Yes, you just say things like 'Good girl!'"

Pike stared down at the little red puffball. "Good girl."

The dog wagged her tail and trotted back over to him. Pike picked her up and held her at eye level. "You are a cute little sucker, but I'm still not keeping you."

Pike pulled out his phone and took a picture of him and the dog, making sure to scowl for the camera. He sent a message to Anthony with the selfie attached.

This is why I hate my sister.

His phone beeped seconds later.

LOL what is that thing?

Pike tapped out his response one-handed, tucking the dog against his chest. Apparently, my new dog.

The three message dots popped up. Congrats, man.

I'm not keeping it.

You should. It kind of looks like you.

Pike scowled at his phone and then at the dog.

Jerk.

Just stating facts, man.

Since he had Anthony's attention, he decided to change the subject. I'm taking Alia and her crew out tomorrow morning. When will you be back?

Probably around nine. What time are you meeting them?

Pike hadn't solidified the plans with Alia and Ryler yet. Not sure. I'll confirm and let you know. As an afterthought, Pike asked, Are you having fun with your brother?

It's been a good visit.

Cool. See you tomorrow.

Pike carried the dog back into his apartment, his fingers twitching to find out if Anthony was still at his father's house. Should he ask him about it, just to put his mind at ease?

This is your best friend. You have no reason not to trust him.

It wasn't Delilah and Anthony's interest in her that bothered him. It was the numerous times he'd asked Anthony if his friend had feelings for Delilah and he'd assured Pike he didn't. It was the possibility that his best friend was lying to him that had him on edge.

"What are you doing out there?" his mom called.

"Nothing," he said, putting his concerns to the back of his mind. Whatever the truth was, it would come out eventually. It always did.

Chapter Fourteen

"It's finally starting to look a little like Christmas in here," Alia said from her perch on the couch.

Ryler and Kit had come back from town with their arms loaded down with Christmas décor, and they had to make three trips up and down the stairs to get everything inside. Alia and Neil had been sitting in the living room when they'd arrived, and although Neil helped, Alia told them she wasn't feeling great.

Ryler, Neil, and Kit got to work decorating the tree, while Alia sat on the couch, directing where the ornaments should be hung. The stockings wouldn't be ready until Monday, but they covered the top of the fireplace with garland and four stocking holders that spelled out *NOEL.* Ryler put a little figurine of a Christmas gnome holding presents in the middle of the kitchen table and lit two of the same scented candles that Holly had been burning in the store, placing them at opposite ends of the house. Now that the rental smelled like her mother's kitchen and the decorations were all in place, it was really starting to feel like Christmas.

"All you need is stockings and a Santa hat, and this will be the jolliest place on Earth," Alia joked.

Ryler laughed. "And it only took four hours."

"What should we do tonight?" Neil asked.

"We went to a little bar and grill the other night," Ryler said. "It had a dance floor and darts."

"And animal heads on the wall," Alia said.

Ryler stuck her tongue out at her cousin. "But the food was good."

Neil pulled up his phone. "I'll see what our options are. Brews and Chews."

"That's the place we went," Ryler said.

"There's axe throwing."

"That could be fun," Kit said, pantomiming throwing something overhand.

"There's another bar that sounds a little sketch," Neil said.

"Why does it sound sketch?" Ryler asked.

"It's called the Wolf's Den."

"Yeah, let's not go there," Alia said.

"Looks like we're either axe throwing or Brews and Chews," Neil said.

"We can axe throw before we go get dinner and drinks," Kit said, checking his watch. "It's still early."

"I know we're getting a guided tour tomorrow, but we could go explore the outskirts of town now," Neil said.

Alia groaned. "I really don't want to be stuck in a car for hours if it's all the same."

Ryler frowned at her cousin's pale face. She really didn't look like she felt good. "Are you going to be okay for tomorrow?"

Alia shrugged. "Neil got me something to help with my stomach, so hopefully that takes care of it."

Ryler thought about Kit's revelation that Alia didn't want to be the face of the podcast's Instagram anymore. Could the stomachache be a ruse so she didn't have to admit to Ryler that she wanted to quit?

Ryler said, "What if I asked Pike if he knows of any fun things to do on a Saturday night? I bet there's lots of events he knows about that we wouldn't."

"Sounds good," Neil said.

Ryler squatted down next to her cousin and placed a hand on her knee. "Why don't you go lie down and rest while we figure out tonight's plans?"

Alia got up from the couch and nodded. "Thank you."

"Do you need anything?" Neil asked in a surprising show of concern.

Alia smiled. "No, I'm alright. Thank you."

When Alia left the room, Ryler raised her eyebrow at Neil. "Since when are you worried about my cousin's well-being?"

"Just because I think she is a pain in the ass doesn't mean I don't care about her." His tone was admonishing, and it left Ryler immediately contrite.

"I'm sorry, that was shitty of me."

Neil laughed. "It's all right, we haven't always been the best around each other, but I'm trying to be better."

"That's really nice, Neil," Ryler said, wondering at the change of heart but afraid to ask.

"Why don't you go ahead and text your friend, and I'll hop in the shower?" Neil suggested.

"Okay," Ryler said.

"I'm going to go make a snack," Kit said, leaving the room and heading into the open kitchen. Ryler sat on the couch and pulled out her phone to text Pike.

Hey, it's Ryler, Alia's assistant. What are some things to do in town on a Saturday night?

The three little bubbles flashed, and when she read his response, Ryler laughed.

How did you get this number? (Pensive emoji)

Holly gave it to me. I told her we were supposed to meet tomorrow and I forgot to grab it from you. Why, did you not want me to have this number?

I just didn't remember giving you a card.

Oh, you have business cards. Sophisticated.

Lol I'm a sophisticated guy.

Well, are you a sophisticated guy who knows what the haps are on a Saturday night?

The haps are a live band at Brews and Chews and that's about it.

Is the band any good?

I guess it depends on what kind of music you like. This one tends to play mostly country and classic rock.

Oh, and at the Wolf's Den they have karaoke, but it's a rougher crowd.

How rough? Coyote Ugly no water in the star rough or Sons of Anarchy toss you out a window rough?

Leaning more toward *Sons of Anarchy*. The local biker club hangs out there a lot. If you pick the wrong song, you might get heckled.

I don't think my friends are gonna go for that. I guess live band it is.

I guess I'll see you there then. My friends and I usually meet there around eight.

Is that an official invite to join you?

You all are welcome to join us. Don't make it weird.

Ryler laughed, and Kit asked over her shoulder, "What's so funny?"

"Nothing," she said, exiting the chat. "Pike invited us to join him and his crew at Brews and Chews."

"Sweet," Kit said, hopping over the back of the couch to sit next to her. "Are Holly and Merry gonna be there?"

"Um, I don't know, but their significant others probably will be."

"That's fine, I just like to look at them," Kit said.

"Creeper."

"Besides, if one woman in this town looks like that, I'm sure there are more."

Ryler shook her head. "I've barely heard you say two words to any woman. Even with Mae, I wasn't sure you guys ever had full conversations."

"Sometimes talking is overrated." Kit waggled his eyebrows, and Ryler laughed.

Neil came out with pants on but no shirt. "Where are we going, so I know what to wear?"

"We're meeting Pike and his friends at Brews and Chews," Ryler said.

"Alright, so how does one dress for this place?" Neil asked.

"Casual T-shirt and jeans," Ryler said.

"So, no coonskin hat, then. Got it."

"Actually, that might work, and I bet you could pull it off," Ryler said.

"Get the fuck out of here." Neil laughed.

"I'm going to get in the shower now," Kit said.

"You showered this morning."

"Yes, but if I meet the love of my life, I want to be extra clean."

"What is he going on about?" Neil asked.

"Kit got a glimpse of some of the local women folk, and now he's fixin' to find himself a bride," Ryler said with a fake country twang.

"That's weird. Especially since he'll have to leave her before Christmas."

"Maybe he'll take her home with him to meet his family," Ryler said.

"Well, as long as he's happy, I wish him the best," Neil said. "I am going to go get on my shirt. I'll be right back."

"I'll be here," Ryler said.

Neil left the room and Ryler's phone beeped. It was another message from Pike.

Are you guys going to join us? If so, I'll make sure to get a bigger table.

We will be there.

Chapter Fifteen

"Tell us more about these Californians you invited to come out with us," Sam said, leaning back in his chair. His blond hair was tousled effortlessly, and Pike found himself envious of Sam's Nordic good looks. Sam was the kind of guy who commanded a room when he walked into it, causing every woman to sit up and take notice.

Pike pulled out his phone and opened Instagram, clicking on the *Excursions* page. He passed it to Sam. "This is Alia, the host of the podcast, and she's bringing along her assistant, her producer, and her photographer."

"Damn, she is fine," Sam said, handing the phone off to Clark, who didn't even glance at it. "Single?"

"I didn't ask," Pike said.

Merry grinned at Clark, taking the phone. "You didn't want to check her out?"

"Why would I need to do that when the most beautiful woman in the world is sitting right next to me?" Clark said, kissing her.

"That's my sister, dude," Nick groaned.

"So?" Clark said, grinning at Nick. "She's my wife."

"Is the rest of her crew cute, too?" Sam asked.

"There is only one other woman, her assistant. The producer and photographer are men," Pike said.

"And?" Sam asked.

"And what?"

"Tell me about the assistant," Sam said, waving his hand impatiently. "What's she like?"

"Would that be the assistant you helped with the tree yesterday?" Nick asked.

"Ryler," Holly said, leaning into her boyfriend Declan's side. "She is super cute."

"Single?" Sam asked.

Pike's spine stiffened at Sam's line of questioning.

"I'm not sure, but I think so," Holly said.

"Hmmm, I've never dated a California girl before," Sam said.

Pike clenched his jaw. "I don't think she's your type."

"Oh yeah? What's my type?" Sam asked.

Pike didn't have a good answer, but Holly jumped in to add, "I feel like she might be too introverted for you."

While he wouldn't have called Ryler introverted, Pike appreciated Holly's attempt to dissuade Sam's interest. Although, maybe Ryler would be excited at Sam's interest. Every other woman in town, including his ex-girlfriend, fawned all over the elder Griffin.

"I like the quiet ones. They can be the freakiest."

Pike's vision blurred around the edges, and his fists clenched. Pike didn't want Sam talking about Ryler like she was just one of his groupies, someone to use up and throw away. "She's more than just a piece of meat, you know."

"Whoa, what's wrong with you?" Sam asked.

"Nothing, I'm just saying, she isn't some lust bunny you can use and then forget about."

"Lust bunny?" Sam laughed.

"Uh, Sam, I think you're upsetting Fish," Noel said, taking Pike's phone and looking at the screen. She handed it to Nick, who simply held it out to Pike, just like every other attached man at the table.

Pike slipped it back into his pocket, trying to keep smiling as all the attention turned to him. "No, I'm fine."

"If you're interested in the assistant, pal, no worries," Sam said casually.

"I'm not interested in anyone. The only thing I want is for the podcast to share Adventures in Mistletoe favorably with the world."

"You heard him," Sam said. "He isn't upset, and he isn't coveting the assistant either."

Noel shot Pike a look of concern, but he ignored it, focusing on finishing his beer so he could order something stronger. Pike didn't want to think of Sam or anyone else getting close enough to talk to Ryler, let alone sleep with her. It didn't matter that they weren't interested in each other or planning on hooking up, it was about Pike feeling responsible for her. She and the rest of the *Excursions* crew had come in on his suggestion, and he wanted to make sure that they were all treated with the utmost respect.

Even Ryler, who could press every last button he had.

Pike downed the rest of his beer and got to his feet. "I'm going to get another round. Anyone want something?"

"I'll come with you," Nick said, climbing to his feet.

The two of them walked over to the bar and leaned against it. Pike signaled Ricki, who gave him a nod and held her finger up to signal she'd be over in a minute.

"So, are you going to be honest with me or tell me another whopper?" Nick asked.

"What are you talking about?" Pike asked.

"Ryler. I know you're attracted to her, but I'm not sure why you're denying it."

"I'm attracted to a lot of people, but that doesn't mean I want to hook up with them."

"Fair enough," Nick said, bumping Pike with his shoulder. "I do feel like Ryler is different though and you actually do want to hook up with her."

"Have you talked to Anthony?" Pike asked abruptly.

"Just a few texts, why?"

"I got this feeling that something is going on with him and Delilah," Pike admitted.

"I don't think so, but even if there was, she turned you down, right?"

"Yeah, but I asked him point-blank about her several times, before I even made a move on her, and he swore he wasn't interested."

"Maybe he changed his mind," Nick said.

"Which would be fine if he'd manned up and talked to me about it before anything happened."

Nick shrugged. "I don't know, man."

"You're right, it's probably just my paranoia." Pike laughed.

Ricki approached them before Nick could respond.

"Evening, boys. Another round of beers?"

"Actually, I'd like a whiskey on the rocks," Pike said.

"And you?" she addressed Nick.

"I'll have another beer."

"You got it." Ricki turned her back on them to grab a whiskey bottle off the shelf and a glass from under the counter.

Nick tapped Pike's arm, drawing his attention away from his drink being made and toward the door. "Looks like your guests have arrived," he said.

Alia was in the lead with her hair falling in loose waves around the shoulders of her cropped, cream sweater. Her jeans sat low on her hips, showing off her belly button ring.

Neil came in next in jeans and a button-down Hawaiian shirt under his jacket; he stood over a foot taller than Kit, the photographer, who wore a blue collared sweater and jeans. Ryler brought up the rear in an off-the-shoulder black sweater and wide leg khaki cargo pants. Her hair was swept back in a high ponytail, showing off the bare sun-kissed skin of her neck and shoulders.

Ryler spotted him and waved, saying something to her group, who started heading toward the bar. Alia reached them first, smiling.

"Pike, good to see you. And Nick, right?"

Nick nodded. "That's me. Nice to see you again."

"Nick, this is Neil, *Excursions*' producer, and our cameraman, Kit. This is Nick. His family owns the Christmas tree farm outside of town."

Nick stood up and took their hands. "Nice to meet you both. What do you all want to drink?"

"Can I just get a Shirley Temple?" Alia asked.

"I'll take a Corona with a lime," Neil said.

"A Moscow mule," Kit said.

"Pike, do you got that? I'll take these guys over and start introducing them."

"I'll help him," Ryler said.

The trio followed Nick to the table, and Ricki set the beer and whiskey down on the bar, announcing the total.

"Hang on, Ricki, I've got four more drinks for you. A Shirley Temple, Moscow mule, Corona with a lime, and—"

Pike looked at Ryler expectantly, and Ryler said, "Sex on the beach."

"I'm on it."

Ryler set her small black purse on the bar and started to pull out her wallet, but Pike shook his head. "This round is on me. You can get the next one."

"Thanks."

"No problem," he said, turning around to put his back to the bar. "So, the big guy with the dark hair next to Holly is her boyfriend, Declan. They host a TikTok together where he teaches her how to cook."

Ryler laughed. "That's cute. I'll have to ask them what their handle is."

"The blond guy is Sam. He's sitting next to his brother, Clark, who is married to Merry. Clark is the foreman on the Winters' tree farm, and Sam is a tattoo artist."

"Huh, is he any good?" she asked.

"Why, you looking to get a tat?"

Ryler shook her head. "No, but I like to look at them. It takes a lot of talent to draw on human skin."

"I suppose it does," Pike said grudgingly, handing Ricki his card when she set the rest of the drinks on the counter.

"I'll get you a tray when I come back with this," she said, holding up his card.

"I could start delivering them," Ryler said, picking up the Shirley Temple and Moscow mule. "Be right back."

Pike watched her walk away, his gaze drifting down to where her pants hugged her curvy ass. God, she was sexy without even trying. She set down the drinks in front of Kit and Alia, and Pike's jaw clenched when Sam held out his hand to her, saying something that made Ryler throw back her head and laugh.

Ryler came back to him, shaking her head with a smile on her face. "Whew, that Sam is a trip, huh?"

"He's something, alright," Pike grumbled. "What did he say to you?"

"Asked me if I had any tattoos he couldn't see. I told him no, and he said, do you want one? All low and seductive-like. He must be a real winner with the ladies."

"I've heard he gets around," Pike said, knocking back his whiskey in one swallow.

"What about you?" Ryler asked, grabbing her drink and the Corona. "Do you get around?"

Pike scoffed. "I date. I don't have a different girl to warm my bed every day of the week."

"So just one for the weekends?" she joked.

"No," he said, picking up Nick's beer and signaling Ricki for another whiskey. "I mean, I don't have any women to warm my bed."

"I'm sure that's not true," Ryler said.

Pike shot her a suspicious look. "What have you heard?"

Her wide-eyed, innocent expression matched her tone. "I have no idea what you're talking about."

They reached the table, and Pike set Nick's beer in front of him. "Alright, which one of you big mouths has been feeding this woman dirt on me?"

"I told you, no one said anything." Ryler laughed, handing Neil his Corona. "I just figured that you're a relatively good-looking guy. If Sam has a girl for every day of the week, it makes sense you'd have a couple waiting in the wings."

"Whoa, what now?" Sam said, turning toward them. "How did my sex life get brought into this?"

"I asked how you scored with the ladies," Ryler said, winking at Sam.

"Ah, trying to scope out the competition, huh? For you, darlin', I'll clear the way as long as you're in town."

"Smooth talker," she teased.

"I'm going to get my drink," Pike muttered, turning his back on their flirtation. When he reached the bar, Ricki was just setting another whiskey down for him.

"The look on your face says this should have been a double," she said.

Pike inhaled the golden liquor, ignoring the burn in his throat. "Keep 'em coming."

Chapter Sixteen

Ryler sat at the table with all of Pike's friends, watching him as he came back to the table and took an empty chair next to Nick. Kit and Declan were having an intense conversation about art. Neil was telling Merry, Clark, and Sam about their trip to Australia last year and how both Alia and Ryler panicked over the snakes and spiders. Alia sat next to him, jumping in to contradict and argue with Neil. Pike's friends were so welcoming and fun, and yet, he looked as if he'd rather be anywhere else.

"Ryler, you're awfully quiet," Nick said, drawing her out of her thoughts.

"Sorry, I was just listening to everyone."

"How are you enjoying Mistletoe?" he asked.

"It's beautiful. I'm really excited to get out and start exploring."

"Where do you live?" Sam asked.

"Right now, Alia and I have a condo in El Dorado Hills, which is in the Northern California foothills below Tahoe. Funny story, I actually grew up in Idaho until I was twelve, but I'd never heard of Mistletoe before."

"What part of Idaho?" Merry asked.

"Boise."

"Where did you move after that?" Holly asked.

"I moved in with Alia and her parents in LA after my parents died."

"Oh, I'm so sorry," Holly said.

"I lost my parents when I was sixteen," Noel said, giving Ryler a small smile. "I'm sorry for your loss."

The rest of the table chorused something similar, and Ryler shook her head. "I appreciate that. Thanks. Lucky for me, my cousin and I had each other. It's been the two of us against the world for sixteen years."

"With a little help from your friends," Neil interjected.

"Yes, we wouldn't know what to do without you and Kit," Alia said, gazing at Neil warmly. The intimate look caught Ryler off guard, and she watched Neil bestow a tender smile on her cousin.

Holy shit. They're sleeping together.

How had she missed this? She was with these people three out of four weeks a month, twelve months out of the year, and yet she hadn't realized something had shifted between them. How long had it been going on? Ryler wasn't upset about it, but knowing how much they'd always fought and argued, it was weird to think of them crossing that line.

Unless what they said was true, and enemies really did make the best lovers.

"I'll be back shortly," Ryler said, climbing to her feet.

"Do you want me to come?" Alia asked.

"No, you stay put. I'm just going to get some air. It's hot in here."

Ryler thought she saw Sam move out of the corner of her eye, but then Holly pushed him back into his seat.

"Ow, what was that for," he grumbled.

"I thought I saw a bug," she said.

Ryler missed the rest of the exchange as she made her way through the crowd of bodies and down the hallway to the back patio, pushing the door open. There were several groups out tonight, a haze of smoke lingering in the air. Mixed scents assailed her nostrils, and she made her way to the farthest corner, away from the people smoking and vaping.

Ryler stared out into the darkened tree line, wondering at her obliviousness to the people around her. Alia and Neil, even Kit breaking up with Mae. Was she really so self-absorbed? Ryler had always thought she was generous and observant, but she hadn't known the two people closest to her were unhappy. That they were sleeping together.

She needed to do better, starting with figuring out how to talk to Neil and Alia about everything. She didn't want it to come off like she was accusing them of something, but Ryler wanted to clear the air and know where they stood.

"Hey, you okay?"

Ryler turned around at Pike's loaded question, laughing softly. "I'm not really sure. I realized that I might just be the most oblivious person on the planet."

"Why do you say that?" he asked, leaning against the fence next to her.

"Because I'm pretty sure Alia and Neil have something going on, but they're keeping it quiet."

"And that's a bad thing because . . . ?"

"It's not a bad thing," Ryler said. "It's just weird that they didn't say anything."

"Were you and Neil ever a thing?" Pike asked.

"A long time ago and for a very short amount of time."

Pike shrugged. "Maybe they weren't sure how you would react."

"Maybe," Ryler admitted.

"How do you feel about it?" Pike asked.

"Fine. Happy if they're happy."

"Then that's all you have to tell them," he said.

Ryler nodded. "What crawled up your butt tonight?"

"Excuse me?"

"You got all surly when Sam was talking to me."

"You mean when you were flirting with Sam?" he said dryly.

"Wow, so this is what jealousy looks like on you?" Ryler nudged him with her shoulder. "You're all broody and taciturn."

"Don't those mean the same thing?" he asked.

"They are semantically related. Not technically the same thing."

"Fine. Maybe I'm a little sore about Sam."

"Why is that?" she asked.

"Because when my ex dumped me, she chased after him, looking for a rebound."

Ryler winced. "Did he go for it?"

"Surprisingly, no. He actually avoided her."

"Sounds like he's not such a man-whore then."

"Maybe not. I guess I can't really hold a grudge against the guy just because he's got the height and the looks. That air of trouble all the women go mad for."

"Honestly, super tall guys are overrated."

Pike laughed. "Get the fuck out of here."

"No, I'm serious. It was one of the biggest turnoffs about dating Neil in college. My calves and arms were always sore from trying to reach his lips—"

Pike held up his hand. "I'm good with the visual."

Ryler grinned. "I'm just saying, not every woman wants a six-foot-tall Thor to come home to."

Pike's gaze lingered on her face, and she caught her breath when he reached out, his fingers trailing against her cheek. "If not Thor, who is it you think about?"

Ryler caught her bottom lip between her teeth, knowing this was a bad idea, but his lips were so close, those blue eyes hooded and glittering in the dim patio lighting. "It varies, but since coming to Mistletoe, I've developed a thing for bearded men." Ryler reached up, pinching the side of his blue bow tie between her thumb and forefinger. "Especially if they have a tendency to wear bow ties."

"That is a very specific type," Pike murmured, his mouth inching toward hers, and she closed her eyes, tilting her head as she waited for the press of his lips on hers.

"Ryler?" Alia called, breaking the spell, and Ryler jumped back from Pike. She spotted her cousin just outside the door, scanning the crowd.

"Over here," she called.

"I better let you two talk," Pike said, pushing off the fence.

"To be continued?" she murmured.

Pike grinned. "Just let me know when and where."

He passed Alia and stopped for a second, saying something to her that Ryler couldn't hear, but her cousin smiled. As Alia approached, Ryler could tell her cousin was pale. She stepped off the fence to meet her, touching her arm.

"Hey, are you still feeling sick?"

"Yeah, but I wanted to check on you. Everything okay?"

"Yeah, just a little overwhelmed in there. Lots of people," Ryler said.

"Come on, you talk to thousands of listeners every week and socialize with strangers daily."

"Must have been something else, then," Ryler said, linking her arm through her cousin's. "Do you want me to run you home?"

"No, I'll be okay. I don't want to give people a negative impression of *Excursions*."

"You know your personal well-being is more important than the podcast, right?" Ryler said abruptly.

Alia started, her eyes wide. "What brought that on?"

"I just want to make sure you know that."

"I do," Alia said, wrapping Ryler in a hug. "I love you."

"I love you, too."

They broke apart, and Alia grinned. "So, out of curiosity, did I interrupt something between you and our tour guide?"

"If I say yes, are you going to come clean about you and Neil?"

Alia's mouth dropped open. "How did you know?"

"Because for the first time in six years, you two aren't at each other's throats. He was sweet to you, and you didn't insult him. It's weird but a dead giveaway. How long has it been going on?"

"A couple months," Alia said softly.

"Wow. I really am just a blind idiot."

"No, you aren't. It just happened, and once we crossed the line, we kept doing it and realized we didn't want to stop. We did everything we could not to let it interfere with the podcast."

"So, is it serious or just hooking up?"

"It started as casual, but now . . ." Alia trailed off. "Are you mad?"

"No, of course not. Is there anything else you want to talk about?"

"Honestly, there are probably several things we could discuss, but nothing that needs to get hashed out tonight."

Ryler didn't like the sound of that, but she also didn't press the issue. "Rain check, then. Let's get back inside. This courtyard is under some sort of spell where it makes people want to make out under the stars."

"Well, dang, what's so bad about that?"

Kissing leads to complications, and I feel like my life is already chock-full of those.

Chapter Seventeen

"Oh my God, Dog, can you please do your business? It's freezing out here."

Pike stood on the little lawn in front of his apartment in his house slippers, sweats, and a jacket, bouncing from foot to foot. It was the third time he'd been up with the pup since he got home from the bar, and that was when the creature would let him sleep. The only time she'd stopped whimpering was when he'd taken her out of the crate and put her on the bed with him. At first, she'd pounced and attacked his face with kisses until he'd wrapped an arm around her and pulled her close.

"Be still," he said.

She'd obeyed him for a few hours, and he'd fallen blissfully asleep until he'd woken up to her whining again and trying to get off the bed. He checked the time. It was six ten. He wasn't due to meet the *Excursions* group until nine, and hopefully, he could get a few more hours of sleep.

Finally, the puppy pooped, and Pike gave her a slow clap. "Congratulations, you finally did it."

Pike used one of the baggies his sister provided to pick up the poop, then he scooped up the puppy in his other arm. Pike tied the top of the poop bag and tossed it into the garbage can before going back inside. He carried the dog into his room and set her on the bed, heading into the bathroom to wash his hands. When he came back into the bedroom, Pike stripped off his jacket and slippers while the puppy bounced around. He lifted the covers to crawl into bed, and once he was under them, she laid in the crook of his arm and rolled over, gazing at him from her upside-down position.

Pike scratched her belly, fighting a smile. "You think you have me wrapped around your finger, huh?" She pawed at him, and he laughed. "Good girl." He yawned, his eyes fluttering closed, and before he knew it, he'd passed out again.

Pike woke up when his alarm went off, and he took the pup out one more time before putting her in the crate so he could shower. He stood under the hot stream, washing his hair and scrubbing his body, his mind drifting to Ryler. They'd almost kissed, but once she and Alia returned to the table, he hadn't had another moment alone with her. It seemed like everyone at the table vied for her attention, and she fit right in, teasing the guys and bonding with the girls. When their group had taken off around eleven, Holly and Merry had fawned over her, inviting their group to the Winters' joint birthday party for Nick, Merry, and Holly the first week of December. Pike offered an awkward good night, and when they disappeared out the door, Holly had smacked him and called him an idiot.

I did all that work to keep Sam away from her, and you couldn't close the deal. Stupid!

Despite their chemistry, Pike still had hesitations about getting involved with Ryler. What if they slept together and she regretted it? Anthony could always step in with them, but what if she decided to bail instead? She and Alia acted more like sisters than cousins. If Ryler wanted to leave town, would Alia really stick around without her to finish the podcast for Mistletoe?

Pike didn't think so.

When he got out of the shower, the puppy was yowling loudly, and his upstairs neighbor was beating on Pike's ceiling.

"Shut that mutt up," the old coot hollered.

Pike flipped off the ceiling and opened the crate, freeing the puppy. "You are just a pain in the ass, aren't you?"

The puppy stood on her back end with her paws up, and Pike took her into his hands, lifting her into his arms and holding her against his naked chest.

"What am I going to do with you today? I can't leave you here to terrorize the neighbors."

Pike put her down and used his towel to finish drying off before he got dressed, trying to avoid stepping on the puppy, who was underfoot. He finally picked her up and tossed her on the bed. She followed him as he moved around the room. When Pike sat down to get his shoes on, he found himself dodging the darting puppy tongue again. "We're going to have to work on that licking stuff. I can't stand licky dogs."

Apparently, the licker didn't care, because she rushed him again, swiping his hand. "You know what?" Pike rolled her over onto her back and gave her a raspberry on her stomach. "How do you like it?"

She squirmed away and launched herself at him. Pike caught her and carried her into the bathroom so that he could finish doing his hair and beard. While he got ready, his phone rang. He tapped the talk button and greeted Ryler. "Good morning."

"Good morning," she said. "We're grabbing coffee and breakfast. You want something?"

"Thanks, that's nice of you. You at Kiss My Donut?"

"We are," she said.

"I'll take a cinnamon roll latte and a ham and cheese croissant. I can Venmo you if you text me—"

"Don't worry about it; it's on us," she said. "You're technically off this weekend and still taking us out to explore."

"Alright, thanks. I'll meet you at Kiss My Donut, and you can follow me out to the first landmark."

"Is your partner going to meet us, still?" Ryler asked.

"Yeah, I think so. I just need to check his location." Pike smoothed his beard oil over the strands, using his comb to shape them.

"What do you mean check his location?" Ryler asked.

"We have a GPS app that tracks our locations."

"Seriously?" She laughed.

"Yeah, it's for safety in case we're out with clients and something happens. Don't you do that with your family?"

"Alia is my only family, and we are always together."

"It's still weird to think of you two as cousins."

"If you say you can't see the resemblance, I'm hanging up now."

Pike laughed. "That wasn't what I was going to say— No!" He hollered when he saw the puppy taking a whiz on his bath mat. "Bad dog." The puppy tucked tail and rushed for safety at his harsh tone, knocking over the wastebasket. "Damnit."

"Everything okay over there?" Ryler asked.

"Not at all! My sister thought it would be a good idea to get me a dog, and the creature doesn't let me sleep and pees all the time on everything."

"Aw, what kind of dog?" she asked.

"A Pomeranian, I think."

"Aw!"

"It's not aw, like 'how cute.' It's a small fluffy demon."

"Are you going to bring her?"

Pike got down on his hands and knees and pulled the dog from her hiding spot with a grunt. "Only because I'm a little afraid to leave her home and find an eviction notice on my door when I get back." The puppy trembled against him, and guilt tightened his chest. "Hey, I'm sorry I yelled and scared you. I didn't expect you to use my bath mat as a toilet."

Ryler chuckled. "Alright, I'll let you deal with that. See you in a bit."

"See you."

Pike put the puppy in the crate while he picked up the bath mat and took it out to the laundry room, ignoring the pitiful howl and the neighbors hollering as he threw it into the washer and hit start. Pike went back to the bathroom to finish getting ready, and when he got his hair and beard the way he wanted, he took the puppy out of her crate and carried her out to the kitchen where her supplies were.

Pike found the doggy harness his sister had included and put it on the puppy. "I'm gonna have to call you something other than *Dog*. Who is a female with red hair. Julia? Nah. Wynonna? Hmmm. Oh, I got it! Jolene."

Pike started humming the song under his breath as he took the leash and tried leading her, but she refused to walk, dragging her back end.

"Alright, dude, none of that." He picked her up and took one of his kayaking bags and started filling it up, including a small bowl, two food pouches, and a couple bottles of water. He put the roll of poop bags in the bag and zipped it up. "We have our puppy bag. What do you say we show a couple flatlanders around?"

She tried to lick him, and he put his hand out to block it. "Yeah, we're definitely going to have to work on that."

It took Pike less than five minutes to get to Kiss My Donut, but when he arrived, he didn't see either rental car. But he did see Ryler out front, holding two coffee cups and a pastry bag.

"Hey, where is everyone?"

"They wanted to check out a historical site twenty minutes away, and I said we'd catch up."

"Okay, hop in."

Ryler climbed into his red Dodge Charger and passed him the coffee. "There you are."

"Thanks," he said, setting it in the cup holder.

Jolene whined from the back seat, and Ryler turned around, her face melting into a smile. "Well, hello, sweetheart," she said, setting the pastry bag down on the floorboard and her coffee in the other cup holder before reaching for her. Ryler pulled her into the front seat on her lap, snuggling her and dodging Jolene's frantic tongue.

"Jo, stop being a licky dog!" Pike said firmly.

Ryler laughed, rubbing the puppy's ears and kissing her on top of the head. "She is darling."

"She certainly thinks so," he said mildly, watching Ryler love on the dog for several moments before he cleared his throat. "Which historical site did they head to?"

"I'm not sure, but it sounded boring, so I passed. It was where some massacre took place."

"Ah, I know where they are. We'll probably end up passing Anthony on our way to them. Want to text Alia and let her know we're coming to them?"

"Sure." As she furiously tapped on the screen, Jo pawed at her fingers, making her giggle. "You are just a silly puppy, aren't you?"

Pike pulled out onto the road and made a left at the next street, circling back to take the highway out of Mistletoe.

Her phone beeped, and she set it in her lap. "They are going to wait for us by the sign."

"Perfect." Pike took a drink of his coffee and hummed. "So good. Want to try?"

"That's okay, I actually got the same thing as you."

"Well, good, because I really didn't want to share," he teased, glancing at her out of the corner of his eye. She went to take a drink of her coffee, but Jo tried to jump for it. "You can put her back there so you can enjoy your coffee in peace."

"Just until we finish eating, baby." Ryler lifted the dog into the back seat once more and pulled sanitizer out of her purse, cleansing her hands.

"I also got us the same breakfast," she said, grabbing the pastry bag and reaching inside, handing him a ham and cheese croissant.

Pike took a bite and groaned. "I actually think these are better than the donuts."

"I hope so because I saw a cream-filled one that was calling my name," she said. He caught the look on her face out of the corner of his eye as she took a bite of the croissant. "Hmmm, that is good."

"I told you."

"No one likes a know-it-all, Pike," Ryler admonished.

They ate in silence for a few moments, Jo whining in the back seat. When Ryler finally finished her breakfast, Pike stopped her from grabbing the puppy right away. "Wait until she stops whining, please. I'm trying to teach her some patience."

"Are you keeping her, then?" Ryler asked.

"No, but I think dogs should learn patience at a young age," he said quickly.

"Mm-hmm."

Ryler did as he asked, and when at least thirty seconds had passed, he nodded, "You can grab her now."

"Aw, your daddy thinks he's a hard-ass, but I think he's warming up to you."

Despite the baby talk, Pike's ears perked at her use of the word *daddy*, and while he knew it made him a complete perv, he liked the way she said it.

"Speaking of warming up to things, should we talk about last night?" he asked.

"About almost-kisses on moonlit patios?" Ryler asked.

"That would be the subject at hand."

"It depends on how the conversation's going to go. Are we saying it should or shouldn't have happened? If it shouldn't, then there is no need to talk about it, and we can forget it even happened."

"And if it should have?" he asked.

"Then I guess we need to explore the subject further."

Pike chuckled as he took a right onto Hwy 20, opening his mouth to do just that, when a car crested the hill in the distance. As it drew closer, trepidation made Pike's heart rate quicken. He did a double take as they passed Delilah's car, recognizing Anthony in the driver's seat. "Son of a bitch!"

"What is it?" Ryler asked.

"A lying rat bastard." Pike pressed on the gas, and at the next turnout, flipped the car around, tearing back toward them.

"Pike, what are you doing?"

"I'm going to have a little chat with my business partner."

Pike whipped his car into the space off the road in front of Delilah's car and threw it in park. "Just stay put, okay? I won't be a minute."

He climbed out and marched back toward the front of the car. He stopped in front of the hood and pointed his finger at Anthony through the windshield. Delilah stared out at him from the passenger seat with wide eyes, while Anthony's guilty expression told Pike everything he'd already suspected was true.

"I fucking knew it!"

Pike turned away from the car and stomped back toward his, ignoring the opening and closing of a car door. The sound of running feet preceded Anthony's desperate call. "Pike, hold up. It's not what you think."

"I'll bet," Pike scoffed, twisting around and shoving Anthony backward. He must have caught Anthony off guard because he stumbled a few feet but caught himself. Pike was beyond caring if he looked like an emotional idiot. His best friend, his partner, had been lying to him for days.

"I asked you point-blank if you were interested, and you said no."

Anthony held his hands up in a pleading motion. "I can explain everything, but I don't want to do this on the side of the highway."

"I don't want to do this at all," Pike snapped. "I just had to make sure it was you because I thought I was making myself crazy. Telling myself it was a weird coincidence that you changed your mind about visiting your dad."

"That was all true!" Anthony protested.

"When did it start? How long were the two of you fucking around and laughing at me?"

"Wednesday night."

"After she rejected me?" Pike scoffed. "So, while I was waiting at the bar for you to show up, you were together?"

"It wasn't like that—"

"Then explain it to me, man, because I knew you liked to razz me, but I always thought you respected me."

"I do respect you, which is why I didn't tell you about us over the phone. It's why I said I wasn't interested when you asked, even though I've been into her for almost a year."

That was something he hadn't been expecting to hear.

"The fuck are you talking about?" Pike asked.

"We kissed last year at Merry and Clark's party. I knew she liked you so I stopped it, but I didn't forget."

"Why didn't you tell me that when I was going on and on about dating her?"

"Because I thought she wanted you, too!"

"And the minute you found out she'd turned me down, you made your move."

Anthony hesitated. "I honestly didn't expect you to be so invested, man. It had only been a couple of days."

Pike laughed. "I can't believe you're trying to turn this around on me. Forget the fact that you made a move on her behind my back, you're my business partner. My brother. And you fucking lied to me. That's what I can't get over."

Pike opened up the driver's side door and slammed it shut, regret seizing him at the ill treatment of his car, but he was too furious to care at the moment. Pike checked to make sure it was clear and pulled back onto the highway, flipping around at the closest turnout.

Ryler and Jo sat quietly in the passenger seat, and he hated that she'd witnessed his humiliation. She probably thought he was having a jealous meltdown, when it had nothing to do with Delilah and everything to do with Anthony going behind his back and lying.

Trust was everything in any relationship, and if you were doing something that would hurt someone you cared about, you shouldn't be doing it.

"I'm sorry if I scared you," he whispered.

"It's okay. I'm more concerned with how you're feeling now that you've put some distance between you and him. I was afraid for a moment you were going to get into a fistfight."

"I wanted to hit him, but not because he was with her. It was that he lied rather than just came clean."

"Maybe he wanted to tell you in person."

"They hooked up on Wednesday before he met me at Brews and Chews."

Pike saw Ryler wince out of the corner of his eye. "Ouch."

"Like I said, not about her. This is about him and me."

"Are you going to be okay taking us around today, or would you rather take a mental health day?" she asked.

"No, I want to hang with you guys today. Being around people who are genuine and honest will do me some good."

Chapter Eighteen

Ryler kept glancing over at Pike as he drove, her hand stroking the puppy's soft fur. She wasn't sure what to say to Pike, especially since he hadn't spoken a word for a good ten minutes. While the situations were different, Ryler couldn't help comparing Alia's confession about Neil to Pike discovering his best friend hooked up with the woman he was interested in. Although Neil and Ryler had dated, she had no lingering romantic feelings for him, and the only concern she had was one or both people she loved getting hurt.

Pike's best friend had lied and snuck around behind his back because he hadn't wanted to hurt him. Or get caught. Either way, Ryler could only imagine what was going through his head.

"The historical site is just over this hill," Pike said.

"Okay. Where to after this?"

"I thought we'd head west, check out the lake and maybe get some lunch at the lodge. It will be cold, so I don't know how the rest of the group will feel. I could also take you east to Ketchum. It's about an hour out of the way, but there are lots of shops and restaurants. Plus, it's the winter destination for lots of celebrities, so you might get to see one or two. The only issue is a lot of places are closed because it's Sunday."

Ryler laughed. "Places still close down on Sunday?"

"In Idaho they do."

"Honestly, you've had a rough morning, so we can keep it simple. Explore the lake and get lunch. Maybe take the long way back?" she suggested.

"Sure." Pike pulled off the road across from the historical site, where the rented SUV was parked.

Ryler set the puppy down in the back seat, ignoring her whining protest. They got out of the car and waved at the group across the road, who were taking pics in front of the sign.

"Where have you two been?" Neil asked.

"Pike stopped to talk to his business partner," Ryler said quickly. "Pike offered to show us the lake, and then we can grab lunch. Kind of play the day by ear."

"I'm down to get some scenic shots," Kit said, holding up his Nikon camera.

Alia stood at the back of the SUV with her arms wrapped around her body. "Is it always so cold here?"

"Usually from October until May," Pike said.

"That's horrifying."

"You can follow me," Pike said, heading back to his car. The other three gave Ryler a look as if to ask, *What's his problem?*

"I'm going to ride with Pike because he has a puppy in his car."

Alia perked up. "Puppy?"

"Yep! Super cute Pomeranian."

"Aw, I want to see," Alia said, following Ryler across the road to the car. Ryler opened the door, and her cousin bent down, leaning into the car so only her butt stuck out.

"Well, hello, pumpkin. Aren't you sweet?"

Ryler smiled. Although her aunt and uncle hadn't liked animals in the house, Alia had been allowed one dog, a long-haired Chihuahua named Lucile. She'd been a spoiled, sweet creature who passed away when Alia was seventeen. She hadn't wanted to get a dog since.

Alia leaned back out of the car with the puppy in her arms, cuddling and kissing her. "What's her name?" Alia asked Pike, who had stopped next to the driver's side door.

"Jolene. Jo for now."

"Hello, Jo," Alia said, letting the dog kiss her nose.

"Isn't she darling?" Ryler said.

"Yes! I want her to ride in the car with me."

Ryler glanced over at Pike, who shrugged. "That's fine with me."

"Yay," Alia said, wrapping the leash around her wrist. "Don't mind Neil's driving," she murmured to the dog. "He just likes to follow all the rules because he can't ruin his perfect record."

Pike shook his head, and Ryler asked, "What?"

"Nothing, I was just thinking that talking to animals thing really does happen to everyone."

Ryler laughed. "Are you trying to tell me you've been talking to your dog?"

"First of all, temporary guardianship doesn't make her mine, and second of all, yes, I absolutely have, especially at five a.m. on the front lawn when the damn thing won't take a piss."

"Oh boy, you're a goner," Ryler said, climbing into his car. "Deny it all you want, but the minute you start talking to animals, they've got their hooks into you. There is no escaping that little fur ball now."

Pike settled into the driver's seat. "So you say, but I'm not really a dog person."

"Ew, you did not just say that," she groaned.

"What?" he asked, starting the car.

"Saying you're not a dog person is like saying you drink the blood of babies."

Pike burst out laughing. "What the fuck? It is not!"

"Actually, it kind of is!" she said, watching the side mirror as Pike pulled out. When Neil flipped around safely and fell in behind them, she added, "According to scientific research, people who don't like animals show a lack of empathy and disconnect, which makes it difficult for them to form lasting relationships."

"While that does describe my dating history, I didn't say I didn't like dogs, I said I wasn't a dog person. That just means I don't want one pissing and crapping in my house."

"That is why you teach them not to."

"Yeah, but when? I'm out with clients or at the store eight hours or more a day. That's not fair for a dog. And while Idaho is a dog-friendly place, I can't take her everywhere, especially in the summer when it gets hot."

"Oh my God," Ryler said, slapping his arm playfully. "You *are* a dog person!"

"I just said—"

"All the reasons why you couldn't keep her have to do with her happy and healthy mental and physical being! You, Pike Sutton, have been giving this a lot of thought because you're really falling in love with

Jo and want her in your life." Ryler turned in her seat to watch him, the seat belt stretching to accommodate her new position. "Plus, adorable dogs are a great way to meet women."

Pike scoffed. "No, thank you. From all the things you said, it's obvious I am too dysfunctional to be in a relationship."

"Who said anything about a relationship?" she asked.

"I'm thirty-one. I'm a little old to be playing the field."

"I'm sorry, I didn't realize there was an age limit for how long someone could be single and enjoy dating."

Pike shook his head. "Even George Clooney eventually gave up the game."

"Not until he was in his fifties." Ryler settled back in her seat with a grunt. "I don't care what anyone thinks, if I am not completely, one hundred and fifty percent in love with someone, there is no way I'm settling. Even if I never find the one."

"Do you believe in soul mates?" Pike asked.

"I don't know. To me, soul mates are so limiting. You find the one and they die, so then what? You're stuck alone and loveless for the rest of your life?" Ryler shook her head. "I think there are varying degrees of love, and it depends on where you are in life. In college, I was too scared to open myself up to anyone fully, and my relationships were fleeting."

"And now?"

"I like my life, and I love exploring with *Excursions*. But if I met someone who made me want to put down roots, I'd be open to it." Ryler saw Pike's jaw tighten as he pressed down on the gas, and the engine roared as he crested the hill. Ryler sucked in a breath as she took in the view. "Wow! I didn't expect it to be so high on the other side."

"Welcome to Idaho, where the landscape can change in just a few miles."

Ryler stared down at the twisting road that descended the mountainside and rounded a gorgeous lake with pine trees surrounding it. Craggy peaks reached for the sky on the other side of the lake, snow-capped and imposing. The landscape was heavenly and raw, and she wished she could capture the view to do it justice.

"I can see why you love it here," she murmured.

"Don't get me wrong, it has its pitfalls. Small town. Cold weather eight to nine months out of the year. Some parts aren't so pretty." He sighed loudly. "But it's home."

Ryler put her hand on his arm. "I'm trying not to bring up what happened, but if you do want to talk about it, or maybe find a canyon or mountain and scream into the void, we can do that."

Pike shook his head. "If it's all the same, I'd rather try to forget about it and just enjoy today before I have to deal with reality. Right now, I get to hang out with one of my favorite podcasters, her crew"—Pike took a left down a treelined lane and shot her a grin—"and you."

Ryler made a face. "So glad I made the list."

He reached out and touched her hand briefly. "I'm only kidding. I appreciate you distracting me from all the drama in my life."

"Happy to help."

Chapter Nineteen

"This is gorgeous!" Kit said, his camera clicking rapidly as he took pictures of the mountains and trees. The sky above the group was blue, but Pike was keeping an eye on the gray clouds drifting over the mountain. It wouldn't take long for them to get caught in a snowstorm, and although their rental SUV had four-wheel drive, Pike couldn't guarantee that any of the Californians knew how to drive in snow.

Pike watched Ryler approach Neil, who had his cell phone out, presumably taking personal pictures to share. Ryler's puffer coat hung open, revealing the sweatshirt underneath that read *Leave me alone.* He appreciated the fact that she hadn't made things weird after witnessing his personal meltdown. Would she tell Alia? God, would that be something they included in the podcast? The last thing he needed was for her to tell Alia that Adventures in Mistletoe was rife with issues.

Although, if she was going to do something like that, wouldn't she have cut the tour short? He'd been trying to keep up a pleasant façade and push Anthony's betrayal from his mind, but what would happen tomorrow when he went into the store? How would he keep himself from knocking out his best friend the minute he opened his mouth?

Alia approached with Jo in her arms, holding the puppy out to him. "She went potty, although she really does not like the leash."

"No, she doesn't," he said, taking the dog from her. "Thank you. You didn't have to do that."

"I didn't mind. Keeps me busy and out of my own head. Got a lot on my mind."

"Oh yeah? About the podcast or life?" Pike asked.

"Both, I suppose," she said. Pike watched her profile, following the line of her vision as it passed over the lake and landed on Ryler and Neil. Alia shivered, and Pike noticed the thin pea coat she wore, frowning.

"You've got to be freezing in that getup." He shrugged out of his jacket, transferring Jo from one hand to the other, and held the jacket out for her. "Here."

"Oh, you don't have to do that," she said.

"Aren't you already not feeling good? All you need is to get worse because you weren't dressed for the weather."

Alia slipped her arms into Pike's coat and gave him a grateful nod. "Thank you. It's really warm."

Pike shoved one hand into his sweatshirt pocket, grateful he'd decided to layer up today. Jo's stomach was warm in the palm of his hand as he held her against his rib cage. "It's not a problem. You're my guest."

"It's nice to know that not all men are selfish jerks," she said, and although none of the others were standing near, Pike thought that might have been a pointed comment.

"I have my moments, too, believe me." Pike caught Ryler watching them and wondered what she thought of him. Was he just some jerk, bouncing from woman to woman?

"Hey, Pike," Kit asked, pointing in the distance. "Is there a way to get to that waterfall?"

"Waterfall?" Ryler repeated, her smile wide. "Where?"

"We can take the trailhead there, but it's about a four-mile hike round trip."

"I'm good with that," Kit said.

Ryler nodded. "Me, too."

Alia looked over at Neil, who was nodding. "I guess I'm coming, too."

"Just give me a minute. I need to grab something from my car."

Pike jogged back to his trunk and set Jo inside before he removed the holster with his gun and bear mace from the lockbox inside. Although the chances of seeing a bear this time of year were slim, there was still a chance they weren't hibernating yet. In addition, the quiet of the trails could sometimes put hikers into the path of a hungry juvenile cougar or wolves. Even a bull moose could be a danger out here. The crew would be in their territory, and after Pike had been chased by an aggressive coyote on the ski slope last year, he didn't go hiking unarmed.

"What are you doing?" Ryler asked, coming around the backside of his car. He unzipped his sweatshirt and took it off, slipping his holster up his arms and over his shoulders. "Is that a gun?"

"Yeah, but don't worry. I've got a concealed carry permit," he said, slipping his sweatshirt back on over it.

"But why do you need a gun?"

Pike quirked an eyebrow. "Ever been hiking in the woods before?"

"Yes, in India, South America, Africa—"

"And none of those guides carried a weapon?"

"Well, yes, but that's because there were lions and tigers and dangerous people."

"This is Idaho, Kitten. We have mountain lions, wolves, bobcats, wolverines, and even a few dangerous characters cooking shady shit." Pike picked up Jo and gave her a reassuring smile. "We're going to stay on the trail, but I'm always cautious. When the tourist season dies down and hunting season is over, the critters around here aren't used to seeing humans."

Ryler stared at him for several seconds before taking Jo from him. "I'll carry the baby so at least your hands are free."

Pike closed his trunk, following her back to the group. When he stopped between Alia and Ryler, he addressed everyone. "Make sure you make noise as you walk in case there's an animal nearby. We don't want to spook it."

Alia stared at Pike with wide eyes. "What exactly are we going to spook?"

Pike was surprised by her apprehension. "Like I was telling Ryler, there's always a chance of encountering animals when we're in the woods, especially near a water source. I just want all of us to be cautious, and if you do see an animal, make yourself large and imposing."

Neil snorted. "You're doomed, Alia."

"Shut up, Neil," Alia snapped.

"Whoa, okay, don't make me separate you two," Ryler joked.

"Oh, please do!" Alia said, marching back to Pike. "I'll walk with you."

Pike glanced toward Ryler, who held his puppy in her arms, and pushed down the disappointment in his stomach. "Alright, we'll lead the way, but you three stay close to us. No stragglers."

Pike took off, Alia keeping pace beside him. The first part of the trail was relatively flat, but about halfway down, it would start to climb as they drew closer to the waterfall.

"Are you okay?" he asked.

"Yeah, why?"

"You're wearing Nikes instead of a shoe with ankle stabilization and tread for hiking. I just don't want you to roll an ankle."

"I didn't expect us to hike today. I thought we were going sight-seeing."

"Fair enough," Pike said, following behind as she pulled ahead. Pike glanced behind him, and Ryler smiled. Jo seemed perfectly content for Ryler to hold her as they walked the trail. Pike noted that Kit and Ryler wore heavy-duty hiking boots, while Neil had on simple sneakers. He must have thought the same thing as Alia.

Alia was nothing like how he'd imagined her to be after listening to her podcast for six years. He'd always assumed she'd be tough, level-headed, and personable, but she almost came across as a whiny princess. While Alia wasn't a jerk, he'd noticed that she wasn't as charming as he'd expected, especially when it came to people helping her. When she'd gotten up last night to grab another drink from the bar, Ricki hadn't seemed terribly impressed. He'd overheard her telling Holly that Alia was a diva. Not exactly the description he'd expected after some of the interactions she'd described on her podcast.

"Is this where we start singing *The Ants Go Marching*?" Kit called out.

Pike chuckled. "Depends on if you've got the voice of a dying cat or not."

"Nah, Kit's got the voice of an angel," Ryler said.

"Who you talking about?" Neil asked. "'Cause I've been out with this man when he gets a couple beers in him, and he sounds like a cow looking for a mate."

The group laughed, except for Alia, who continued to march ahead. Pike ended up next to Ryler and Jo, who strained toward him. He took the dog from her and held her against his chest, scruffing her ears.

"Your cousin doesn't seem to like hiking."

"She does," Ryler said, brushing a hair off her forehead. "She's just been under the weather the last few days."

"Ah, okay." Pike took a deep breath; the scent of pine trees and crisp, cold air was comforting. "This is what I needed today."

"I'm glad I could provide a distraction for you," Ryler said, her full lips stretched into a smile.

I'd be happy to let you distract me any way you want.

Pike didn't know where the thought had come from, but there was no way he was going to make a move on Ryler, especially given what she'd witnessed between him and Anthony. He'd said that they would keep things professional, and that was exactly what he was going to do.

The trees cleared ahead, and Pike heard the thundering of the waterfall before he saw the rocky base. A cloud of mist rose from the water, obscuring the bottom of the cascading liquid. A collection of excited reactions came from the group as they took in the sight, followed by the rapid clicking of Kit's camera shutter.

"Let's get some pictures," Kit said, waving at Alia. "Come on, A, we'll start with you."

Alia stepped up in front of the waterfall and flashed a dazzling smile, changing up her stance with each take.

"You'd never guess she used to model." Neil laughed.

"She did?" Pike asked.

"Mostly print stuff," Ryler said, watching her cousin. "The business was brutal for her."

"Really? Seems like she's a natural at it." Pike caught the sharp look she gave him and frowned. "Something I said?"

"She knows how to smile and pose for a camera, but the demands and the pressure really took their toll on her."

"How long after that did she start *Excursions*?" Pike asked.

"Yes, Ryler, how long after?" Neil asked.

Ryler scowled at Neil before she sent Pike a smile. "It wasn't long. The summer after we graduated from college."

"Alright, the rest of you get over here. You, too, Pike!"

"Oh, I don't need to be in it—"

"Nonsense, you brought us here, and we're going to tag Adventures in Mistletoe for taking us on this gorgeous hike," Kit said, pulling out his phone. "Although, someone with longer arms is going to have to do the selfie."

"Gimme that, Tiny," Neil said, holding out his hand for the phone.

Kit placed it in his hand, muttering, "Jerk."

Pike chuckled. "I'm the shortest in my friend group, too, man, and they never let me forget it."

"I think being tall is overrated." Ryler echoed what she had told Pike the night before, stepping in next to him.

"Says the short girl," Neil teased.

"Shut up." She laughed.

Pike was keenly aware of Ryler's full breasts pressed against his arm as they squeezed together to fit into the frame.

"Alright, everyone, smile." Neil held up his hand, and the camera on the phone clicked.

When they all moved apart, Pike was still only a foot away from Ryler, so close he could see the hint of gold in her dark eyes.

"Why are you looking at me like that?" She laughed softly.

"I just—"

Alia suddenly screamed, shoving into Pike as she took off running. Pike flayed his arms, trying to stay upright, but fell backward into the freezing cold pool. The water splashed up and over him, soaking his clothes from neck to shoes.

Fuck this day.

Chapter Twenty

Pike!" Ryler handed Jo off to Neil before kneeling on the side of the shallow pool, reaching for him. "Here, let me help you."

"Thanks," he said, his teeth chattering. His hand gripped hers, wet and icy.

"Alia!" Neil yelled, cupping his free hand over his mouth. "It was a fucking bunny! You nearly killed Pike over a wrascally wrabbit!"

"Shut up, Neil," Ryler snapped, grunting as she pulled. Kit swung his camera onto his back and reached for Pike's other hand, helping her lift him out of the water.

"How's the water?" Kit asked, the corner of his mouth twitching.

"Like ice."

"I think I'll pass, then."

Ryler was about sick of all her friends right now. Worry twisted her gut up like a corkscrew, and she stroked a hand over Pike's forehead. His lips looked a little blue to her, and he was shivering.

"I've got no service," Neil said.

"What . . . the hell hit me?" Pike whispered.

"My cousin," Ryler said dryly.

Pike blinked, and Ryler was struck by how beautifully blue his eyes were. "Are you telling me I got knocked out by a hundred-pound woman?"

"Would you rather I lie to you?" she asked.

"I'm going to catch up to Alia before she takes off with the car and leaves us stranded," Neil said, passing Kit the puppy. "Hopefully, I'll have a better signal down by the cars."

"I'm alright," Pike said, his arms wrapped around his soaking wet frame. "Don't call anyone. We can just go to the lodge."

Ryler saw something that looked like blood and grabbed him by the chin.

"Ow, my beard!" Pike said as she turned his head to the right.

"You've got a cut above your ear. Does it sting?"

Pike reached back, his fingers coming away bloody. "I didn't notice it until you said something."

"Shit, I've heard about moms lifting up cars to save a trapped child, but never a woman knocking a man four feet into the air when she's scared," Kit said, waving at Alia and Neil when they came into view. "Good news, Alia. You didn't kill him."

"Not yet anyway, but the hypothermia in my extremities is definitely becoming an issue," Pike chattered. "If I freeze to death, it's par for the course for how my day has gone so far."

"You should strip off your clothes," Kit said, and Ryler's jaw dropped.

"I'm not stripping here and walking naked back to my car. I have a blanket in my trunk that will at least save my dignity."

"How far is the nearest hospital?" Ryler asked.

"We don't need to go to the hospital," Pike said, taking a step toward the trail. "They have a doctor at the lodge down the road."

"Damn, what kind of bougie hotel has their own concierge doctor?" Neil asked, coming in on the conversation.

"They don't. He bought the place when he retired."

Ryler shook her head. "Pike, he won't have any medical equipment—"

Ryler quieted when he covered her hand with his and gave it a squeeze. "It's just a bump on the head and some wet clothes, Kitten. Get me back to the car, and I can fix half my problems."

"I am so sorry, Pike," Alia said, her voice hoarse. "I heard the bushes rustle, and this brown thing poked its head out, and I just panicked."

"Yeah, I figured that out after I went flying through the air and ended up in the pond," he said, shuffling down the trail. Ryler could only imagine how those wet jeans were rubbing against his skin if he wasn't wearing boxer briefs.

"I'm still concerned about the weather turning," Pike called over his shoulder. "You guys should probably head back to town."

"You can't drive like this," Ryler said.

"I'll be fine. Like I said, I have a blanket in my trunk. I can strip down and drive the ten minutes up the road."

"Your cut is still oozing. What if you pass out because you have a concussion?" she asked.

"I don't have a concussion."

"But you might have hypothermia," Kit said, holding his phone in front of him. "Hypothermia can take up to thirty minutes to fully develop and starts with shivering."

"We are still twenty minutes from the car," Ryler said.

"Oh God, did I kill him?" Alia shrieked.

"You are all panicking over nothing— Oof! What the fuck!" Pike hollered as Neil grabbed the shorter man and lifted him over his shoulder, carrying him like a sack of potatoes. Ryler couldn't believe Neil had the strength to pick him up, let alone head down the trail at a brisk pace.

"Dude, put me down!" Pike growled.

"You're shuffling too slow, my guy. Just relax and enjoy the ride."

"Give me your keys," Ryler said. "I'll run ahead and grab the blanket and turn on the heat."

"What the hell is that digging into my shoulder?" Neil asked.

"It's either my bear mace or my gun, and no, I'm not giving you my keys!"

"Why not?" Ryler asked.

"Wait, did he say gun?" Kit asked.

"It was in case we saw a bear," Ryler said.

"That's comforting," Neil said.

"Pike, just get me the keys. I'm doing this for you."

"I have them," Alia said, pulling a set of keys from Pike's jacket. Ryler had forgotten she was wearing it. Ryler grabbed them and took off, jogging down the trail ahead. She could hear Pike bellyaching and complaining, and while she knew this was probably embarrassing for him, his health and safety trumped his discomfort.

Ryler was sweating buckets despite the chill in the air by the time she made it to the car, hopping into the driver's seat and starting up the engine. She turned the heater all the way up and got out to retrieve the blanket from the trunk.

By the time the rest of the group reached the cars, the red Charger was toasty inside. Neil dropped Pike onto his feet. His teeth were still chattering, but his cheeks were flushed.

"Thank you for the lift," he deadpanned, taking the blanket from her. "You can all head back to town."

"What about the lodge?" Ryler said.

"If you leave now, I don't think you'll hit any weather. I can make it to the lodge on my own, but I would like to get out of these wet clothes first, preferably without an audience."

Neil patted Ryler's shoulder. "Let's give the man some space."

"I am really sorry," Alia said.

Kit handed Jo over to Ryler, but she didn't give him the puppy or get into the SUV with them. Instead, she walked over to the passenger door and said, "Go on ahead. I'm going to make sure he makes it there safely."

Neil looked like he was about to protest, but Alia cut him off. "Let me take the puppy. I'll give her plenty of love and snuggles, and you can concentrate on him."

Ryler handed Jo off. "Thanks."

"Text me when you're heading back."

"I will," Ryler said.

Neil backed the SUV up, and Pike looked around the trunk of his own car, cursing when he saw Ryler. "I told you I'd be fine."

"Well, I didn't believe you, so you're stuck with me." Ryler opened up the driver's side and climbed in.

Ryler caught movement in the side mirror and saw a flash of thigh and buttock as Pike pulled off his pants and underwear. Ryler's cheeks burned, worried that he would catch her watching, so she looked straight ahead. From the brief flash, he was nicely put together, but she'd already guessed that.

When Pike opened the passenger door and climbed inside, he glared at her.

"Stop giving me that death stare." Ryler started the car and put it in reverse. "You doing okay?"

"Getting there," he said, buckling his seat belt over the blanket. "Where's my dog?"

"Alia took her back to our place."

"That's probably good." Pike settled in and closed his eyes, but Ryler poked him. "What?"

"Just keep talking to me. If you start to feel tired or—"

"Don't worry about me, Kitten. I just need a glass of whiskey, some dry clothes, and a warm fire, and I'll be back to my charming self."

"I'm sorry, whoever called you charming lied to you."

"Man, give a guy a break. Today I lost my best friend, my business is on the rocks, I got taken out by a tiny woman, and then I was carried back to my car by another man. The only way my day would be more emasculating is if you looked at my junk and laughed."

Ryler blushed.

"What's that look?" he asked.

"What look?"

"The red-faced, guilty look . . ." Ryler saw Pike turn in his seat out of the corner of her eye. "Did you peep on me when I was changing?"

"What? No! I—accidentally saw your thigh in the mirror, but I wasn't actively looking."

"I can't believe sweet little Ryler is a peeper." He chuckled.

"I am not!"

"Sure, sure." Pike leaned his head back against the seat and closed his eyes. "I'd ask if you liked what you saw, but I'm afraid I won't appreciate the answer."

Ryler pressed her lips together, fighting a smile. "No need to be scared of that."

"Oh yeah?" he asked.

"I said what I said. Now, be quiet and save your strength."

"I thought you wanted me to talk?"

"I changed my mind."

Chapter Twenty-one

As if Pike hadn't suffered enough humiliation for one day, Doc Patten's raucous laughter upon seeing him walk inside the lodge wrapped in a blanket was the cherry on top of his shit sundae. The retired doctor was a friend of his dad's and had been his primary care physician for most of his life.

"What the heck happened to you, kid?" Doc asked, coming around the counter to greet him. Pike kept the blanket clutched in one hand as he shook the doctor's outstretched one, annoyed by the amusement on the older man's face.

"You probably won't believe the truth," Pike said.

"Try me."

"I took a group out to the waterfall at Lake Pine, and one of them got spooked by a rabbit. Knocked me into the pool."

"That sounds so unbelievable, it must be true," he said, grinning as he ran a hand over his silver buzz cut. "Let's get you and your lady friend into a room before one of the other guests sees you."

"Oh, we're not going to stay," Pike said.

"I'm not his lady," Ryler said at the same time.

"I just need a place to dry my clothes and for you to take a look at me," Pike said.

Doc ignored him, addressing Ryler. "Since Pike here has forgotten his manners, hi, I'm Doc Patten."

"Ryler."

"She's one of the people from the group I was showing around the area," Pike muttered.

Doc gave her a once-over, eyes wide. "Not the one who knocked him out, right?"

"No, that would be my cousin."

"Is your cousin a big gun?" Doc asked.

"No, she's tall and thin."

"Whewy, Pike, you better start working out some more if you're getting laid out by tiny women."

"Thanks, Doc," Pike grumbled.

Doc put a set of keys in his hand. "Head on up to room fourteen. It's the only one available, I'm afraid, because we got a full house for the holiday. Family reunion." Doc held out his hand to Ryler, who had Pike's wet clothes in her arms. "If you want to hand me that stack of clothes, I'll go wash and dry them while you get him settled. I'll be up to check on you in a bit."

"Thank you," she said, passing them over to him.

"Thanks, Doc," Pike said, leading the way up the stairs.

"Let me have the keys since I have two hands."

Pike gave her the keys, too cold and tired to argue. He'd wedged his feet back into his boots and the soaking wet footwear was like encasing his feet in blocks of ice. As he climbed the stairs, his feet squished inside the shoes and he gritted his teeth.

Ryler unlocked the door and pushed it open. Pike rushed inside, kicking off the shoes and crawling onto the king-size bed. His feet were pale and shriveled from the moisture in his shoes, and he pushed down the blankets to get under them.

"Do you want me to wait out here?" Ryler asked.

"No, you can come in," he said, pulling the comforter over him and burrowing down. "I'm decent. I'm just trying to get warm."

Ryler walked in and took a seat in a chair by the window. "You know, I've seen several shows and movies where they say the fastest way to get warm is another person's naked body heat."

"Are you offering to strip down and warm me up, Kitten?"

Ryler blushed. "No, I was just sharing information."

"I knew that already. I also would have been better off stripping off my wet clothes immediately and running naked back to the car, but I didn't want to make things awkward."

"Why would it have been awkward seeing you naked?" Ryler shrugged. "It's not the first time I've seen a naked man, you know."

"It was the first time you'd have seen me naked, and I definitely didn't want to experience that in front of two other men and your cousin."

"I get that. I probably wouldn't have stripped either if the roles were reversed. Then again, your lips did look awfully blue there for a while, so it depends how cold I was."

"I'm freezing. I can hardly feel my feet."

Ryler got up from the chair and crossed the room. "Are you serious? You can't feel anything?"

"Not well. They're kind of tingling."

Ryler grabbed the end of the comforter, pulling it out from its tucked position at the end of the bed.

"What are you doing?"

"I'm going to help get your feet warm."

Pike tucked his feet up and away from her as she reached under the blanket. "That's okay, you don't have to do that."

"Oh, for fuck's sake, it is no big deal. They're just feet."

Ryler climbed onto the bed with her head facing the footboard and took his feet, sliding them under her shirt. When she sucked in a breath, Pike tried to pull away, but she wrapped her arms around his legs, keeping his feet against her stomach. Pike was afraid to move, aware of how close his feet were to her breasts.

"Is this any better?" she asked, rubbing his feet through the outside of her sweatshirt.

"This cannot be comfortable for you," he said.

"I'm fine, but how are you? Any warmer?"

The heat of her skin was penetrating his cold feet, and her touch was firm, the press of her fingers into the muscles in his feet wonderful and painful at the same time.

There was a knock at the door, and Ryler got up to open it, letting the doctor in. He came over to the side of the bed and checked Pike's vitals before looking over his hands and feet.

"You're lucky it wasn't lake water, or you'd have been worse off," Doc said, tucking him back under the blankets. "Ryler, why don't you turn on that electric fireplace and get some more heat in here? I want you to stay like this and warm up. I'm going to send up some whiskey and lunch for you while your clothes dry. Hopefully a few hours in a warm bed will get you all toasty and good as new."

"He's also got a cut on the side of his head," Ryler said, and Pike shot her a disgruntled look.

Doc looked at it and prodded it a bit with a grunt. "You got a little bump back here, so I'm going to suggest you stay awake for the next six hours. Watch a movie, tell stories, whatever tickles your fancy, but keep him entertained so he doesn't doze off."

"I will," Ryler said.

The doctor cleaned his head wound, clicking his tongue. "At least you won't need stitches."

He got up from the bed, cleaning up his supplies and carrying his medical bag out of the room with him. "You're welcome to stay the night, of course, free of charge. I'll get the food and drink sent up shortly."

When the doctor left, Ryler grabbed the remote and sat down on the bed with him, turning on the TV. "Do you want me to keep warming your feet?"

"Nah, I'm good." Pike watched her flip through channels until she found a rom-com and settled back next to him. The sweet, floral scent of her hair drifted around him like a hug, and he found himself inching closer to her. "That was nice of you."

"What was?" she asked.

"To ignore me while I stripped and then drive me here," he said, watching her cheeks redden. "To warm my feet and offer to stay with me."

"I think if our positions were reversed, you'd do that and then some."

"I would have, but I was responsible for you. You don't owe me anything."

"It's not about owing anyone," Ryler said, meeting his gaze. "It's about being a decent human being."

Pike touched her hand briefly. "I appreciate that about you." He snuggled into the blanket and yawned. "Thank you for taking care of me."

"You're most welcome."

Chapter Twenty-two

Ryler arched her back, staring up at the ceiling as euphoric pleasure swept through her body. She was in her room, but it didn't look exactly like her room, and whoever had his head between her legs was doing the most incredible things to her. Ryler grabbed the bedspread in her hands, gripping the fabric as she thrashed her head wildly. The sensation of his tongue lapping at her pussy, flicking across her clit in quick, circular motions left her dizzy, gasping, reaching for that little push she needed to fall right over the edge.

The man between her legs looked up, blue eyes glittering, and her stomach flipped as she stared into Pike's grinning face.

"I knew you wanted me."

Her eyes popped open, blinking rapidly against the flashes of light from the TV that illuminated Pike's face as he lay on his side next to her. He cradled his head in his hand, watching her with a smirk.

"Good dream?" he asked mildly.

Ryler's pussy still throbbed in the aftermath of her sex dream, and she hoped to God that he couldn't tell she was blushing.

"I—um—was eating ice cream with no calories, but it tasted like the real thing. So good."

"Wow, your ice cream noises sound a lot like sex noises," he said.

"Well, some people think that eating ice cream is better than sex."

"Then they are having the wrong kind of sex," Pike said.

"And what is the right kind of sex?" she asked.

Pike grinned. "The kind that elicits ice cream noises and leaves you too weak to move."

"Hmmm, I don't remember ever having that kind of sex," Ryler said, rolling up on her side to face him. "Must be why ice cream is so good."

"That's a damn shame."

"I take it you're feeling better?" she asked.

"Yep. All toasty warm."

"What time is it?"

"Around six."

"At night or the morning?"

"Night."

"I was going to say, I didn't think I was that tired." She laughed.

"Tired enough."

"So, should we get in the car and head back to town?" she asked.

"We could do that," he said, pointing to the window. "Or, we could wait until tomorrow when the snow lets up."

Ryler sprang from the bed and ran to the window, staring out at the few parking lot lights that lit up the area, showing the white dusting across every car. Large flakes swirled in the air, and Ryler sighed.

"It's been so long since I've seen snow. It's so beautiful."

Ryler sensed his body heat as he came up behind her, stopping several inches behind. "You hungry?"

Her stomach gurgled, and she laughed. "Apparently."

"They have a pretty great in-hotel restaurant," Pike said, the heat of his breath tickling the hairs on the back of her neck. "Doc brought my clothes up a little bit ago, if you want to go down there."

Ryler turned around, noticing that he was fully clothed, his hair mussed and standing on end. On impulse, she stood up on her tiptoes and smoothed his hair back. "Sure, although I need to use the bathroom first."

"Go ahead."

Ryler wasn't used to sharing a bathroom with anyone, least of all a man. Would he hear her through the thin walls of the hotel?

Ryler turned on the faucet and went about her business, keenly aware that Pike knew she'd been dreaming about sex and had been hovering over her, watching her. For a moment, she'd almost thought he was going to offer his services and show her what she was missing, but that would have been a turnoff. Men who bragged about how good they were in bed never measured up, and she'd already imagined what Pike would be like in bed enough, especially subconsciously.

Ryler washed her hands and exited the bathroom to find Pike still standing by the window in his hoodie and jeans. "I'll text Alia and let her know we're waiting for the storm to pass."

"The weather shows snow until seven a.m., so we might be stuck here."

All night, alone with Pike in a king bed now that he was 100 percent? "Alright."

"I can ask Doc if he's got another room now," he said.

"Sure, but if not, no worries. We're both adults." Ryler grabbed her phone off the side table and texted Alia. Pike is better but we're going to wait out the storm. Be back in the morning.

The three little bubbles popped up. Oh, are you two sharing a room?

No.

Boo, that is boring!

I like my sex life boring and predictable. Cuts down on complications.

Snore.

Goodnight.

I love you!

I love you too. Ryler slipped her phone into her pocket with a shake of her head. "You've got a sister, right?"

"Yep. Biggest pain in the ass of my life."

"Sounds about like having a cousin."

Pike got the door for her, waiting as she passed through. "My sister is the one that thought I needed a companion. I swear, that puppy would have been bouncing all over the place had she been in the room with us."

"You're going to try to tell me you don't like that dog at all?" Ryler asked.

"Of course I like her. Still trying to figure out how she'll fit in my life."

"You're worried about your job?" Ryler asked, descending the stairs next to him.

"And my living situation. If the upstairs neighbor banging on the ceiling every time Jo makes a peep is any indication, I'm going to have to move. My mother has been trying to convince me to buy a house—"

"So, why don't you? You want to stay in Mistletoe, don't you?"

"Yes, but it seems like a waste to buy a house for just me and possibly Jo."

"What about in the future when you meet someone? You should buy a house based on how many kids you want."

"Seems like I need a partner to help make that decision. If I buy a four-bedroom house, and my partner only wants one kid, I'll have two extra rooms."

"And she'll get an office and you get a home gym."

"You saying I need to work out?" he teased.

"No, you look like you like to work out."

"More like I have to. I was a pretty chubby kid. Puberty helped, but I also started hitting the weights freshman year."

"I do a lot of walking and hiking, but I don't worry about it. As long as I'm eating enough fruits and vegetables and I feel good, that's what matters to me."

Pike chuckled. "I like pizza and beer too much to not hit the gym five times a week."

"That's interesting," she said.

"What is?" he asked.

"The girl with Anthony, the one you were interested in. She's plus size."

"And?" he said flatly.

"A guy who cares that much about his appearance, I'm surprised you wouldn't be obsessed with women who looked more like my cousin."

Pike shook his head, stopping outside the restaurant's entrance. "Why would I look at women superficially when I've experienced that behavior my entire life?" Ryler couldn't come up with anything to say and he added, "Do you really think I was popular with this hair color? People called me Lucky Charms growing up, and that was after I lost weight. Delilah is gorgeous just the way she is."

Ryler wanted to sink into the floor. She'd made a lot of assumptions about this man's character, and the more time she spent with him, the more she realized his Instagram showed him best. He was well-liked and respected by the people who knew him. He was hardworking and adventurous. He was funny and raw.

Shit, it was one thing to be attracted to the guy, but to like him?

That spelled trouble.

"I'm sorry for how that came off. I am far from perfect, but I guess I just assumed she'd be—" Ryler shook her head. "Listen to me sounding like a superficial shithead."

"Listen, I get it. You see it on social media, in movies, on television. You can't help who you're attracted to. I just happen to be a guy who likes variety." Pike winced. "That came out wrong. I just mean I don't have a type. I want who I want."

"Fair enough," she said.

The hostess seated them by the window, and Ryler was surprised that a booked-up hotel was so empty. "I wonder where the family reunion is."

"There's a ballroom at the other end of the lodge. They probably rented it out to have their party down there."

"Ah, makes sense."

The waiter came back to take their drink orders, and when he left, Ryler looked around at the wood walls and rustic atmosphere. Several animal heads adorned the walls, and she shook her head. "Alia would definitely have something to say about the animal heads."

"I'm not surprised. I remember the episode when *Excursions* was on a safari tour and discovered a poached lion. Given the anger and emotion during that podcast, I can't imagine she takes well to seeing animal trophies."

Ryler had never talked so much with someone about her podcast as if it wasn't her behind the mic. Most of the people they met in countries she visited had never listened to *Excursions* and just thought they were a group of Americans touring. No one cared who said what or how they felt. Choosing an American city, especially where Pike was such an avid fan, may not have been the best decision, but she couldn't regret being here.

"Are you a hunter?" she asked.

"No. I went when I was in my teens, but I don't love venison, so it doesn't make any sense to go out hunting something I don't want to eat."

"I'm not a fan either. Too gamey. I did have alligator in New Orleans."

"How was that?" Pike asked.

"Tasted like chicken. I could not do the frog legs, however."

"My sister got me chocolate-covered crickets and shoved them into a regular chocolate box. After that, I would never accept anything edible from her."

Ryler laughed. "I never had a sibling to torture, but it sounds like a delight."

"For her, maybe. Nick's sisters were the same with him, although they were younger. Holly was evil when it came to pranks. I woke up covered in glitter once after drinking too much with Nick. I was finding that crap in my hair for weeks."

"Sounds awful," she said. "Alia and I tease and mess with each other, but nothing that extreme."

"At least my sister can't do too much damage from two states away."

"Where does she live?" Ryler asked.

"Arizona."

"Are you ready to order?" the waiter asked.

Pike nodded. "I'll take the sirloin, medium, with a baked potato and a dinner salad with ranch."

"And you, miss?"

"I'll have the lemon-crusted chicken with fries and a dinner salad with ranch."

"Perfect, I'll take those menus and be back with your food when it is ready."

They handed their menus to the waiter, and Ryler caught Pike watching her. "What?"

"I was just thinking about the night we met."

Ryler blushed, remembering their kiss. "Oh God, what about it?"

"You following me out to the courtyard to make a move."

Ryler spluttered. "That is not what happened!"

"Right, you were just returning the mistletoe I dropped." Pike leaned forward, balancing his chin on his hand. "You know, I saw some in the front lobby if you need another excuse."

"If *I* need another excuse?" she scoffed. "Pike, honey, if you've been thinking about kissing me, then at least have the stones to admit it."

"I've been thinking about kissing you again." Ryler started at his admission, and he chuckled. "You asked for it."

"I suppose I did," she murmured, reaching for the bread basket in the center of the table and taking a roll. He'd told her that they needed to keep things professional, and yet, here he was admitting that he'd been thinking about kissing her.

"I guess the question hanging in the air is, have you been thinking about kissing me, too?"

Ryler took a bite of her roll, chewing slowly to give her time to make a choice. If she admitted that she hadn't stopped thinking about it since the first time, she'd be opening herself up to the possibility of him putting on the breaks again.

Then again, if she lied and he thought that was the end of it, would she regret it? Would they spend the night lying awkwardly in the room, totally aware of how close they were and what they could do to each other if they only took the chance?

"I have, quite a bit, actually. It's becoming a real problem, and I feel like the only solution is to get it out of our systems."

"You think that will work, huh?" he asked, smiling.

"I feel like it's a chance I'm willing to take. What about you, Pike?" She set her roll on her plate and reached across the table, trailing her finger over the back of his hand. "Feel like taking a chance on me?"

Chapter Twenty-three

Although Pike was starving, it was hard to sit there for the next thirty minutes and finish his meal. He couldn't stop thinking about getting Ryler alone and kissing every inch of her body, starting with her lips and ending at her pussy. When the waiter finally came back with the check, Pike pulled his wallet out and set his card down, ignoring Ryler's protests.

"You don't have to pay for my dinner," she said, picking up her purse off the floor. Technically, you are my guide."

"Not tonight I'm not," he said. "Tonight, I am a man taking out a beautiful woman."

Ryler blushed. "We don't have to make this anything more than what it is."

"And what is this exactly?" Pike asked.

"It's two people who are attracted to each other and have an irresistible itch that they need scratched."

"I don't know how I feel about being compared to a mosquito bite."

Ryler laughed. "It's just an expression. I only mean that we can keep this casual and fun, and we don't have to turn it into anything more complicated. I'll be gone by Christmas, and everything in Mistletoe will go back to normal after I leave."

"Yeah, my new normal," Pike said bitterly, thinking about Adventures in Mistletoe and Anthony, something he'd been trying to avoid. What would happen when he returned to town tomorrow? Would he pull out of the business, his dream? Could they continue to run the place, even if they were no longer friends?

"I think we should have some ground rules for this," she said.

"Fire away," Pike said, keeping his attention on the subject at hand.

"I think that as long as we're together, we should only talk about happy things, so it doesn't kill the mood."

The waiter took Pike's card and went behind the counter to run it.

"Fair enough," Pike said.

"In addition, I don't think we should share this with anyone, especially the rest of the *Excursions* crew."

Pike nodded in agreement. "Completely doable."

"And if at any point either one or both of us wants to end this, we need to be completely honest," Ryler said. "We don't need to make it awkward after the fact. We just rip off the Band-Aid."

"We're just casually hooking up to stave off the holiday lonelys," Pike joked.

"It works for me," she said.

"Are there any rules for what we do together?" he asked.

"Define *do*," she said.

"Like we're not gonna tell anybody that we're having extracurriculars," he said, "but are we going to go to dinner like we are now? Or is this more of a late-night text, quickie on my lunch break kind of thing?"

"I think it would be pretty suspicious if we were doing date-like activities together, don't you think?" Ryler asked.

"Noted," he said. "So this will be our last dinner just the two of us."

"I think that's best," she said. "And if either one of us finds the experience tonight to be not as gratifying as we expect, no hard feelings in the morning."

Pike almost spit out his drink. "I think we're going to be fine."

"Just because we had one good kiss doesn't mean we'll have the right chemistry for sex. I just want you to know that if there are no fireworks, we're good."

If Ryler thought that she was going to get a lackluster performance, she was going to be in for a shock.

"Anything else?" he asked gruffly.

"I think we've established the main boundaries."

Doc walked into the restaurant and waved at them, making his way over. "How was everything?"

"It was good, Doc," Pike said.

"Are you going to stay the night?"

"Yeah," Pike said, waving his hand toward the dark window. "With the snow coming down outside, I think we're going to wait it out until morning and give the road crew time to plow."

"Do you happen to have another room?" Ryler asked.

"I don't, but if you're uncomfortable, I could have a cot brought up," Doc said.

Pike shot Ryler a quizzical look, his eyebrow arched. What was she doing? They'd just agreed to cross the line, and now she wanted to move out of the room?

"No, that's fine. I was just wondering," she said.

"Alright, then," Doc said, crossing his arms. "I hope the two of you get some rest." Doc pointed his finger at Pike. "Stop letting girls push you in waterfalls to get my attention. If you want to come visit, just make the drive."

Pike laughed. "Will do."

"It was nice to meet you," Doc said to Ryler.

"You, too," Ryler said.

Doc left the restaurant, and the waiter came back with Pike's card and the receipt. Pike signed the receipt and set it aside.

"Ready to go?" Pike asked.

"Absolutely," Ryler said.

They got up from the table, and Pike placed his hand on the small of Ryler's back, guiding her out the door. As they climbed the stairs, Pike's heartbeat kicked up the closer they got to the room. This was the moment of truth, whether their next few moments would be spent in pleasure or fizzle out.

When they were standing outside the door, Pike stuck the key in and twisted it to the side. It released with a telltale click, and he'd no more than pushed the door open, when Ryler grabbed him by the front of his shirt and dragged him in after her.

Pike kicked the door closed seconds before Ryler wrapped her arms around his neck, pulling his face down to hers. Their mouths melted in a passionate fusion, tongues tangling and circling. Pike's hands gripped her lower back, sliding down over her round ass and squeezing her cheeks. Ryler gasped against his mouth before opening hers wider, and he deepened the kiss, loving her eager thrusts and parries against his.

Pike let her push him back toward the bed, and when the backs of his knees hit the side, he sat down. Ryler followed him, straddling his lap without breaking their contact, and he closed his eyes at the warmth of her pussy branding his cock through their jeans. Pike reached up, tangling his hands in her hair, and he pulled her ponytail holder out in one quick pull.

Ryler broke their kiss with a gasp. "Ow! Gentle! My hair is attached to my head."

"Sorry," Pike said, massaging the back of her head with his fingertips, tracing the lines of her neck to her shoulders, when his fingers dug in there.

Ryler moaned, her head falling back. "Oh my god, that feels amazing."

Pike leaned forward, kissing the lines of her throat as he kneaded her muscles, working his way down her arms and around to her back. When he reached the area above her ass, his mouth trailed kisses along the column of her throat and down until he encountered the collar of her T-shirt.

"We have got to get some of these clothes off," Pike said.

"I thought we were just coming up here to kiss," Ryler teased.

Pike tangled his fist in her hair, his mouth gently connecting with her jaw. "Is that all you want Ryler?" he whispered against her skin. "Do you just want me to kiss you?"

Pike's hands gripped the bottom of her T-shirt and lifted it up, dragging it over her stomach, exposing her gorgeous body inch by inch. She stretched her arms above her head, making it easier for him to divest her of her T-shirt. When she sat before him in just her bra, her full breasts nearly overflowing the cups, Pike licked his lips in anticipation.

"Mmm, beautiful."

He dropped his mouth to her collarbone, showering her skin with light kisses. "Is this all you were looking for?" he asked. "Do you just want me to kiss you here?"

"No," Ryler murmured, and his mouth drifted lower, his lips caressing the curves of her breast.

"Should I stop here?" he asked.

He felt her move and watched as she reached behind her and undid her bra, sliding the straps down her arms. To his surprise, she cupped her breast, her thumb gliding over the nipple.

"I think you should keep going," she said.

"Do you now?" He reached out and covered her right breast with his hand, squeezing the soft flesh. With his other hand, he pulled her hair slightly, and she followed his lead, leaning back to give him better access to her left nipple. Pike sucked the hard peak in his mouth, tonguing it with quick strokes.

"Oh," she whispered. "Yes."

Pike continued to squeeze her breast, increasing the pressure as his mouth sucked her nipple deeper. Afraid the pressure would be too much, he let off, but she whispered, "Harder."

Pike's dick twitched at her plea, and he obliged, squeezing her until she gasped, "Enough." Learning her threshold, he nipped at her nipple, and she bucked on his lap. The fact that Ryler wasn't afraid to tell him what she wanted made her all that much hotter, and he wanted to push her to her limits to find out exactly what pressed all her buttons and make her scream his name.

Pike released her breast and flipped her onto her back, sliding off the bed to stand at the end of it. He reached for her pants, but she pushed his hands away, slipping to her knees in front of him. To Pike's utter shock and anticipation, Ryler grabbed his belt, pulling it through the loops and working his jeans open. When she pushed his jeans and his underwear past his hips to his knees, his cock sprang forth, bobbing inches from her face.

Fuck, he liked her down there, staring at his cock like it was a lollipop she couldn't wait to lick. Her hand wrapped around his length and traveled upward and over the head, his breath caught when she glided her thumb across the tip. Pike threw his head back, eyes closing, losing himself in the feel of her touch.

When her mouth closed over the tip, he cradled her head in both hands as she lapped at him with that eager tongue. Fuck, he wanted her to take more of him. To thrust deeper. He wanted to sink all the way in until he hit the back of her throat and felt the muscles spasm around the head of his dick. But he held himself back. He kept a tight rein on his control. Her tongue massaged his shaft as he pulled back out, and her mouth came off him with a pop.

"If I do something you don't like," he said, stroking his thumb over her cheek, "tap my hip twice."

Ryler laughed. "So don't bite down?"

Pike spluttered. "Keep talking like that, and he's gonna go away."

"We wouldn't want that," Ryler said, cupping his balls, rolling the orbs in her hand.

"Hmmm, fuck."

"Although a little bit of teeth might make you nervous, I like it," she said, running her tongue over his balls, before looking up at him with luminous eyes. "You're not gonna break me, and I swear, if you do something I'm not into, I won't hesitate to say something."

Oh, that was the wrong thing to say.

Pike's fingers dug in slightly behind her ears, and he pulled her back to his cock, pressing against those full lips until she opened them over his head. Her mouth widened as he thrust inside, her lips closing over him as he pumped in and out. His length disappeared when he pushed all the way in, biting his lip as her fingernails dug into his ass and she met his motions, making guttural moans that vibrated against his tip, traveling up his dick to his balls. They tightened with happiness at the sensation, and he wanted to feel it again and again.

Pike usually let a woman set the pace at first, but with Ryler, he wanted everything at once in case this was their only time together. He'd been dreaming about her mouth for days, those dick-sucking lips wrapped around him, making him melt. That sweet little tongue swirling his length. Ryler pressed all the way down on him, and he felt the back of her throat convulse against his tip, nearly undoing him, and he pulled out of her mouth with a shudder.

"Fuck me," he said, breathing hard as he stroked her cheek. "You're fucking perfection."

"Thank you," she said, licking his tip once more, making a big show of her tongue gliding over his flesh, and he couldn't take it anymore. Picking her up by the armpits, he tossed her onto the bed. Kicking off his pants and underwear, shoes and socks, stripping madly, until he was completely nude, Pike was extremely aware of her watching him from her prone position.

"Take your fucking shoes off," he growled.

Ryler didn't hesitate, unlacing the boots and dropping them off the side of the bed. When she didn't move fast enough for him, Pike took her by the ankles and tugged her closer. He removed her socks, rolling them down her feet and tossing them aside. Pike grabbed the button of her jeans and flicked it open, working the zipper down next until they were loose enough to remove. Pike yanked them all the way off, tossing them across the room, taking her panties with them. Without giving her a moment to catch her breath, he dragged her to the end of the bed and dived between her legs with his mouth covering her sweet pussy with his lips. His fingers spread her open, his tongue finding her clit and flicking it rapidly before nipping at her labia. Pike had always enjoyed going down on a woman, listening to her likes and dislikes, what made her tick, but with Ryler, he was driven by a desperate need to possess her. To absorb everything about her. Listening to her sweet cries as he curled his fingers inside her, rubbing at the rough skin just inside her pussy. He circled her G-spot as his lips closed over her clit, sucking it into his mouth with reverence and heat.

"Holy fuck, yes, please, so good!" Ryler cried out, a prelude to her body convulsing under his mouth, the sweet taste of her come on his lips, his tongue slurping up every bit of her pleasure.

"Pike," she breathed out, her voice trembling. "That was . . ."

He grinned when she didn't finish, obviously at a loss for words. If Ryler thought he wasn't going to give her his absolute fucking best and leave her walking away from this bed with wobbly knees, she'd underestimated him. Just because she'd come didn't mean he was done.

Pike didn't stop licking and kissing her until she finally sighed, her body going limp under his mouth.

"Fuck, that was so much better than my dream."

Pike stopped, his eyes rolling up to meet hers, which were wide, and he realized she hadn't meant to say that out loud.

Oh, this was going to be so much fun.

Chapter Twenty-four

Ryler froze, realizing a second too late what she had said. How could she have been so stupid, so lax? Pike latched on to her face with curious eyes, watching her with a small smile from between her legs.

"What dream was that?" he murmured, his hot breath rushing over her sensitive flesh, and she shuddered.

"Nothing, it was just an idle thought," she said.

"Are you sure?" he teased. "I'm beginning to think those weren't ice cream noises earlier."

"No, those were definitely ice cream noises," she said.

"Really?" he drawled, crawling up her body, only to flop onto his side. Pike leaned his head onto his hand, his other palm caressing down her body and covering her pussy. "Because the sounds you were just making were awfully similar, only more intense."

Ryler blushed. "Or maybe I just realized that certain aspects of sex could be better than ice cream."

"You can keep lying if you want to," he said, his fingers dipping in between her lips and grazing her sensitive clit. Ryler moaned as heat shot from between her legs to the rest of her body, warming her up. "But now I know exactly what to do to get the truth out of you."

Pike dipped down, his mouth covering hers, and she tasted Pike and the sweet musk of her arousal as he deepened the kiss, his finger continuing its torturous strokes over her swollen clit.

"Pike," she gasped against his mouth.

"Yeah, baby?" His mouth trailed along her skin until it reached her breast, his finger still doing deliciously evil things to her body. "Do you have something to say?"

"I just was hoping— Oh! I want— We could move on— Holy f—" She whimpered as he pressed harder, making tight circles against her. "To the new. I mean the next—"

"Spit it out, baby. Tell me what you want."

His mouth covered her breast, sucking the nipple sharply into his mouth, and she arched her back, lifting her hips, which only made the pressure on her clit intensify.

"I don't know whether I want you to stop or keep going," she cried, threading her fingers into his hair and tugging the strands. "I can't make up my mind."

Instead of doing either, he switched to the other breast, rolling the hard nipple between his lips before grazing it with his teeth. He released it with a hard pop, increasing the speed of his circles on her clit until her legs shook.

"Tell me about your dream, and I'll make an informed decision on whether to stop or make you finish," he said.

"I-I was— Oh god," she moaned.

"Did you dream about me doing this to you?" he asked, leaving her clit to slip his fingers inside her, adding a second one when he pulled out and pushed back in again.

Ryler shook her head frantically. "No."

"Hmmm, not that? Let's see, what else could it be about?" Pike slid down her body, kissing his way from her belly button down. "Did you imagine me doing this to you?" He ducked between her legs and swept his tongue along her seam from the bottom all the way back up to her hooded clit.

Ryler cried out loudly, covering her mouth with her hands in an attempt to quiet herself. What if someone passing by heard her?

"Is that what you dreamed about, Ryler?" he asked firmly, taking her labia into his mouth and tonguing her, and she gave in.

"Yes," she whispered.

"Good girl," he said. He kissed her between her legs once more and then slid off the bed, reaching for his pants.

"Where are you going?" she asked, bereft without him.

"Just grabbing a condom, baby," he said. "Don't you worry, I'm not done with you yet."

Ryler's pussy still tingled, and she reached between her legs with her hand, fingering her clit to ease the tension. She watched him search his wallet, and when he looked up with a condom in hand and saw what she was doing, he froze.

"Fuck me, that's a beautiful sight." Without further comment, Pike ripped opened the condom with his mouth and glided it over his straining cock. "I could fucking watch you do that all damn day."

"Really," she said recklessly. "Because what I really want is your fucking cock inside me."

Ryler had never been so vocal in the bedroom. Most of her experiences had been men asking if she was okay, tentatively touching her, and never taking charge. Pike wasn't afraid to be in control, relished in leading her into pleasure, and she loved it.

Pike crawled over her, spreading her legs wide, almost too wide as her hips protested his hands on her thighs pushing them farther. With his cock firmly in his hand, Pike dragged the tip over her, teasing her, smacking her clit with the head playfully. Ryler's eyes rolled up into her head, and she spread her arms out, grabbing the bedspread in her fists.

"What do you want, baby?"

"Everything."

"Then come here and fucking get it," he said, flipping onto his back. "Climb on top and ride me."

Ryler scrambled to her knees and threw a leg over him, hugging his sides with her knees as she sank down, the tip of him stretching her. Pike was thick and rigid, stretching her body to accommodate him in the best way possible, and as his length slipped inside inch by inch, she placed her hands on his chest to drag it out, to torture him the way he had her.

"No, baby, that's not what we're going to do now," he said, gripping her hips in his hand and thrusting upward, slamming her down on his cock. She cried out with joy, and he lifted her up and over and over in rapid succession, giving her no chance to slow down. She'd thought by letting her be on top, he was giving her some kind of control back, but in reality, he wanted to be the boss, and fuck, she loved it. It felt so fucking good.

"Fuck, I love watching your tits," he said, bouncing her faster. He rolled his hips up and across her G-spot, the motion more intense than any she'd ever experienced. Ryler had no idea how he knew exactly what and where her G-spot was because no one else had ever found it before, but it was almost like he was going above and beyond so she'd never forget tonight. He took her like he was claiming her, like he was showing her exactly why she wanted this, wanted him. Why sex with Pike was better than any fucking ice cream ever had been in her entire life.

When she came for a second time, she fucking dragged her nails over his chest, her hips pumping, crying out with abandon. Pike gave no quarter as he kept moving, the rapid rolling strokes continuing until his own motions became erratic. Yelling her name, he pushed into her as far as he could go, one, two, three times, and she loved it. Loved everything about it.

Ryler fell forward against his chest, her cheek resting there. His chest hair tickled her nose as she listened to his heart pounding against her ear. How did any woman experience this with Pike and walk away? Did he get lazy with them as the relationship went on? Maybe he stopped trying so hard. The thoughts racing through her head were far too serious for if they were going to keep it casual. She was going to be gone soon, and that would be the end of this. They would have several glorious weeks, and she would say goodbye.

Ryler wasn't going to think about that now. This was just the beginning of something great.

She trailed her finger along his chest, running the tip of it over his nipple as she breathed, "Are we good?"

"Good?" he asked.

"Are we one and done?"

Pike's fingers twisted in her hair as he pulled her head up to look at her. "Do you want to be one and done?"

"I was just asking," she said breathlessly.

"Ryler, once is not gonna be enough for me," he said. "But if you really don't want this, then—"

"No, I was just joking. I was just playing."

Suddenly she found herself on her back with Pike looming over her, his expression thunderous.

"You can joke about a lot of things, Ryler, but until you get on that plane and leave Mistletoe, I want this pussy as much as possible," he said, sliding his hand between her legs. "Do I make myself clear?"

"Crystal," she said. Anticipation coursed through her body. Although they planned on this being casual between them, Pike's possessive and assertive claim on her did things that she'd never expected. She loved it. The raw want on his face was intoxicating and addictive.

"And what about you?" she asked.

"What about me?"

"Are you going to be kissing other women?" she asked.

"Would it bother you if I did?" he asked.

Yes, she thought.

But instead of being honest, she shrugged. "You said we're casual, right? And since we are a big secret and no one is supposed to know about us, it would look weird if you suddenly stopped being interested in other women."

"So, you're saying you want me to continue to date other women?"

"We've got to keep up appearances, right?" she said, wondering why she was saying any of this, because the last thing she wanted was for him to date anyone else and take any time away from her. But her self-destruct button had been flipped, and now she was saying all kinds of stupid shit.

Just stop talking, Ryler, she thought.

Pike leaned closer and gave her a hard, fast kiss. "I don't give a fuck about appearances. These lips and every other part of you are mine until we're done."

Ryler quivered, but in a light tone, said, "We'll see."

Pike kissed her again, groaning against her mouth, "You're gonna be the death of me."

What a way to go, she thought.

Chapter Twenty-five

Pike dropped Ryler off Monday morning, resisting the urge to kiss her goodbye. Although they had been clear about the rules, he couldn't stop wanting to touch her.

"I'll see you Wednesday for our snowshoeing adventure," Ryler said.

"Do you want me to come to your rental, and you can all follow me out there?"

"Sure, that would be great." She hesitated before opening the door and whispering, "I had a really good time."

Pike chuckled. "Just once?"

Ryler blushed. "Fine, more than once."

"That's what a guy wants to hear."

"Don't go getting a big head," she said.

"Dang, way to tear down the man's ego."

Ryler laughed. "Your ego is indestructible."

"Do you think so?" he asked softly.

Ryler leaned across the seat, and for a second, he thought she was going to kiss him. Instead she paused a few inches away and said, "It is taking everything in me not to lean across here and kiss you, but if I do that, everyone's gonna know what we've been up to."

"I could do another turn around the block and find someplace private."

"Oh yeah, that won't be suspicious. You pull up to drop me off, and then we suddenly leave again."

"So does that mean we're gonna be waiting a few days, or do you think you could sneak away later?" he asked.

"Maybe I'll have to go grocery shopping," she said. "We might need some whipped cream for sundaes."

"I know what else whipped cream is good for," Pike teased.

"Stop it!" Ryler laughed. "I'm getting out of here."

"Wait! What about my dog?" he hollered.

"Oh, I almost forgot. Hang on." She climbed out of the car and shut the door.

Ryler ran up the stairs to the house, returning a few minutes later with Jo under her arm. As she passed the dog through the window, Ryler leaned in and whispered, "You know what goes good with whipped cream? Chocolate syrup."

Despite her protest, Ryler gave Pike a brief kiss, and before he could even react, she was halfway up the stairs.

He put Jo in the back, watching Ryler stop at the top of the landing and wave at him before she disappeared inside. Jo barked from the back seat, and Pike sighed. "I know, Jo," he said. "She kind of grows on you."

Pike made a three-point turn out of the driveway and headed to his apartment. He showered and packed Jo's crate in the car. At least if he tried crate training at work, his uptight neighbor wouldn't have anything to complain about. Since it was his turn to be in the office, he was trapped if Anthony decided to come in. He didn't wanna deal with the aftermath of his best friend's betrayal, but there was no way to avoid it. Pike was not going to let their personal business interfere with Adventures in Mistletoe. They'd both worked too long and hard to bring their dream to fruition to bail now. He was at least going to make it through the new year before he made any big decisions on whether or not to leave and start something up on his own. There were people out there who were business partners without being friends. He could be professional.

Then again, could you really trust someone after they screwed you over personally?

Pike put Jo inside her crate in the car and carried her to the front door of Adventures in Mistletoe. He set her down to unlock the door and heard Nick call out behind him. Pike turned and saw Nick coming up the sidewalk with two coffees in hand.

Pike grinned. "Is one of those for me?"

"Yes, it is. It's a cinnamon roll latte for my very good friend Pike."

Pike hiked an eyebrow at Nick's cheery tone. "What's your deal?"

"What do you mean? I'm just a friend bringing a cup of coffee to my good buddy."

"So long as that friend isn't trying to butter me up to talk about our other former, mutual friend," Pike said.

"We share many friends, so you're going to have to be more specific."

Pike pushed open the door, carrying Jo's cage inside. "If you want to talk about Anthony, you are barking up the wrong tree. He made his bed, and now he's got to lie in it."

Nick shook his head. "Can't you at least hear him out?"

"I heard him out on the side of the road, and each excuse was worse than the last." Pike set Jo down behind the counter and leaned against it, watching Nick intently as he said, "Anthony can tell me that she's a witch who cast a spell on him, and it still wouldn't change the fact that he lied. That he didn't have the balls to tell me he wanted Delilah and I needed to back off. Instead, he let me make a fool of myself, then went behind my back and hooked up with her. That was beyond cruel and not what friends do."

"Playing devil's advocate," Nick said, holding his hands up as though Pike were armed, "have you ever had feelings for someone that you weren't ready to talk about yet with your friends?"

Pike thought about his little arrangement with Ryler, but it wasn't the same thing. They had a casual relationship and weren't going for anything more. Anthony had spent the weekend with Delilah and her parents. You didn't go home and meet someone's parents unless you were serious about them.

"I've always been very open about people I am serious about, and I make my feelings known. I make my intentions known. I don't skulk around and blow my best friend off. I don't leave him hanging. And I certainly don't laugh about him behind his back."

"You know that Anthony didn't laugh at you," Nick said.

Pike threw his hands up. "Why are you taking his side?"

Nick shook his head. "I am not taking his side. We've all been friends for a long time, and maybe he had a reason for his behavior. It might not be a good reason. It might even come off as stupid, but maybe in his mind it was the right thing to do at the time."

Pike shook his head. "I am not interested in his logic. All I want is to do my job. I don't wanna deal with any of this personal stuff yet.

I am having a good morning, and I don't want it ruined by Anthony's bullshit."

"Fine," Nick said, setting Pike's coffee on the counter. "I've got to get ready for my presentation today. I just don't like all this strife between you guys."

"I've got nothing against you. My only issue is the man who picked a chick over his best friend."

Nick nodded. "Fair enough. When did you get a dog?"

"My sister's early Christmas present," Pike said. "It was the start of my very difficult weekend."

"What else happened?" Nick asked.

"Nothing, just got stuck out near Lake Pine yesterday and had to wait out the storm at the lodge."

"Oh, how is Doc doing?" Nick asked.

"Keeping busy," Pike said. "He had a full house with only one room left for me."

"I thought you weren't working this weekend," Nick said.

"I was showing the *Excursions* crew some places outside Mistletoe. I sent them back to town before the storm hit."

"Well, we were thinking about getting dinner tonight if you want to join us," Nick said.

"Who is 'us'?" Pike asked.

"Noel, me, Anthony—"

Pike shook his head. "I'll pass, but thanks for the invite."

Nick sighed and pushed the door open. "We love you, man."

"I love you, too," Pike said.

As Nick disappeared outside, Pike thought about how hard the next few weeks were going to be as he acclimated to not being friends with Anthony. Nick and Noel were always *their* friends and now he would have to split their time with Anthony. It was going to be like a divorce, except they would share custody of their friends instead of their kids.

Around lunchtime, Noel showed up with two French dip sandwiches and a smile.

"Hey, Fish. Look what I brought you."

Pike eyed her suspiciously. "Interesting. Nick brought me coffee this morning, and now you're bringing me lunch."

"What? Can't a friend just feed another friend with no ulterior motives?"

"Yes, a friend can, but you don't normally leave your bed when you're working nights. So the fact that you dragged your happy butt out of your sleep time to come bring me lunch means that you wanna talk about something."

"What could I possibly want to talk about?" she said.

"I don't know," he said sarcastically, "but if it has anything to do with Anthony, you can save your breath."

Noel huffed. "Come on, Pike, be angry for a week and then hear him out."

Pike shook his head. "You act like he didn't pay me back for lunch or something. He lied to me. He humiliated me. He gave absolutely zero fucks about our friendship while he was away having God knows how much sex. So, no, I'm not just gonna get over it like that." Pike snapped his fingers to emphasize his point. "This is the man who has always had my back, and in a split second, he throws all that away."

"Well, maybe he really likes her."

Pike shrugged. "Maybe. I wouldn't know. He never told me."

Noel set the sandwich container down on the counter with a sigh. "Well, I thought that if I came by and kind of put everything into perspective, you might hear Anthony out, but I guess you're just too stubborn."

"Yes, that's exactly what it is. *I'm* the problem. I am so stubborn, and that is why I cannot forgive Anthony for going behind my back, sleeping with a woman I was interested in, and not having the balls to tell me."

"And what if he really cares about her, and he couldn't help himself? What if he wanted to tell you, but not over the phone? What if things just progressed, and he was stuck in a love bubble and wasn't ready to come up for air?"

"When you have sex with someone, it doesn't just happen. You have to weigh the pros and cons and then decide that you want to. You make a choice, knowing the consequences, and you accept them. He made his choice." Pike scoffed. "'Love bubble.' Has being a happily married woman made you mushy?"

"It is absolutely a thing," she said.

"Yes, but I never thought those words would come out of your mouth," he said.

"Fine, I tried; that's all I can do." Noel paused, looking behind the counter at Jo's cage. "By the way, when did you get a dog?"

"My sister bought it and gave it to my mom to give me as an early Christmas present," he said.

"Well, that was sweet," she said.

"Not really, since she's already pooped and peed in here."

Noel laughed. "You should take her out more often."

"And leave the store unattended?" Pike said.

"Why don't you hire somebody to be in the store to make appointments and sell product while you and Anthony take people on tours? Wouldn't that make more money in the long run instead of taking turns?"

"Yes, but I'm not gonna be thinking about any new additions to the business until I figure out what I want to do."

Noel reeled back, eyes wide with surprise. "What does that mean?"

"That means that I don't know if I want to be in business with a man who has such little regard for me."

Pike heard Noel counting under her breath before she exploded. "Oh, come on!"

Pike scowled at her. "If you can't understand and respect how I feel, then you don't have to come by and check on me."

Noel didn't say anything for several beats, and Pike regretted being so harsh with her. Noel had been his person for a long time. While he'd secretly been in love with her since high school, he knew that she would never love him back. When she and Nick got together, he'd been happy for them, but Pike needed to admit how he felt about her. Weirdly enough, they'd had the heart-to-heart in Brews and Chews after Noel discovered him moonlighting as a stripper. She'd finally acknowledged that Pike's feelings were real for her, and they'd moved on. But just because he had a soft spot for her didn't mean that she or Nick could put Anthony's well-being above his.

"I'm sorry," Noel said. "I know it isn't fair what Anthony did. He should've been honest with you no matter what his reasons were. I just hate to see you guys lose a twenty-five-year friendship without even talking about it."

"Like Terri Clark says, maybe I just need to be mad for a while," Pike said, probably giving her false hope, but he was relieved when Noel smiled.

"Don't think I'm going to give up convincing you to forgive him."

Pike chuckled. "I'd expect nothing less."

Chapter Twenty-six

I can't wait to kiss you again.

Pike's text to Ryler came through after she and her friends had just finished dinner and everyone was relaxing in the living room, watching a movie.

Ryler texted back. I am looking forward to a little bit more than that.

Pike fired off a reply. Well when do you think you can get out of there and tell me all about it?

Ryler had been trying to escape for twenty minutes, but she hadn't been able to come up with an excuse that wouldn't lead to somebody wanting to come with her.

I'm trying to come up with something that will get me out of here, but I'm afraid if I say I wanna go to the store and get ice cream or go get a drink somewhere that someone or everyone is going to want to come with.

Pike sent back a 😉 followed by the suggestive, Depending on who shows up I guess we could open up the welcome wagon.

Ryler made a face. No this is between you and me. There will be no ABC ED.

You sure? Cause I already got the D 🤪

Ryler tried to smother her laughter, but Neil heard her, shooting her a questioning look, his brow furrowed. "Who are you texting?"

"No one," Ryler said, ignoring the burning in her cheeks.

"Then why are you blushing?" Kit asked.

"I'm commenting on funny memes on Instagram," she said, tapping on the app quickly in case somebody got the big idea to snatch her phone.

"Why is that making you blush?" Neil asked.

"Because it was a dirty meme."

"You should send it to me," Neil said, his gaze flicking briefly to Alia and back to Ryler. "I need a good laugh."

Alia was curled up in the recliner, staring at the TV and not contributing to the conversation. Ryler had noticed her cousin barely ate anything for dinner and that she'd been pale and sluggish today. With this consistent stomach bug for almost a week, Ryler was seriously considering making her a doctor's appointment and having her checked out. It would suck if she had gotten some kind of parasite in Bali, and they let it go for weeks or months.

"Alia, are you still not feeling great?" Ryler asked.

Alia shook her head. "Just queasy."

"Maybe we should make a doctor's appointment," Ryler said.

"I'll be fine," Alia said, wrapping her arms around herself. "It's just a bug."

"You keep saying that, but most stomach bugs go away in twenty-four hours," Ryler said.

Alia got up from the couch with a huff. "God, it's my body and it's my bug, so why don't you just back off and let me deal with it?"

Ryler's jaw dropped as her cousin stomped out of the room and slammed the bathroom door. Ryler looked from Neil to Kit. "What was that about?"

Kit shrugged.

Neil just kept staring at the TV.

"Does anybody know what's going on with her?" Ryler asked.

"That time of the month?" Neil offered.

Ryler's eyes narrowed. "You know that blaming a woman's period for every mood swing is a good way to get yourself kicked right in the nuts."

"Well, you're the one talking about how she's been off for a week, and isn't that how long it lasts? Seems like simple logic."

"Careful," she said. "I love you, but I will not hesitate to throw you out that window and watch you fly through the air."

Neil chuckled. "I'd love to see you lift me."

Ryler's phone beeped again, and when she checked out the message, it was a picture of Pike shirtless, lying on the bed with Jo.

I'm just lying here waiting for you.

Ryler slipped her phone into her pocket, her heart thudding excitedly. "I'm thinking we need something sweet and maybe some ginger ale for Alia."

"There's Oreos in the pantry," Kit said.

"I don't feel like Oreos," Ryler said, climbing off the couch. "I'm going to head to the store."

"Hey, will you grab another case of Gatorade?" Neil asked. "The blue one."

"Sure, anything else you guys need?" Ryler asked.

"I want those taffy cookies," Kit said.

"I thought we had Oreos?"

"Yeah, but the taffy ones sound better. And you might want to get a bag of Jolly Ranchers for your cousin. I heard sour candies help with nausea."

"How do you know that?" Ryler asked.

"My brother's wife. When she was pregnant, she used to suck on them all the time. It made her feel better."

Ryler paused with her purse over her shoulder, glancing toward the hallway where the bathroom door was. Could Alia . . .

Ryler shook her head. No. There's no way that Alia was pregnant. If they were just hooking up, neither one of them would risk it by going bareback, and things had ended with the last person she'd dated three months ago.

Ryler walked down the hallway and knocked on the bathroom door. "Hey, Alia. I'm going to the store and was going to pick you up some ginger ale. Do you need anything else?"

"Yeah," Alia said quietly.

"What is it?" Ryler asked.

"I'll shoot you a text," Alia said. "I have to think about what it's called."

Ryler almost sighed, thinking about how complicated it was going to get now that all of them were shooting out suggestions on what she should buy at the store. At least having to buy multiple things gave her plenty of time to drive across town to Pike's place.

When she got out to the car, she sent a text to Pike. What is your address?

Her phone beeped a few seconds later with his address, and she popped it into her GPS. The directions sent her across town, and as she made the drive, her phone kept beeping with messages, presumably from either Pike or the *Excursions* crew. She didn't bother checking them, anticipation coursing through Ryler as she drew closer. She imagined crossing the threshold of his home and immediately dropping to her knees, relieving him of his pants and underwear to suck him into her mouth. She could imagine the sounds he'd make, and her pussy throbbed, her panties growing wetter as her GPS announced, "In one thousand feet, take the next left."

She pulled into an empty parking spot that wasn't covered and climbed out, crossing the parking lot. Before she even reached the sidewalk, Pike threw open the door, holding on to the top with his hands. He was shirtless and barefoot in just a pair of sweats. Ryler licked her lips as her eyes glided from his feet all the way up to his smiling face.

"What took you so long?" he asked.

"I had to find a good enough reason to leave," she said.

"Getting laid is not a good enough reason?" he asked.

"I thought we were going to be discreet." Ryler placed her hands over his chest, the hair tickling her fingers. Pike circled her waist with his arm and hauled her inside, slamming the door behind her with his foot. Someone above them knocked on the ceiling and yelled, "Stop slamming the door!"

"Your neighbor sounds like a peach." Ryler sighed.

Pike cradled her face in his hands and kissed her, his tongue thrusting inside. Ryler opened wider, giving him better access, and the kiss deepened. Her knees trembled as he sucked her tongue, his fingers tangling in her hair. When he finally pulled away, he murmured, "I've been waiting all day to do that, and I don't give a fuck about that asshole upstairs. All I wanna do is strip you down and feel your tight pussy around my dick."

Ryler never thought she'd be one for dirty talk, but Pike's guttural need spurred her into action, and she whipped her shirt over her head, roughly tossing it to the side.

"Where is Jo?"

"She's in her crate. But the minute she sees you, she is not gonna be happy there."

"Then maybe she shouldn't see me," Ryler said, pushing her yoga pants down. "Your couch looks comfortable."

Pike grinned, dropping his sweats to his ankles. "We should probably sit on it and find out."

Ryler reached out, wrapping her hands around his thick, hard cock, reveling at the softness of his skin, and smiled.

"All this for me," she teased.

"Absolutely," he said, picking her up by her thighs and lifting her against him, carrying her to the couch. He sat down with her straddling his lap, and Ryler leaned forward, positioning herself over his cock.

Pike took his dick in hand, rubbing it against her labia, pressing inward. Ryler felt him at her opening, the pull of her muscles welcoming him, and fuck, he was warm. She whimpered with need and he cursed. "Fuck, I need a condom."

Ryler shuddered, realizing she'd been so caught up in her lust for him, she'd almost let him take her bareback, something she'd never done with anyone. She was always so careful, and yet here she was like an out-of-her-mind teenager, ready to roll the dice.

"I'm not on the pill, so that's probably a good idea," she said.

Pike kissed her hard and fast before moving her off his lap and onto the couch. He got up and went to a side table across the living room, and Ryler enjoyed watching the globes of his hard ass move.

Pike pulled out a condom from the table drawer, and Ryler laughed. "You just keep them everywhere around your apartment?"

Pike grinned. "You never know where the mood might strike."

Ryler unhooked her bra and slid the straps down her arms, freeing her breasts as he swaggered back to her. She loved watching his eyes darken as he stared at her chest. She could tell by his reaction that Pike was definitely a boob man and was happy he appreciated her attributes.

"I'm starting to think you're a bit of a man-whore," she said.

Pike opened the condom with his teeth and sat down next to her, rolling it over his turgid cock. "I have experience."

"Oh, so I am not off the marker, then," she teased.

"Does that upset you?" he asked.

"Would it upset you if I said I've had dozens of lovers?"

Pike shook his head. "Sex is a natural occurrence and something that our bodies crave." Pike picked her up and moved her over to him again, taking his dick in hand to rub it along her seam, circling her clit with his tip. "Besides, practice makes perfect, and I want to make sure you never have to say ice cream is better than sex again."

Ryler's laugh was cut off as Pike thrust inside her, filling her easily despite their lack of foreplay. The anticipation of being with him had made her wet and ready before she even got out of the car, and she closed her eyes, enjoying the fullness of him inside her.

Pike took her breast in his mouth and sucked, and she bounced on him, rolling her hips. Every time she pressed forward, there was a delightful zing that shot up to her stomach. A current that spread through Ryler's limbs, tightening her nipples as he switched his ministrations to the other breast. Her hands tangled in his hair, tugging at the strands, bringing him closer to her, and Pike's hands gripped her ass as he moved her faster and faster, his dick sliding in and out of her in a swift, steady rhythm. She rode him at a gallop, her breath coming out in rapid pants. She'd never imagined that an orgasm could come on so fast, but as it washed over her, waves upon waves of pleasure shaking her with every thrust, she cried out in bliss. As she rode out the sensations, Pike continued to thrust, his motions becoming jerky and uneven until finally, he released her breast and groaned, his head thrown back against the couch, watching her with heavy-lidded eyes. The intense expression on his face was arresting, and she couldn't stop staring. She always thought it was strange to watch men come, oftentimes laughing at the stupid looks on their faces, but with Pike, it was empowering to study his parted lips and hungry eyes locked on her, and she didn't want it to end.

Ryler leaned over and kissed his lips softly, her arms circling around his neck. "So that's a quickie, huh?" she murmured.

Pike laughed. "You've never had one before?"

"Not in the same sense," she said. "Usually they're very quick, and I'm left unsatisfied."

Pike opened one eye. "You can't say that this time."

Ryler laughed. "No, I can't."

Pike opened both eyes and threaded his hands in her hair, bringing her mouth down to his, his tongue roving over hers slowly, deeply. The kiss was sensual and caressing, making her moan.

Pike pulled away and kissed her jawline and her neck. "Can you stay awhile?" he whispered.

Ryler moaned, her hands running over his shoulders. "I told everyone I was going to the store. They're going to wonder where I am if I take too long."

Pike continued kissing her, moving along her collarbone. "I wish I could keep you here." His words lit through her like lightning, and she froze. Was he asking her to stay in Mistletoe?

Pike must've realized what he had said, and his hands dropped to his sides. "I just mean that I want more time with you. I'm not ready to let you go."

Ryler relaxed, laughing. "Believe me, I'd stay if I could."

Ryler climbed off his lap, her legs wobbly. She gathered up her clothes from the floor. "Can I use your bathroom?"

"Yeah, it's through the bedroom at the end of the hall," he said.

Ryler followed his directions, passing by Jo's cage. When the dog heard the footsteps, she started whining. Riley didn't say anything, afraid of setting her off. She ducked into the bathroom, surprised by how clean and organized it was. She giggled when she noticed that Pike had more hair and skin products than she did. It made sense though, considering how much pride he took in how he looked.

She used the facilities and then started dressing, ignoring her vibrating phone. When all her clothes were back in place, she looked at the messages from Kit, who also wanted sherbet, and Neil, who wanted a case of Mountain Dew in addition to the Gatorade. And finally, Alia. The two word text message her cousin sent hit her like a fist in the chest, making it hard to breathe.

Pregnancy test.

What in the actual fuck had happened to her easy, drama-free life?

Alia was pregnant? If she was asking for a test, she didn't know for sure, but she suspected. What was she going to do? What was her plan?

Ryler burst out of the bathroom, causing Jo to bark excitedly. Pike came into the bedroom, frowning. "Everything okay?"

"Yeah, I've just got to get going. Thanks, this was great." She gave him a quick kiss, bolting for the door. "I'll see you."

"Ryler, what—" Pike called after her, but she didn't stop to listen to the rest of his question. Her cousin needed her.

Chapter Twenty-seven

Ryler sat outside the bathroom door the next morning, waiting for Alia to emerge with an answer on whether or not she was expecting. Alia read somewhere that the first pee of the morning is the strongest for early detection. She'd sent Kit and Neil off to go snowshoeing with Pike, and although she'd been disappointed about missing out, Ryler hoped that after Alia discovered the truth, they'd be able to join the guys.

The door opened, and Ryler studied Alia's tear-stained face, her stomach sinking.

"What do you want to do?" Ryler asked.

"I don't know. I've never been pregnant before, so this is new territory for me," Alia said, walking past her to the front door with the box in hand.

"Where are you going?" Ryler asked, climbing to her feet.

"I am taking this out to the trash can so Neil and Kit don't see it."

"Even if they see it, what does it matter? If you decide to keep the baby, they'll find out about it."

Alia didn't answer her, just walked out the front door, and a lump formed in Ryler's throat. *No. No way. No fucking way.*

When Alia came back inside and closed the door, Ryler ran a hand over her face.

"Does he know?" Ryler asked.

"No, but I'm going to have to tell him."

"And how do you think he'll react?"

"He probably won't be too happy about it, considering—"

"Fucking Neil!" Ryler hollered, grabbing a pillow off the couch and beating its side with rage. "I cannot believe he pretended to not like you, all the while sleeping with you!"

"It was my idea," Alia said. "It just happened one night, and when it kept happening, we didn't want to make things weird. Plus, we weren't sure how you would react since you two used to date."

Ryler laughed. "Neil and I have always been better off friends, but how could you two roll the dice on unprotected sex?"

"We didn't!" Alia said, sitting down on the couch. "A condom must have broken."

"And you weren't on the pill?"

"You know the pill makes me gain weight," Alia protested.

"So does pregnancy!" Ryler cried.

Alia sniffled. "You are supposed to be my person, and you're making me feel worse."

Ryler flopped down next to her, closing her eyes. "I'm sorry. I just don't know what to say! This is the last thing I expected from either one of you."

"I think we were just lonely, and one night, we had a few drinks and started talking. One thing led to another and bam."

"Sex doesn't just bam," Ryler said.

"It does when it's good. We said that would be the only time and that we weren't going to talk about it, but then I couldn't stop thinking about it. Every time I was around him, he smelled so good. I kept thinking about the way he kissed and how good things had been." Alia cleared her throat. "I guess he was thinking the same thing, because suddenly, he was knocking on my door at one in the morning, and we were ripping each other's clothes off."

"Too much information," Ryler said, although Alia's description of events had a familiar ring, and she found herself thinking about Pike. The desperation. The need. How much she wanted him and just thinking about his touch could make her throb with desire.

"How long has it been going on?"

"A little over two months."

"But he hasn't talked about anything more than hooking up?" Ryler asked.

Alia shook her head. "No. And I'm afraid when I tell him, he is going to freak out. He's already been looking at—" Alia clapped her mouth shut, but Ryler caught it.

"He's already what? Been looking for a new job?" Alia didn't say anything, and Ryler shook her head. "It's alright. I already know you both are over *Excursions*."

"I'm sorry, Ryler. I loved modeling, and you gave me a safe space to do it, but I want to be me. I want to live my life out of the spotlight." Alia touched her stomach hesitantly. "Maybe this is my sign."

"What made you change your mind?" Ryler asked.

"I'm thirty, and a few months ago, someone commented that my breasts were starting to sag."

Ryler remembered the comment but thought she'd deleted it before Alia saw it. "I'm so sorry."

"It's the facts. I'm getting older, and my body is changing. If I keep this baby, there are going to be stretch marks and who knows what else. I don't think I can go through all this under a microscope."

"That's why I never wanted to step in front of the camera," Ryler whispered.

"I don't mean to be insensitive, but the difference between you and me is that people never saw you as perfect. They weren't jealous of you. It is going to get ugly, fast. I'll be like the girl who fell out of favor with the popular crowd, and now they're coming for me."

"That's a bit superficial, but I take your meaning," Ryler said.

"Don't get me wrong, Ryls, you are beautiful. I've always thought so. I used to be so jealous that you got the good boobs and I got these dinky tits." Alia laughed. "Do you think they will get bigger if I stay pregnant?"

"Maybe, but that is not a reason to stay pregnant."

"I know. But honestly, I'm considering keeping it. I mean, why not? I've got my trust fund and can buy my own place if you don't want us living with you."

"Alia—"

"No, I mean it. I know you didn't sign on for this, and if you're mad at me, I understand."

"Why would I be mad at you? You are allowed to sleep with whomever you want and live your life on your terms. I just don't want you to feel like you have to move out. I'm hardly at the condo as it is, so if you want to stay with me, I would love to have you both." Ryler cleared her throat. "Of course, Neil might have something to say about that."

"I don't know," Alia said, nibbling her lip. "Sometimes I think he feels more for me than just sex, and other times, it's like nothing's changed between us."

"Well, you're going to have to tell him about the baby, even if he wants nothing to do with any of it." Ryler hoped that wasn't the case, because if Neil turned out to be the type of guy to use her cousin and walk away, Ryler didn't know if she could forgive him. Ryler reached out and tucked a piece of Alia's hair back. "Do you think we should drive out and catch up with the guys? See if we can't put your anxiety to rest?"

"Ugh, you're really going to make me go snowshoeing in the forest when I feel like ass?"

"Maybe the fresh air will do you good," Ryler said while calling Pike, but it went straight to voicemail. "Damn."

"What's wrong?"

"Pike didn't answer his phone."

"Ooh, Pike," Alia teased, and Ryler rolled her eyes, trying Neil and Kit, but there were no answers either.

"Please, you can't say anything to Neil-lover." Ryler looked up Adventures in Mistletoe and called the store number.

"Adventures in Mistletoe, Anthony speaking."

"Hi, this is Ryler from the *Excursions* podcast."

"Oh, hi there. Aren't you supposed to be out snowshoeing?"

"Yes, but my cousin wasn't feeling well, so I stayed behind to wait with her, but now that she's perked up a bit, we thought we'd join the guys. Only Pike isn't answering his phone. I know you two have the GPS app to track each other and was hoping you could point me in the right direction?"

"He told you about that?" Anthony asked.

"Yeah, he seemed surprised I didn't do it with my friends."

Anthony chuckled. "Let me see."

It was silent for a few beats before Anthony hopped back on the line. "I know where he went, but it's a little tricky to find if you don't know the area. How about I drive to you, and you can follow me out there."

"Oh, but don't you have to watch the store? I don't want to put you out or in a bad position with everything—" Ryler snapped her mouth closed.

"I'm happy to do it. Just give me about fifteen minutes."

"Thanks," Ryler said, swallowing past the uncomfortable lump as she ended the call.

"Everything okay?" Alia said.

"Yeah, he's coming here so we can follow him out to where the guys are."

"I can always wait until Neil gets back."

"Oh no, we are getting everything out in the open, especially this baby business. Neil was part of the production process and should be part of the finale."

"You make our lives sound like your podcast."

"Oh, *Excursions* was never about the drama, but I have a feeling today we are going to see all the plot twists."

"Why is that?"

"Let's just say Pike isn't going to be happy when I show up with his partner in tow."

Chapter Twenty-eight

Pike recognized Anthony's familiar outline in the distance being trailed by Alia and Ryler. Pike's jaw clenched in frustration when he realized that Ryler had contacted Anthony, knowing everything that happened, and asked his former friend to track him so that they could join Kit and Neil. Although it made perfect sense and under normal circumstances, he would have understood, all he felt now was intense betrayal.

"Hey," Anthony called, stopping a few feet in front of him. Pike had taken Neil and Kit along Lamb Ridge, introducing them to the breathtaking views of the mountains and valleys around them, but they were heading back down through the trees when the trio caught up to them.

"Hi. Who is watching the store?" Pike asked.

"I put the sign on the door letting customers know we'd be right back."

"Oh, that's what we need right now—to lose business by not sticking to our original agreement. If I'm in the field, you're at the store, and vice versa."

Anthony's eyes narrowed. "Look, your clients couldn't get a hold of you, and I knew where you were, so I brought them out. Now that we're all here, I will leave them in your capable hands."

Anthony turned on his snowshoes and nodded at Alia and Ryler as he passed back by them on his way down the hill. "Ladies, have a great time."

"Thanks," Ryler said, meeting Pike's gaze. He kept his expression neutral, even when she mouthed, *I'm sorry*.

"I thought you weren't feeling well," Neil said, addressing Alia.

"I was feeling better and didn't want to miss out on another activity."

"Why not? You hate outdoor activities," Neil said, pointing at her face. "You said the sun gives you premature wrinkles."

"What, you hate outdoor activities but started a travel podcast?" Pike asked.

Alia's eyes widened, and she glanced at Ryler, who was glaring at Neil. Kit was the only one out of the lot with a decent poker face.

"Does someone want to explain exactly what's going on here?" Pike asked.

"I, personally, would like to head back to the car and get some water," Kit said, tilting his head. "Pike, you want to come join me and leave these people to figure out what kind of drama they need to work through?"

"There is no drama, Kit," Ryler said, taking Kit's arm. "How was the hike?"

Pike trailed behind them, glancing back at Alia and Neil, who seemed to be invested in a heated discussion.

"The hike was great. Beautiful views. I'll show you the pictures when we get back to the car," Kit said.

"I feel like I'm missing something," Pike said to their backs, unsurprised when they ignored him.

"Are you serious?" Neil erupted behind them, and Pike stopped and turned, watching Alia reach for him.

Ryler was suddenly beside him with her hand on his arm. "They need a few minutes."

Pike watched Alia wring her hands, speaking quietly to Neil. "I didn't realize they were a couple," Pike said.

"Neither did I," Ryler said. "I don't even know if that's how to describe them." Pike stared at her and she shrugged. "It's complicated."

"I'm getting a lot of that lately in all aspects of my life, and I'm getting a little tired of hearing it."

"I'm sorry that I asked Anthony to bring us out here, but you weren't picking up, and he offered to lead the way."

"You could have declined," he grumbled, brushing past her. "I would have taken you out to see the ridge free of charge."

"Pike, come on, don't be that way."

Pike was aware that Kit was already standing by the cars, taking random pictures, and that Anthony's truck was slowly backing up, as if hoping that if he lingered, Pike would want to talk to him, but he didn't. It felt like the whole world was lying to him, and he was sick of it.

Suddenly, something struck him and he spun around. "You."

"What?" Ryler said, taking a step back.

"You haven't missed a single thing. You were excited to be here, to learn everything you could about Mistletoe. You wear proper hiking shoes and clothing. You're level-headed, good to those around you, kind to the locals, and you are personable and funny and people naturally like you."

"Thank you?" she said huskily.

Pike snapped his fingers. "Your voices. Alia can't get hers quite as low as yours, but they sound similar."

"Pike, what are you going on about?" she asked, her voice trembling.

"Why are you lying about Alia being the host of *Excursions*?" he asked.

"I—" Ryler cleared her throat. "I don't know what you mean."

She started down the hill toward Kit, but Pike shook his head, reaching for her arms to spin her around. "Yes, you do. Why did you lie to me?"

Ryler paled. "It's not about you. After we started the Instagram, people wanted to know what I looked like. They were calling me out online, and I didn't want to expose myself to it. I just wanted to talk about the amazing places I'd been and show everyone why they should visit them. Then Alia lost her modeling contract, and I offered her a chance to do what she loved, to be in front of the camera, and it gave me the freedom to continue as I had been. The world got a beautiful podcast host to enjoy. No one knows I'm the voice of *Excursions* except Kit, Alia, Neil, and now you."

"But you would have let me keep believing that she was the host if I hadn't figured it out, right?"

"Why not?" Ryler asked. "I'll be flying out of here on Christmas Day to regroup at my condo in California before I take off for my next destination. If I told one person in every place I visited, it wouldn't be much of a secret."

"I guess it would have been nice to know exactly who I was fucking."

Ryler sucked in a breath, and Pike knew he'd crossed the line, that he was being a dick, but between the appearance of Anthony and finding out that Ryler had been hiding this from him? He'd made such an idiot of himself, fawning over Alia and her podcast, meanwhile it was Ryler all along. Was she laughing at him? Mocking him for being a fanboy?

"I am exactly who you see. I love traveling. I just also happen to talk about it on a show I'm passionate about. Do you know how *Excursions* started? It was me and Neil in a van, driving around the U.S., visiting places that no one else was talking about. Then we got some national sponsors, but they didn't want to know about smalltown America. They wanted bigger destinations that would really get people talking. Suddenly, we were hitting all the same places as everyone else, but I still wanted to be different. I pushed the boundaries, find the local hole-in-the-wall place no one talked about. Discover the secret swimming hole where the water was cerulean and sparkled in the sunshine. Still, I got bored, jetting off to the next destination filled with sand and light.

"When I put that post up on Instagram, I wanted something different because I'd already sensed a change these last few months, and I knew *Excursions* needed to go back to what it was before in order to survive. I came to Mistletoe not just to find that passion to explore again but also to remember who I was before I lost my parents. After I lost them, I changed and adapted to my new way of life, to the opportunities I was afforded, and I had the positive feedback from my therapist that I should show the world that I had gone through all the grief steps and come out on top.

"The only things that have been mine were Alia and knowing I created *Excursions*. So, I'm sorry that we slept together a couple times and I didn't divulge my whole life story to you, but I'm not an open book. I like my privacy, and if that bothers you, then maybe we should rethink our little arrangement."

Pike's mind whirled, her monologue replaying in his head.

"What arrangement?" Neil asked, joining them. Alia kept walking, tears streaming down her face, and Ryler glared at her producer.

"The one where I paid him to take us out and show us what Mistletoe has to offer," she snapped, rushing after her cousin.

Pike watched her, his mouth pressed in a thin line.

"Are you trying to make a move on Ryler?" Neil asked, his voice laced with warning.

Pike turned to face the bigger man, smirking. "If I was?"

"Don't."

Pike studied Neil's pinched expression, surprised by the other man's interest. "I thought the two of you were just friends?"

"As a friend, you're not what she needs," Neil said.

"And you know what that is? Because a few minutes ago, you were fighting with her cousin at the top of the hill, and that sure looked like something." Pike crossed his arms over his chest. "Based on the look she just gave you, I suspect she knows what it was about, too."

Neil glanced down the hill, pain etched on his face. "Fuck me."

"Let me guess . . ." Pike shook his head. "You've landed yourself in a river of excrement without a paddle. So, maybe worry less about me and Ryler and more about yourself."

He only managed to make it a few feet before he heard Neil mutter, "Prick."

Pike could live with Neil thinking that about him, but Ryler's dark glances were another matter. He'd let his anger at Anthony bleed over into his relationship with her. While he didn't like that he'd been unknowingly fanboying over her for the better part of a week and she hadn't put him out of his misery, she was right. Ryler didn't owe him that part of her. He hadn't earned it, especially if they were just two people having sex without any strings attached.

Pike watched Ryler, Alia, and Kit get into the blue SUV and take off, leaving the silver SUV for Neil and Pike's red Charger.

Pike saluted Neil as he took off his snowshoes and climbed inside. He still had three appointments left with *Excursions* and plenty of time to figure out how to make things right with Ryler.

Chapter Twenty-nine

Pike pulled into the supermarket parking lot, considering his next move. Ryler had left snowshoeing angry and upset, which meant Pike needed a gesture to show her how sorry he was. Although they'd spent the last five days together, Pike didn't know her all that well, especially not her likes and dislikes. Unless he wanted to go back through six years of podcasts to trigger something, he needed to look for a universal romantic gesture.

Flowers. Candy. Card. It could all be found behind the automatic glass doors of Mistletoe Market.

Pike got out of the car and headed inside, smiling and greeting anyone who called out to him. He should have gone back to Adventures in Mistletoe to see how it was going, but that would mean talking to Anthony. Pike had seen enough of his former friend for one day.

He headed for the corner of the store where there were several buckets of bouquets, looking through each of them, but they were pretty wilted. He made his way to the candy aisle, searching for something to strike inspiration. He grabbed a bag of Dove and kept walking, debating on a bottle of wine from the front.

When he rounded the corner, he nearly crashed into someone's cart. "Sorry about that."

"My fault." Delilah stared up at him, nodding. "I wasn't looking where I was going."

Pike's gaze traveled over the contents of her cart. "Looks like you're having a party."

"Book club," Delilah said. "Don't ask me how I got roped into hosting. It was supposed to be Holly's bag, but with the lights displays on Evergreen, she was afraid no one would be able to get in."

"Makes sense," he said, glancing behind her. "I should let you finish. Enjoy your night."

Pike started to step around her cart, but she said his name, and he stopped.

"I'm sorry for coming between you and Anthony. You should know that we aren't . . . seeing each other anymore."

Pike shook his head. "When did that happen?"

"About five minutes after your fight on the side of the road." She cleared her throat. "He loves you, you know? Anthony and I had a moment, a long time ago, but he didn't want to get in the way."

"So he said." Pike couldn't believe Anthony had spent the weekend with Delilah and risked their friendship for that relationship, only to turn around and blow it. "Exactly what did he do to drive you away?"

"He wanted to take a step back with me and fix things with you. I told him that he was trying to fix the barn after the animals got out, but you're important to him. You should think about that before you throw away your friendship."

"Anthony lied to me. Just because he regrets it now doesn't change the fact—"

"Oh, jeez, do you hold yourself to those standards as well? Did you ever make a mistake or hurt someone and regret it after the fact? When you tried to make it better, did they forgive you or drop you? Maybe consider how you would feel if the roles were reversed and Anthony wouldn't forgive you."

"If you're so angry at him, why are you defending him?" Pike asked.

"Because I can't turn off my feelings as well as you, apparently," she said, pushing her cart away from him and disappearing down the snack aisle.

Pike headed toward the wine aisle, Delilah's words heavy on his mind. Yes, Anthony had lied, had pursued Delilah after she rejected Pike and not come clean about it, all of which he deserved to twist for, but was it worth completely obliterating their friendship? Destroying their business?

He had a lot to think about, but first he had to figure out how to make a woman forgive him.

RYLER

Ryler and Alia walked down Main Street toward A Shop for All Seasons, drinking their shakes from Lord of the Fries with gusto. Alia was still spitting fire over Neil's reaction to her pregnancy, especially his worry that Ryler knew. She'd tried to assure her cousin that there was nothing going on with Neil and hadn't been for many years, but she wasn't sure if Alia believed her.

"I can't believe the stones on that son of a bitch. If he's at the house when we get home, I might just kick him for being a flipping idiot!"

"I can see why you might be tempted to do that," Ryler said, thinking about Pike and his obnoxious affront to not being party to her business. Ryler was pretty sure she'd set him straight, but still, the unmitigated gall.

Ryler grabbed the shop door for Alia and let her cousin walk through first. Ryler followed behind and waved at Holly, who was talking to a young Black woman behind the counter.

"Hey, Ryler, welcome back!"

"Thanks. My cousin hadn't seen your shop, and we've had a pretty awful day, so we figured it called for shakes and some Christmas cheer."

Holly laughed. "Well, this is my support system, Erica Pace. She keeps me from losing my mind."

"Unless I start talking about hockey, and then all bets are off," Erica said, grinning at them.

"Maybe Neil should play hockey," Alia said, an evil glint in her eye. "Then some big, burly enforcer could knock him into the wall."

Ryler smiled. "Her special friend is being a douche."

"A total d-bag," Alia agreed.

"If you're looking for somewhere to get away from your worries and blow off some steam, you should come to book club with us," Holly said.

"Don't we need to have read the book to attend?"

"No, it's not that kind of book club. We all read something different and then come together to enjoy wine and conversation and talk about the books."

"Holly came up with the idea because my dark romance picks would scare some of the older ladies. But if you're into the morally gray heroes, I got some book recs that would blow your mind and break your vibrator."

Ryler laughed. "Now that sounds intriguing."

"We'll talk later," Erica said with a wink.

Ryler glanced over at Alia, who was examining a Baby's First Christmas ornament. "What do you say, Alia? Want to go have a girls' night?"

Alia nodded rapidly, dropping the ornament back on the tree. "More estrogen and less testosterone, yes, please."

Chapter Thirty

Pike sat on his couch with Jo sprawled across his lap, holding his phone in his hand. He should text Nick at least and rap out how he was feeling after Delilah's truth bomb. Pike dialed Nick, but he sent him to voicemail after one ring.

"Fine, jerk, I'm calling your wife," Pike said aloud. Jo lifted her head and looked up at him, staring at him with unblinking dark eyes. "It's not what you think. She's just a friend."

Jo laid her head back down again, and Pike dialed Noel.

"Yello," she said brightly.

"Well, you sound like you're in a super mood."

"I am. I get to go to book club at Delilah's tonight instead of heading into work. What's not to be happy about?"

"Well, great," Pike said, stroking Jo's fur. "Listen, I tried calling your husband first, but he sent me to voicemail, so you're my backup plan."

"Insulting, but continue."

"I bumped into Delilah at the store, who told me that Anthony broke things off with her because of what happened with me."

"I heard something similar," Noel said.

"Which I can't understand, because if he wanted her so badly it was worth lying to me, why lose the both of us?"

"Maybe he couldn't be happy with her until he fixed things with you?"

"That is ridiculous," Pike grumbled.

"I'm also pretty sure it happens to be true," Noel said. "Listen, I don't want to end up on your bad side, but Delilah might be on to something. Anthony is miserable, and although I think losing you is a big part of it, I don't think it's the only thing that's making him a wreck. I think he knows that his feelings for Delilah are real, and he doesn't know what to do about them."

Pike spluttered. "Are you trying to tell me that Anthony Russo, Mr. I Can't Fall in Love, is besotted with Delilah Gill?"

"That is exactly what I'm telling you. He is head over heels for her, and he gave that up for you."

"I didn't ask him to do that!"

"You didn't have to. You're his person, Pike. We're all human, including Anthony, but we rely on the people who love us to realize that and be there when we screw up. Especially when it doesn't happen often."

Pike grumbled under his breath about guilt trips, and Noel said loudly, "What was that?"

"I asked if you had any idea where Nick and Anthony are now?"

"Nick said they were going to the gym after work. Of course you'd know that if you'd bothered to call Anthony."

"Thanks, Noel," Pike said.

"Anytime, Fish."

"Are you ever going to stop calling me that?" he groaned.

"It's a term of endearment at this point, but if you really want me to, I will try to curb the urge."

"Nah, that's okay," Pike said, smiling. "Thanks."

Pike ended the call and texted Nick. Where are you and why aren't you answering your phone?

Pike put Jo in her crate, ignoring her protests, and changed his clothes to jeans and a T-shirt. He snatched his jacket off the hook before leaving the house and heading into town, tracking Anthony's location as he headed to the gym from the store.

A text came through from Nick, and he pressed the button on his steering wheel, playing it over his stereo in a high electronic voice. "At the gym with Anthony. I think he's going to kick Brodie's ass. The guy keeps talking about Delilah. You should come help. We can grab a drink after. Winking face emoji."

Anthony was going to start a fight? Pike had seen him jump in to help a friend or defend someone he cared about, but Pike had never seen him throw the first punch. He definitely wanted to watch that.

His mood lighter than it had been in days, Pike parked as close to the gym entrance as he could get and got out of his car, heading down the sidewalk to the front door. He saw Anthony and Brodie facing off through the glass, and he opened the door, coming up behind Anthony and taking his arm before he let his fist fly.

"Whoa, cowboy," Pike said in a cheery tone. "Let the Neanderthal go before you catch a case."

Anthony looked down at Pike with wide eyes and dropped Brodie's shirt. The minute he was free, Brodie shoved Anthony, who stumbled back into Nick.

"Next time you come at me, Russo, we're going to finish this outside."

"Brodie, Brodie," Pike tsked. "You don't want to bite off more than you can chew."

"What the fuck are you talking about, Pike?" Brodie asked, posturing like an aggressive dog. Pike had always thought the big ox was an idiot, even in high school, but by the tense set of Anthony's jaw, Pike could tell the other man was walking on thin ice.

"I can't have you putting hands on my boy or his girl," Pike said, giving Brodie a nod. "You understand? Delilah Gill is off-limits to you and anyone else in this town."

"I think that's up to her, don't you?" Brodie asked.

"You can think that, but then again, I still have a certain photo you probably wouldn't want going viral on social media." Pike grinned when Brodie's face paled, and Pike slapped his shoulder. "Glad we understand each other."

Pike turned to face Nick and Anthony, cocking his head to the side. "I thought we were going to get a drink?"

"We are," Nick said.

"Great, let's vamoose." Pike pointed at Anthony. "You're buying every round."

Pike walked out the door with Nick and Anthony trailing behind.

"What is going on?" Anthony asked. "I thought you were pissed at me."

Pike stopped next to Anthony's truck and shrugged. "I took some time to sit with the situation and reflect."

Nick cleared his throat.

"And listened to the advice of a few friends. Here is what I realized. You said that even though you wanted her, you took a step back when you thought that she and I were feeling each other. That's what makes you an amazing friend. Just because I had you up on this pedestal, thinking you were this paragon of virtue, doesn't mean you can't ever fuck up. She wasn't my girlfriend—hell, she'd been pretty clear that she wasn't interested in me at all. I pulled out some moves, too."

Anthony held up a hand. "I don't want to hear about it, thanks."

Pike chuckled. "Fair enough. Besides, it's obvious you love the girl. I can't stay mad at you when you're in love for the first time and already fucking up. You need me."

"I don't—" Anthony paused, considering. "How do you know?"

"That you need my help?" Pike asked.

"No, that I—"

"Can't get it out yet? It's always hardest the first time." *Or the second and third time,* Pike thought. "As to how I know, you were about to tear Brodie apart for talking about your girl. You've either lost your mind or you're in love." Pike opened the passenger side door and waved a hand. "Now, get in the truck. Considering how pissed off Delilah was, this will require several mixed drinks and careful planning if you're going to win her back."

"You saw her?" Anthony asked.

"Oh yes. That is one angry woman."

"Speaking of angry, why were you at the gym?" Anthony asked.

"I was talking to Noel about some things and suddenly needed to see you. I texted Nick to find out where you were and Nick texted back that something was about to go down I'd want to see, so I raced on over here to check it out. Watching you lose your cool? Priceless."

Anthony grunted. "You're both a couple of meddlesome fuckers."

"I think the word you're looking for is friends." Pike pulled himself up and pounded the top of his truck. "Now move! Time's a-wastin'!

PIKE

Stereotypically, the world portrays women sitting around eating ice cream and watching movies when they're struggling romantically. Men go out drinking and try to meet someone new.

Hollywood got half the formula right.

Pike sat at the table with Anthony, Nick, Clark, Declan, and Sam, listening as they each tried to give Anthony advice on winning Delilah back. There was talk of mixtapes and flowers, but Anthony had axed them all. Pike took mental notes of his own, thinking about Ryler. Would a simple bouquet and apology do the trick, or would she need more?

Clark leaned forward next to Pike, drawing him out of his own thoughts.

"What does Delilah like?" Clark asked.

"Her Corgi, Leia," Anthony said.

Pike laughed. "We could kidnap it and make her think it's lost, but Anthony could find her like a damn hero, return her, and she is forever grateful," Pike said, rubbing his hands together. "Jo could use a playmate for a few days."

"You are a sick man," Sam said, tossing a balled-up napkin at him.

Anthony shook his head. "I'm not doing that."

"Fine, no dognapping." Pike said, holding his hands up. "What else do you got?"

"What about a favorite song?" Nick chimed in.

"Oh! Her name. That song that has her name . . ." Anthony paused for several seconds, and then he belted out, "Hey there Delilah—"

Talk about a grand gesture! Anthony was a genius.

"That's better than a boom box!" Pike exclaimed, shooting to his feet with his glass held high. "We shall march to her house and romance her with the power of song."

"How do you ever get laid, Fish?"

Pike startled at Noel's appearance, as if she'd come from thin air. When she leaned over to kiss Nick, her husband asked, "Hey, what are you doing here?"

"Picking up Ricki for book club now that her bartending shift is over." Noel checked her phone. "She gets done with her bartending shift at six."

"Since when are you in a book club?" Anthony asked.

"As of today," Noel said, hanging on to the back of Nick's chair. "I figured with you boys out plotting and scheming, I'd join the girls and see what kind of trouble we can get into."

Pike scoffed. "Trouble at a book club? Book clubs are for sipping wine and gossiping."

"How do you know?" Sam asked, smirking.

"My mom used to host one every Tuesday," Pike said, grinning. "I snuck out of my room and listened in once. I was traumatized."

"Sounds like fun," Noel said, giving Ricki a hug when she joined her. "See you later, boys. Behave."

"Never," Pike crowed, and the other men echoed him, except Anthony. Pike noticed him staring at his phone, but before he could bring Anthony back into the conversation, Pike looked up and saw Brodie and Trip walk through the door.

"Ah hell," Pike said.

"What?" Nick asked.

"Trip, Brodie, and the goon squad just walked in."

Brodie made a beeline for Anthony, and Pike was so tempted to burst into song to throw the guy off. *A little Taylor Swift maybe? "Bad Blood"? "Trouble"?*

The group of burly men dressed in varying colors of flannel shirts stopped like a wall of plaid next to their table.

"Russo," Brodie said, smirking at Anthony, "I heard you and Pike are in charge of the winter games?"

"Yeah? What about it?" Anthony asked.

Brodie put his hand on the table, leaning over between Sam and Declan. "I just wanted to tell you that I'm going to enjoy kicking your ass."

"Ha," Pike said, pointing at the group of men. "You couldn't kick a can if it was right in front of you."

"You want to wager on that?" Trip asked.

"Absolutely," Anthony said firmly, much to Pike's surprise.

"If we win," Brodie said, thumbing at his group, "you're going to buy each of us a snowmobile."

"And if we win," Anthony said, leaning back in his chair casually, "we want your boat."

"Deal," Brodie said, holding out his hand, which Anthony took. Pike realized he was holding his breath and didn't release it until the group of men walked away, laughing.

"That was a little too cocky," Nick said.

Despite his reservations about making such a large bet, Pike scoffed, "I'm not worried about those clowns." Pike stood up, grabbing Anthony by his arm. "It is time!"

The group of men stood up, whooping and hollering. Sam started chanting, "I don't know but I've been told." The group repeated after him, and he continued, "Mistletoe men are mighty bold." He continued to pause, giving them a chance to follow along as they walked out of Brews and Chews. "We play for keeps and get the girl. Except for me, 'cause romance makes me hurl."

The rest of them booed Sam while Pike sent Ryler a text, his buzz making the words fuzzy on the edges. I miss your smell.

"So, we're going to walk all the way to Evergreen?" Clark said skeptically.

"Actually, Delilah is hosting," Declan said, pointing to the left of the parking lot. "Holly was afraid people wouldn't be able to get in with all the cars waiting to see the lights display."

"Follow me!" Anthony called like a general commanding an army. "To victory!"

Pike laughed, skipping along with them. And to think, he almost missed out on all of this. The group slowed down, and Pike found himself falling in step with Sam. Anthony, Nick, and Clark were practicing the song ahead of them, while Declan walked in between them, typing on his phone. Maybe giving Holly a heads-up they were on their way? It would take them at least a half an hour of drunk walking, maybe longer, to get there. Pike didn't want to spend the whole time in silence.

"I'm surprised you're coming along on this little adventure," Pike said, segueing the conversation.

Sam shrugged. "I've got nothing better to do tonight."

"Really? I'd think you'd be out with whatever woman caught your eye this week."

"Why do you act like I'm some lady-killer, when you've got a reputation yourself?" Sam asked, his voice gruff with irritation.

Pike reeled back in surprise. "What? I'm not judging you."

"Sure feels like it. Every time you open your mouth. Not all of us are made for a happy ending, you know," Sam said, shoving his hands into his pockets.

"I didn't think you wanted one. I thought romance made you hurl, as you so eloquently put it."

"We always scorn that which eludes us," Sam said.

"Are you telling me the great Sam Griffin is looking for love?"

"Even if I was, I'm the bad guy. Women don't look at me for long-term commitment. I'm the guy they use for a good time."

Pike experienced a strange kinship with Sam, realizing that he'd thought women felt the same way about him. That was before Ryler and everything they'd been through.

"If you weren't that guy, and you were trying to get back into a woman's good graces, what would you do?"

Sam swiveled his way, frowning. "Are you asking me for relationship advice now?"

"No, I was just making friendly conversation, since we're on a quest to help our friend woo his girl. Like you, I'm not exactly the guy women want to settle down with."

"Maybe don't tell them they snore like a trucker, and you'll get a little further with them," Sam said, smirking.

"Who told you that?" Pike asked.

"Sally, after the two of you broke up. She wanted a rebound, and I wasn't in the mood to oblige, but apparently, spilling her guts about what went wrong between you was the next best thing."

Pike had known about Sally chasing Sam, but where it used to bother him, now he really didn't feel anything. Not even regret for how things ended.

"Yeah, well, my issue with telling women exactly what's on my mind without sugarcoating it seems to be a pattern I need to break."

"You can be honest with women about the important shit, like feelings and whatnot, but if they ask you how they look in an outfit, use finesse before answering." Sam clapped him on the shoulder. "And if you fuck up, I'm a firm believer that being earnest and vulnerable with any woman is the way to get back into her good graces. Especially if you care about her."

"For a guy who isn't relationship material, you make a lot of sense," Pike said.

"Maybe that whole saying that ends with 'those who can't, teach' has a point."

Chapter Thirty-one

Ryler stood against the wall of the living room, watching all the women laugh and mingle, including Alia, who had connected with Merry Winters over their opinions of Instagram algorithms and hadn't stopped talking for over an hour. Ryler had gotten bored with their conversation and walked around for a while, smiling and nodding at people she passed, but no one stopped her to talk.

Out of the corner of her eye, she saw a gorgeous plus-size woman hanging back, sipping from a wine glass. Ryler recognized her from that day on the side of the road with Anthony and Pike and thought about joining her, but what would she say?

Hi, nice to meet you officially. I was Pike's rebound after you rejected him. More wine?

Although Ryler knew that nothing was going on with Delilah and Pike, would it be weird to go talk to her now that there was something going on between Ryler and Pike?

Ryler's phone buzzed in her pocket, and she pulled it out, checking the text from Neil.

We need to talk.

"Not right now, we don't," she muttered. Of all the people in the world who Neil could hook up with, why would he choose her cousin? And furthermore, what was he going to do about the baby?

Ryler saw the new text from Pike below Neil's and clicked on it. He'd sent it a half an hour ago.

I miss your smell.

Ryler frowned at the message. As far as segues go, it wasn't the most ingenious opening, so she fired back.

That's all you've got?

The nerve of the guy to act like the biggest dick in Dicktonia and then have the brass to text her some sweet, sentimental bullshit?

Ryler waited several minutes to see if he would text again, and he did. I'm a little drunk and afraid of saying the wrong thing.

As long as you're honest, it can't be wrong, right?

The bubbles pulsated across her screen. So, if I say I miss your naked body, that isn't going to piss you off more?

It should, but what she almost responded with was, *Same.* It had only been a day, but she was already burning, missing Pike and every feeling he brought out of her with a touch, a kiss, the thrust of his cock inside her.

Damn, when had she become a lust-crazed woman?

Ryler put her phone into her pocket without responding and made her way over to Delilah, coming up alongside her. "You're Delilah, right?"

Delilah jumped, spilling a little wine onto the tablecloth. "Shit."

"Sorry, didn't mean to sneak up on you." Great, she was already making an ass of herself. "I'm Ryler Colby. I'm the personal assistant to Alia Cole." Ryler held out her hand, and Delilah took it.

"Nice to meet you," Delilah said, giving her a once-over. "Your outfit is so cute."

"Thank you. I'm a huge thrifter, so the jeans I snagged for six bucks, and the sweater was five. Still had tags on it."

"That's awesome," Delilah said, giving her a rueful smile. "Unfortunately, most clothes I find thrifting look like something my grandma would wear."

"Not where I shop. You ever want to take a trip, I'll show you some hidden gems with fantastic finds." Ryler pointed to Delilah's wine. "Can I get a glass of that?"

Delilah poured her a glass and passed it to her. "So, I apologize, but who is Alia Cole?"

"Ah, Instagram travel blogger Alia Cole? She's the gorgeous blonde over there. She's my cousin and boss." The lie still rolled off her tongue with ease, but it seemed shallow now. With Alia facing a world-changing decision with Ryler's producer slash best friend, what was the point of keeping up the charade? She might as well tell everyone, *Oh yeah, it's my podcast. Alia's been posing as me for years so I didn't have to put myself out there.*

"Is that weird?" Delilah asked, and Ryler blinked at her, forgetting what they'd been talking about for a second.

"Sorry, is what weird?"

"Working for family," Delilah clarified.

"Oh, sometimes." Ryler swallowed a gulp of wine, the lie that she didn't know exactly who Delilah was hovering over her head. Finally, she swallowed and leaned closer to the other woman, lowering her voice. "Full disclosure?"

"Um, sure."

"I was in the car with Pike on Sunday. When he saw you with . . . what's his name? Anthony?"

"Oh, yeah. That was—"

"None of my business," Ryler said, trying to put the other woman at ease. "We were on our way to meet Alia when he saw you."

"I didn't get out of the car until you were gone," Delilah said, cocking her head to the side. "How did you know it was me?"

"I heard your name and put two and two together." Ryler took another drink, searching for something to say to make this less awkward and instead blurted, "He was on a pretty good tirade on Sunday."

Delilah blushed. "Just to be clear, I'm not in the habit of causing issues between friends. I try to avoid drama."

"Are you kidding?" Ryler laughed. "You were not the issue. He had nothing negative to say about you at all. Anthony, on the other hand, was getting a lot of heat."

"Well, I hope they make up soon," Delilah said. "I tried to talk to Pike about what happened. They've been friends a long time and shouldn't give up on each other so easily." Delilah smiled. "Sounds like you've been spending a lot of time with Pike."

And there it was. Why else would she have opened her big mouth about other people's drama unless she had a vested interest? "Yeah, he's taking me and the rest of the crew around Mistletoe so we can do research . . . for Alia, I mean."

"And how do you like Mistletoe so far?" Delilah asked, her smile broadening. At least she wasn't trying to run away from the nosy outsider.

"It's beautiful," Ryler gushed. "I've heard all about your holiday festivities, and I'm excited to hang around and join in."

"Where are you from?" Delilah asked.

"Boise originally, but I've got a condo in Northern California I stay in when I'm not off somewhere exploring."

"Well, if there's one thing Mistletoe goes all out for, it's Christmas," Delilah said.

"Not a fan?" Ryler asked before taking a sip of her wine.

"It's not about being a fan. I'm just not as diehard as my best friend, Holly."

"Which is an amazing Christmas movie, by the way."

"Pardon?" Delilah asked.

"*Die Hard.* Great holiday film for the whole family. Also, Holly is awesome."

"Yes, she is." Delilah laughed. "Don't say that too loud about *Die Hard*, or you'll start a rumble. That is a hot-button topic."

"Gotcha," Ryler laughed. "I love your shirt, by the way."

Delilah was wearing an electric blue off-the-shoulder sheath that made her eyes brighter. Between the eyes, the hair, and the chesticles that put Ryler's full C cups to shame, she could see why Pike had his eye on her.

"Thank you. It made me feel pretty." She shared a small smile with Ryler.

"You're gorgeous."

"I appreciate that. You're not trying to butter me up and sell me something, are you?"

Ryler laughed. "No, I just call it like I see it. And I'm trying this new thing where I don't hold back. Everything I think, I'm saying it."

Delilah tapped her fingers on her wine glass and smirked. "That could be dangerous."

"Maybe." In actuality, it could be dangerous, but Ryler was sick of all the secrets. She wanted to live life without holding back and wondering what might have been, starting with her relationship with Pike. "I've spent a lot of time keeping everything close to the breast, afraid of offending someone or embarrassing others. I've finally decided I don't give a shit. If someone doesn't like me, warts and all, I'm fine on my own."

"Damn, girl. I need that energy in my life." Delilah waved her glass around the room, still grinning. "I got persuaded to play hostess at the last minute when I really wanted to escape into my room."

"Hey, if you want to do that, I'll totally cover for you." Ryler feigned confusion. "Oh, you're looking for Delilah? I think she's in the kitchen. Not there? You know what, I think she had to pee."

"You're good," Delilah said, taking a sip from her glass.

"That's why Alia keeps me around. I'm the best."

Delilah suddenly looked around the room, frowning. "Do you hear that?"

Ryler paused, trying to hear anything strange over the buzz of conversations. "What am I hearing?"

"It sounds like singing."

Ryler frowned, standing perfectly still.

Suddenly, there was a pounding at the door.

"Delilah!"

Delilah covered her mouth, eyes wide. Ryler couldn't tell for sure, but she'd bet her last dollar it was Anthony pounding on the door. The entire house of women quieted, gathering in the dining room doorway to watch.

"I think that's for you," Ryler said.

Delilah set her cup down and crossed the room, Ryler following behind. When Delilah opened the door, Ryler saw the group of men standing in the yard with Anthony front and center, looking sheepish, and Pike by his side. When Ryler met Pike's eyes, he grinned wickedly, setting her panties ablaze.

Damn him.

"What are you doing here?" Delilah asked.

"We have come courtin'," Pike said.

"No, we've not," Sam said.

Delilah grabbed her coat off the hook and stepped out onto the porch, wrapping her arms around herself. "Again, why are you all gathered on my lawn?"

"I'm getting to that," Anthony said, clearing his throat. "Nick?"

Nick held his phone up, and the first notes of "Hey There Delilah" sounded, and suddenly Anthony was singing at the top of his lungs, the men behind him humming along.

"Oh, it's what you do to me!" Anthony belted. He wasn't bad, but he was slightly off beat and obviously a little drunk. Holly stepped out onto the porch between Delilah and Ryler, her mouth agape.

"Oh my God," Holly said.

The crowd of women thickened on the porch as more of them came out to watch the spectacle.

Anthony threw his hands out to his side as he sang, "And you're to blame!"

The men chorused, "Oooooooh," and Ryler bit her lip to keep from laughing at Pike, who was waggling his eyebrows at her as he crooned. Delilah's neighbors had all stepped out into their yards to watch, some of them laughing. Others shaking their heads.

The song ended, and Delilah didn't move as Anthony took a few steps toward her, grinning. Ryler gave them space, keeping her eyes on Pike as he backslapped and congratulated his friends. Seeing him among them again made her think back to that Instagram stalking she'd done and how his relationship with his friends was the first thing that fascinated her about him.

"Aren't carolers supposed to sing Christmas songs?" Delilah asked Anthony.

"Not when they're trying to win back their girl."

An eruption of feminine "aws" echoed throughout the women on the porch, including Ryler, who couldn't resist the romance of it all.

Anthony seemed to finally realize how large his audience was and blinked at them. "I didn't know you were having a party."

"It's a book club," Delilah said.

He climbed up on the first step, swaying with a smile. "What book are you reading?"

"Stay focused, man! I am freezing my balls off!" Declan said.

"Right, sorry." Anthony cleared his throat. "Delilah Gill. I like you and want to take you out on a date. 'Cause I like you."

"You already said that," Delilah whispered.

Anthony leaned in, towering over Delilah. "I thought it bore repeating. I like the hell out of you, and I will shout it to the world any time you doubt me."

"Would you kiss him already?" Holly hissed.

"I swear, if you don't, I will!" Another woman called from the doorway of the house, and Ryler shot her a dirty look. *Find your own man, hussy.*

"Will you date me, Delilah?" Anthony asked.

Delilah laughed. "You are very drunk."

"That is a statement of fact but not what I'm looking for."

"And you'll get an answer when you're sober."

"Boo," the men on the lawn hollered.

"Sloshed or not, that was pretty epic," Ryler said, leaning against the railing. "Although the redhead was pitchy."

Pike glowered at her. "Witch, I have the voice of an angel."

"A fallen angel."

Suddenly, Pike bent over and gathered up a handful of snow, letting it fly. It missed Ryler and hit Holly on the side of her face. Delilah's mouth dropped open as Holly dived off the porch.

"You're a dead man, Pike!"

"I wasn't aiming at you!" he protested, hiding behind one man after another. "Declan, control your woman!"

"I don't know, man. I kinda wanna see what she does when she gets you."

Ryler jogged down the steps to join Holly in her pursuit of Pike, picking up a handful of snow. She ignored the stinging cold as she snuck up on Pike from the other side, using the rush of wives and girlfriends who had joined in the fun to hide in plain sight. There were whoops and cheers as snow exploded against the side of Delilah's house and windows. The door slammed on a group of women who ran back inside, but Ryler was in this, stalking Pike as he pleaded with Holly, holding on to Nick's shoulders to keep him between them.

Ryler pressed the snowball into the back of his neck, laughing as he danced forward with a yell, nearly knocking Nick off his feet. When he spun around and spotted her, he said, "You're dead, woman."

Ryler took off as soon as he bent over.

The female officer she'd been introduced to earlier, Officer Wren, hollered, "We're going to get the cops called on us if we don't simmer down."

"Officer Wren, is that you?" Sam called. "I didn't think you knew what fun was."

"Smug son of a bitch." Ryler watched the woman hop off the porch from her hiding spot behind the trash can. Officer Wren's blond hair was up in a high ponytail that swung as she bent over for a handful of snow. "You've been asking for this for weeks."

"Well come on, hot stuff! Catch me if you can!"

Ryler saw Pike coming and stepped back into the darkness of the side yard, hoping he wouldn't see her, but a motion light clicked on, and Pike whirled, grinning at her.

"Gotcha," he said, launching a snowball that caught her on the shoulder.

Ryler laughed. "Truce, I'm unarmed."

"You yield to me, then," Pike said, advancing on her until the side of Delilah's house stopped her. He pressed into her, trailing his fingers along her cheek. "Hmmm?"

Ryler's breath caught as she stared up at him, the intensity of his gaze too arresting to speak. "Yes," she managed.

Pike took her hands, pinning them above her head. His mouth dipped, his lips settling against the shell of her ear. He kissed Ryler along the side of her neck, and her eyes fluttered closed.

Pike leaned back, his blue eyes boring into hers. "Should we take this discussion somewhere with more privacy?"

"I brought Alia with me," Ryler murmured.

"You could drop her off and come back to me."

"Delilah and Anthony fought, and he serenaded her. I feel like you need to sweeten the pot."

"Oh, I'll sweeten it alright. I bought you a packet of chocolate and a bottle of wine with the intention of groveling for your forgiveness, but got distracted by trying to help Anthony win back his girl."

Ryler licked her lips. "Let me see what I can do."

"Even if you can't come now," he said, releasing her hands and threading his fingers with hers, "I'd like to go back to our original arrangement. I want to spend as much time with you as possible before you go."

"Still keeping it between us?" she whispered.

"Is that what you want?" he asked.

"I think it's best."

"Then that's what we'll do."

Chapter Thirty-two

I'm trying not to be a bitter Ben, but I wish you could have come over last night.

Ryler stared at her phone, smiling at Pike's Wednesday morning text. Alia had wanted to stay until the end of book club, having far too much fun hanging with Merry, but it turned out that book club was cut short due to Anthony vomiting all over Delilah's front porch. Ryler had driven Alia back to the rental, but instead of being able to escape, Alia asked her to stay and watch movies with her. Ryler had texted Pike with her regrets last night, and he'd responded with a deliciously naughty pic and caption. I guess I'll have to take care of this myself.

Ryler had tapped out a response, glancing over at Alia, who had fallen asleep on the other couch in the middle of *Dirty Dancing: Havana Nights*. While it might be the campiest of the *Dirty Dancing* films, Ryler had always been partial to the romance between Javier and Katey.

Neither Neil nor Kit had stirred yet this morning, so Ryler silenced her phone, and using her finger, pulled the neckline of her night shirt down to expose an expanse of breasts. She took the picture and captioned the photo, Good morning. Would it make you feel better if I admitted I wish I'd come over too?

Her screen lit up with his next message, a shirtless picture of him in a pair of sweats and—

"Oh my," Ryler whispered aloud when she realized his dick was creating that tent in his sweats.

This is what you do to me. I just have to think about your smile, and I'm hard as a fucking stone.

Ryler grinned as she texted, Maybe you should imagine me frowning.

Doesn't help. It's just you.

Ryler could get used to this kind of flattery and swung her legs off the couch, fully intending to use the bathroom and take a shower. Before she turned on the water, another text came through, this one from Neil.

I need to talk to you.

Ryler washed her hands and opened the bathroom door, then saw Neil peeking out of his room down the hall. He made a motion for her to come to him, and she did so reluctantly, allowing him to close the door behind them.

"What's up, Neil?" she asked coolly.

"Look, I know I should have told you about Alia and me, but I thought it was nothing. Just the two of us hooking up when we were bored or lonely. I didn't plan any of this."

"I know you didn't, but that doesn't change the fact that you slept with my cousin. For better or for worse, you're the father of her baby, and whatever you're doing is hurting her. You're making her feel small and sad, and I hate it."

Neil ran his hands over his face and took a seat on the edge of the bed. "You know, for years I thought it was going to be you and me? I mean, we tried it in college, but this podcast was about us and our love of the world. Of discovering new things. When did we lose sight of that?"

"Neil," Ryler whispered, sitting next to him on the bed. "You're my best friend, but I don't—feel that way about you."

"Especially now that I've impregnated your cousin."

"Definitely didn't win you any points, but I'm more concerned about what this means for the two of you. I know that you've been looking at other shows." Ryler almost laughed at his horrified expression. "What? You should be careful what you say. Your voice carries."

"Why aren't you angrier with me?" he asked.

"Because this is life. You are well within your rights to get bored and look for something else, whether that be a new job or a relationship. We've been friends a long time, and I'd like things to stay that way. I don't want you to resent me for holding you back."

"I was going to talk to you about it, but I applied to produce the *Crime Lords* podcast, and I got it."

"The mafia family podcast?" Ryler chuckled. "Just don't offend anyone and end up with cement shoes."

"They're turning the show into a TV series, and I know you've never been interested in that, but this is my chance to break into television."

"I think that's great, Neil. When do you start?"

"I was going to wait until after the New Year, but now . . ." He trailed off, and Ryler picked up the conversation.

"What are you going to do about Alia and the baby? Do you have feelings for her?"

Neil groaned. "Yes, I do, but it's new. We spent so much time picking at each other and hating each other that when things changed, I wasn't expecting our relationship to do a complete one-eighty. And what if we try, and it gets bad again?"

"Have you told Alia any of this?"

"No, I just flipped out over the baby."

"You two don't have to rush into marriage, but if you care about her and want to give this a real shot, maybe you can start by asking her on a date?" Ryler said.

"A date you say?" Neil said in a British accent, stroking his jaw. "What a novel concept."

"I know," Ryler said. "I'm sorry, Neil, if you were holding out for me. I never meant to lead you on."

"You didn't. I guess I just always thought that friends make the best lovers. Turns out that isn't the case for us."

Ryler squeezed Neil's hand. "It has been an honor and a privilege working with you, and I hope this doesn't mean we stop being friends."

"No, I will always be your friend. And hey, we'll always have Paris."

Ryler laughed. "If you are referring to Paris, Texas, that is a trip I'd rather forget!"

"What? I thought that was a fun trip."

"It was," Ryler said.

Neil got up from the bed with a determined expression. "So, where is Alia?"

"On the couch in the living room. We were watching movies and fell asleep."

"Alright, I'm going to talk to her," Neil said firmly. "Wish me luck."

"First, let me duck into the shower in case you two start fighting again."

Ryler exited Neil's room and went back into the bathroom again, picking up her phone to read her most recent text, Will I see you later?

Ryler heard the door to Neil's room close and a few minutes later, lowered voices. I'll let you know after my shower. It depends on how things shake out.

Ryler finished her shower, drying off her hair and wrapping the towel around her. When she walked out of the room, she found Neil and Alia sitting on the couch, her head resting against his chest. They looked happy and contented instead of the two people who had been at each other's throats just yesterday.

Neil looked up and spotted her, giving her a thumbs-up. Things were about to look really different for *Excursions* in the coming weeks, but Ryler was so happy to see her cousin smiling again, she didn't care about how the changes would affect her. The two people she loved most were going to try to be together for real, to stop holding back and live life on their terms.

It was something she could get behind.

Ryler closed the door to her room and texted Pike. All signs point to yes.

Chapter Thirty-three

Pike leaned back in his chair on Saturday night at the Mistletoe Community Center, wishing that Holly, Merry, and Delilah would hurry up and get the show on the road. Anthony and Pike had carpooled to the bachelor auction meeting, but Pike had plans to pick Ryler up from her rental and take her out for a surprise. Maybe not a real date, since they weren't supposed to be doing that, but the next best thing.

Pike just hoped she liked it, because he had never got around to asking if it was her thing.

"Listen up!" Holly shouted.

Most of the men quieted down except for a few whisperers who received withering looks from Holly. Once the room was dead silent, Merry nodded toward her sister, addressing the crowd with a strained smile. "Thank you. Next week after the Parade of Lights, you'll come straight here and get ready backstage. Please dress appropriately in a coat and tie. We'll call your name alphabetically, and when you cross the stage, smile, dance, show off, whatever you want to do." Merry pointed to the elevated stage behind her before continuing, "You'll see onstage we have a backdrop and a camera set up because we want to get everyone's picture for the program, plus a brief bio. Delilah, Holly, and I are going to call your names and gather that information while you're waiting for your picture. Once you are finished with your picture and bio, you are welcome to take off and enjoy the rest of your evening. I want to thank you again for being here. Your participation is going to make a world of difference for our school extracurriculars this year." The room erupted in applause, and Merry's smile became a genuine one. "Let's get started. Trip!"

"Pike!" Holly hollered.

Pike climbed to his feet and grinned. "If she doesn't call you next, I'm ditching your ass," he said to Anthony.

"Funny, you came in my truck. I guess you're walking back."

"Pshaw, I got so much swagger, you know all this is getting picked up," Pike joked, exaggerating his walk all the way to Holly. When he stood in front of her, he grinned. "I am ready and waiting!"

"Name, age, occupation, height, hobbies, and your idea of the perfect date."

"What, no bank code?" Pike said.

Holly hit him with her clipboard. "Just give me the deets and get out of here. You've got places to be, don't you?"

"How do you know about that?" Pike asked.

"A little birdy told me. We've become friends, you know." Holly leaned forward, scowling at Pike. "I really would hate for anyone to hurt her, because I might be tempted to seek retaliation."

"Whoa, there is no need for vengeance! Both Ryler and I are open and honest about what we want."

"Good, then. Pike—" She wrote it down. "Thirty-one. Business owner. Snowboarding. Bullshitting. Downing mixed drinks. Playing with his dog—"

"Hey, I don't like your interpretation of me. After snowboarding, I like hiking, camping, dancing, and playing pool. My perfect date"—Pike grinned—"getting snowed in together. We'd snuggle up on the couch, watching movies and eating dinner by a fire."

"Well, isn't that a romance novel answer," Holly said, giving him another playful whack with her clipboard. "Thanks for being here, Pike. Enjoy the rest of your ni— What in the world?"

Pike turned and saw Anthony holding Delilah away from Brodie, carrying her off her feet. Pike shook his head, wondering at the strange ways love worked. Anthony had been a reasonable, single man two weeks ago, and today, he was a jealous caveman.

Having felt the sting of that foul emotion before, Pike refused to be overwhelmed with it. If a woman didn't want to be with him, he wouldn't fight over her like a wolf guarding a piece of meat. She could flirt and dance with whomever she liked.

Pike texted Ryler when he returned to his seat. I just finished and Anthony should be done soon. Where can I pick you up?

I'm at Brews and Chews with Kit, Alia, and Neil having dinner. Care to join us?

I'd actually like to spend time with just you tonight.

Then I'll leave here when I'm done and meet you somewhere.

Come to my place and we'll leave from there.

Can't wait 😘

Pike grinned, impatiently tapping his foot as he waited for Anthony to finish his interview. When he came back over, Pike clucked his tongue.

"Really? Making a spectacle of yourself again?"

"He tried to kiss her," Anthony growled.

"And you didn't lay him out? I say that shows restraint." Pike cracked his knuckles. "Come to think of it, I'm pretty sure I told him that your girl was off-limits. We might need to catch him by his truck."

Anthony chuckled. "I'm glad to have you on my side again."

Pike's chest squeezed. "No more secrets and lies, and we'll be golden."

"Does that mean you're going to tell me why you're in an all-fired hurry to get out of here tonight?"

"Oh wait, I wasn't clear, you can't keep any more secrets, but I can."

Anthony playfully pushed Pike's shoulder. "Get the fuck out of here."

"You're not going to stay and watch your girl?" Pike teased.

"I think everyone got the message to stay away," Anthony said, heading for the exit. As they pushed through the door and the cold air stung Pike's face, he shivered. Maybe it wasn't a good idea to take her to an ice-skating pond. Freezing to death didn't exactly lead to romance.

Practically everything he had in his dating rolodex took place outside, and it was cold as hell tonight.

"I need a date-night idea. It's too cold to go ice-skating."

"Wait a second, back up!" Anthony said, pulling up short. "Who do you have a date with?"

"Um . . . I can't tell you that."

Anthony hit the unlock button on his truck fob. "You preach to me about secrets, and then you keep a secret girlfriend from me?"

"She is not my girlfriend."

"Oh yeah? So, this is a new development." Anthony sucked in his breath. "It's not the podcaster you've been showing around, is it?"

Technically, yes, since Ryler is the voice of Excursions *but—*

"Nope, not Alia."

"No, the other one. Ryler!"

Pike grinned sheepishly.

"Dude! I thought the whole point of inviting them here was for publicity. We don't want bad publicity!"

"Relax, we have an understanding, and that's all I'm going to say because this was supposed to be between her and I."

"You're having a secret relationship with the podcaster's assistant? Oh yeah, this is going to end well."

"Back to the matter at hand, where do I take her? And don't say Brews and Chews."

"What about the Wolf's Den?" Anthony said before he climbed into thc driver's seat.

"No, we don't need to listen to bad karaoke."

"It's warm, it's inside, and I bet you'd have fun."

Pike shook his head. "I'll consider it. You got anything else in that big brain of yours?"

"You could take her through Holly's neighborhood first. Grab some tacos, eat them in the car as you check out the Christmas lights, and end the night with drinks and an off-key rendition of 'Pour Some Sugar on Me.'"

As far as ideas go, it wasn't the worst one he'd heard, although he was a tad concerned. He wasn't joking when he'd told Ryler that the Wolf's Den was a rougher crowd, and bringing a beautiful, curvy girl like her in there would be asking for trouble.

Then again, if someone messed with her, Pike imagined his Kitten could handle herself.

His Kitten? When had he added the possessive "his" to her nickname?

About the same time thoughts of her took over every free moment of the day?

Pike shook his head, refusing to acknowledge the little voice's antics. He and Ryler were enjoying each other's company. If he had an off-color thought, that was completely natural when he liked someone. No need to read too much into it.

Chapter Thirty-four

"Are you trying to get me killed?"

Ryler stopped walking at Pike's greeting, cocking her head to the side. "Um, no?"

"Then why are you wearing that?" His eyes swept over her from the toes of her boots to the top of her head, and Ryler self-consciously tugged her jacket closed. She'd put on the black in-case-of-an-emergency dress she always packed with the sole purpose of making Pike lose his cool in a good way.

Apparently, she'd missed the mark.

Ryler looked down at the tight black dress that dipped into a low V in the front, showing off a generous amount of cleavage and then addressed Pike waspishly. "I thought I looked good in it."

"You do! Too good. I'm going to get my teeth knocked out for just walking into a room with you."

Ryler laughed. "Okay, you don't have to lay it on so thick."

"Sorry," Pike said, taking her hands and pulling her in for a kiss. Ryler melted into him, inhaling the woodsy scent of his cologne. He wore his heavy winter jacket, but she could see the collar of his shirt peeking over the top. He'd dressed up, too.

For a non-date night, they'd put in a lot of effort. Ryler had even put on a full face of makeup and curled her hair. Alia and Neil had believed it was because of their celebratory dinner, but when she'd ducked out to go hang with Holly, Kit had given her a rather knowing look, and she wondered how much her cameraman had picked up on.

Pike's hands moved under her jacket, cupping her butt through the dress, and she laughed. "Hey now, it took me hours to look this good, so we are not just going to waste it staying in."

"Believe me, it wouldn't be a waste," Pike said.

Ryler's knees weakened at his rough voice, and she placed her hands on his chest, giving him a light push backward because if she didn't put some space between them, they were never getting out of here.

"We have plenty of time for that after. Right now, I'm starving and can't wait to see what you have planned for us."

"Well, I hope you're not disappointed, but I grabbed some tacos from my favorite place because for our first stop, we don't even have to get out of the car."

"I'm intrigued," she said, watching him open the passenger door and hold it open for her. Sure enough, there was a white bag in the middle console that had a happy taco cartoon on the side and two drinks in the holders. Ryler slipped into the seat, and he closed it after her.

Pike climbed into the driver's seat and handed her the bag. "Help yourself while I get us going. I didn't know if you prefer beef or chicken, so I got both."

"I like both." Ryler pulled out the first taco she grabbed and a napkin, a little afraid of eating something so messy in her dress. The fixings inside were liable to fall out and drop right down her neckline into her bra.

She fashioned a makeshift bib with her napkin to cover up her chest, then unfolded the taco wrapper carefully in her lap.

"What you got going on over there?"

Ryler smiled, leaning over the wrapper so as not to spill anything on her dress. "I don't want to end up with anything down the front of my dress."

Pike opened his mouth but then snapped it shut, smothered laughter sputtering from between his lips.

"What?" she asked.

"I was going to say something, but on reflection, don't think it was very sexy after all."

"Oh my God, were you going to tell me that I was just saving it for later?"

"No! I was going to say I'll find it later."

Ryler laughed. "You're a sick man."

"That's why I wasn't going to say it," he said, making a left. There was a line of brake lights in the distance, and Pike slowed down, getting in behind the last car.

"What is this?" Ryler asked.

"The best Christmas lights display in Idaho."

"Really? Is this Holly's street? I've been wanting to check it out but haven't had the chance."

"Yep, she's the first house on the right. It shouldn't take long to cruise through, but I thought we could eat dinner as we check out the lights before moving on to our next stop."

"And what would that be?" she asked.

"It's a surprise."

"Fun," she said. "I love surprises."

Pike adjusted the radio until jolly Christmas music filled the inside of the car. Ryler passed him the bag of tacos as she nibbled delicately at the one in hand. They moved up faster than she expected and when the street finally came into view, Ryler sucked in her breath.

"Wow!"

"Right? People from all over the state come through to see this. Even some out-of-staters."

"It's gorgeous, but dang! Do they do the same setup every year?"

"Nope, they change it up. A few years ago, that house"—Pike pointed to the house across from Holly's—"did a display dedicated to their cat."

"That's Christmassy, I suppose." Ryler laughed. She stared at Holly's home as they drove past at a crawl, admiring the extravagance. It was made up to look like a giant gingerbread house with a forest of lollipops stuck into the front lawn. Several lit-up gingerbread men and women danced between the colorful candy stalks.

Each house had an elaborate theme, as if trying to outdo the one next to it. "Is there a competition for the best design?"

"Oh yes, the same for the window displays in town. We take our holiday festivities seriously. This year, Mistletoe is hosting their first winter games, and Anthony and I are in charge of it."

"That must be a big job. When is it?"

"The weekend before Christmas."

"Wow. I guess it's a good thing the two of you made up, huh? Otherwise, you might not have been able to pull it off."

"I would have pulled it off, with or without Anthony."

"So cocky," Ryler said, finishing her taco and cleaning up the wrapper and napkin.

"You're only having one?" he asked.

"I told you that we were celebrating Neil and Alia's happy news. I had dinner with all of them, but I am grateful you let me try your favorite taco place." Ryler reached for his hand and covered it with hers, squeezing it. "And for bringing me here. It is truly beautiful."

When she started to pull her hand away, he caught it, threading his fingers with hers. "I'm glad you like it. Which one is your favorite?"

"I think Holly's is adorable, but this one," she said, pointing to the Hogwarts-themed home, "would put Universal to shame."

"I've never been to Universal or Disneyland. Or World, for that matter."

"I think you would enjoy it," Ryler said as they rounded the circle and the last house's display left her puzzled. "Are those raisins?"

"Yeah, I think they're from California, and they kept talking about some California Raisin Christmas special."

"That's an obscure theme to pick," Ryler said.

"Hey, at least they participated. A lot of these streets are dying out because people don't want to invest the time or money into them," Pike said, making a left out of the circle.

"Well, where to now?"

"To the Wolf's Den," he said.

Ryler frowned. "Isn't that the biker bar you said was too rough for Alia and me?"

"Yeah, but you're going with me. They have karaoke and a pool table. It will be grand," Pike said, mimicking an Irish accent.

Ryler chuckled. "If you say so, then I believe you."

"What do you mean?" he asked.

"I have to spell it out for you? I trust you." They were honest words, but by the way he stilled beside her, you'd think she had professed her love for him. "What's wrong with that?"

"Just the way you said it made me happy, is all."

"Well, I live to please, but just so we're clear," Ryler said, leaning across the middle console, "if there is any danger, I will not hesitate to trip you and save myself."

"So, shoving people out of the way to save yourself is a family trait you and your cousin share?" Pike said dryly.

"Uh-huh."

"And you're telling me when shit hits the fan, I better run faster than you?"

"Absolutely. Survival of the fastest and the most devious."

Pike laughed. "Now that's a movie I'd like to see."

I'm already living it, Ryler thought, realizing that in two weeks the credits would roll on this little romance of theirs, and her time with Pike would be another adventure she could look back on.

Why did that thought make her so bereft?

Chapter Thirty-five

The minute they crossed the threshold of the Wolf's Den, Pike knew he'd made a mistake. Not only were several men homing in on Ryler with obvious interest, but a familiar face called out to Pike, jovially crossing the bar floor to embrace him.

"Pike Sutton!" Davis Lamb slapped his back several times and pulled back, grinning down at him. His long blond hair was loose around his shoulders, and he wore a fitted blue T-shirt that hugged his bulging muscles like a second skin. "How the hell are you, friend?"

"I'm great, Davis. This is my friend, Ryler Colby."

Ryler held out her hand, and Davis took it, pumping it vigorously. "So very nice to meet you," Davis said.

"It's nice to meet you, too. How do you know each other?"

Before Pike could fully mouth the word *no*, Davis said, "We were part of an all-male review about, what would you say, Pike? Four years ago?"

"Male review, like stripping?" Ryler asked, wide eyes swinging toward Pike as if searching for confirmation. He didn't have time to fix his face before she realized that she'd hit the nail on the head. "Oh my God."

"It was just a few months," Pike said.

"Yeah, they canceled the group when interest died off, but it was fun, right? Also gave me a foot in the entertainment business. I got a part in an indie film after a producer saw me at one of the shows, and I've been in a dozen or so short films all around Idaho. Eventually, I'll land that big role, but I'm going to have to relocate to LA or Georgia. Just not a lot going on in the Potato State."

"Well, we're going to get a table and order some drinks. It was good to see you, man," Pike said, accepting another hug.

"If you get some time, you should come to an audition with me. You have no idea how many roles are out there for a ginger who can dance."

Pike was keenly aware of Ryler's curious gaze on him. "Maybe if my business folds, I'll look into it. Great to see you."

"You, too," Davis said, heading over to a tall blonde and throwing his arm around her before the two of them headed for the exit.

"So," Ryler drawled. "You failed to mention your former career as an exotic dancer."

"It would have come up eventually," he said, holding out a stool at a tall table. "Take a seat, I'll grab us some drinks, and if you want the whole sordid tale, I'll tell you all about it."

"I'll take something fruity."

Pike went to the bar and ordered their drinks, worry gnawing at his insides. Would she be repulsed by him? Several women he'd been out with had mocked his stint as a dancer, but he wasn't ashamed of it. He'd started dancing after his ex-girlfriend cheated on him and he'd worked out like a fiend, his confidence growing, and he'd come out of it stronger and happier.

He returned to the table and set the drinks down, taking the seat across from her. "I don't usually tell people about it because some people judge me for it."

"I'm not. I just find it fascinating," she said, removing her jacket and laying it over the back of the chair. "There are so many different parts to you, and I want to know them all."

"It was just a whim that turned into a fun way to mend my broken heart. It was mildly humiliating when people discovered what I was doing and proceeded to tease me, but it was something I needed to do."

"Have you retained any of your exotic moves?" she teased.

Pike took a deep draw of his beer and shrugged. "I might remember a thing or two."

"Maybe you could show me later?" she asked.

Pike chuckled. "You looking for a lap dance, Kitten?"

"Only if you're the one giving it," she said, leaning on the table and pressing those beautiful breasts together. Pike imagined sticking his face between the soft mounds, and his mouth went dry.

"Next up onstage is Larissa singing all about falling 'Accidentally in Love.'" Larissa, with her leather pants and straight black hair, jogged up onto the stage and belted out the first few lines in a smoky voice that was delightfully melodic. Pike found himself tapping his foot along to the beat as Ryler took another sip from her straw.

"You really don't come here often?" she asked.

"No, we like Brews because the atmosphere is more relaxed. Sometimes the people here take themselves too seriously."

"Whew, sweetheart," someone called out, and Ryler and Pike turned toward the voice. Pike didn't recognize the man approaching them, but he did a double take when he saw Sam Griffin leaning against the bar. Sam gave him a nod, his attention on the man who stopped next to Ryler, his gaze locked on her. "Where have they been hiding you?"

"I haven't been hiding," Ryler said, holding out her hand with a small smile, "but this is my first visit to the Den since getting to town."

"What a terrible shame. You brighten up the place for sure." The man gave Pike a feral smile. "You mind if I dance with the lady?"

Yes, I fucking do, he thought, but that wasn't how he was supposed to react. Ryler was her own person, and behaving like a possessive barbarian was sure to drive her right back to her rental and far away from Pike.

"The lady only wants to dance with him," Ryler said, pointing to Pike.

The burly guy shrugged. "You must have a footlong in your pants, Red."

Pike's jaw dropped at the same time Ryler burst out laughing. The big guy walked away, and Pike leaned across the table, whispering, "That's not funny. He thinks the only reason you're with me is because I'm hung like a horse."

"Who cares what he thinks?" Ryler asked, sipping her drink. "Are you going to take him home tonight or me?"

Pike pretended to consider her question. "He does rock that shaved head."

"Ew, you could do so much better than Temu Jason Statham."

Pike burst out laughing. "Fuck, that was good."

Ryler grinned. "I know. And while I appreciate you giving me the freedom to turn him down myself, if any more would-be suitors approach, you have my permission to tell them to fuck right off."

Pike took a drink of his beer with a grimace before he set it back down on the table. "Maybe I'll find a gentler way to reject them, as regardless of whether it is you saying it or me, it's going to get me punched in the face."

"And we wouldn't want that." Ryler reached across and trailed her fingertips along the side of his face. "I quite like the way your features are arranged. Wouldn't want any teeth to go missing or a nose to get smashed."

"I appreciate you looking out," Pike said.

Ryler leaned farther across the table and whispered loudly, "What do you say we finish these drinks and head back to your place for that private dance? While I wanted the chance to show off my makeup and dress, I think I prefer it being just you and me."

"Hey, you two," Sam said, coming up alongside Pike. "What's shaking?"

Pike gave Ryler an arched brow, and she nodded. Pike turned to Sam and grinned. "Not a whole lot. We were actually about to head out. Seems like crowded bars aren't really our thing."

Sam sighed. "Well, hell, I guess I'll go home, too. I was excited to see familiar faces, but I don't want to interrupt your night." Sam downed the rest of his drink and set it down. "I'll see ya."

Ryler gave Sam's back a pitying look. "Maybe we should—"

"No," Pike said.

"I just mean, we could—"

"Uh-uh."

Ryler huffed. "You don't even know what I was going to say."

"If it involves Sam, the answer is always no. The man is sex on a stick, and he already thinks you're cute."

"Really?" Ryler drawled.

"That's it," Pike said, finishing off his beer. "No dance for you."

"Oh, come on, I was just kidding."

"Nope."

Ryler sucked down the rest of her drink and wrapped her arms around his neck, pouting. "Please, I was only teasing."

"You're gonna have to do a lot better than that to win back my dance moves."

Ryler smiled up at him seductively. "Then let's get out of here so I can show you how very contrite I am."

Pike's cock jerked with anticipation, but instead of taking her hand and leading her out the front door, he headed for the back.

"Where are we going?" she asked, sucking the last of her drink and abandoning it on the bar as they passed.

"I'm giving you what you asked for. A dance. Just keep your eyes forward."

"What does that even mean?" she whispered.

"Trust me."

When a burly man stopped them before a black curtain, Pike gave him a wad of cash and said, "Moonlight changes man."

The man nodded and opened the curtain, pointing to a wall of keys. "Number thirteen."

"Thanks," Pike said, holding tight to her hand as they walked through the curtain. Pike picked up the keys, and they walked down a red-lit hallway.

"What is this place?" Ryler asked.

"It's the den." Pike opened the door to number thirteen and led Ryler inside before he locked it. Inside the small room was a couch, a chair, and an open door in the corner that revealed a small bathroom.

"Is this like a pay-by-the-hour hotel or something?" she asked.

"I told you the den is rougher. Most of the motorcycle guys are just passing through and want a place to just chillax before they move on. You just have to know the password to get in, which only members get via text every Friday night."

Ryler shook her head. "This is very sex dungeon-esque."

Pike pulled her in close and kissed her. "If we go home, Jo is going to need to go out, and she is going to cry and whine if I put her in the cage. At least this way when I dance for you, I won't have a dog jumping all over me or making a whole lotta noise."

"This is very *Sons of Anarchy* of you." Ryler sat down on the couch, crossing one leg over her knee. "Where do you want me, big boy?"

Pike shrugged out of his jacket and tossed it over the back of the chair. "On the couch."

He watched her all the while he unbuttoned his shirt, the dim light casting a warm glow over her, making her eyes brighter. He shrugged out of the shirt and it landed on top of his jacket.

"Mmm, now that is a pretty sight," she murmured, placing her elbow on her knee and cradling her chin in her hands. "Let's see the rest."

"Absolutely, but let me lay down a few ground rules," he said, slipping off his shoes.

"Rules?" Ryler pouted. "We don't need no stinking rules."

"Oh yes, we do." He dropped his pants and stepped out of them. "First off, I can touch you, but you cannot touch me. Number one rule of stripping."

"That's garbage."

"Next, and I cannot stress this enough," Pike said, swaggering over to her. "Enjoy the ride."

"Oh, I'm sure I—" Pike slid down her body in a fluid motion, ending on his knees between her legs. "Will," she finished, right before he buried his head between her legs and lifted her off the couch. She squealed as he gripped her ass, her skirt riding up and exposing her thighs. When her hands landed on his shoulders, Pike lifted his head and clicked his tongue.

"Uh-uh. Grab the back of the couch, baby, and hold on."

Ryler did as he commanded, and Pike rolled his way back up her body, stopping to bury his face in her cleavage. Ryler released a breathless laugh as he hopped up, both of his feet next to her on the couch, and he rolled his stiff, boxer clad cock into her face.

"Oh my God, Pike!" she gasped.

He jumped back before somersaulting across the floor and twisting his body, landing spread eagle in her lap in a handstand. He humped her lap a few times and then rolled off, climbing to his feet. Pike picked her up and turned her around to face the back of the couch, lifting her skirt and grinding against her ass. Ryler wasn't laughing now, a low moan escaping her as he reached around and cupped her breast, pinching her nipple through the fabric of her dress and bra.

"Not fair. You can touch me, but I can't return the favor?"

"Not this time, Kitten," he murmured against the side of her neck. He ran his tongue down the column of her throat and bit her shoulder at the same time he realized she wasn't wearing panties.

"You forgot something."

Ryler was desperate with need as Pike pressed against her bare ass, her hands cramping as she gripped the back of the couch. The top of the love seat was wood, with dark velvet covering the cushions. When they'd walked into the room initially, Ryler's first thought was taking a black light to every surface, but after getting stripper-fucked by Pike, she was in a fog of lust. The only thing she wanted was his cock in her, and he continued to rub that hard length against her instead, playing with her.

Pike suddenly lifted her into his arms and carried her over to the lounge chair in the corner of the room. When he sat down, he pulled the lever and leaned back slowly until the chair was nearly horizontal. He didn't let her settle over his lap, but hiked her higher until her knees buried into the cushions next to his head. His nose nuzzled against her, and she let out a slow, shaky breath. Pike's hands cradled the globes of her ass, rocking her forward.

"Sit on my face, Kitten. I wanna make you scream."

Ryler shivered as she leaned into his mouth, his tongue flicking across her sensitive flesh. Ryler loved sex, but anything remotely adventurous hadn't been on her radar. Doggie style was about as spicy as she got, but this was hot. He pressed her firmer against his mouth, lips and teeth and tongue creating a tornado of intensity she hadn't been prepared for, and when he sucked her clit into his mouth, flicking it rapidly with his tongue, Ryler exploded with a cry.

When her back arched sharply, Ryler suddenly pitched to the side, and Pike grabbed her right before her head hit the floor.

"Shit, are you alright?" he panted.

"I was amazing until I almost did a face-plant. I thought you had me."

"I wasn't expecting you to jackknife backward when you came." Pike chuckled, pulling her back up until she sprawled on top of him, nearly nose to nose. "I'm sorry I almost dropped you."

Ryler sat up, straddling his lap in the chair. "But you caught me, so in my mind, almost doesn't count."

Pike arched against her, his cock still hard under his briefs. "Did you finish?"

"Kind of. I was in the process when I took a tumble."

"We can't have that," he said, reaching between them. When several of his fingers thrust inside her, stretching her muscles and curling inward against her G-spot, her eyelashes fluttered.

"Pike," she sighed, searching for the top of his boxer briefs and pushing them down. Her breathing hitched as his internal massage quickened and her pussy muscles squeezed. "I want you inside me."

"I don't have a condom, baby," he murmured.

That alone should have sent alarm bells through her brain. She barely knew him, but she was too far gone. Too caught up in his woodsy cologne and his hard body pressed against hers. The way he called her Kitten. The effort he put in to please her, to make sure that she enjoyed herself.

Euphoria spread from her core outward, like a butterfly opening its wings, and she screamed his name, a loud, guttural sound that dissolved into a chant of pleasure.

"Please, now, inside, me."

Pike withdrew his hand, and for a moment, she thought he was going to agree. Instead, he wrapped his arms around her and brought her against him, her cheek pressed against his chest.

"You're not on the pill, remember?" Ryler stiffened, realizing what she'd almost asked him to do, and his hand ran over her hair softly. "As much as I'd love to keep you, I don't want an unplanned pregnancy to be the reason."

Ryler's heart raced as his words sank in and she whispered, "You want to keep me?"

Pike's lips brushed the top of her head. "For as long as I can."

Chapter Thirty-six

On Sunday, Ryler stood at the bottom of the hill watching Pike and Kit race down the slope neck and neck. Ryler could spot Pike's yellow puffer vest from outer space, and although she'd mocked him for it, he'd waved her off.

"At least if something happens, they can always find me," Pike had said.

Alia and Neil had left yesterday, having booked an early flight so she could meet Neil's parents. Ryler was sad that this was the end of an era for *Excursions*, but Kit was staying on as her photographer and asked if he could have the chance to be her producer. Although he didn't have any experience, Kit had been a huge part of *Excursions'* rise to fame. At least she could give him a chance and see.

Ryler had seen Anthony and Delilah show up earlier and watched for them on the bunny hill. Delilah seemed to be having trouble getting up the nerve to go down, and while Ryler's first reaction had been to encourage her and cheer her on, she didn't want to make her more nervous that someone was watching.

Ryler returned her attention to the two men racing down the hill closely, her mind wandering back to last night. After they'd left the den, Ryler had spent the night in Pike's arms after he'd retrieved a blessed condom and finished what they'd started in that dimly lit room, but his words kept coming back to her.

I'd love to keep you.

What would that look like for either of them? Could this be more than a temporary holiday fling?

Ryler shook her head. "No, absolutely not." She hadn't meant to say the words out loud, but it was hard enough to maintain a relationship with someone, let alone a man who could make her body burn with a word or a glance.

Pike was dangerous to her life and heart, and yet, she couldn't bring herself to cut things off between them. She didn't want to.

Kit beat Pike by a foot, and Ryler gave him a slow clap. "Wow. You're supposed to be the guide, so shouldn't that mean you're better than the clients?"

"He's lighter than me. Makes for a faster ride," Pike said.

Ryler laughed. "I don't really think that's true but keep telling yourself that."

Pike gave her a firm smack on the butt. "Smart-ass."

Ryler blushed, her wide eyes flying to Kit at the same time that Pike realized his mistake.

"Shit," he said.

Kit chuckled. "Please, the two of you aren't exactly discreet. I've known for a few days now."

"You have?" Ryler asked. "Why didn't you say anything?"

"I mind my own business." Kit pulled his goggles off and grinned at them. "On that note, I think I'm done for the day. Will you make sure she gets a ride back to the house?"

"Yeah, I will," Pike said.

"I figured as much."

"Wait, where are you off to?" Ryler asked.

"You aren't the only one with a secret," Kit said, gliding away from them.

Pike laughed at Ryler's shocked expression. "He sure told us."

"Who do you think it is?" she asked.

"No clue. I can't remember seeing him talk to anyone."

"I guess we have a mystery to solve, Daphne," Pike teased.

"I prefer Velma." Ryler placed a palm on his chest briefly, this need to touch him becoming a real issue with keeping their relationship a secret. "I'm going to the bathroom. Be back in a bit."

"Okay."

Ryler took off, relieved that there wasn't a line. As she used the facilities, she thought about the last few days of sneaking around and grabbing illicit moments together. Now that Kit knew, they could spend the night together without worrying. Getting up and leaving Pike's arms had become a real chore of late.

How are you going to feel when you leave him forever?

While she'd recorded the first of a two-part Mistletoe episode yesterday, Ryler thought about how different the show was going to look with just her and Kit. She'd thought about putting up another Instagram post but hadn't felt the drive to go anywhere. It was odd, but in a short amount of time, she'd made friends here. Holly, she'd become especially close with, and then there was Pike.

There wasn't a place she'd visited, not even her month-long stay in Ireland, that had ever felt like home. Not until she'd explored this quiet little town. But moving here and getting a place—now that Neil and Alia were taking over her lease—that would be insane, right? She'd have to talk to Pike about staying; what if he flipped out?

Alia and Neil tried to talk her out of moving, offering to share the condo with her so she didn't rush into anything, but from the moment she'd arrived, Mistletoe had felt different. Like coming home. And even if Pike wasn't feeling the same, this is where she wanted to be.

For the first time since she was twelve, Ryler was vulnerable, and she didn't think that she liked it.

Ryler left the bathroom, looking for Pike, and she found him hovering over a prone figure.

"Oh my God, Delilah!" Ryler yelled, gliding over to where they stood, stopping next to Pike. Delilah blinked as if trying to place her, then flashed her a reassuring smile.

"I'm alright." Delilah rapped her knuckles on the side of her helmet. "Anthony made sure I was wearing noggin protection."

"Can you help me get her to that chair?" Anthony asked, pointing to chairs in front of the hot cocoa hut. "I'm going to run back and get my equipment. I kind of threw it in a panic."

"We've got her," Pike said, taking her hands from Anthony's and gliding her over the snow to the closest chair.

"First time snowboarding?" he asked as she plopped into the seat.

"How'd you guess?" She laughed.

He chuckled.

Ryler put a hand on Delilah's shoulder. "Do you want something to drink? Chocolate always makes me feel better."

"A water, please?" Delilah said.

"You got it."

"Not gonna ask me, Kitten?" Pike called out as Ryler got in line.

"I already know what you want," she shot back.

Pike chuckled again, the deep rumble shooting a spark of need in her, and Ryler looked at him, wishing she could come back with his drink and kiss him, admit all the things she needed to get off her chest.

Instead, Ryler blushed and hurried over to the hot cocoa shack, turning her back on them before either one of them saw it. Ryler kept glancing at them conversing as she stood inside, her stomach twisting up when Delilah smiled at Pike. Did he still have feelings for her? Ryler knew his beef with Anthony was about the lies rather than Delilah, but did he regret not getting a chance with her?

Since when did she get jealous?

Since you found someone you wanted to keep.

Oh, shit. How did she let this happen?

Ryler got their drinks and headed back, balancing them in her hands.

"Water for you," Ryler said, handing her a clear cup with a bright pink straw. "Cinnamon roll latte for you," she said, handing Pike his cup. His fingers grazed hers as he took it, his lips curving into a smile, his eyes warm and tender.

"Good memory."

Ryler sat on the edge of Pike's chair before her knees dissolved. Dang, she needed to get control of herself. She sipped from her coffee cup before asking, "What did I miss?"

Neither of them had a chance to answer, as a group approached them, laughing obnoxiously. They stopped a few feet away, a big burly man with dark hair at the front of the pack. The nasty sneer he leveled on Delilah threw Ryler off, as the other woman seemed so sweet. Why would this guy have beef with her?

"Guess you should have stuck with me, huh, Delilah? Not crashing at the bottom of the bunny hill is lesson number one."

Ryler was tempted to throw her lukewarm coffee at him, but Anthony was already doubling back like a raging bull, snapping, "I've got a lesson for you, motherfucker." He dropped his gear, his fists clenched at his side. Ryler stiffened as she realized that he might just throw a fist, and she almost took Delilah's hand to move her out of harm's way.

Pike shook his head with a smile. "You better uncork my boy soon. I think everything being pent up is what's making his fuse so short."

Ryler rolled her eyes and muttered, "Not helping," but Delilah hadn't seemed to hear her, her eyes glued to Anthony.

"Anthony," Delilah called softly, trying to climb to her feet but dropping back down with a whimper.

"Pike's got him," Ryler said, patting Delilah's knee with her free hand, trepidation making her chest tight as she watched Pike step between the two bigger men.

"You two wanna keep slinging insults or settle this like men? Brodie? Anthony?"

"What are you going on about?" Brodie asked.

"You two stop this pissing contest until the winter games. No more making moves on his girl," Pike said, poking Brodie in the chest before pressing Anthony back with both hands, "and you stop trying to get yourself thrown in jail for assault."

Ryler would have laughed at his attempt to hold Anthony back if she wasn't worried about the idiot getting knocked out by mistake.

"What happens after the games?" Trip asked.

"Same bet we made at Brews and Chews," Pike said, keeping a hand on Anthony as he addressed the other men. "Either we have a new boat, or you have new snowmobiles. Somebody's going to be happy."

"I want one more thing if I win," Brodie said, smirking. Ryler caught Pike's resigned expression and waited for the other man to strike the fuse that would send Anthony over the edge.

"No, we agreed," Pike said.

Brodie pointed past Pike's shoulder at Anthony. "That was before this prick humiliated me."

"It's really that easy?" Anthony scoffed, slapping Brodie's hand out of his face.

"Stop it," Delilah said softly.

"What did you say?" Ryler asked Delilah.

Delilah opened her mouth, but nothing came out. Ryler squeezed her knee reassuringly, freezing at the next words out of Brodie's mouth.

"If I win, your girlfriend is going to give me a victory kiss," Brodie said, puckering up at Delilah. Trip and the rest of his crowd laughed and jeered while Anthony tried to go over Pike.

"Over my dead body," Anthony snarled.

Pike wrapped his arms around Anthony's middle, hauling him back with a grunt, and Ryler started to climb to her feet, looking for something she could use to clobber one or all of them.

"Hey, you heard him, Pike." Trip laughed. "Your boy's got a death wish. You should let him go!"

"Um, hello! This isn't the eleven hundreds!" Ryler said loudly. "Consent is sexy, and we don't use women as bargaining chips."

"Whatever, I don't even need a prize," Brodie said, cracking his knuckles like a bully from an eighties movie. "I'm going to enjoy kicking your ass on principle."

"Stop it," Delilah said, getting to her feet unsteadily. She hobbled over to the group of men, and Ryler followed behind, worried the other woman would keel over. "Whatever you guys have going on, grow up and leave me out of it."

Brodie's dark expression dissolved into one of malice. "Hey, no worries. I just wanted to see what it was like to fuck a fat girl."

Delilah reeled back like he'd slapped her, and Ryler clenched her fist. Anthony was right. This dude was a motherfucker.

"Sorry to disappoint," Delilah said dryly, and Ryler wanted to cheer her on.

"As soon as Anthony's done with you, he'll share with the class if you were worth the effort."

Ryler watched Anthony take Delilah's shoulders and moved her out of the way. "Take care of her for me, would ya?"

"Anthony, don't—" Delilah told him, but it was too late. Pike wrapped his arms around Delilah and hauled her backward seconds before Anthony threw the first punch. Pike lost his footing and almost stumbled, but Ryler placed her hands at the small of his back, keeping him upright. Pike looked at her over his shoulder, his expression fierce.

"Both of you get out of here, alright? I'll come get you when it's over."

Ryler nodded, catching Delilah when Pike dropped her out of harm's way after Trip sent a swift upper cut into Anthony's stomach. Pike yelled, "Ah, hell no! No tag teams!"

Pike grabbed Trip and flipped him onto his back. Another of Brodie's crew went after Pike, and he cracked the guy across the jaw, sending him spinning away. Ryler's heart seemed to stop when Pike turned back around with a grin, taunting the remaining men with a come-on motion with both hands. "Step up, kiddies. I've got plenty to go around."

Ryler heard Delilah's groan and noted the disgusted look on her face, wishing she could feel the same. Watching Pike's cocky exuberance shouldn't be turning her on, but as he took out one after another of them, Ryler wanted to whoop and cheer.

Delilah, on the other hand, whimpered, and Ryler followed her line of sight to Anthony, who had Brodie in a headlock, kicking at another goon.

Ryler put her arms around Delilah's shoulders. "How about we go to urgent care while they sort this out?"

Delilah nodded, letting Ryler lead her away.

"Why are men such idiots?" Delilah asked.

"If I had that kind of information, do you think I'd be an assistant? Girl, I'd be president, saving the idiots of the world from themselves."

Chapter Thirty-seven

Hey, man," Anthony said, clearing his throat. "Thanks for jumping in."

Pike rested the back of his head against the wall with his eyes closed, thinking about the hours he could have been wrapped up with Ryler. Taking a hot shower to ease his aching muscles, then convincing her to give him a back rub that he would gladly return with tax. Instead, he was sitting in the Mistletoe police station, in a jail cell with Anthony, all the while sitting next to the smelly, bloody, and beaten idiots they'd been fighting with. Every part of him hurt, especially his face, but at least Anthony was happy with his comradery.

"Sure, what are friends for but to have your back when you start a fight with six guys?" Pike heaped a hefty dose of sarcasm into his tone so his friend wouldn't miss his irritation.

Anthony gave him a hard nudge with his shoulder. "Hey. What's your problem?"

Pike opened his eyes to glare at him. "You're supposed to be the smart, level-headed guy in this friendship. Instead, you're betting our equipment and getting into fights that lead to us sitting in a jail cell facing possible charges. It's like you've been replaced by a pod person!"

"So, because you have me to curb your spending, you think volunteering us for everything is fine because I'll create a budget?" Anthony snapped. "News flash, sometimes the budget is too much."

"Uh-oh. I think the lovers next door are fighting," Trip said, earning a chuckle from a few of his friends."

"Will you shut the fuck up?" Pike hollered.

"Why don't you make me, Lucky the Leprechaun?"

"I thought I already did," Pike said, pointing to his mouth. "Nice lip, Trip. Looks like it split open again."

Trip touched his fat lip, which had split open and started oozing blood. "You'll pay for that later."

"Stop your whining, you big boobs!" Officer Wren barked from the other room, the stomp of her boots growing louder before she cleared the hallway and stood with her hands on her hips, glaring at them. Her blond hair was pulled back in that severe bun that reminded Pike of an angry librarian instead of an officer of the law.

"If you weren't fighting like a bunch of middle schoolers," she said, her tone acidic, "you wouldn't be hurting so damn bad."

Pike laughed. "You tell them, Wren."

"I'm talking to you, too, ya idjit," she snapped, approaching their cell, her gaze focused on Anthony before swinging to Pike. "You are supposed to be leaders in this community. Leaders control their damn tempers."

Pike shrugged. "We tried to take the high road, but he started talking shit about Anthony's lady."

"They're just words," Officer Wren said, lowering her voice to add, "and he's dim-witted anyway."

Brodie hollered, "Hey!"

"Hey yourself," Wren said without turning Brodie's way. Her entire focus was on Anthony, who shuffled his feet under her disapproving gaze. "Why would you care what he thinks? Do you like the guy? Respect his opinion?"

"No," Anthony said.

"He's a douchebag," Pike added.

Brodie smacked the bars with his hands. "I am sitting right here!"

"Yeah, we can see you." Pike grinned at Wren, pain erupting from his eyeball, and he groaned. "Admit it. The shiner makes me look tough, huh?"

"Idjit," Wren muttered again, turning her back on him and disappearing back down the hall.

"I think Officer Wren likes me," Pike said.

Anthony shook his head. "I think Officer Wren wants to take us all out back and tase us. Can't really blame her."

"What are you talking about? We are the victims here. Innocently making sure your girlfriend was okay and then, blam! They walk up on us and start talking shit."

"It was stupid of me to let that dick get to me," Anthony said.

"So, why did you?" Pike asked.

Anthony closed his eyes. "I guess I've just been on edge. Stressed out."

"I'm sure you have been," Pike said, every muscle protesting as he sat on the bench. "And sounds like I've made things worse. But I think you went off on Brodie because he was saying hurtful things to Delilah."

"Obviously, Pike," Anthony said. "Any man would have reacted to a woman being verbally attacked."

"But only a man in love would have pummeled the idiot the way you did."

Anthony stiffened, silence stretching between them. Did he really not see how in love he was with Delilah Gill?

Brodie muttered, "I think I'm going to puke."

"God, can you ever just keep your mouth shut? Or do you have to hear yourself talk to pretend you're relevant?" Pike asked.

"Watch yourself, Pike. You're no better than me."

"Actually, I am. I don't alienate women when they reject me or tear them down. I accept the rejection with dignity. Walking around like you don't care if people think you're the biggest douche in the world is not a good look for you."

"Fuck you," Brodie said.

"Witty retort." Pike turned his back on the other man and sighed.

Anthony wiped a hand over his face. "I hope Nick gets here soon."

Pike nodded. "I am ready to blow this Popsicle stand." He sat forward, his forearms resting on his legs. "I'm sorry, man. I know I can be moronic, and I need to learn to slow down and ask you before I agree to things for the business. I just get excited, and I'm still getting used to having a partner."

Anthony smirked. "Me, too. I did a lot of research before we got into this, and there were a lot of people saying that going into business ruined friendships for them. I don't want that for us."

"Agreed." Pike got up, holding out a hand to him. "Forgive me?"

Anthony took his hand and pulled him in for a hard hug. "Always."

"Someone get these assholes out of here before I lose my cookies?" Trip hollered, with Brodie and the rest of their friends shouting in agreement.

Wren appeared through the hallway again, jingling a set of keys. "Your wish is my command." Wren unlocked Anthony and Pike's cell. "It's your lucky day, boys. You've been sprung."

"What about us?" Brodie asked.

"Can I call my father again?" Trip bellowed.

"I'm sure it will be any minute now," Wren said, smirking. Anthony and Pike picked their jackets up off the bench and followed her. Once they passed through the hall, she whispered, "You've got a ten-minute head start before I release the goon squad."

"Thanks, Wren," Anthony said.

Wren pointed at each of them in turn. "You can thank me by staying out of trouble. You're lucky no one wanted to press charges."

Pike's laughter died when he saw Anthony's expression fall and followed his line of sight to Delilah and Ryler standing next to Officer Wren's desk, wearing identical frowns. Pike wanted to rush Ryler and wrap his arms around her, grateful that she'd shown up after watching him throw down in a brawl, but he couldn't blow their ruse with anyone else.

"Hey, you don't get to give me that look," Pike said, pointing at Ryler. "You ain't my girlfriend."

"Thank God for that." She laughed, but her eyes scanned his face, worry heavy in those beautiful brown orbs. "No man of mine would get into a fight wearing snow pants." Ryler shot Delilah an apologetic smile. "No offense."

"None taken." Delilah took a step closer to Anthony and reached up, her hand hovering over his cheek; it was bruised and swollen. Pike could only imagine what a mess he looked like to Ryler.

"You look terrible," Delilah said.

Anthony tried to smile, but it split his swollen lip open. "I know, but really, you should see the other guys."

Delilah shook her head, but Pike saw her small smile, and relief flooded him. After all that Delilah and Anthony had been through, he'd hate to see this be a wrench between them.

"I have your truck outside," Delilah said.

"You're all good to go," Wren said. "And I wouldn't worry too much about those idiots changing their minds about pressing charges. I think they're too ashamed that the two of you kicked all six of their asses."

"You're good people, Wren," Anthony said with a wink. "Don't let anyone tell you differently."

Wren's cheeks flushed unexpectedly, and she scoffed. "Get them out of here."

Anthony and Delilah walked ahead of them out of the police station, conversing quietly.

Pike took a step closer to Ryler, his hand brushing hers.

"Are you okay?" she asked quietly, and Pike could have sworn her voice trembled.

"Yeah, Kitten. Just a little banged up."

Delilah called over her shoulder to Ryler, "Do you have Pike?"

"Yeah, I'll take him home," Ryler said, rolling her eyes. "He's so tore back, I'm afraid he might pass out if I made him walk."

Pike snorted, rounding to the passenger side of the rental car. "Don't act like I'm a chore to be around, when we both know I'm a fucking delight."

"You're more like a de-blegh," she said, making a gagging sound.

"That's mature," Pike deadpanned.

"Says the man who looks like he went five rounds with a badger." Ryler waved at Delilah and Anthony before climbing into the driver's side, hitting the unlock button.

Pike got in, watching her buckle up. "This is the second time you've rescued me after having a spot of bad luck."

"I wouldn't call this bad luck. More like a poor decision."

"Hey now, I am the injured party here. I was just protecting my friend," he said.

"I know," she agreed, backing the car out of the space. "Plus, watching how scrappy you are in a fight was pretty hot. You should join the WWE."

Pike shook his head, wincing at the shooting pain in his head. "If I never get into another fight, I'll be a happy guy."

Ryler reached out, placing a hand on his knee. "In all seriousness, do I need to stop at the store and get anything for you? Pain meds? Ice pack?"

"I have all that, but I can honestly say, while I was sitting in that cell, all I could think about was how being with you would make me feel a hell of a lot better."

"Are you asking me to stay and take care of you, Pike?" she asked softly.

Pike knew this was more than what any casual relationship would require, but he couldn't help it. He wanted her with him, all the time. He needed her.

"Yes, that's what I'm asking."

"Then I'll stay."

Pike only wished she meant forever.

Fuck, when did you go and fall in love with Ryler Colby?

Chapter Thirty-eight

Ryler stepped out of the rental car, lifting the skirt of the floor-length dress she'd purchased from Amazon on Monday in anticipation for the bachelor auction. The dress was a sequined black-to-silver ombre, off the shoulder with a sweetheart neckline, which showed off her smooth shoulders and the tops of her breasts. Holly had helped her twist and braid her hair back, leaving small strands to frame her face, while the rest of her hair was curled around her shoulders. She'd artfully applied her makeup, highlighting her eyes and lips, and she couldn't wait to see Pike's face. If he thought the other dress was going to kill him, he would pass out when he saw this one.

And what was underneath.

Kit got out of the passenger side, adjusting his tie. "How do I look?"

"Very handsome, but I am still shocked Holly asked you to join the bachelor auction."

"Just because I don't live here doesn't mean I can't be a part of it. I'm not leaving until Christmas. Besides, it's for charity."

Ryler laughed. "Well, you better hurry. I think the bachelors were supposed to be here half an hour ago."

"I thought I'd at least make sure you got inside safely. Those heels look deadly," Kit said, holding out his hand to her.

Ryler took it and let Kit lead her into the community center. Holly greeted them with a delighted smile. "Ryler, you look fantastic."

"Thank you."

"Kit, they are waiting for you. Thank you for doing this."

"No problem. Where should I go?"

"Just head up the stairs to the left and disappear through that door," Holly said.

Ryler took a program and looked around the room at the linen-covered tables, the twinkling lights hung from the ceiling, and the smartly dressed people mingling together. She didn't see Pike, which meant he was probably backstage already. She had no idea how much bachelors usually cost at these things, but she had a stack of cash burning a hole in her purse. Of course, would Pike want her to bid on him if they were keeping things on the down-low?

Unfortunately, the thought of letting another woman bid and win him turned her stomach, so she would take his irritation if it came to that.

"Are you okay?" Holly asked.

"Yeah, I'm just not sure what to do next."

"If you plan on bidding for one of the bachelors, you need to register and get a paddle number. If you're just here to have fun, you can take a seat at one of the tables, and dinner will be served shortly."

"Thanks," Ryler said, heading over to the table and registering. She got the number twenty-three. Ryler took a seat at a table at the edge of the room, watching people as they engaged in exuberant debate on each man's attributes, how good the food was, and how much they had to spend to take home one of the men being auctioned off.

A waiter filled her water glass and asked for her menu card. Ryler filled it out quickly, choosing the pasta dish and an iced tea.

"Ladies and Gentlemen," Merry greeted the room from onstage, a black wireless mic in her hand. She wore a long black dress that hid her adorable baby bump until she turned to the side. "Please find a seat and get ready for an evening of charity, conversation, and Mistletoe's finest bachelors!" The room erupted with excited screams, and Ryler picked up her water glass, taking a healthy drink as several women made their way over and sat at her table. They smiled at her, and a few even introduced themselves, making friendly conversation, but they were soon pulled back into their own anticipation for who would be the first bachelor onstage.

The waiter came back with a side salad and Ryler's pasta, while another filled her second glass with tea. Ryler thanked them and took a bite of her pasta, the creamy sauce delightfully delicious.

The lights flickered overhead, and music exploded from the speakers, signaling the start of the show, and everyone who was still standing started moving at once, scrambling to find their seats. Merry came back on the mic, waving at the crowd. "Thank you, everyone. This evening, I have the pleasure of introducing you to some of Mistletoe's finest specimens of the male species. Handsome. Hardworking. Intelligent. Athletic?" The last was said with a playfully suggestive tone, and the crowd woo-hooed, only quieting down when Merry continued. "Remember that every bachelor is a prize and that we are raising money for our children and our community, so dig deep and bid hard. Are you ready?"

The crowd erupted with wild hoots and hollers until Merry read the first name. "Sam Griffin, come on out. Sam is a thirty-eight-year-old tattoo artist with ambitions to own a shop of his own again. He is over six feet with dreamy eyes and tattoos in all the right places. Shall we start the bidding at twenty-five dollars?"

"Twenty-five."

"Thirty!"

"Forty!"

The aggressive bidding continued as Ryler enjoyed her meal, not at all surprised by the amount Sam sold for. He was an attractive man, after all, and his bad-boy allure was appealing to some.

Merry held up the next card and read from it. "Anthony is a thirty-one-year-old local business owner, who stands six foot three in his bare feet. In his spare time, he likes to partake in outdoor activities like quad-riding, snowmobiling, or waterskiing, and spending time with his beautiful girlfriend, Delilah."

Ryler looked around the room, finally spotting Delilah with her mouth hanging open, and Ryler couldn't believe she was surprised. It was incredibly obvious that Anthony was head over heels for her.

"As Anthony is in a serious relationship, he does not feel comfortable being auctioned off," Merry said, ignoring the boos and hisses from the crowd. "However, his company, Adventures in Mistletoe, has agreed to donate generously. Not to mention his bachelor replacement is a young, virile firefighter, who is new to Mistletoe and graciously donated himself tonight! Please give a big round of applause for Bladen Moon!"

After Bladen got picked up, Merry clapped along with the crowd as he exited the stage and then spoke into the mic. "It is my pleasure to announce our celebrity guest, who is visiting Mistletoe as part of the *Excursions* podcast. He is a wizard with a camera and says his dream date is to explore the beauty in nature. Give it up for Kit Park!"

Ryler clapped loudly, whistling around her fingers as Kit stepped onstage.

"Shall we start the bidding at thirty dollars?"

A paddle went up in the crowd, and Ryler strained to see who it was. Another paddle popped up as Merry called out each new dollar amount, until the other bidder gave up at one hundred and thirty-five dollars.

"Sold, to Ricki."

Ryler started as she watched the tall bartender head toward the stage to greet her newly acquired bachelor. Kit climbed down the stairs to join her, and the two embraced with a familiarity Ryler hadn't expected. Suddenly, everything clicked into place.

"Why, you sly dog," Ryler said, watching Ricki pay and then the two of them head out the front door with their arms wrapped around each other's waists. Two of the women at her table shot her strange looks, and she grinned sheepishly. "He's a friend of mine."

"Next, I am happy to present Pike Sutton." Hundreds of cheers exploded when Pike stepped onto the stage in a tux and green bow tie, spinning across the platform. "Pike is a local business owner who enjoys the great outdoors and dancing with the right woman. Who will start the bidding at twenty-five dollars?"

Before Ryler could raise her paddle, someone shouted, "Twenty-five."

"Thirty," another woman yelled.

"Thirty-five."

"Forty!" Ryler said, waving her paddle.

"Forty-five," the woman across from her said loudly, flashing the number six in the air. Bidding on Pike was as breakneck as Sam, and Ryler was going to have to say something to him about how ridiculous his lack of confidence was. Especially when the bidding went way over a hundred.

"One hundred and sixty," Ryler called out.

"One seventy!"

Ryler's jaw clenched as more women joined in, and when the bidding started slowing around three hundred, Ryler raised her paddle. "Four hundred dollars!"

"Do I hear four ten," Merry asked, but the room remained silent. "Four hundred going once. Going twice. Sold to the lady in the sequin dress, number twenty-three."

Ryler put her fork down, forgetting about the rest of her meal as she went to claim her prize. When Pike met her at the bottom of the stairs, he grinned. "I think people are going to get the impression you might like me, Ryler Colby."

"Or that I really wanted to donate to charity." Ryler went to the table and paid for Pike. "Are you upset that someone else didn't win?"

"Why are you asking stupid questions," he asked, leaning over to place a soft kiss on the skin of her neck. "I'm going home with the most beautiful woman in the room. That dress is sure something, Ryler, and I can't wait to see it on the floor of my bedroom."

Ryler looked up into his roguish expression, his eye and cheek still slightly bruised from the fight, and she grinned. "First, I believe you owe me another excursion. That is what I paid for, isn't it? Your time and expertise."

Pike pressed his mouth against her ear and whispered, "How about we skip the excursion, and you let me spend all night showing you some of my other talents?"

"You're sounding a little like a male hooker, sir," Ryler teased.

"Whoa now, I was going to teach you some dance moves. What were you thinking about, dirty girl?"

Ryler laughed. "Naked dance moves."

Pike kissed her temple. "Your wish is my command."

Chapter Thirty-nine

Ryler walked up to Delilah with a white coffee cup in her hand and stopped alongside her. "Hmmm, this better not be boring, or I'm going to chuck a snowball at Pike's head."

Delilah laughed. "I guess if it is, they won't have another one next year."

"Oof, don't put that out into the universe. I actually want them to do well."

Delilah shot Ryler a curious glance. "I do, too, but I'm surprised you feel that way. I thought you and Pike hated each other."

"'Hate' is such a strong word," Ryler said, taking a sip of her coffee. "I prefer to think of it as mild dislike with a friendly dose of animosity."

Delilah shook her head. "Whatever you say."

"Everyone, get ready to cheer on your favorite holiday trio. The first team to complete the final task wins! On your mark. Get set." A loud bang sounded in the distance, and Ryler kept her eyes peeled on the crest of the hill, watching for a flurry of motion.

"If he comes in last, I'm never letting him live it down," Ryler said.

"Look!" Delilah pointed to a redhead on a blue sled, zipping down the hill. She bumped Ryler with her hip. "I guess you can't torment him now, huh?"

"Don't think that doesn't piss me off," Ryler said with no real heat. What she really wanted to do was scream at the top of her lungs and cheer Pike's name, but they'd already sent the gossip mills spinning with their exit at the auction. No way was she causing any more drama.

Holly came back with Declan and Sam in tow, asking, "How are they doing?"

"Pike just handed off the bag of goods to Nick, who has to put on skis."

"Who came up with this idiocy?" Sam asked.

Ryler glared at the pretty boy and bent over, forming a ball of icy snow in her hands. The snowball caught him on the side of the head, and he frowned at Ryler. "Did you just nail me with a snowball, girl I barely know?"

"Why would I hit a stranger with a snowball? That would be really odd."

"Go Nick!" Delilah yelled.

Holly's employee, Erica, returned with a corndog in one hand and a churro in the other, all smiles until Sam tried to take a bite.

"Hey now, get your own! You ain't pretty enough to share my food with."

Ryler was ready to scream at all of them to shut up as she watched Nick ski down the road, stopping every ten feet or so and picking something up. Someone in an orange parka was gaining on him.

"You can see them?" Erica asked.

"Barely," Delilah said, pointing. "I'm watching between a couple trees."

"Go, go, go!" Holly cheered, her voice fading as she squinted. "Wait, is that Anthony in an inflatable reindeer costume?"

"That had to be Pike's idea," Delilah said.

"I think it's genius," Ryler said, her smile widening as Nick slipped and slid, his puffy body shaking.

Nick came around the corner and hopped up onto the lawn toward Anthony. Once Nick was within arm's reach, Anthony grabbed the bag from his hand and took off running toward the pile of snow just before the finish line, the inflatable suit several inches too short on him. Another reindeer was bouncing up and down like a frog behind him, and when they hit the snow-covered lawn of the park, they were neck and floppy neck. Anthony rolled each ball of his snowman into position and started removing items from bags. The inflatable suit looked awkward, and by the sound of his curses, it was making the situation more difficult.

"Isn't that the jerk from the ski slope?" Ryler asked, pointing at Brodie when he skidded across the snow-covered ground.

"Yes, it is," Delilah said.

Brodie started picking up the snowballs to set them one on top of the other, but they kept rolling off. Finally, he looked over at Anthony and seemed to realize he was packing snow around each section to keep them in place, because he followed his lead. Brodie started gaining ground on Anthony, and Ryler heard Delilah whisper, "Come on, Anthony," right before he stood up with his hands in the air and yelled, "Finished!"

The last man hadn't even made it to the snowman section yet when he heard Anthony, and he waddled off in a huff.

Brodie started bitching and hollering about how Anthony must have practiced the course and had an unfair advantage since he created it. Anthony said something about Brodie being a sore loser, and Brodie stood up and stomped away, yelling over his shoulder, "I'll see you on the ice."

"I know! I set up the match!" Anthony called after him.

Ryler stood on her tiptoes, searching the distance for Pike.

"Anthony!" Delilah called, and the rest of the people around her, even Sam, who wasn't exactly an enthusiastic guy, started cheering and hollering. Anthony spun their way in the blow-up costume and spotted them, waving back with a grin.

"I wonder how he pulled the short straw," Sam asked.

Anthony jogged over to them, the material of the reindeer suit creating a high-pitched noise. Delilah giggled when he wrapped his arm around her, burying her in the material, and Ryler's chest squeezed. She wanted her guy, but he was slower than molasses—

Whoa, back up, "your guy"?

Anthony released Delilah and fiddled around with something inside the suit until the low hum of the fan stopped. The material deflated around him, creating a brown, wrinkled mess, and he spun around, giving her his back. "Could you get me out of this thing before Sam and Declan start slinging zingers my way?"

"Wouldn't dream of it, buddy," Declan said, coughing to cover a laugh.

Delilah pulled down the zipper and held it open while he stepped out. He was wearing a blue thermal shirt and jeans, his hair damp and plastered in every direction. He looked like an adorable mess, and she reached up, waving him down so she could fix his dark hair.

Anthony obliged her, their noses nearly touching as she ran her fingers through his hair and tried to create some semblance of style.

"I'm going to be playing hockey in an hour, love. No sense in wasting your time when I'm going to just mess it up again."

Delilah gave up with a sigh. "Fine, but the mussed hair is supposed to be for my eyes only when you first wake up."

"This is different hair," he said, pointing at his crown. "This is 'I just got done running in an inflatable reindeer suit' hair versus 'waking up next to my beautiful woman' hair."

"My God, are they always like this?" Sam asked.

"Worse," Holly joked.

"Gross," he said, walking away from them without another word.

"See, if that had been you," Holly said, addressing Declan, "I would have chased you down for being rude, but that is only because I love you and care about what other people think about you."

"So, Sam can be an ass and get away with it, but I can't because you love me?" Declan asked.

"Exactly."

Declan shrugged. "Makes sense."

"I'm going to hike my butt across the park and settle up with the redhead," Ryler grumbled.

"Settle up?" Delilah called after her retreating back.

Ryler turned to face her, walking backward. "I may have bet against him, and now I have to pay the piper."

"I'll see you when I get back," Delilah said, and Ryler waved in response.

When she reached the sidewalk along the main street, Ryler spotted Pike jogging across the street with a wide grin on his face. "What did you think? Pretty awesome, right?"

"It certainly was." Ryler wrapped her arms around Pike's neck. "When do you want to collect your winnings?"

"After the hockey game. You're coming to watch, right?"

"I wouldn't miss it for the world."

Chapter Forty

I still can't believe we lost," Pike grumbled for the millionth time. It was Christmas Eve, and still he kept bringing up the winter games and the horrible hockey game. Luckily, they hadn't had to honor that stupid bet and give up their snowmobiles.

However, Ryler did have to follow through with putting on the reindeer blow-up and giving Pike a private dance, all because she'd jokingly bet against his team. At least the consolation sex had been worth it.

"I thought you were going to your parents' tonight?" Ryler said, playing with a strand of his hair. They sat on the couch, snuggling as *How the Grinch Stole Christmas* played on the television. Kit was in his bedroom, talking to his parents about missing Christmas Eve with them, but he'd be home tomorrow. And Ryler, well, she would be spending the holiday with Neil and Alia, far away from Mistletoe and Pike.

The thought of leaving created a hollow sensation in the pit of her stomach, and she hated that after vowing to say exactly what she was thinking, Ryler was chickening out.

"I am going to my parents', but I kind of thought you might like to come with me."

"Visiting parents?" Ryler's heart raced, emotions warring inside her. "That sounds like something a girlfriend would do, not the woman you're casually hooking up with."

Was Pike trying to tell her that he wanted more?

"I was thinking," he said, running his hand over her thigh, which was curved over his lap, "that maybe when you get done after your next destination you could come back here and visit. Stay with me and Jo."

Her hopes deflated at the word *visit*. Pike didn't want her to come back and build a relationship. He wanted a situationship, and while that had worked for her in the past, it couldn't with him. "I would go with you tonight, but I have to pack. Kit and I are taking off early to make our flight in Boise," Ryler said, noting his disappointment. Ryler leaned in and kissed him, wanting to wipe away any discomfort. This was their last night together, and if he needed to leave for his parents', time was running short.

The kiss deepened naturally, as it always did between them, and before she knew it, Pike got up from the couch and carried her into the bedroom. Her suitcase was open in the corner with half her clothes already laundered and neatly folded inside, but she didn't want to focus on that. Ryler wanted to be with Pike, to hold him and melt into him one more time.

He closed the door, and they both stripped off their clothes silently, watching each other from a few feet away. His blue eyes were heavy, and she opened her mouth, ready to tell him everything that had been building inside her since their first kiss, but if she told him now and he rejected her love, they wouldn't have this. Their last time.

Pike reached for her, gloriously naked and stunningly beautiful, and they fell across the bed in a tangle of legs and arms. The usual passionate, hurried caresses and kisses had been replaced by slow, searching touches and butterfly-soft brushings of lips across skin. Tears pricked Ryler's eyes when Pike leaned over her, his hand between her legs, and he never took his eyes from her face as he caressed her, circling her clit with strokes learned through complete trust. Despite their short amount of time together, Ryler trusted Pike with her body.

If only she could be sure of his heart.

As she crested, rocking against his fingers with a sharp, joyful cry, Pike dipped down and covered her mouth with his. His tongue circled hers in lazy waves before removing his hand and breaking their kiss with a groan.

"I didn't expect this to be the last time. I-I'm not prepared."

Ryler knew what he was saying, but nothing was going to stop her from having this moment with him. This memory, which was going to hold her, because who knew if she'd ever love anyone as much as Ryler loved Pike Sutton.

She reached for him, tugging him over her body, and moved her hands up and down the length of his muscular back.

"I understand, and I still want this. I want you. All of you."

As Pike sank into her, Ryler's eyes fluttered closed, memorizing his heat, the way her body stretched around his girth. She vowed to remember his mouth on her neck and the sweet sound of her name on his lips as he thrust into her slowly, long strokes that teased her to the point of madness. Ryler's fingers massaged his shoulders when his motions quickened, his hips pumping against hers, and the pressure built in her core, rising with every stroke until she quaked beneath him, murmuring her love too low for him to hear, smothering her confession against the skin of his shoulder. Pike jerked against her, shouting her name, and she smiled, clenching her eyes shut against the tears escaping.

"Ryler, I'm sorry. I shouldn't have—"

"Shh," she said, opening her eyes and smiling up into his worried gaze. "I'm crying because that was amazing, not because I regret anything."

"Oh," he said, dropping his head to her shoulder with a muffled, "Thank God."

Ryler giggled. "I picked up the pill after our first time together. So I don't want you to worry that I'm trying to trap you or anything."

Pike stiffened, jerking back to stare down at her. "I wasn't thinking that."

"Sorry. I wasn't trying to offend you."

"Would you stop apologizing?" Pike snapped, rolling away from her and sitting on the edge of the bed with his back to her.

Ryler sat up and scooted over to him, laying her cheek on his back. "I had a lot of fun with you, Pike. Thanks for inviting us here."

Pike's laugh had a bitter edge. "I'm glad you came."

You don't sound glad.

Suddenly, he turned and pulled her into his arms, holding her on his lap. When he kissed her, locking his arms around her as if afraid to let her go, Ryler tangled her hands in his hair.

When he pulled away, she was ready to take back everything and agree to anything he asked, but that wasn't fair. Not with how much she cared for him.

"You'll call?" Pike asked, his forehead pressed to hers. "We can still keep in touch, right?"

"Sure, I'll call you." Ryler extracted herself from his embrace and climbed to her feet. "We'll still be friends."

Ryler thought he flinched as he stood. "Yeah, friends."

They dressed as quietly as they'd stripped, Ryler's mind heavy with everything she wanted to say but was too scared to. She led him out the door and said good night again. When she shut the door after him, she almost crumpled into a heap on the floor. Kit's door opened, and he came around the corner, watching her emotional meltdown grimly.

"You know we could stay, right?" Kit asked, leaning against the wall. "Come back after the new year and not renew our sponsor contracts. Hang out in the cold, snowy north and enjoy being with people who make us happy?"

Ryler laughed. "Let me guess. Ricki."

"Yes."

"What if they don't want that, though? What if we stay, and after a few weeks or even months, they decide they made a mistake picking us?" Ryler wiped a tear from her cheek.

"Then we move on but know we tried."

Ryler pushed off the door and headed to the bedroom. "We need to pack."

"I'm already done, but while you stuff your clothes into a suitcase, think about what I said."

Ryler closed the door behind her and sat on the bed, picking her phone off the side table. Instinctively, she called Alia, but when she didn't answer, Ryler tapped on Neil's contact.

He picked up on the second ring.

"Ryls? You alright?"

His deep voice, so filled with worry, reminded her why he'd always been her second-in-command. Her best friend and partner.

"No, but I wanted to see what you and Alia were up to. Have you told your parents yet?"

"Yes, and funny enough, they took it really well. We were going to head down and spend a week with them after we pick you up from the airport."

Oh goodie, spending the holidays with my cousin, her boyfriend, and his parents. It didn't matter that Ryler had spent plenty of holidays with Neil's parents. This time, she wouldn't just be the friend who had nowhere else to go, but the third wheel.

"Ryler? Are you going to tell me what's going on with you and the outdoorsman, or am I going to have to guess?"

Ryler sniffled into the phone. "I think . . . I mean, I love him."

"Yes, I got the feeling that was what this sad phone call was about. So what's the issue? He seemed to feel the same way."

"He doesn't though. He asked if I wanted to visit and stay with him and Jo when I was on break."

"Who is Jo?" Neil asked.

"His dog."

"That doesn't sound like a bad thing. He's respecting your job but asking to be a part of your life," Neil said.

"No, he's suggesting a situationship, and that is the last thing I want from him."

"Did you tell him that?" Neil asked.

"No."

"And why not?"

"Because if he doesn't feel the same way I do, then I don't want to know."

"I will never understand how someone so smart could be such an idiot," Neil muttered.

"Excuse me?" Ryler gasped.

"You would rather say goodbye to the man you love and get on a plane tomorrow than take a leap of faith and tell him the truth?" Neil huffed into the phone. "You're a scared little chicken! Scared of owning the podcast, scared of embracing everything that is great about you, and furthermore, you are scared of professing your love for a man who, frankly, I want to punch in the face, but who is so obviously gone for you I will forgive him for being an unbearable asshat at times."

Ryler choked out a laugh. "He really isn't an asshat. I think he's just jealous of you."

"As he should be, for I am taller and flyer than he will ever be, but let's focus on the facts. You took a chance on bringing me with you and seeing where a busted-up van could take us. You chased your dreams with your whole heart. Where is that girl now? If you want him, tell him. Otherwise, when you get on that plane tomorrow, you'd better not act like a mopey sack, because you will have only brought it on yourself."

"While I really want to hit you with something, I've missed these talks."

"Me, too."

"Thanks for listening, Neil. It means a lot after everything."

"I'll always be your friend, Ryler. No matter what or who we're with, that's not going to change. But if that idiot does not immediately sweep you up and run away with you, I might find a mountain to shove him off of."

"I appreciate the sentiment. Hug my cousin for me. Where is she, by the way?"

"Currently pouting in the bathroom," Neil said, his voice exhausted.

"Why?"

"Because I got the wrong brand of cookie dough ice cream."

Ryler laughed. "Oh, Neil."

"Wish me luck?" he deadpanned.

"You don't need luck. You're Neil."

"Thanks for reminding me. Whatever you decide, own it and be happy. Because if you lose your spark because of him, I'll—"

"I get it. He's toast."

Ryler said goodbye, and as soon as she hung up, she called out for Kit. He poked his head in and said, "Yeah?"

"Feel like doing a little podcasting?"

Kit grinned. "Sure. Who needs sleep? Let's work a Christmas miracle."

Chapter Forty-one

Pike had picked up Jo from his apartment and taken her over to his parents' for a visit. After imbibing one too many glasses of his mother's deadly eggnog, Pike crashed in his parents' guest room.

When he woke up the following morning to his mother singing *We Wish You a Merry Christmas*, Pike was aware of two things. It was Christmas, and according to the time on his bedside alarm clock, Ryler was already gone.

Pike squeezed his eyes shut, ignoring Jo's squirms against his side. Although he knew she probably had to pee, she seemed to sense his mood and hadn't started whining yet. Pike couldn't get last night with Ryler out of his mind, and he kicked himself over and over for not speaking up. For not telling her that he wanted her to stay with him, forever. He'd settle for being the guy at home waiting for her to return from every trip if that's what she needed, but he wanted more. Pike wanted everything she could give and then some.

Only when he was faced with her beautiful brown eyes and her impending departure, Pike couldn't do it. He couldn't ask her to choose between the podcast she'd worked so hard for and him. Pike was a guy Ryler had known less than a month. How could he ask her to wager her future on such a short acquaintance?

There was a knock on the bedroom door, and he called out, "Yeah?"

His mom poked her head in. "Merry Christmas, honey. Do you want me to take Jo out so you can sleep?"

Pike sat up and picked the puppy up in his arms as he slid off the bed. "Nah, I got her. Thanks, though." Pike paused to kiss her cheek as he passed. "Merry Christmas, Mom."

"I'll be in the kitchen making breakfast when you're done outside."

Pike slipped on his boots and his jacket by the front door before he harnessed Jo up. He grabbed his phone from the wireless charger next to his dad's chair and walked out, squinting against the bright morning sun. It had snowed a little last night, and the ground sparkled.

He let Jo down on his parents' front lawn and scrolled through his phone, noting the merry Christmas texts already coming through and the social media tags. He clicked on an Instagram mention and found that Ryler had posted several times from the *Excursions* page. Pike tapped the first reel and watched Ryler stare into the camera. She wore light makeup and a red, cowl-neck sweater, her waves loose around her shoulders.

"I apologize that my Christmas gift to all of you this year is exposing a lie. I wish it were raindrops on roses or whiskers on kittens, but it's that I am human. I make mistakes, and I've been scared to own them until now."

Ryler took a deep breath, staring into the camera with those brown doe eyes. "My name is Ryler Colby, and I'm the host of *Excursions*. My cousin, Alia, agreed to be the face of my podcast because I was scared that the internet wouldn't be kind to someone like me. Someone so incredibly ordinary, who just loved to travel and wanted to share her passion with the world.

"Only, I've spent the last few weeks somewhere that to the rest of the world may view as ordinary to the extreme, but being there breathed life back into my soul. I realized that my passion had gotten lost in the beaches and the long plane rides. I'd let myself be controlled by others, by their money and influence, instead of being confident in what made *Excursions* such a blast to record in the first place: the destinations in America that no one else was exploring. Just me and my producer in a van, traveling around the U.S. and discovering hidden gems.

"That's what *Excursions* started as, and in the new year, we'll be going back to our roots, starting with a sneak peek of our newest episode, Adventures in Mistletoe. This little mountain town stole my heart, not just with its beautiful, craggy mountains and snow-covered trees, but with the people who pour their hearts and souls into making the holidays special. To the events that bring joy to people, especially the extravagant lights display at Evergreen Circle. And to the men at

Adventures in Mistletoe, who take tourists out to explore all the fun that Mistletoe has to offer, who put on one heck of a winter games this year, including blow-up reindeer races, I want to thank you. You reminded me what made this podcast great."

Jo scratched at Pike's leg, and he stooped to pick her up without looking away from the screen, swiping to the last reel he was tagged in.

"My final thought before I leave you this Christmas morning is don't go into the new year with fears and regrets. I told myself I was going to start saying what I mean. I was going to be honest and aware of myself, but I've already failed to follow through. You see, I didn't just fall in love with the town of Mistletoe, but also the man who brought me there." Pike sucked in a breath, his heart pounding so loudly he almost missed her next few words. "Pike Sutton, I love you. I don't want to just come back and visit you. I want you to be my home. The place I belong, which is something I've been missing for nearly twenty years, but I found it with you. So, if you feel the same way, just drop a comment below. I'll be waiting."

Pike continued to walk as he scrolled, but when he stepped onto the sidewalk, his foot caught a patch of ice that sent him and Jo flying backward. He managed to bear the brunt of the fall, but his phone had sailed out of his hand.

"Fucking smooth, Pike," he groaned, stretching away from Jo's seeking tongue. Pike realized when he stood up that not only had his phone landed in the only yellow snow in the yard but that his butt was covered in Jo's number two.

"Mom!" Pike yelled. Although he should have been concerned about waking up the neighbors, he had more pressing issues. He shuffled across the lawn to retrieve his phone, wiping the pee-soaked snow off on his jacket.

His mom and dad burst onto the porch, talking at once.

"Are you alright?"

"What's all the hollering about?" his dad asked.

"Sorry, but I slipped on some ice and I have shit on my back and my phone landed in pee. Do you have some clothes I can change into and maybe a towel for my phone? I really need to use it."

"Oh, yuck! Here, give me Jo," his mom said, coming down the stairs and holding her arms out. "I'll be back in a minute with a towel and some clothes."

When his mom disappeared inside, his dad grunted, "Hopefully you didn't wake up all the neighbors. I'd hate for them to get a look at your goods while you're changing out here."

"Thanks for those nightmares, Dad," Pike said, thinking about how long it would take him to clean up and hit the road.

When his mom returned, the first thing Pike did was strip down and change his clothes. He slipped his dirty ones into a bag his mother provided and went inside to put on fresh socks and his boots.

"Can you watch Jo for me? I'll be back in a few hours, hopefully with a guest," Pike said, smiling at the thought.

"Who are you talking about, Pike? And why do you suddenly have to go rushing off?" his mother asked.

"Because it finally happened, Mom. I found the love of my life, but I've got to catch her before she leaves."

"This sounds like a bunch of overdramatic bullshit," his dad grumbled, crossing the room to his favorite chair.

But his mom's face lit up at the mention of love, and she waved him off. "You go on. Go get her. If she's got you willing to run out the door and chase her down on Christmas, I can't wait to meet her."

Pike kissed her cheek, petted Jo's head, and yelled, "I love you, Dad!" before slamming out the front door, avoiding the ice this time. Pike dialed Ryler first, but it went straight to voicemail, so he commented on the last reel, typing out in all caps, I LOVE YOU, TOO! DO NOT GET ON THAT PLANE!

Pike kept trying to call Ryler, but her phone was shut off. He tried Kit's, too, but it was the same thing. By the time he pulled out in front of Anthony's house, he was stress sweating his way through the I Heart Santa sweatshirt his mom had given his dad as a gag gift last year. He needed someone to drive so he could type and call. Hopefully, somehow, she would see either his texts or comments and call him back soon, but either way, he was heading to Boise. Even if he had to chase her back to California, he wasn't spending another day away from her until she knew how he felt.

Pike called Anthony, and when he picked up on the second ring, he said, "Shouldn't you be celebrating with your parents?"

"Listen, I need your help," Pike said. "I know you're with your brother, and normally I wouldn't ask, but I'm in fucking love, and she's about to leave the state."

"I'll be out the door in twenty."

"Can you make it two? I'm right outside."

Anthony opened the front door a few seconds later and jogged out to the car. Pike got out, tossing Anthony the keys as he rounded the hood to get into the passenger seat.

"Where are we headed?" Anthony asked.

"Boise Airport," Pike said, typing out the same all caps message on all of her reels from today.

Anthony took a left at the stop sign, heading back through Mistletoe toward the main highway.

"What exactly triggered this urgent need to catch her?" Anthony asked.

"She posted several reels this morning, admitting that she loved me."

"Jeez, couldn't you just be honest with each other without the dramatics?"

Pike laughed. "Come on, you know me! What is life without a little drama?"

Anthony shook his head but kept driving. Pike squeezed his shoulder. "Thanks for coming out, pal."

"Friends to the end, right?" Anthony said, pressing down on the gas once they cleared the town limits.

"Right."

Pike wasn't sure exactly what he'd say when he reached her, but he had at least two hours to come up with something good. Of course, it didn't matter what it cost. Even if he had to drive all the way to California, he'd do it. There was no way he'd be able to live without her knowing that he felt it, too, that he'd wanted to tell her for so long but had been scared, too.

They crested the hill outside of Mistletoe, and a familiar silver SUV passed by. Pike recognized Kit in the driver's seat, and he spun around with a whoop.

"What?" Anthony asked, and Pike slapped his friend's shoulder. "That's them."

Anthony pulled off and turned around, chasing after the SUV. Kit had pulled over on the other side, waiting for them.

Pike got out, his heart racing as Ryler opened her door. He had no idea what she was doing coming back to town, but he couldn't let her leave without telling her everything. Despite all his precautions and fears about loving someone more and getting hurt, he didn't care. Even if Ryler never felt what he did, Pike couldn't lose her.

Before she could say anything, he had her in his arms. "I love you. Don't go anywhere. Or if you have to go, I will follow you on every future trip. Or if I can't, I'll be here waiting for you to come home. We will make it work because you are my everything, Kitten."

The seconds ticked by like hours as he held his breath, staring into her face and waiting for her to say something, anything. Ryler's cheeks were pink and streaked with tears, but she was also grinning broadly. Her arms wrapped around his neck, and she said, "Funny story. Kit and I agreed that Mistletoe is somewhere we both feel at home, and you're a big part of that. I love you, Pike. I want to go all in with you."

Pike hugged her hard, murmuring against the side of her neck. "You are the second best thing I got for Christmas this year."

Ryler reeled back with a scowl. "What was the first?"

"Jo."

Ryler laughed. "I knew you were going to fall in love with her."

"And you? Did you know I was going to fall head over boots for you?"

"I hoped so, but I couldn't be sure."

Pike kissed her, pouring all of his love and happiness into their molding of lips. "And now?" he whispered. "Are you sure?"

"About being with you? Yes. I've never been surer."

About the Author

Codi Gary is the author of thirty contemporary and paranormal romance titles, including the bestselling *Things Good Girls Don't Do* and *Hot Winter Nights* under the name Codi Gary and the laugh-out-loud Mistletoes series under the pen name Codi Hall. She loves writing about flawed characters finding their happily ever afters because everyone, even imperfect people, deserve an HEA.

A Northern California native, she and her husband and their two children now live in southern Idaho where she enjoys kayaking, unpredictable weather, and spending time with her family, including her array of adorable fur babies. When she isn't glued to her computer making characters smooch, you can find her posting sunsets and pet pics on Instagram, making incredibly cringey videos for TikTok, reading the next book on her never-ending TBR list, or knitting away while rewatching *Supernatural* for the thousandth time. Codi is represented by Sarah Younger at NYLA. To keep up with all Codi's hijinks, join her newsletter at codigarysbooks.com.